SHADES OF DEATH

J.M. MULLER

This story was derived from a mind that enjoys fantasy a little too much, and is completely fictitious. Any similarities to living people (or dead, for that matter) is entirely coincidental and should be deduced as pure happenstance. The opinions expressed by the protagonist (who isn't real) or the villains (who REALLY aren't real)—and every character in between—belong to those characters and not the author. This work is fiction and should be treated as such.

For CJ. The friend I never knew I needed, and the one I can't live without.

A MESSAGE FROM THE AUTHOR

Dear Readers,

Following the epilogue there is a chapter titled, "The Legend." It's a a bonus short story that is incredibly important.

I daresay it's the most important part of the entire book. And if I'm being real, it's my favorite too.

It shifts the story into a new light—and although I could've placed it in the front, I feel like it has more power in the back.

Furthermore, it's important I mention that the *Colors of Immortality* series is dark, and often deals with heavy topics and tragic situations. That wasn't *always* my intention, but it's how the characters deemed their path—and I'm one to let the story unfold as I feel it should.

So don't let the starting age of my character fool you. Lots of big things happen as he grows up.

Please read with care.

Lastly (but definitely not least), I wanted to say thank you. I know there are lots of books out there, great books, fantastic books, pressing TBR piles that seem to grow and never shrink, yet you're here—opening these pages and starting to read these words of mine.

It means a lot.

Thank you for taking a chance on this story and for taking a chance on me. May this story and journey surprise you. Happy reading.

Sincerely,
J.M. Muller

CONTENTS

CHAPTER 1
DEAD DREAMS

I plucked a hatchet from the pegboard, enjoying the feel, how the handle's curvature fit perfectly in my hand. I rocked it in my grasp, letting the heavy head propel it forward. Someone had recently sharpened the blade. It looked primed for killing.

If I could have removed my gloves to run my finger along the edge, I would have, just to feel my skin breaking, to know part of me still lived despite Narivous' attempt to break me.

But by orders of the elite, i.e., Thorn, my gloves were ordained to stay and—so I wouldn't get any wild ideas—adhered to my skin. *Literally*.

Overkill, like everything else in this appalling city, but the toxin touch had an ugly bite, and no one wanted to take any chances with me.

I twisted the handle, the thin mesh shrouding my fingers allowing for a deeper grip, and took a step forward. With a small smile, I cocked the hatchet behind my head and thrashed my arm forward, flinging it at a straw-stuffed target.

It hit right above the bullseye. My aim was improving.

Immortality sure as shit wasn't kind. It'd been five weeks since my transformation. Five damned, soul-sucking weeks. Thirty-seven days if I wanted to get specific—and each day was worse than the one before it. My own personal hell, on its own personal cycle, and in that mess of time, a birthday slipped in—although I wasn't entirely sure it counted since I was undead. Forced into isolation, the only reprieve I'd received was access to this medieval gym, evenings only, when no one else wanted to use it. And if someone did, I was automatically required to leave.

My illusory noose only tightened.

Unlike every other gym I'd been in, Narivous' version of a fitness center included deadly weapons and obstacle courses. The room was imposing, large, and somehow, despite its expansive space, suffocating. The gymnasium was on the Animal side of the castle, tucked toward the back, blooming far and high to accommodate all their special training tools.

Aka torture devices.

I wasn't going to dress up the truth with bullshit labels. You can call a knife a letter opener and it doesn't make it true.

Screw that.

Velores, of all shapes and sizes, came with special gifts. The Animals reigned in martial arts and physical superiority, and the gym was catered to their skill sets. Designed to hone their abilities and make them more dangerous than they already were.

Unnecessary, since they had claws and superlative senses to begin with.

The walls were made of gray slate, leaving everything cold and somber—with only climbing ivy to break up the muted tones. Above me, twenty-five feet in the air, rested long balance poles, with bars for acrobatics and upper body strengthening.

To be part of the cool club, one had to make friends with heights.

There were sparring stations, and rock walls with hand and foot holds set impossibly apart—unless you were a giant, which the male Animals most certainly were.

Along the perimeter, embedded within the polished wood floor, was a track. To run it during peak hours, however, would be to risk impalement, since there were a dozen targets flanking the far wall and a large collection of weapons to throw at them.

The past few nights I'd been favoring the hatchets. The one I'd just flung had quickly risen to the top; it was better balanced than the others.

But variety and practice, that's what separates the amateurs from the pros, and if I wanted to excel in my newest craft, I needed diversity. I grabbed an axe and held the long handle high above my head.

The poison pumping through my blood made me an outcast. I wasn't supposed to exist. They hadn't even bothered to rename me ... at least, not yet. Thorn wanted the task, to choose my new identity, and just the thought of it made my blood pressure jump.

Not to mention, my transformation had wielded cruel punishments on everyone I cared about.

Each harsh injustice flashed through my mind. I hurled the axe at another target, and as it found its home on the outer rim of the bullseye, I started to tally each lousy "behavioral modification" doled out to everyone involved in the creation of, well, *me*.

Polar, my grandfather, was sent away.

A second axe went flying.

Thud.

Ferno, Polar's eldest brother, was sent away too, both

banished to the Southside. A royal statement was issued, claiming they were monitoring the growing army, when really the sight of them disgusted Thorn, who couldn't stand to leave them unpunished.

I cut the room with a skinny-handled hatchet.

Thwap.

Chanticlaim—the Brilliant responsible for injecting the cure—was whipped, his skin split, while he was on his hands and knees in forced subservience. I was told he kept his screams contained and took the punishment in stoic silence. No small feat, since he was given a hundred lashes. His back opened easily toward the end, vulnerable as softened butter.

A knife sliced the air.

Schwaap.

Plague's punishment was worst of all. Thorn gave him a lesson in blood, taking a chunk of his soul in retribution. His face, partially hidden by a mask, bleached to bone when he informed me Thorn made him kill a human. And not just any human. A good one. A father of three young girls, a man so good that when he went missing the community rallied together. But hunters have a way of going into the forest and not coming back, and since he was pulled from an area well beyond Narivous' borders, his loved ones would never know his end was of a gruesome sort.

I think his name was Derek. Or Daren. Or something like that.

I shuddered and severed the space with a machete.

Thud.

Fantasia. Thorn was clever with her. I did my best to banish any and all thoughts of the raven-haired beauty who'd disappeared from my life. Of how she must be suffering—on account of me.

Each painful thought exasperated the buzzing in my skull. I threw a dagger. It whistled before landing on a target fifteen feet from where I stood.

Hitting the mark brought another smile.

But it wilted when my thoughts circled back to Fantasia and the harsh rumors swarming the castle. Even isolation couldn't keep the truth from reaching my ears, and the whispered voices made my blood scream.

The buzzing increased and I ran my hand along my pants pocket, feeling for the small vial I kept there, for emergencies only. My translucent phase—the state in which my powers came into full effect—was still unpredictable. It made me a liability. The vial was my backup plan. In it was a small collection of Dexitrol dust. If I ever started to slip, I was to inhale it immediately, to subdue the energy trying to clamber free.

Because my powers were perhaps the most deadly in all of Narivous, and Thorn couldn't look past it. My presence took away from her authority.

It ate at her.

Another reason why I was ordered into isolation. Thorn didn't want to compromise her darling undead society, and she couldn't stand the sight of me.

I'd been following orders meticulously ever since my transformation, because even though I couldn't undo Thorn's punishments, I could at least stop more from happening. *Hopefully.*

I grabbed a knife, bone-handled and serrated, and stalked to an empty target. I was clenching the weapon so fiercely, had it not been for the gloves I would've seen my knuckles shining.

All the while, the rattling in my skull continued to gain momentum. I rolled my tongue around my mouth, checking for texture, and was relieved to find none. That meant I had more time—but the thrumming at the base of my neck told me it wasn't much, perhaps a minute, maybe a little more. My translucent phase and the indicators that went with it were becoming familiar.

It seemed like a waste to use the Dexitrol to push my powers back since the gym held other tools to help me decompress.

I took deep breaths, stilling the buzzing, and began to pummel the target, stabbing it, forcing it to absorb my pain.

Chuck, chuck, chuck.

I pretended each hit was one right in my heart, destroying me when nothing else could.

The knife slid in and out, puncturing the cover, eradicating the red outlines and spilling the stuffing. My violent thrusts escalated, my arm working like a piston until my muscles started to cramp.

Even then I didn't stop.

I kept at it, jabbing, ripping, tearing, reducing the target to nothing but shredded hay and wire cording.

When I was far past spent, my energy depleted, I collapsed to the floor atop the carnage. The buzzing retreated, my translucent phase shoved into dormancy. I'd managed to force the rattling drone into a deep well. Not bad for a Velore as new as me.

It was a minor win, but one worth savoring.

I took in the ruined target. It was the third one I'd destroyed in as many days, and I wondered when someone would talk to me about it. Destroying Narivous property had to be a punishable offense—because *everything* was a punishable offense.

I guess I wasn't toeing the line *completely*....

Even with the overheads dimmed to the lowest setting, the light hurt. I clamped my lids shut to block the glare. Life had become too damned convoluted, and my brain's synapses were shorting out.

A flutter and soft tapping snapped my eyes open. Wading in the straw was a tiny, yellow canary. The bird cocked its head to the side and chirped.

"Where the hell did you come from?"

Almost as if he understood me, he fluffed his feathers and chirped again, prancing back and forth, his delicate nails clicking against the polished floor. He grabbed a strand of straw and held it like a dog showcasing a bone. I sat up as he continued to twitter and flutter in small spits never more than a few feet away, completely unafraid.

"You're a brave little thing," I said.

His chirping intensified as he sang and danced. A smile—a real one—cracked my face.

"His name's Fred, and you're not allowed to touch him."

Dreams stood at the gym's entrance, leaning against the door, having snuck in while I was in the middle of my temper tantrum. Fred chirped and took flight, landing comfortably on her shoulder. She'd changed since the last time I'd seen her. Her blonde hair was twice as long—which seemed inconceivable. It now reached well beyond her waist. She'd dyed the underbelly a shade of hot pink and wore a bizarre get-up somewhere between steampunk and princess, lace tutu and skull tank included. Fred ran along the bridge of her shoulders, diving behind her hair, forcing his beak through the silken strands as if it were his own private veil.

I stood up and patted the straw off my clothing. "How'd you get in here?" I asked. The castle, after hours, was only open to the Seven, their direct descendants, or guards—and since Dreams was none of those, she had to have either slipped past the sentinels or been willingly admitted.

"I have my ways," she replied, coming closer. Her blue eyes

scanned my chaos. "So, the rumors are true—it's been you assaulting these blameless bullseyes. I've heard they've had to replace a few."

I shrugged. "Yeah, well, they had it coming."

She shook her head, fighting a shadow smile.

"Why are you here?" My tone wasn't unkind, but it wasn't eager, either. Truth be told, I was happy to see her, but with the shitstorm my transformation stirred up, her presence freaked me out. Dreams was Fantasia's sister and too closely connected for my liking. It made me grossly aware of every word, knowing any screwups could potentially fall back on Fancy.

"Just got back, and Fantasia asked me to check on you."

My gut twisted into an angry knot. It was one thing to think her name, it was another to hear it aloud.

"Is she okay?" I asked.

Dreams looked away and shrugged her shoulders. "Okay as she can be under the circumstances."

The knot twisted tighter. It was all my fault. Talking about her was too much, especially considering the buzzing had only just retreated. I pivoted the conversation, reaching for sarcasm to distract.

"So, you know Halloween's still a ways out." I raised an eyebrow, and it earned me a smile.

"Yeah, well, this is how I like to dress when I'm not recruiting."

I repositioned my weight. "Uh, dumb question, but ... why would that matter? You can make people see what you want anyway. You should be able to wear what you'd like." Dreams was part of the Doppelgänger clan, the group that specialized in mind manipulation—reading thoughts and casting mirages as fast as a blink.

Dreams snickered and tugged at her half gloves—the type

that served no purpose other than to make the wearer look ridiculous. "It takes a lot of energy to put up an illusion full time. And I'm pretty enough to use my own appearance to lure people in, so, yeah."

Fred fluffed his feathers and danced onto Dreams' hand.

"Anyway"—she peered around me, eyeing the target—"do I dare ask how you've been?"

"Oh, things have been great. Everyone's really happy to have me here. Someone sent a fruit basket."

Dreams rolled her eyes. "You can save the sarcasm. No one likes a self-deprecating asshole."

"Sorry," I said honestly, shoving my hands in my pockets. "It's just sucked ... everything's really sucked." My shoulders dropped. "I don't mean to be a dick. I think my social skills have suffered in purgatory."

"Whoa, whoa," she scoffed, holding up a hand. "Who said you had social skills?"

I almost laughed. "Now who's being sarcastic?"

She smiled, one I matched. "You must be rubbing off on me."

"You're welcome."

She actually chuckled, and we both let our edges dull.

"Immortality suits you," she said. "I like the eyes. They're, like, an ultramarine now. I don't think I've seen that before. And the gray streak's a nice touch, too."

I shrugged, not entirely convinced. "I feel like a freak."

Which was true, in a sense. It wasn't that I'd changed a lot, it was more like I couldn't miss the differences with my refined sight. My blue eyes were darker, my blond hair had a lock of ash, and my skin went from normal to pearlescent depending on my level of toxicity, just enough to remind me I wasn't human.

And enough to avoid mirrors.

"Believe it or not, I think that's pretty normal." Dreams gave me a kind smile, and I saw hints of Fantasia in her expression.

"Noted," I mumbled, untucking my hands. I gazed toward the door, and Fred chirped. I finally mustered the courage to speak the thoughts screaming in my head. "I want to see her, ya know? To know she's okay."

"She's been trying to find a way to get to you." Dreams grabbed a strand of her hair and began to pet it in long, nervous strokes. "But it's not all that safe right now." She took a step closer, her head glancing up at a camera tucked in the corner. "That's why I'm here. If someone walks in on us talking, no one will think anything of it, but if Fancy came and someone walked in, they could twist it and use it against you. Against *her*. Even if it's nothing more than innocent chit chat.

"They like to do that," Dreams continued. "Build lies to serve their own agendas. She's off limits, so she has to be careful whenever she's alone with a male." I winced, and she softened. "She's really worried about you. Rumors run rampant around here, and your little ... tizzies"—she indicated the deconstructed target—"have made it to her ears."

"Well, let her know I'm fine. I'm more concerned about her. Has it happened yet?" I couldn't force the words out, my thoughts tangled with my tongue. Too many hurts lingering below a very thin surface.

Dreams shook her head and pinched the bridge of her nose. "I don't wanna talk about that," she mumbled, more to herself than to me. "We're getting off track anyhow."

"Oh, so there's an itinerary?"

"In a sense, yes." She looked toward the ceiling, searching for words—or maybe reaching for lies—and when she dropped her gaze, my stomach turned to ice. Her expression was so dire, it seemed as if she were looking into the eyes of death. I went rigid.

"Daniel, I didn't just come here to check on you. There's something else I need to tell you." She looked down, losing her confidence, and mumbled, "But if I do, you mustn't say anything. This has to be kept secret, I'm not sure I'm even supposed to know about it."

"What is it?"

"Give me your word." Her head shot up, her eyes boring into my own. My mouth went dry, so I simply bobbed my head. She took a breath, so deep her ribs strained, and surveyed the room in a quick glance. "They're rebuilding the toxin testing lab."

I blinked a few times, confused. "I don't know what that means."

"It means you need to make Thorn like you. This"—she gestured again toward the dismembered target—"has got to stop."

"I feel like I'm missing something."

Her face hardened. "The toxin testing lab has been decommissioned for years. *Years.* It was set up ages ago, long before you were born, to see if they could get answers to the poison running through your blood."

Thorn forbade the making of Velores in the Poison clan because it was the one group she couldn't defeat. Not having the upper hand, even for a few select Velores, grated her ego. She wanted to own her citizens, make them bend to her will, and nothing short of a hundred percent was good enough.

Whispers of a solution, either to eradicate the poison entirely or find a way around it, had whirled for years—or so I'd been told. Thorn would stop at nothing to regain ultimate supremacy. She wanted to stop our toxic wails. Stop our power. Placing herself at the top of the hierarchy, as she so rightly saw fit.

"And you're getting at what, exactly?" I asked.

"So, the fact they're rebuilding it means one of two things: they're either going to use it to perform tests on you, or to resurrect a safe place to kill you. And considering you haven't been named, and it's been nearly a month, my bet is on the latter." She jabbed me in the chest, her words urgent. "If you want to live, you need to make Thorn like you."

"But I thought I was indestructible." That was the whole point of my creation. Enraged over the execution of my friend Tony, Plague sought a way to make me stronger. Better. He utilized the forbidden combination, without Thorn's approval, to make me a permanent sliver in her side.

But now ...

Dreams gave me a slick smile. "Oh, you simple fool. You think she'd give up that easily? Your head is as removable as everyone else's. They just need a safe place to sever it. A room equipped to suck up the mean particles and easy enough for your executioner to vacate. The Brilliants think" —she waved a hand across me—"a Poison Velore will expel for days following their death. So they need a room with proper ... *ventilation* ... to handle such an overhaul." She edged closer and repeated herself. "You need to make Thorn like you, or else your head will be on her mantel. She doesn't give up."

"Better my head than someone else's."

Dreams' face fell. "You'd really rather die? That's what you want?"

It was. Dreams, regardless of her intentions, gave me a morsel of hope. *A way out.* My muscles uncoiled at the mere thought of it. I even smiled.

End me—end the problem.

I looked at Fred, his yellow plumage so vibrant it was a blight against the dismal backdrop. "Yeah," I said. "I would."

"How can you say that?"

"Because I'm not worth it." I threw my hands into the air. "Think of it, Dreams. Really think. Look at all the pain I've caused. I'm a burden."

"No, you're—"

"Don't even try." I attempted to soften my words, make them less biting. "Look, I know you want to help. And I really appreciate it. But you're not gonna convince me, 'cause you and I both know it's a shitty-ass lie. I'm a bartering tool—and a pitiful one at that. People are getting hurt trying to keep me alive, and it hurts like hell."

"So you're gonna give up?" She looked hostile enough to spit. "Let all their punishments go to waste? News flash, Daniel, you can't undo what's already been done. Chanticlaim will have the scars, Plague will have the pain, and Fantasia will have the guilt. You can't take that away, but if you give up then you're letting *Thorn* win." Her voice dropped an octave. "You'll have let them take those punishments for *nothing*."

"But at least that'll be the end of it."

Dreams snorted. "You're an absolute idiot if you think your death will be the end of their pain."

"What am I supposed to do, Dreams? I want to fix this, all of this, but I don't know how. I can't ..." I rolled my fingers into a frustrated fist. "I just can't let anyone else get hurt on account of me. If this is my chance to make it right, then I'm gonna take it."

"And your death will make it right?"

"Yeah, whack my head off and I fade into a memory. I've been locked in my room for weeks because the higher-ups can't even stomach the sight of me. If I'm dead, problem solved."

"Listen up, moron." Dreams' lip curled. "Even memories here have power. So if that's the best you can do, then you've failed." She crinkled her nose and added, "*Miserably.*"

"C'mon, Dreams—"

"Stop thinking about yourself."

"Excuse me?" I stepped back, surprised. "How do you figure?"

"Death, you jackass, is easier on the dead than it is on the living. It's the people you leave behind that'll suffer for it. They'll have to live with the pain. And that type of guilt can really beat someone down—I thought you cared about Fancy, but it seems you only care about yourself."

It was a hard hit. The blood drained from my face, and Dreams shifted. Regret stole her light.

"I'm sorry," she said, kinder. "It's just, Fantasia cries every night. She misses you. That's what I meant. Don't leave her. And I gotta say this." She ran her tongue across her lips. "I think this connection you two have, well, I think you shouldn't ignore it."

"What are—"

She held up her hand. "Just because it's weird doesn't mean it isn't real." Dreams shrugged and bit the side of her cheek. "I remember your human thoughts. Don't be a skeptic this time, okay? If Fancy trusts it—I think you should too. And right now she needs you."

I stilled, my nerves calming. The room lost its weight, and it dawned on me I was fearful Fantasia no longer cared. That she wasn't longing for me the way I longed for her.

All I managed to get out was, "She cries?"

Dreams nodded. "Every night."

"Because of the human she's recruiting, right?" Rumor was Fantasia'd been ordered to pull in a target to please Thorn. The task would wear heavy on her heart. She'd done everything in her power to keep me out of Narivous' clutches, and now she was being used to bring more humans in.

Clever punishment indeed.

"No," Dreams said. Fred fluttered to a beam near the door, and Dreams' oversized eyes grew bigger. She leaned in. "It's over you," she said in a hushed whisper, clipping along with urgency. "It's your name she says in her sleep. It's your name she cries when she wakes up in the middle of the night."

"She says my—"

"She's scared." Her eyes shot toward the door, and the hollow of my stomach fluttered.

We were running out of time—I felt it.

"Because they're rebuilding the lab?"

Dreams shook her head. "Not just the—" she started, only to clamp shut as the door to the gym was thrown open and a masculine Velore stepped in. I recognized him as one of Amelia's boys.

But which one, I wasn't sure. Amelia had herself quite the litter, and aside from the gingered demon, Cheetoh, Amelia's two other boys looked the same. They were carbon copies of their father. Tall, statuesque, with raven hair and muscular frames. I was only able to tell them apart when they were standing next to each other. One was shorter by an inch and liked to contort his face into comical expressions. I simply hadn't been let out of my rooms long enough to distinguish who was who. Unlike their father, Amelia's dark-haired boys still had a kindness about them. They weren't afraid to smile, whereas Cougar's face was carved with disappointment, nothing but hard lines and bitter expressions.

He cleared his throat, his enormous palm on the door handle, and inclined his head toward the hallway. A chorus of voices seeped beyond our line of sight. The castle was awake—more so than usual.

Dreams respectfully tilted her head in my direction, sealing her lips and pretending our conversation was of little consequence. She scuttled out of the room, Fred landing on her shoulder as if on cue.

The giant nodded kindly toward me and closed the door softly behind them.

Leaving me to wonder what Dreams was going to say.

CHAPTER 2
SINS WE KEEP

Unassuming as a shadow, I crept along the corridors. The castle never truly slept, although there were times it liked its occupants to think so. But no matter how black the night, how silent the stones, there was always someone awake. I knew it from the energy, the way my skin rolled and the air tasted—a combination of musk and iron—of the restless undead.

I'd stayed in the gym for another hour, until the voices faded. Being the new guy equated to a beacon, and I hated the sensation of eyes boring into my back.

When I entered the main hallway, the one with the macabre ornaments on a high shelf of concrete, I followed a steadfast rule.

Don't look up.

Tony's skull was bound to be up there, the taxidermy beetles having done their work, crawling over the flesh of his decapitated head, eating away his muscle, skin, membranes, until all that was left was pristine bone.

Thorn mandated how her skulls were handled, an order

directly decreed to feed her sadistic cravings. All heads sat on her mantel, both humans and Velores. She'd leave them on display so visitors could admire her handiwork, bask in her power, until the decay made the stench too unbearable or attracted too many flies, whichever came first. Then she'd order the skulls removed and placed in a glass box kept underground, where her insects would be waiting for their next meal, ready to gnaw away all identifying marks.

Making it a featureless shell.

Only after the bones were free of rotting flesh would she place the head back in its original spot. A courtesy of sorts. So we'd know whose skull it was.

Thorn wanted to remove the rank, but not the horror.

The hallway reminded me of the events directly following my transformation, how Thorn staged a counterattack, how her impatience spared me the sight of Tony's fresh head on that shelf.

No one expected her to move so quickly, and the ambush blindsided us all. She had her guards seize the room, each equipped with biochemicals engineered to shove us into a state of unconsciousness.

They called it Purple Magic, aka blackout dust.

Chanticlaim was finishing up on the details of my transformation when a knock came at the door. Everything became a blur after that.

I remember screams and plumes of eggplant-colored ash. How men in forest-green clothing emerged through the haze, masks covering their faces, gloves shielding their hands. How angry voices, vaguely muffled, shouted orders in a language I didn't understand.

The last thing I remember was Fantasia crying out my name.

It was chaos.

Absolute chaos.

Then it all went dark, and I was gone. Vanquished into a deep sleep.

When I awoke days later, I learned of Thorn's harsh punishments and that the gloves I wore were a permanent fixture. Glued on until my toxin eroded the adhesive—only to be reapplied, over and over.

At least I was out long enough to never see Tony's placement. And even though I didn't know which skull was his, I didn't want my imagination picking one out. So I kept my gaze down on the polished marble floor and not on the death lingering above.

I grabbed the latch of the Poison Quarters and ducked inside.

THE POISON ROOMS were palaces in their own right. The main entry point, as formality dictated, was a Throne Room where two regal chairs sat on a pedestal, so no matter the height of the Velore, everyone was forced to look up at their betters, stationed well above them in merit and logistics.

Scream's throne was larger and more opulent than Plague's. Both were elegant, the polished mahogany gleaming no matter how little light leaked in through the windows. Someone had taken great care in crafting their seats, insignia of webs and spiders so detailed they were close to scuttling away.

The walls were draped in black, the floors covered in black, the curtains black. Even the mantel, crafted in a wood so dark it, too, looked black.

Black. Black. Black.

There was only one plant in their quarters, and it was such

a contrast to the dark decor it always made me pause. A yellow rosebush, the very same that grew on the two oaks leading into Narivous, bloomed around the fireplace, clambering up the stonework, giving the room some much-needed color.

And the sick part was, I actually liked it, even though it represented death in my eyes.

It was Thorn's favored weapon, after all.

Behind the Throne Room were the private quarters, set up like a luxurious apartment.

Very few saw the inner-workings unless they were a servant or part of the noble circle.

I was neither. I was more like slime slipping through the cracks.

The rooms were comfortable, but still reeking of money and power, the type of space where you sat on the edge of your chair, always aware one slip-up could cost a fortune. Spilling a drink on one of their pricey rugs, for example, or knocking over a valuable vase would cost a normal person's annual salary.

Just the thought made me sick.

I asked once where all the finances came from and was told the mind-reading capabilities of the Doppelgänger clan made theft easy. We were living in the midst of extravagance, bought with stolen money, selected by Velores with only the finest taste. Stealing was a minor infraction in the grand scheme of things, considering they dabbled so frequently in murder and death.

I started through the room, passing a pair of stiff couches —black, of course—and shelves lined with rare books, limited editions, the spines so soft they were edging near total disinte-gration, when an unmoving silhouette in one of the chairs hit the corner of my eye.

"How was the gym?" My joints locked into place. Plague

didn't turn his head, he was still as a corpse, staring at the far wall and seeing nothing.

I took a step into the room. "It was fine."

He nodded and lifted a drink to his lips, the amber liquid sloshing against the decanter, the ice rattling as he swallowed it like water.

It wasn't water, but you'd never know it by how casually he slugged it back.

Very few people can take their alcohol like that. Mom was one of them. I winced, thinking of her and her worthless, wasted life.

"Why are you sitting in the dark?"

Plague had acted strangely since my transformation. Avoiding me as if my presence unnerved him. I'd catch him sitting by himself, his gaze far away in some internal plight, only for him to notice me and quickly excuse himself from the room.

So for him to initiate a conversation was a big deal.

He set the drink in his lap, his hands wrapped tightly around the glass, and swirled the spirits.

"I happen to like the dark," he said.

"I happen to prefer the light."

"That's a good thing. That means there's still hope for you." He finally looked at me. He wasn't wearing his mask, and even the blackness of the room couldn't hide the disfiguration of his face.

A shotgun carefully placed in the crook of his eye had turned his flesh to hamburger, leaving behind a gaping hole—and skin so shredded—not even the healing properties of Narivous' cure could stitch back together.

I sat on the couch. "What do you mean?"

Plague studied me for a moment and then indicated his face. "I never wanted to be brought back. And I've never gotten over it." He pointed to the door casing, where tally marks had been etched into the wood. "If they'd just left me well enough alone, those wouldn't be there."

I remember how his face twisted when he first told me about those marks. He was standing in front of the door, his hand resting on top of the etchings. He knew I'd walked into the room, even though he refused to look at me.

"This is my list," he said. "My list. I keep it here so I'll never forget. Because ... because I don't deserve to forget. Each one of these marks is a person who didn't deserve to die. See this one here?" He tapped a mark so well worn it could've passed for a natural flaw in the wood. "This was a child." His voice grew quieter. "A little girl who died because I was too new, too young, to control it. All it took was a touch." He turned and looked at me. "She rotted in front of me. Her hair fell out, her skin melted, and I watched her dissolve. You know what it's like to see someone so young dissolve?" He swallowed, not expecting an answer, and pressed his finger harder on the casing. "It's a sight that stains you. I wanted to take it back, but I couldn't. It was over so fast...." He removed his hand and glowered at the mark. "So I just watched and listened to her scream. She screamed until she couldn't scream anymore, and then ... she just stopped existing. And it was because of me."

Plague's whole body fell—shoulders, head, spirit—before he wrung the back of his neck and stalked out the door.

The image left its mark.

And now he sat in the dark, reliving past lives.

He put the cup on the table and looked at his hands, as if they'd betrayed him too many times and he'd happily sever them from his body. He looked at me with his one dead-filled eye and said, "I'm an abomination."

A phrase he favored.

Here in the dark, his words weirdly held more weight. A

cringe, so deep it rolled through my organs, hit me like a wave. Plague often partnered with melancholy—he had the moves memorized in a haunting dance. It always started with sorrowful memories and ended in shit self-worth.

I wanted to help, but my stupid brain only came up with a pitiful comparison. "If you're an abomination, so am I...."

He surprised me by nodding. "And I'm the one who made you. What was I thinking?" he groaned, and raked his fingers through his hair. "Now I worry ... I worry I'll never die. That this will be my life, only every year will be worse than the one before it. And that you're destined to suffer the same fate."

I opened my mouth, and he waved it shut. "Don't try and tell me otherwise, I've had decades to think this over." He stared at his glass. "I think the thing that pisses me off most is that I let one weak moment condemn you. I should've let them turn you into an Animal, or a Doppelgänger. Anything other than this."

I shook my head. "It's okay."

"No, it's not. Time, Daniel. In time you'll come to hate me. You'll realize the lack of touch is a starving state to be in. And the ones you do touch and kill"—he pointed to the doorframe —"those deaths will be mine too."

His pain ran deep. Years of memories and painful regrets clung to him.

And for the life of me, I didn't know what to say.

Because there wasn't anything *to* say. No words could chisel away even a fraction of his shackles. He spared me the stilted words when he swung back his drink, offered me another apology, and disappeared into the depths of his rooms, leaving me to wonder where his guilt would stop.

If it even could stop.

Scream was at my door the following morning.

"You need to get your rage in check," she said, as a Velore servant girl, her aura so drab it appeared whitewashed, placed our morning tea on the nightstand. She curtseyed on her way out. Scream barely acknowledged her, flicking her hand as if shooing away a fly.

The moment she left, I grabbed the cup and took a sip, not waiting for it to cool. It was one of the vices I looked forward to. Something about the drink was soothing—they called it a balm tea, and it calmed my overworked brain.

I couldn't get enough of it.

"When you have a problem, you use the screaming room and not the targets." Scream's onyx eyes narrowed in my direction, her tone biting as an asp. "I was hoping you'd stop on your own, but it seems you need more ... *encouragement*. We have an image to keep up, and behavior like that has a way of undermining our authority."

"But no one even sees me." The cup's heat was bleeding through my gloves, and Scream took a step closer.

Even though Scream had been the one to decorate my room, she never looked like she belonged in it. As an apology for all the crap I dealt with prior to my transformation—and directly thereafter—Scream used scraps of my former life to piece together my space. A bit of a welcome-to-our-horrible-undead-society type of thing.

She had Velores sneak into Gram's house and bring back posters, books, pictures, one of Gram's hand-stitched quilts, all to ease my homesickness. It had the opposite effect. It reminded me of how much had changed.

I was surprised by the gesture, considering my orders were to take as few items as possible. Aunt Marie would notice the missing pieces. Scream simply shrugged and said they'd think I'd come back in the middle of the night to raid the house.

She was probably right.

"You're a member of this clan," Scream continued, "and a blood relative of my husband. You'll be obedient—and will not reflect our lineage in a negative light."

She had her thick, black hair knotted at the base of her neck and a pair of finely crafted spider earrings dangling from her earlobes. Each time she moved her head, the diamond-encrusted ornaments caught the light and sparkled like someone vomited glitter on them. Her gaze bored into me as she took a step forward, the slant of her jaw arched so I was forced to look up at her from where I sat. She never bent her neck and walked as if the world owed her for simply existing. "Do we understand each other?"

I nodded and was rewarded with a glow of approval.

"Good. But as a punishment you're no longer allowed to use the gym."

Figures.

And as if she could read my mind, she threw in an unexpected tidbit. "It's not only because of your destructive tendencies."

"Oh?"

"The Dawning Rose Celebration is almost upon us. The gym will be used more frequently. Actually"—her eyes scanned the room, and she smoothed the sides of her dress, taking her time, languidly dishing out information—"the whole castle is going to be more active. And if I had to guess, I'd say your confinement will soon be at an end."

"I'm gonna be free?"

She laughed, her siren powers pulling. "Free is a foreign concept here. But you'll have more room to roam. Thorn's anger is extinguishing."

My face twisted. Thorn's anger was fizzling because she

was preparing my funeral, not because time had mended her wounds.

Scream misread my expression and went off on a tangent.

"I know this hasn't been easy, Daniel. Being locked away was never our intention, but you must understand where Thorn's coming from—her image was jeopardized." She sighed. "Appearances are important to her, almost too much so. It's how she was programmed. This"—she gestured to the room—"is hard for her. You're hard for her. She needs her citizens to see her as she is—all powerful. But, you'll be happy to hear she's preparing your official welcome. It's almost over. Your new name, station, all of the necessary arrangements are under way. Soon, we can put this unfortunate chapter behind us."

Lies. Lies. Lies.

Her open face, the way her lines spilled without a hiccup, told me she was either a practiced storyteller or she didn't know about the underground lab. Unlikely, but possible, since Dreams most likely heard from Fantasia, who probably acquired the knowledge through illegal means.

Fantasia could read Velores' minds, a forbidden talent—which meant she was privy to top secret information. And if Thorn ever found out about her gift ... I shuddered, and Scream narrowed her eyes.

"Um," I started, "that's great. Do you know—"

She held up a hand. "The details are still being worked out, so I can't give you much more. You'll have to wait." Her eyes flickered, and she cleared her throat. "Just stay put until then."

"Sure."

She seemed eager to leave, and I couldn't help but wonder how much she knew.

I suppose it didn't matter, anyhow. I was a dead man walking—literally—and I was okay with that.

Solitude does strange things to people. For one, empty hours allow the mind to play evil tricks, letting anxiety turn your head into a paranoia-generating machine.

It makes you question everything and, in my case, everyone.

I wished for the gym back. Anything to keep the thoughts at bay.

Because days passed, and the voices only got louder and their tales more farfetched.

So I paced.

Then paced some more. Wearing tracks into the floor, prowling like a feral animal circling the perimeter of its cage.

And when I wasn't pacing, I was sleeping. My body craved it, something Scream told me was normal—it had to do with a massive cellular overhaul and rapid regeneration.

Blah, blah, blah.

I think, honestly, I willed myself to sleep so I wouldn't have to face reality.

Not that sleep was much better.

Because every time I slept, I dreamt. And every dream was loaded with violent imagery. Deathly pictures and horrifying memories. The constant feeling of spiraling uncontrollably in a bottomless pit.

My imagination worked up snapshots of Gram, pinned by briars, held in place by a woman wearing a crown of thorns, her eyes colorless, making her demonic appearance match her evil soul. Gram's face, so carefully carved with love, would be frozen in a look of horror, before she'd open her mouth in a desperate attempt to scream—only no sound would come. Her mouth would hang on loose hinges, the black hole taking up her lower face. And Thorn, with her powerful magic, would smile.

In my dreams it wasn't a quick death. Polar was nowhere to be found, and he couldn't end it with his merciful kiss—the one that froze blood in the veins and turned marrow to ice. Thorn had time on her hands and she made use of it, killing Gram slowly, forcing the vines into Gram's eyes and mouth, suffocating her, choking her, bringing unnecessary pain because it brought Thorn overwhelming joy.

The dreams would always jolt me awake, and I'd be covered in a sheen of sweat.

Sleep was where Tony visited me, too, his death on repeat. But unlike Gram's, I didn't need my imagination to work out the details. I'd seen the light fade from his eyes, witnessed the dissection while he was still alive and could feel each and every puncture.

The memories made it difficult to breathe, and the air would always have a texture to it, changing it from a life force to one of death. I'd dart from my bed and bolt for the sanctuary of the screaming room, the buzzing so powerful no amount of willpower could suppress its energy.

What made it worse was when I had the urge to laugh, when I found their deaths absurd, when I wanted to release a maddening chuckle to litter the atmosphere with the incongruity of it all. It was a trick, a ruse to get my mouth open, a way for my body to instinctively twist my emotions.

Adaption at its finest.

My translucent phase would make the room pulse and tilt. My lungs would pump out textured particles of toxin while my tongue adhered to the bottom of my mouth, priming my jaws to unlock.

The screaming room was the size of a closet, soundproof, with restrictive ventilation to catch particles. Clearly, not enough to handle a dying Poison Velore, but capable enough to handle releases in smaller doses.

The four walls and ceiling were coated in a black substance somewhere between paint and tar.

The toxin's residual mark.

I was told if I ever started to lose control, to make it there as quickly as possible. And even though my legs moved with a supernatural speed, I'd always find the latch clicking just in the nick of time.

Then I'd feed the walls with pieces of my wrath.

DESPITE RUMORS my time of confinement was nearing an end, the days passed in monotony with no word or indicator of when I was to be released. Life ticked by, and I wanted the lab to be built, damn near willed it. Anything to end this ongoing, dull existence where remorse trailed me.

And then, in the middle of a sleepless night, a clatter outside my window grabbed my attention.

Someone was peering in.

And time stuttered. The moon shone down on a face covered in white plastic—a mask that once brought fear but now only resurrected hope.

Fantasia had come for me.

CHAPTER 3

THE CHUMP

I was out of bed in a flash. But as soon as the mask appeared, it vanished, as if it'd never been—making me wonder if my eyes were playing a cruel joke.

But it must've been real because every cell bolted alive, dancing on energy, crackling in my veins. I shoved my feet into my old, worn sneakers and went to the only operational window in my room—all the others were solid panes with no moving parts, decorative stained glass. I turned the latch, then hesitated.

Scream had said fresh air was out of the question, at least for the time being.

"What if you accidentally turn while the window's open? Can you imagine the devastation?" Scream's mouth had twitched at the corner, remorse dulling her complexion. "You'll just have to deal with stuffy air a little while longer. It's for the best."

She'd patted me gently on the arm and left the room before I could build an argument.

And now, aside from the demolished targets, this would be my first act of disobedience.

My brain decided to recognize the monumental event by functioning clearly—a first in its dimwitted life—by slamming into overdrive.

In rapid succession, before a clock's second hand could move ten spaces, I had a list that was reasonable and arguable —and all in favor of going after her.

1. Fantasia would never hurt me.

2. If she came, it meant the coast was clear.

3. Fantasia wouldn't risk my life, especially since she knew firsthand about the underground lab.

4. 'Cause she could read minds.

5. And reading minds meant knowing everything.

6. And knowing everything meant, well, knowing every-thing. Meaning I could follow her, and she could get me back with little trouble.

7. I wanted to see her.

8. Being locked up all the time was absolute bullshit.

9. Screw it.

I pushed the window up, and the casing groaned from being closed for far too long. The fresh air filled me with life. It made me feel semi-normal. I looked behind at my closed door and leapt before I could question my judgement.

It was easier that way.

I landed on soft ground and had it not been for the promise of Fantasia, I would've savored the moment.

I'd been starved of uncirculated oxygen for so long I'd forgotten how it tasted, the cool, crisp feel of un-ducted air. *Clean*. I'd never experienced it as an immortal and wondered if everyone reveled in the same sensation—drinking in air when you've been unwittingly starved of it. My nostrils detected everything: leaves, needles, earth, animals, traces of cinnamon—Fantasia's scent. I wanted to swallow them in deep gasps.

But urgency took precedence. My gaze pried into the trees, searching the shadows. Despite the heavy canopy, rays of moonlight trickled in, enough to give parcels of the city a pearlescent glow. The city wasn't completely asleep despite the hour, my enhanced vision and sharp ears told me that, but everyone was far enough away I doubted they knew I was outside my cell.

Along the back wall I captured movement, and my gaze landed on a mask and patchwork cape. A cape so unique in a land of uniformity, it made identification easy. Fantasia motioned for me to follow.

She didn't have to tell me twice. I started in her direction as she scaled the wrought iron fence, not waiting for me to catch up.

I doubled my speed, but she had too much of a lead. By the time I reached the base of the fence, she'd leapt over and darted into the shadows of the forest. I didn't dare call out. Instead, I clutched the metal and ascended, careful to avoid the pikes at the top.

Life would go straight down the crapper if I nicked my skin and let poison particles out.

When I landed on the other side, notably free of cuts, I allowed myself a glance back—more of a visual jab, really—to make sure I'd alerted no one to my escape. The pause couldn't have lasted more than a blink, before a hiss emerged from between the trees. Fantasia's mask caught the moonlight, shining like a beacon, before she ran farther into the forest. I continued after her, thankful for the scattered light, since Thorn's powerful magic made the terrain near impossible to navigate.

When we hit the trail, I spotted the swift billow of Fantasia's cape as she rounded the corner and disappeared at a full tilt.

I went after her with all I had, using my arms as leverage to push me forward, faster. Fantasia was a phantom, sprinting at full speed, and she quickly greatened the divide. We were pulling away from Narivous, each step a stride toward freedom.

The trail was endless, branching off from time to time, and Fantasia moved right along with it, far ahead of me but still within my sight. Out of the corner of my eyes, I'd catch the glint of a statue embedded in the forest, but we were moving too quickly to make out defining features.

It felt good to move my arms and legs, to let them have full range, to move as they were built. To experience a moment of liberation, even if it wasn't real.

The farther we went, the more the trees relaxed, altering from tight supernatural density to a sparser, more natural landscape. My breathing was even, surprisingly unlabored, as my newly transformed body took to exertion as though it were made for it. Now that we seemed far enough away, I figured it was safe to call out.

"Fantasia, slow down! Lemme catch up."

Only silence, and the smacking of feet hitting soft earth. Her rhythm didn't falter as she continued at an impossible pace. She had years of practice with her immortality and the talents that went with it. Her half Animal blood didn't hurt either.

It even seemed as if she were clipping along faster, and I struggled to keep up. I rounded a corner just as she dove off the path. Only the tail end of her cape was visible as she accelerated.

I followed her footsteps, pushing every muscle in my body harder, longer, faster. Tree limbs blurred, their gnarled branches clawing my shirt, grabbing my hair, slowing my stride. Ferns and brambles slashed at my pants. Had I not been wearing head-to-toe clothing, I would've been tattooed by their touch, slices of skin exposing the toxin and jeopardizing every living creature around me.

She hit a swift-moving river and followed along the bank. Trees parted and the sky opened up. We were high enough in the mountains it made the stars attainable—and they shone brighter for it.

But Fantasia saw none of it. She kept moving at her stupid, relentless speed, without so much as a glance back.

And I was a failing kite ribbon, frayed at the base. Soon she'd be so far ahead I wouldn't be able to see her.

I'd be lost.

Why wasn't she letting up? But I trusted her, and I knew her actions were always cemented in reason. After what seemed like miles sprinting parallel to the river, I detected the roar of crashing water and could see only blackness ahead. That sound and visual effect was synonymous with one thing: waterfall.

And Fantasia was running right for it.

"Stop!" I screamed, as she continued barreling forward. "Waterfall!"

I knew—*she knew*—she was running toward a precipice, but for whatever reason logic fled and my damned protective nature took over. The tingle I now recognized began to pull on my senses, as I continued to push myself forward, even though the effort was futile. There was no way to catch up. If she wanted to go over the cliff, there was nothing I could do to stop her.

And that's just what she did.

One instant she was there, and the next she was gone. Swallowed by the night.

Seconds later, I followed right behind, not even stopping to see how far I was going to fall because, honestly, I didn't care.

And because I'm stupid and wasn't using my weak-ass brain.

It was a massive drop, far beyond my expectations. The moment I jumped, and the air whipped my face, I realized I'd made a mistake. Fantasia must've really leapt to avoid the rocky boulders on the way down, while I pussyfooted my jump, letting the distance, height, and lack of light get the best of me.

And, again, because I'm stupid.

My reward was an onslaught of vicious slams, as my rag doll body made contact all the way down, each hit more brutal than the last. My legs caught the jagged edge of rock and flipped me forward. Water sprayed over me on my somersault descent, the wetness mixing with angry pain. My arm ricocheted back and knocked my nose, the cartilage caving with a crunch. It mercifully ended as I landed with a splash into the waiting river, the coolness both welcoming and frightening as I struggled against the force of rushing water, fighting to keep myself afloat.

I surfaced like a bobber, only to be pushed back under by icy cascades. Water stung against every open wound, and my poison ran into the river, probably killing umpteen fish downstream.

But at least the water kept it from the air.

Swimming was never my strong suit, but damn, it's like my body knew how to self-preserve. I choked on water, spat it out, choked on it again, spat it out, all the while fighting my way to land.

I managed to crawl onto the bank—spent and exhausted—only to collapse against a mammoth boulder. The water I coughed up looked like tobacco chew. It was black and rancid.

My mind went on holiday as my body forced life back into my numb appendages and shocked brain.

When the air stopped burning, I took stock.

And not a damned thing made sense. What was Fantasia thinking? And, more importantly, was she okay?

That brought me out of my fog, and I sat upright, craning my neck to see how far we'd jumped. It was high, so high it would've killed me had I been human, and every protesting muscle informed me I would've been dead had I not been, well, undead.

Hanging off to the side, about where Fantasia had jumped, was a rope. It still moved with residual force. I'd missed it in my reckless attempt to catch up.

Was this another cave she was leading me to? Did she have more than one? Back when I was human, Fantasia took me to her favorite place—a hole in the side of a mountain. She used a rope to get to it—maybe this was another place of sanctuary.

But where was she?

I stood up and searched the waterfall, looking for an access point. Seeing nothing, I moved to the forest line, and that's when I spotted her cloak and mask, carelessly discarded, as though they were trash. As I moved toward them, I realized it wasn't her mask at all. It was a replica—too clean, too new, to be the well-worn accessory Fantasia donned as penance for her mother's transgressions. Hers had scratches and marks, it was polished but slightly beat-up around the edges, and although she was forced to wear it, she'd told me herself of her strange fondness for it. It wasn't so much a burden but a bizarre security blanket. She wouldn't toss it haphazardly to the side.

Only someone with zero attachment would do that.

I grabbed the cloak and inhaled. The cinnamon scent lingered, but it was mixed with a stench I couldn't place.

That's when I pieced it together—I was set up by some shitface stranger.

And I was the dumbass dillhole who fell for it.

The thrumming at the base of my skull rattled along my hairline. A swarm of anger and rage pulled on my translucency. The sight of that lure pissed me off.

Not only was I unwelcome, but it seems others were actively trying to destroy me.

"Come out, you worthless piece of shit!"

My voice had a new edge, a huskiness. My words were beginning to grow texture. I recognized the power thrumming through my veins, but I was past caring. I didn't want to suppress it, not when I had enemies this close. I didn't bother checking to see if I still had the vial of Dexitrol in my pocket. It could be far downriver for all I cared. Soon, if the tempo kept pace, I'd be releasing a monstrous storm of death. The tiny particles in my lungs were festering—readying their escape.

"Coward!"

The silence was deafening.

"I said COME OUT!" I screamed into nothingness.

"Keep it down," a man's voice hissed from beyond the trees. It seems shouting, even a healthy distance from the city, was the only way to get answers.

I honed in on his location, my sharp eyes making out more than one silhouette. It seems I had an audience. "Don't tell me what to do," I said, starting toward them.

"Are you safe?" another shadow asked.

I paused, trying to balance my head, which had grown light, and gave myself a once over. My skin was split in long gashes—forearms, legs, hands, anywhere my clothing had given way—and a few were covered in a crusted mix of purplish black blood. I knew Velores bled purple; the black must've been all venom.

It spelled death—and luckily for them, I managed to clot quickly. But that was the least of their problems.

A smile went along with the vibrations, and I felt both angry and tranquil in that shared moment.

No.

I wasn't safe.

And once I got my hands on them, they wouldn't be either.

My skin warmed despite the frigid water coating it, and my smile grew as their ragged breathing reached my ears.

They were scared.

I liked the smell of their fear—it was a pleasant mixture of sweat and adrenaline—and I wanted more of it. I wanted them to collapse under me. I wanted to rip the patchwork cape and shove the pieces down their throats, choking them until they lost consciousness.

I wanted to turn their skin into charcoal, to flay them, and I wouldn't care if a heartbeat still existed while I did it.

I was going to teach them.

I was going to send them to hell.

And it was going to feel good.

A plan emerged as I mentally calculated the distance between us. I would lunge and, when I was only a few paces away, hit them with toxic air. If I timed it right, I'd incapacitate them all and then could linger over my revenge.

I didn't want a rush job.

Nope. I wanted to dick around, make each moment last. Make them regret.

"No," I said softly, my tone menacing. "I'm not safe...."

My tongue melded, my scream began to build. Their death loomed on the cusp of my lungs.

And just as I was about to leap, a racket of thrashing stalled me.

They bolted. *The cowards bolted.* Running in different directions, scattering like simpering rabbits. I chuckled—with a closed mouth, of course—at their foolish attempts to flee. I wouldn't waste my poison on plants and squirrels. No. I was going to force it directly down their throats.

Another absurd grin split my face. They wanted to play hardball.

Game on.

I took off at full throttle, a hunter running after his prey. Justice was going to taste even better when they put up a fight.

I went after the tallest one, determined to land the best trophy. My eyes took on their translucent light, the whites warming with their glow.

My mouth was dancing with toxic particles, and my speed only increased. Part of me wanted to call out, even with my tongue adhered to the bottom of my mouth—even if what I shouted no longer made sense—just so I could tease my rabbit, but the greedy part wanted to save every piece of death for the moment I unleashed. I pushed my body harder. Inky fissures spread across my exposed flesh, snaking over every inch. I was decay in living form.

Tree limbs split on contact, supersize roots snapped under my feet—the forest was no longer an obstacle, at least not against my anger.

I was a torpedo, and everything in my path was collateral.

His back was growing bigger. I was gaining ground.

Victory was close, I could let loose and still make a grand impact, but it wasn't good enough. I wanted him pinned. Soon he'd feel the full effect. My blackened arms feverishly pumped, eager, desperate, while my legs moved in tandem, and just as I was close enough to touch him, he allowed himself a look back, and when he did, his hand moved with a flash.

He was holding something.

He was prepared.

With a forceful release, he sprung a handful of dust in my path before diving to the side, quick as an arrow, narrowly missing my barreling body. My face hit a plume of suppressing power, and my eyes lost their light as the particles absorbed through my membranes and swept up my nostrils. The Dexitrol took effect immediately. I stumbled forward, surprise stealing my grace, and hit the ground at a roll. I tumbled, each sore muscle smarting, until the base of a tree stopped me.

Behind, the rustling of leaves and crackling of branches grew faint as the Velore retreated into the night—letting the blackness absolve his guilt.

All the fuzz went out of my brain and with it the euphoric aggressiveness that kept my pain at bay.

Now every muscle ached and cut stung. By some miracle, nothing was broken—immortality had fortified my bones. But everything burned, including my scruples. My clothes were sopping rags, and I hurt as much on the inside as I looked on the outside.

How had I become so mean so fast? I was used to pranks, to obligatory hazing. Hell, I'd switched schools often enough I'd become near immune. Even my cousin Eric—who was notorious for pulling that type of crap—couldn't get under my skin. Granted, I'd never been subjected to being tricked off a cliff, but I was immortal now. Stunts should be more intense, especially considering we've all faced death and lived to tell the tale.

So how had I gone from a good-natured person to murderous monster in the blink of an eye? Even worse, how had I liked it?

Now that the high was gone, I was thankful they'd stopped me.

Because I didn't want their deaths on my conscience. Not over something as stupid as a prank.

Fantasia had warned me each Velore's translucent phase was individualistic—that many don't even remember their actions when they've transformed. So I wasn't sure if it was a relief or a burden I could recall each painful, vile, murderous thought. My head, even with the buzzing, seemed crystal clear and all my reasoning justified. I'd become righteous and self-serving. *Vindictive.* What if this was the real me? What if this dormant, angry side was my truth?

What would've happened if I didn't have Dexitrol to save me?

What if?

For the first time since becoming immortal, I felt like a monster. My body was racked with wounds—there was no hiding it.

I was screwed, but maybe in a good way.

Now they'd have the incentive to take me underground and lop off my head. Thorn had her just cause, and I could finally be gone from this stupid society.

I started to stand and head back the way I came, when a spot of moonlight captured my attention. Light, especially in a forest so dense it shut off the sun, was worth pausing for. I limped toward the dappled glow to a break in the trees.

Down in a small valley, an area existed with nothing more than a few trees dressed in shabby moss—a monotonous section of unloved land. The moon's glow touched everything.

Narivous, it seemed, had a graveyard.

CHAPTER 4
THE JESTER IN THE GRAVEYARD

Of all places to stumble into, I never expected a graveyard. Perhaps it was the formality. A dedication to the lives lost. Sacred. And the fact Narivous was a mocking, walking contradiction of what a cemetery represents.

The moonlight gave each tombstone its own nocturnal spotlight. Oak trees and their branches spread decrepit shadowy fingers, as if trying to pluck the dead from their earthy graves. None of the trees showed any signs of life, despite the spring season. They were thick with moss, and vines crawled up their trunks in an effort to choke them out.

But the limbs themselves were naked.

Which told me Thorn kept them that way. It seems even dead plants obeyed her orders.

The cemetery was broken into two distinct parts. From my location on the hill, I could see the divider clearly, a line in the sand. Or, in this case, briars through the dirt.

To the right, the graveyard was smaller, but more grand. Ostentatious. The tombstones tall and ornate, many with carvings of angels and otherworldly images. There were lurching gargoyles, birds perched on orthodox crosses, statues so detailed I could've sworn they were breathing. It sucked me in, and I forgot about being half frozen. I forgot about my wounds and facial features that were most certainly smashed into a new configuration.

I wanted to see more, and made my way to the fancier side where I found paths leading to each burial site, constructed of cobblestone and broken up with pockets of moss. Beautiful in its intentionally fragmented state. The names on the grave markers ratted out their origins. They all belonged to Velores. I saw a Cinder, Raven, Lockneck. In the center of the cemetery, where every path led, stood the two grandest memorials of all. The pair towered well above my head and, unlike the others, were made to scale. They were no doubt life-like replicas of the people buried beneath their feet. One was a man, over six feet tall, with a square jaw and hostile eyes. He was leaning on an axe, his expression just as hard as the stone he was carved from.

Next to him, a delicate woman held a bushel of wildflowers. If I could've picked two opposites, this pair would've been it. Where he was rigid, she was gentle. A smile even played on her lips, something I doubted the guy knew how to do. I touched the cold stone and half expected it to thump beneath my palm. I looked up into her eyes and, somehow, the carver had managed to make her spark.

The inscription below her feet read: *Rose. Beloved wife and mother. Queen of the righteous and great.*

There were no dates. Her death wasn't marked and neither was her birth. It was as if she simply materialized from the heavens and was placed in a plot in the devil's land.

The man's tombstone showed signs of vandalism. Someone had carved out pieces of the inscription and then, almost as if they regretted it, tried to scratch them back. All done in the same reckless fashion. Even damaged, I was able to make out the words: *Urrel: Beloved husband and father. King of Narivous, maker of power.*

The words "Beloved and King" had been the vandal's main target. I ran my hands over the inscription, feeling where they tried to gouge away its existence. Their anger bled through my fingertips.

Deranged laughter shattered the serenity of the moment and I stumbled. I turned to find a man in a stocking cap leaning over a gargoyle grave marker, using it as an armrest.

He was roughly the same size as the Velore I'd chased, and I wondered if it was the same asshat who'd hit me with the Dexitrol powder.

His wild eyes raked over me, taking in my damp, bedraggled clothing, the scratches on my skin, my flesh stained with bruises. When his eyes landed on my smashed nose, a smile—one not completely sane—pulled on his lips. "Why, you look like you've wrestled the rapids. And if you don't mind me saying, I think the rapids won." He laughed again as his eyes swam in their sockets.

I was alone with a nutter.

I dropped my shoulders and forced my expression into one of indifference. "What can I say? I'm clumsy, and the water was refreshing."

"Ah, a clumsy Poison. Not a good combo. Not a good combo at all. If you don't watch your step, you'll tear open your skin and kill half of Narivous." He tapped his lip. "Hmmm ... why, now that I think about it, that might not be half bad. Do you mind if I push you for no reason?" He chuckled at his own joke and I turned away, already exasperated.

"Everyone's talking about you, you know. They think you

might be the deadliest Velore ever made. That's quite the title. I'm jealous."

Behind me, grass collapsed as footsteps approached. He was soon at my side. "So, you have a new name yet? That's one of the best parts."

"Nope. As of right now, I'm still plain ol' Daniel."

"Eh, it'll come. Course, it would be kinda badass if they let you keep your given name. That would make you stand out for sure."

I rolled my eyes. "Then let's hope my new name isn't cringe worthy."

"Not the type who likes attention, eh? I can respect that." He pointed at the two graves. "That there, why that's Thorn's mommy and daddy."

"I figured," I replied, crouching low to inspect the inscription again. "The King and Queen part gave it away."

"Ha! Me senses sarcasm."

"You're a sharp one."

The stranger cackled and actually patted me on the shoulder. I nearly jumped at the touch. I expected him to treat me like a leper.

But he seemed unafraid.

Definitely nuts.

His teeth shone in the moonlight. "I do well with sarcasm," he said. Then he began to laugh again, pointing at my face like my misery brought him enjoyment. "Sarcastic and smashed, you're going to make a wonderful impression at the ball."

I stood up and pulled away, crossing my arms over my chest. With the trickery on the cliff and the abandonment at the bottom, playing nice wasn't in my scope, and I did what I always do when irritation conquers reason—I ran my mouth.

"What's up with all the lunacy?" I barked, stepping close enough he had to feel my breath on his cheek. "Everyone in this forsaken city is insane. And I can't seem to figure out if you're made crazy or come crazy. Care to clarify?"

His grin sliced his face in half, ear to ear. And as I suspected, he was completely unafraid of the toxin pulsing through my veins because, rather than pull away, he leaned in closer until our faces nearly touched. The only separation between us was a flinch.

"Why, I think it's a little bit of both," he said and started laughing again. Then he began to skip ahead. Actually *skip*. Swinging his arms wide, moving his legs in quick little jabs, he looked like a five-year-old frolicking through a meadow, not a grown man navigating a graveyard.

A total basket case.

His clothing hung from his slender frame, ill-fitting and neglected, spots stiff with dirt, and it flapped with each hop and prance. Holes showcased pale skin that rarely saw the sun, and even his aura was faint, as if he wasn't strong or special.

A quarter-way down the path, he turned and opened his arms wide. "But does it matter, really?" he asked. "Once you've gone crazy, you simply stay there. But it's not so bad. Not really. I'd rather be crazy than sane in a place like this."

I rolled my eyes and mumbled, "Noted."

He smiled even bigger and continued to stare. It didn't sit well.

"So, what's it you want?" I asked.

"I dunno, company maybe?"

"Is this how you normally act? Because if it is, I can pretty much tell you why you're alone."

"You make it sound like crazy's a bad thing."

"To the bulk of the world it is." I waited a moment, until the question nagging at me came shooting out. "So, are you the one who lured me out?" His lack of fear told me he was more than capable.

"Lured you out?"

"Yeah. Lured. Me. Out." I indicated my face. "This didn't happen by accident."

His tongue darted out of his mouth, as he tried, in a rather measly attempt, to stifle a smile.

"Why, I don't know what you mean. I thought you were just clumsy." The smirk he gave said anything but.

"Sure, you don't."

"It's true. No one tells me anything. That doesn't mean I don't know a few things though...."

His words dissipated into the air, filling the space with awkward silence. Nervously, I twisted my neck, scanning the graveyard, seeing if other crazies would pop out of the woodwork.

"So, what's your name, anyway?"

"Jester."

"Well, *Jester* ... if you weren't in on it, how'd you know I was here?"

He shrugged his shoulders. "I didn't. This is kind of my turf. Where I come to hang out. You came to me, not the other way around."

"You hang out in a graveyard?"

"Yeah, it's better than hanging out in the city. At least these guys know how to keep their mouths shut."

He chuckled at his own joke and pulled out a deck of cards. Absentmindedly, he began to shuffle, never really losing his gaze on me.

"So, someone played a trick on you, huh? Lured you out? Sounds like you have some enemies. Or maybe it was one of the heathens. Or, even better, both? Either way"—he gestured to my sad state—"you look like the stiff side of shit."

Thanks, Captain Obvious.

"So, hazed or targeted?" Jester tilted his head, appraising

me. "I suppose it doesn't matter. The effect is all the same." He covered his mouth to block his smile.

"Who are the heathens?" I was too new to have enemies—it had to have been a prank. And it would be nice to know who to hate.

"A group of Narivous rebels," Jester clarified with arched eyebrows. "They're a rather unpleasant sub-group. Pricks that laugh too loud and walk with a limp. You know the type, right? They're part of the guard. Thorn loves 'em—and they think because they're favorites it gives them protection." He pulled his shoulders to his ears and let them drop. "I guess it kind of does." He started to bridge the cards, letting them flutter until they folded flat. "So, did they push you in the river?"

I shook my head and looked beyond Jester to the tree line. If he wasn't who I followed, that meant someone else had to be close.

"No, they didn't push me. I jumped off a waterfall."

He let out a low whistle. "That means you're either bonkers or fearless."

"No, it means I'm gullible."

"How'd they trick you?" The cards zipped in and out of sight as he forced them into confusion.

"I thought someone I cared about jumped. I was just going after her."

Jester's hands stilled and his eyes flashed.

"Oh really? Who is it you thought jumped?"

I stowed my hands in my pockets and looked at the ground, silently cursing my ginormous mouth.

"C'mon, man. Don't be shy. I bet I can guess who it was."

"It doesn't matter. I fell for a dirty trick and I'd rather leave it at that."

"Eh." He shrugged. "I don't really care."

"Gee, thanks."

"You're welcome." Jester gave a lopsided grin. "So, since you've had a rough night, how about I give you the grand ol' tour? Is this the first time you've been out, since, ya know?" He mimed a throat cutting.

"Yeah." I looked up. "The air feels nice."

"That it does." He closed his eyes and pretended to savor the sky.

"So, what's with the cards?"

"These?" He held them up before fanning them out.

"Uh, yeah. What else would I be referring to?"

"There's that sarcasm again. I think I might grow to like you."

"What an honor."

Jester fanned himself with his deck. "My cards keep me from going insane."

He missed my eye roll as he stowed his cards in his back pocket—he obviously didn't know the definition of insane. Jester turned toward the more traditional cemetery, stepping through a break in the briars, and pranced like a lunatic to an unremarkable headstone with a thick base and a flat top. It was covered in a layer of filth and history.

He jumped on top of it and spread his arms wide in invitation, a sacrilegious move that rankled me.

I followed, walking past Jester, who was practicing sobriety moves—touching his nose while balancing on one foot.

Jester hopped down, and his footsteps fell into place behind me.

The tombstones on this side were smaller, simpler, and grungier. Moss nearly blocked all the markings, making it difficult to read the inscriptions.

My gloves snagged as I pulled away the plants on one of the tombstones. Ancient from the looks of it. Moss was embedded in each carved impression. It took some work, but I managed to reveal the name and date.

And it wasn't old at all.

"*Albert R. Monroe 1965-2009.*"

"What the hell?" I whispered under my breath.

"A casualty of Narivous," he answered. "This graveyard is full of souls foolish enough to stumble into our neck of the woods. Every marker you see is some sap who crossed paths with one of us. But not everyone ends up here, as you already know. They decide based off the individual. If they can keep 'em, they do. Thorn *loves* her trophies."

"But why? This doesn't make any sense. It's like showcasing murder."

The logic was all wrong. You've identified your victim in stone, out in the open for anyone to discover. If someone stumbled across this location, it would only take basic literacy skills and a web search to know these names belonged to those of the missing.

"It's actually quite brilliant, if you think about it," Jester replied. "When you saw the stones, they looked ancient. Older than dirt. You physically had to clear away the moss to read the name. Thorn can make new graves look old—and humans don't believe in that sort of magic. When they look for fresh bodies, they look for fresh dirt. But here"—he motioned with his arms—"Thorn can make anything look untouched. Then you have cadaver dogs. They pick up the scent of the dead, right? Well, what is a cemetery but a place for decaying corpses? They wouldn't even know where to look."

He was right. About everything. A graveyard would be the perfect place to hide a body—considering, of course, you could make the land bend to your will. Or, as in Thorn's case, grow to her liking. No one would think these ancient-looking burial plots held recent victims.

"And then they'll be in Narivous. Even if they were clever enough to get here undetected, the odds of them leaving are nil to none. And for them to bring people back to inspect an old graveyard would be past impossible. No … this method is not only bold, but pretty smart."

"It's bold, that's for sure." My words left a bitter film in my mouth. "So, people really don't leave Narivous," I muttered to myself. Jester's sharp ears didn't miss it.

"Righty-oh." Jester pulled out the cards again and started to shuffle. "I know they hate letting people leave, regardless if they're alive or dead. I heard your grandmother was one they cut loose."

"If by 'cut loose' you mean returned to her bed so she looked like she died in her sleep then, well, yeah … they cut her loose."

"Well it's better than being here. Alive, dead, or undead." He chuckled to himself. "So, you wanna see something else?"

"No. I've had enough for one day." I could feel my bones turning to gelatin. I wanted a shower and a warm bed. To sleep away this conversation.

"Ah, c'mon, just one more look."

There was something lonely about him. Something told me, even by Narivous' standards, he was batshit. Velores probably avoided him simply because he made them uncomfortable.

Because that's how he was making me feel.

I fidgeted, switching my weight from foot to foot. "Nah, I'm out." I started toward the forest, stepping over graves, on top of graves, not caring who I was stepping on.

"It's special. It's enough to make your blood spurt," he said.

I didn't pause.

"It was Fantasia, wasn't it?" He spoke so quietly I wasn't

sure I heard him correctly. My skin pearled with goosebumps. I stopped, my feet melding to the grass.

"That's who you thought you were chasing, right?"

I finally turned. "What makes you think that?" I asked, hoping my voice stayed steady and he didn't see my hands clench.

He shrugged. "People talk. Even out here by my lonesome self, I hear things. Gossip keeps the boredom at bay."

"Who's been talking?"

"Everyone," Jester replied matter-of-factly. "Don't feel bad, man. It happens. When people are lured here, almost all of them fall for the Velore who brought them. It's natural."

I hated myself for it, but I started toward him. Only now the energy between us had changed. It was static—a strike of flint would've ignited the atmosphere, sending us both into flames.

"Is that supposed to make me feel better?" I asked. "Because if it is, you've missed your mark." Hearing it was common practice to become infatuated with your trapper made me think of all the others before me. Made me wonder if Fantasia really cared or if I was just another notch on her belt.

"It wasn't supposed to make you feel worse." Jester rolled his eyes. "Still, I think you're gonna wanna see this."

I dropped my shoulders. I was in no hurry to go back to the castle and face the music. Jester knew he had me. He tucked his cards away and began to skip again. I followed at a safe distance, letting my eyes glide over the timber. There was a flicker of movement by the tree line, but it quickly vanished into the recesses of the cramped forest.

"I think someone's watching us," I whispered.

Jester didn't slow, but kept tromping along. "So what? We're not doing anything wrong. It's probably the same jerkoff who tricked you."

"Well I kind of want to get back at that jerkoff."

"And what would you do?" He popped his lips, an annoying sound that drifted. "Nothing. That's what. Touching them, in any way, shape, or form, would land you in hot water."

"I don't know if you've noticed, but I'm already in hot water. I wasn't supposed to leave my rooms, and now look at me." I gestured to my beat-up face. "How do I explain this away?"

"Hmmm …" Jester stroked his chin, a smile tugging. "I guess you already jumped into a boiling pot. How will you ever fix it?"

"I can't fix it." *They're building a lab to kill me, anyway, so it doesn't matter.* I wanted to scream it aloud, but seeing as I wasn't supposed to know …

Jester, for being a nutter, was strangely perceptive.

"Surely, you have a plan."

I narrowed my gaze, and a sarcastic lie slipped out. "I'm going to beg for mercy."

"They don't do mercy all that well."

"Well, I guess that means I'm screwed."

Jester tittered and continued to hop along, until he stopped abruptly.

His eyes, for a moment, mellowed. They didn't swim in their sockets. "So, you ready to see my special something?"

"I guess."

Jester ignored my disinterested tone. "Look over there." He drew my eyes to a hole in the ground. An open grave waiting for its occupant.

I walked over—curiosity besting me—and peered inside. It was mercifully empty.

"What's this about?"

"They always keep a grave ready in case of emergencies. You know the type—sudden trials, quick executions. Thorn made the order a long time ago. It's pretty smart if you ask me. That way she can have the body buried and concealed before the blood congeals. It's also a nice *reminder* that we're just one decision away from being planted six feet under." He indicated the human section of the graveyard. "They keep at least two open on that side. You'd be surprised how many humans arrive in pairs. It makes for cleaner work. That, and the smell is horrendous. I know it's uncomfortable for humans when they catch a whiff, but for us, it's downright stomach-wrenching. How Thorn manages to keep a fresh head in her hallway for even half a day is beyond me."

"How do you guys deal with this?" I asked.

"Deal with what? Death?"

I nodded.

Jester squinted toward the moon, giving my question some thought. He seemed, at least for the moment, to be taking me seriously. "I guess it's because we are death. You know what I mean? None of us really fear what's on the other side because we've all had to go there before we got here. And"—he raised his eyebrows—"some of us just don't care. I think the word I'm looking for is ... *suicidal*."

It made sense. I think I was becoming a bit that way myself.

"You know why I'm telling you this, don't cha?"

I shook my head.

"It's because of Fantasia."

Alarm sent my muscles into rigor mortis. Jester's smile grew. He said nothing but started to hum. "What do you mean by that?" I asked.

He hummed even louder.

Long before my time in Narivous, Fantasia committed treason. She never shared the details, only that a Velore, Chugknot, had taken the fall for them both—and died for his involvement. Thorn never got the evidence she needed to sever Fantasia's neck, because Chugknot took her guilt to his grave.

Jester must've meant she was close to her death once upon a time ... surely that was it, but I needed to hear it.

From him.

"Tell me," I demanded.

"You want me to tell you? What fun would that be? Not when I could easily show you." Jester looked toward the far end of the graveyard. Underneath a madrone tree's curtain of moss was another briar patch. A self-contained cluster, growing in a circle too perfect to be anything but forced. There was an opening, small enough to go unnoticed if one wasn't paying attention. "What's in there," he said, "why, that puts the open graves to shame and will answer all your questions."

Jester's smile weakened, the sobriety of what was waiting dissolving his high. There was something else in his face, a sort of longing, as he tilted his head and drank in my expression. He wanted to see my reaction.

He was waiting.

"Go on," he urged. "You're gonna find out sooner or later. This way we'll make a memory together. Take a looksie."

I didn't want to go, I even tried to look away. Something deep within myself—the intuition I knew better than to ignore—told me to stop. But with the point of a finger, Jester kept my attention on the briars.

Jester followed as I neared the thicket. He was practically breathing down my neck. I looked at him before peering inside. His expression was too hard to read before he lit up with an eagerness making him shine.

"Look," he coaxed. Onyx tears were forming at the base of his eyes, as if he'd been waiting on this moment for far too long and, now that it was here, could barely contain himself.

Inside were more tombstones. Beautiful, creepy, and

garish. They were built with the same care as the ones on the Velore side of the cemetery. Elaborate and full of meaning. My breathing rasped in sharp, quick stabs. Sucking in air and throwing it out as if my lungs hated the feel of oxygen.

"Look at the one with the horse," Jester said.

My eyes locked on the haunting marker. A large stallion dominated the archway, his neck bowed, his hoof pawing the monument. Carved around him, black as the marble from which he was constructed, were flowers, clambering up his hind legs, threatening to destroy him.

I didn't want to read the name, because I recognized the carving. I knew that horse.

But I did look.

And as soon as I did, the tingling took over. The onset was so sudden and powerful I lurched back and dug deep in my pocket for the Dexitrol. I grabbed the vial, relieved I hadn't lost it during my cliff jump. I couldn't risk any more lives. *I couldn't.* Everything was worse than I thought.

Way, way worse.

My hands trembled as I undid the cork, as my mind reeled and my heart thundered. I saw spots.

The pressure in my chest grew.

Jester swelled in size—he was edging closer—his attention on the vial. His hand shot out and he knocked it away. It fell to the ground, the damp earth soaking up the powder.

Jester's eyes were alert. His face bright.

Everything was going dark. An overwhelming sensation to open my mouth overtook me. I needed to scream. I had to scream. My lips parted as the flesh of my body rotted to black. The wail was coming from the pit of my stomach. It was bile. It was alive. It was ready to kill.

"Let it out," Jester said, "because she's never coming back. She's dead."

My vision blotted and my brain closed down. I couldn't think. I couldn't feel. This couldn't be happening.

"You killed her," Jester taunted. "It was you. It was all because of you."

No. No. No.

"Let it go." He grabbed the front of my shirt and shook me. "Let it go!"

My tongue melded to the bottom of my mouth and I threw open my jaw, releasing a scream so heavy, so powerful, nothing would survive its path. The poison left in swirling waves, spilling like insects searching to kill.

It wove around us, cloaking me and Jester, shrouding us in a painful veil.

Jester's face eroded, and despite the agony, I swore he smiled. He was sucking in the poison, and it eagerly took to him.

Before everything went dark, all I could think of was the name on the tombstone, and how nothing mattered anymore.

Because Fantasia was dead.

And it was all my fault.

CHAPTER 5
TERRIBLE RESULTS

Someone ripped me from the depths of hell. I'd touched Hades, fallen into the yawning pit, and somehow, when I thought the end was in sight, been yanked back to the living.

I'd been cheated. Hell would've been an improvement over Narivous. Only problem with hell, Fantasia most certainly wouldn't be there. I'd never see her again. Perhaps that was for the best, since my existence was the end of hers.

And all she'd done was try to keep me safe.

Screaming—loud and pitched, the most forceful voice I'd ever heard—leached into my ears. I tried to open my eyes, but my lashes and lids were too heavy, even my supernatural strength couldn't pry them apart.

A flurry of voices broke out. A groan, deep and guttural, pulled from my mangled chest. It burned, as if I'd swallowed a mouthful of acid, and I winced.

Then a smell, soft and familiar, calmed the fire threatening to incinerate my ravaged heart into ash.

It was cinnamon. Fantasia's scent, no doubt conjured by

my wounded brain, a sick taunt to intensify the guilt. The spicy fragrance of warmth and kindness crawled down my throat, and I tried to cough it out, to force it away.

It wasn't real, after all.

Warmth enveloped me as a body pulled close. Then my mind pulled up another punishing trick. Along with her scent, Fantasia's voice, as soft as a fall breeze, trickled into my ear. "It's going to be okay," she said.

A lie.

A terrible, horrible lie.

I moaned.

"Put him under again," someone barked. Unlike Fantasia's voice, this one was real. And it was mean. "I don't want him awake until we have more answers."

The energy in the room shifted, and I tried to force my eyes open again, but they still wouldn't budge.

"Hurry up," the person—a female—shouted. "Get him out NOW!"

A presence pulled next to me. And even though I was already trapped in blackness, the world went dark for a second time.

It was a small miracle.

⁂

THINGS WERE DIFFERENT NOW.

I was somewhere different, somewhere cold.

And the smell was horrid, somewhere between sulfur and cat piss, and I gagged with each breath. My ears felt plugged, no longer the keen receptors they once were, and I was on hard ground—too solid to be dirt, and too uneven to be the polished marble of the castle floor.

Perhaps I was in purgatory.

Nothing was clear, including my mind.

My muscles smarted, and I couldn't breathe. My skin scraped against fabric. Something was obstructing my airways. Each pull of my lungs brought it closer, sealing around my lips and nose. My mental fog was burning off as I slowly realized, with dread, that I was wearing a bag over my head. Panic thrummed through me, making my heart work twice as hard.

Instinctively, I went to reach for the cloth sack, to rip it away, only my wrists were weighted. Metal clanked against stone, and my arms stopped mid-movement. I was anchored in place. Shackles cut against my gloves.

I wanted to scream, claustrophobia closing in on me, but I couldn't move my mouth. Something—within the cloth bag— had my jaw clamped shut. The texture of leather bit into my skin. Beads of sweat broke along my brow, pooling along a vise connected from the top of my head to a strap cinched beneath my chin.

Medieval-type shit.

It took me to a new level of terror. My senses had been stolen from me. I couldn't see, I couldn't move, I could barely breathe.

"He's awake," someone shouted, as footsteps echoed. Dampness and despair leached through my clothes.

"Daniel," a male said. The bag, and whatever drug I was on, made the voice both familiar and alien. "I need you to calm down. I need you to mellow your breathing."

Calm down? I was tied to a wall, pinned like an animal, with a contraption pinching my jaw closed and a cloth bag over my face. How the hell was I to calm down?

As if he understood, he placed a hand on my shoulder and squeezed.

"Slow breathing," he instructed. "Slow and soft ... slow and soft …" His voice was calm, filled with authority. Near hypnotic. "Focus on my voice, and force your heart to steady."

Breathe, breathe, breathe. Not too deep. Not too fast. Don't let the sack close in.

"That's it," the male soothed. "Keep it up. We'll remove the bag once you're calm."

With determination I forced my heart into a slower rhythm. I focused on the blood pounding in my ears, counting each and every throb, willing it to fade. Somehow, after a thousand years, I managed to calm myself to a satisfactory level.

The bag was ripped off, and I blinked a few times. Disorientation made the room spin. Or, rather, made the cell spin.

I took great swallows of air, as a small audience stood grim-faced above me.

Scream, Plague, and Ember waited silently. Ember wore a tiara of ruby-encrusted flames—she was the Fire ruler after all—and even in the darkness of my cage her gems reflected spots of light.

Ember's eyes blazed as hot as the power she emanated.

I was in a windowless, stone room coated in a layer of mildew and ruin. A lone bare bulb, with wattage in the single digits, glowed over a bedding of moldy straw in the farthest corner.

A stench of urine, iron, and vomit permeated from it.

Beside me, with a bag clutched in his hand, was Chanticlaim. A flood of guilt washed over me as I imagined what his back must look like, with scars that were long, puffy, and angry. He stood up, his brown eyes soft and full of concern, and took an apologetic step away.

I sensed others waiting in the shadows, hidden behind concrete walls and steel bars, keeping watch—or playing witness, because this was clearly an interrogation.

Chanticlaim held up the bag. "I laced this with Dexitrol,"

he said, his face tipped toward sadness. "And as you can feel, you have a device strapped along your jaw to prevent any ... *accidents*." He looked at the rulers—all grave, standing tall and firm—then turned back to me. "Do you think you have enough control over yourself to answer a few questions?"

Despite the unsettling circumstances, no humming, buzzing, or thrumming could be detected. The Dexitrol-laced bag, while I was getting my breathing under control, most likely pushed my powers far beyond my reach. I must've inhaled more than ever before.

Most certainly more than what I was exposed to while running through the forest and having it thrust into my face.

The forest. The graveyard.

The tombstone with Barney, Fantasia's beloved horse.

I flinched as grief pierced me. The memories were too haunting, and I clambered toward the wall, wishing for a hole to burrow in, to let the sadness devour the guilt.

The chains screeched against the floor, and Chanticlaim looked to Plague and Scream. Ember's eyes narrowed. Scream stepped closer.

"Take off the strap," she ordered. I clamped my lids closed in an attempt to shut out reality.

I sensed Chanticlaim's hesitation, but then his gloved hands undid the buckle below my jaw. I was free to move my mouth, but instead I centered into myself, trying to manage the grief.

"You may leave, Chanticlaim." Scream's tone was biting, and she held out her hand. "Please give me the Dexitrol dust and send the guards away. If there is an incident, I don't want any more blood on our hands."

I opened my eyes just in time to see Chanticlaim place a vial—bigger than usual—in her waiting palm and give a curt bow. She folded her fingers over it and placed it into a pocket within her black cloak. Chanticlaim looked over his shoulder at me and mouthed, "I'm sorry," before walking into a short hallway and disappearing down a stairwell. Shadows trailed after him as guard members cleared out. All that was left was me and the pissed-off Powers.

A draft wafted around the corridor, chilling the sweat over my body.

Scream thrust a key at Plague. "Unhook him."

Plague removed my shackles, and part of me wanted them back. He stepped away from me.

"Get up," Ember ordered and, somewhere deep, I found the strength to stand. I was amazed my heart still beat, it felt obliterated. *Crushed.*

"I can't even put into words how angry I am," Plague said. "How disappointed. And if you know what's best for you, you'll loosen your tongue with only the truth." Scream and Ember looked at Plague with disgust. As if my mistakes were his mistakes.

Just as he predicted.

My memories were fuzzy and riddled with large holes. I could only collect snapshots.

Plague squared his jaw and looked me in the eye. "Jester's dead," he said. "Because you fed him your poison."

A slow, billowy tendril wove around me, pulling tight. The shackles, the leather muzzle, the bag, all because I killed another Velore. The room spun, and I fell back to the ground, bringing my knees to my chest, trying to steady the sway. My head hurt. My lungs hurt. I dry heaved, empty, hollow retching. Ember and Scream took a step away, as a layer of saliva pooled on the dirty concrete.

Even my spit was black.

I found the energy to sit up and motioned for the vial. Pity momentarily replaced Scream's anger, as she placed the powder in my hands.

I inhaled all of it, sucking it in as if my life depended on it.

"What happened, Daniel?" Scream asked.

I shuddered and wrapped my arms around myself. That's when I noticed all my wounds were gone. Every scratch, bruise, abrasion, each mark I'd earned on my cliff jump had simply vanished. My flesh was back to its normal texture. I touched my nose and it, too, was mended. How long was I out? Now with Fantasia gone ...

Fantasia.

I couldn't think it. I choked on a sob and brought my gloved hands to my mouth.

And somewhere, after moments of heavy silence, I found the strength to tell them what happened.

Aside from Scream's dimmed complexion, their faces remained expressionless, as I came to the close, telling them about the graveyard, about Jester cackling in my face. How sorry I was. An accident. Accident. Accident.

Saying Fantasia's name sliced my vocals, and I winced.

"You were set up," Plague said, his face twisting in anger. "It was all a set-up." He could barely get the words out.

Scream went whiter still. Ember touched her arm, her polished nails squeezing gently, as rage rippled from Scream's core. They knew something I didn't, and I froze as the horrific scene unfolded in slow motion.

Scream's aura flared. Her eyes flashed.

In a matter of heartbeats, Scream's skin broke with hairline fissures, black with decay. They overtook every part, transforming her flesh from perfection to rot. The sight made my own skull thrum with warning. I unfolded my hand to reveal the vial, but it was empty.

Too late.

She moved her mouth, fighting for words, and managed one. "Safe?" Her silken voice now gritty, she strained against the power pulsating beneath the surface.

Plague took a step back and inspected the hallway. He was methodical and efficient. He took off his cloak and handed it to Ember, who remained rooted, her focus on her raven-haired sister.

Plague nodded and said, "All doors are closed."

It was the signal for darker things to come.

Scream's breathing, small and short, blew past charred lips. Her composure and grace, which she had in spades, were tripping toward feral menace.

Ember took a step behind Scream and covered her elegant clothing with Plague's cloak. The poison didn't affect blood relatives, but it could still wreak havoc on fabric.

Scream's power continued to build. Her eyes hit a pinnacle, the whites lighting up, her irises black.

Then she let go.

I was surprised the walls held—surprised any of us were left standing. Scream's toxin exploded, blanketing everything, sending shockwaves through the castle. Ember covered her hair with Plague's hood, so the particles wouldn't attach to her. Plague simply bowed his neck in defeat, allowing it to touch him everywhere.

And I let it hit me.

Many thoughts flooded my system, but one was louder than the others.

They were wrong.

I wasn't the most powerful Velore, not even close. Nor could I be. Scream was death incarnate—the Reaper dressed in lace.

No one was a match for my aunt.

Thorn's desire for a toxin cure became clear as the unbridled power of the Poison clan came into focus. With a power like that, I'd want a safety net too.

Anything to offset the vulnerability.

We may have been unable to kill other Deadbloods—but every other living thing, as well as Velores, was fair game.

TWO THINGS HAPPENED FOLLOWING Scream's explosion. One, I was moved to another prison wing within the castle to await my punishment, since the former was covered in toxin and needed to be scrubbed down. My new lodgings had a window, a private bathroom, and even a bed with some linens, which I took as a good sign. And since there were no rooms in the tower designed to hold Poison members—since we weren't supposed to exist—every hour or so a guard would come in and toss me a vial of Dexitrol powder. They'd cross their arms and wait as I happily sucked it up, since that was the alternative to wearing that awful medieval jaw clamp.

Two, there was an eradication of some, but not all, of my guilt. And it resuscitated my heart.

Jester had lied. Fantasia wasn't dead. The tombstone was just a tombstone, protocol for anyone who ever fell on probation. An effective tool—nothing says death more than your own grave marker. It encouraged obedience. And as abhorrent as it was, it was better than the alternative.

Because she was alive.

She was the one who healed my body and whispered in my ear. She was the scent of cinnamon I thought I imagined. They kept me in a fog of Purple Magic—the coma-inducing knockout dust—so they could sort out the mess I'd crafted in their cemetery.

As for Jester, it seemed he'd chosen suicide by Velore. I was simply the method he'd picked to snuff out his life. Like the depressed woman who steps in front of a semi, or a deranged man threatening an officer with a decoy gun, he'd let me deliver the fateful blow.

It filled me with spite.

That's what I was thinking of as I lay on my bed, counting the pores in the concrete ceiling, when soft footsteps approached.

"Dreams told you to behave yourself, to make Thorn like you, and this is what you do." Torti, Fantasia's oldest sister, sauntered down the corridor. A bird's nest of auburn curls bounced atop her head. She was, like her two sisters, perfectly gorgeous, and she wore it well.

I stood up and went to the bars, but not before looking over my shoulder at the camera in the corner.

"It's off," Torti said. "Seems the electrical system's glitchy. So ..." She surveyed my cell and smiled. "Care to explain why you're enjoying some of our finest accommodations?"

"I was set up."

"You're gonna have to do better than that." Her green eyes stabbed. "You need to think quicker on your feet, because harder questions are coming."

"I feel like an idiot."

"It's because you *are* an idiot, darling," she purred.

"Ah, there's the charming Torti we've all grown to love."

"Eh." Her face twitched with amusement. "How you holding up?"

"Better now I know Fantasia's alive."

She didn't say a word. She just stood there, on the opposite side of the bars, looking as if she were seeing me for the first time.

"Things are gonna be okay," she said with surprising soft-ness. Her face colored to eggplant, Velore blood rushing, unfamiliar with being nice. "I'm sorry, ya know. For what you went through. I imagine it must've been pretty horrific. But I gotta tell you, this isn't all on you. Jester wanted to die. That's why he lied to you, to set you off."

"I just don't get why he used me. Why he couldn't have found a different way." There were plenty of ways to off yourself if one had the mindset to do so. Maybe an epically proportioned cliff with a rocky base? Or a gun from some stupid hunter who wandered too close to Narivous? But me?

Screw that.

It made me wish he were still alive so I could choke the living daylights out of him—with or without gloves.

"Jester's tried to kill himself before. He's failed many times," she said.

"So he sucked at a lot of things."

"Yeah. Just like you."

Truth. "Valid point."

Torti rolled her eyes. "I'm gonna do you a favor, explain a few things, since you're new and all." Her chest swelled with a long breath. "It's not easy to destroy us, and Velores like Jester are even harder to kill. It pretty much boils down to their method of death. You remember how that plays a role, right?" She paused. "You wanna play a game? I'll let you guess how he died."

"I'm not really in the mood."

"Tough. Give me a guess. I wanna see how your dimwitted brain operates."

She had a way of mixing insults into her everyday conversation, a rather impressive quality, since she managed to do it seamlessly.

When I didn't give, she started to tease.

"Oh, c'mon, Daniel. Play with me."

"Fine." Jester's aura was faint, it barely registered, so I edged toward innocent methods of death. "He died of cancer?"

Torti snorted. "That's the dumbest answer you could've given me. Try again."

"He hung himself?"

"Nope."

"Took a bunch of pills?"

"Uh-uh."

"Hit by a car?"

"Getting warmer ..."

"Just tell me, this is getting stupid."

"Says the stupid boy in front of me." She smiled before giving up the answer. "He was bludgeoned to death with a pipe. They smashed everything. His shoulders, kneecaps, head. That's why he wore that hideous beanie. It's padded on one side to offset his lopsided skull."

It was a revolting image.

"Now, what do you suppose would be the ... *talent* ... for a Velore who dies via a brutal beating?" Her brow arched, and a smile tugged at her lips. "Their bones become unbreakable. Their skin builds a layer equivalent to a bulletproof vest. They become strongholds. Impenetrable. Like I said, he's tried to kill himself in the past. He once threw himself off a cliff and landed 150 feet—"

"Can we stop?" I didn't want to hear anymore. I'd had enough of Narivous' horrific stories.

I was starting to feel pity for Jester, when all I wanted was to hate him.

Because hate's an easier emotion. Hate gives you an edge, while pity turns you to putty. Before long, guilt would creep in. And I didn't think I could handle guilt.

"No!" she said. "You have to acquaint yourself with ugly details because that's all Narivous is—ugly details. And you saw for yourself what's at stake." She stepped up to the bars and grabbed them, pushing her face into a gap. "That tombstone ... it rips at me too. But I'm glad you saw it. You needed to see it, to know how close she was to the grave. I need you to keep her out of trouble. I need you to"—she checked the space around her, paranoia too deeply ingrained, and breathed—"keep her damn rebel thoughts away."

"She won't listen to me."

"The hell she won't. There's something strange between you two. I've only seen it a few times, but I can assure you, whatever it is, it's alive. Make it work in our favor."

Her words made me desperate. Color rose to my face. The rush, the heat, was unmistakable.

"It's real, Daniel," she said. "I know you question it. But I can assure you it's not all in your head. Use it to your advantage. To *her* advantage. Keep Fancy safe. Make Thorn like you."

"After this, though—"

"This is the perfect opportunity."

The perfect opportunity? She was nuttier than Jester. Thorn was having a room built to destroy me, all because I was a threat to her society. And what did I do? I fortified her fears the first chance I got. I killed one of her undead, and whether he sought his death or not, it didn't matter. I lost control, showed her I couldn't be trusted.

"How do you figure?" I asked.

"Thorn loves, above all else, power. You *are* powerful, you showcased it in the graveyard. Let her think you're the weapon she's always wanted. Be her pet. Anything to keep Fancy safe. If she grows fond of you, you'll carry weight. She'll honor you with favors. You can give Fancy another layer of protection."

"But this"—I gestured to my cell—"only reinforces I should've never been made. I couldn't control it."

"Only because you're new and were goaded. Jester knew

what he was doing and Thorn will look past that. Now that you've told them your side they'll know how to angle their investigation. What to search for. And trust me"—she let go of the bars—"you have allies who will help you. Jester provoked you. He saw you tipping and he gave the final push. He's the one who knocked the vial from your hand. This is his fault."

"So everyone knows the details."

"Not everyone." She fidgeted with the top of her hair. A nervous move that spoke volumes.

She's protecting Fancy.

I moved on.

"But they're building an underground lab to kill me."

Torti's sharp eyes softened. "Perhaps, but now it's up to you to convince them otherwise. That lab was built long before you were made, and it wasn't used to kill anyone. Make history repeat itself."

"You really don't think it's too late?"

"Not at all." Her smile was gentle. Genuine.

A door down the corridor opened, and Torti took a step away. She was clearing her throat, preparing to bow, when Camille stepped in. A carbon copy of her daughter, aside from the blonde hair and blue eyes. The pair looked more like siblings.

Torti instantly dropped the charade.

"Geeze, Mom," she admonished, "you could've cleared your throat or something ... let me know it was you."

"Watch your tone," Camille snapped and approached my cell. "I'll do as I please. Besides"—she looked at me carefully—"you should always be on your watch around here. I don't need to coddle you."

Torti rolled her eyes.

"And you ..." Camille pointed a well-manicured finger in my direction. "You are quite the problem child, aren't you?"

I mocked a bow, and Torti stifled a laugh.

"I came to deliver a message," Camille said and chewed her lip, debating if I was worth her time. Almost with a snarl, she continued, "Fantasia wants you to know she's counting on you in the next few days to *not* screw up. I know that'll be a challenge, since you excel in your craft of foolishness. So please, try not to be yourself."

That was the message? After everything, the time in solitary, the loneliness, and now ... *this*? That's all she had to give me? A reprimand?

"Mom," Torti groaned. "Don't lie."

Camille's lips pulled at the corners. "That's not the message," she admitted with a wicked grin. "I'm simply paraphrasing."

"Something tells me you're not even paraphrasing. You made that up," Torti said.

Camille shrugged. "Okay, fine. That's *my* message. But I'm her mother and have the right to add my two cents."

"Then what's the message?" I asked.

"Stay strong." Camille placed her hand on Torti's back. "Fantasia told me to tell you to stay strong. That she misses you." Camille snorted and mumbled loudly, "I don't get what she misses, though. Seems like a waste of energy to me."

She turned and gave me a false smile, while ushering Torti toward the exit.

"Thank you!" I shouted, grateful despite the insult. "Tell her I miss her too. And that I haven't lost my charming personality."

Camille paused to glare in my direction.

"That's what she misses," I clarified, gesturing to my face. "My brilliant witticism."

Camille rolled her eyes. "Well, see to it your 'brilliant witticism' doesn't rot to stupid, Stupid." She paused, her hand still on Torti's back. "Don't let her down," she added, her face more open than I'd ever seen it.

"If I get out of here, I won't."

"You'll get out," she replied confidently. "And when you do, you see to it your nonsense stops. There's too much to lose."

I nodded, and they both gave me shadow smiles, very much the same face, and left me to my own demons.

The guards came before sunset. A decision had been made.

CHAPTER 6

POLAR'S UNTHAWING OF A HEART

Two guards brought information and a slip of paper. The former—a briefing on the direction of the investigation. The latter—proof. Camille and Torti were right. Now that they knew what to look for in their investigation, justice moved swiftly.

I recognized one of the guards. His name was Splint and he was built like a bulldog, and strutted like one too. His gait was blocky and short, dropping a hip with every step, the swagger of the overconfident.

"Looks like your story's checking out," he said. "They've been asking around. Seems Jester was kookier than we all thought." He tried to slip me a grin, but it fell short. "They found a journal of Jester's. He had it hidden in the graveyard." He tossed a paper through the bars and it glided to the floor. "And even though we can't let you out, I figured you'd want to know. So you wouldn't be in here ... ya know ... stressing."

"Thanks," I said, as the other guard, one completely unfamiliar, folded his arms with a snort. "Awfully convenient, if you ask me."

Splint shrugged his shoulders. "I don't particularly care if you think it's convenient."

"Seriously, Splint. Think about it. What kind of loony keeps a journal? That's a chick thing."

"Jester's the type of loony to keep one," Splint shot back.

"Such a freak."

"Be respectful of the dead."

"We are dead, Splint. You'll need to be more specific."

"Okay, fine. The dead-dead."

"If you ask me, this dillhole did us a huge favor." The guard shot a finger at me. "Jester was a joke." He snickered, and nudged Splint. "Get it? Jester the joke?"

"You're a sacrilegious shithead."

"I'm a sacrilegious shithead for stating the obvious?"

Their back and forth turned to static. I was all but forgotten and used my invisibility to snatch the paper off the floor.

It was a photocopy of a journal entry, and judging by the number at the top, one of many.

131—

I've heard the new guy's strong, stupid and impulsive.
Maybe he'll visit me.
Death. Freedom. FREE. FREE. Free.
Freefreefreefreefreefreefree

HE FILLED an entire page with those four little letters.

Manic and obsessive—it spoke volumes about Jester and his disintegrating state of mind.

Splint left the copy for me. "To help your troubled conscience," he said.

Fool. The best way to quiet a noisy mind was sleep, and I did just that.

Somehow, either from the lingering effects of the sedatives or pure mental exhaustion, I managed to slip into a coma, waking only when the prison entrance door, far out of sight, groaned open.

A single set of footsteps approached, and as I waited for the person to appear, I prayed for good news. The conversation with Torti, the tombstone engraved with Fantasia's name, all renewed my will to live, if only to keep Fancy alive.

I wasn't going to give up. Not now. Not with so much at stake.

"There you are." Polar walked swiftly to my cell. His white hair and iceberg eyes were a warm relief to the enduring chill of the tower.

I ran to the bars, excitement and happiness flooding over me. Polar was here.

Finally.

He dug in his pocket and produced a key. Unlocking my door, he grabbed me by the shirt and pulled me to him. He was just as I remembered, freezing and solid, his body ungiving, as if he were a sculpture carved of ice. I clutched at him, not caring how he chilled my blood.

"Are you okay?" he asked, pulling away and holding me at arm's length. There was no anger or resentment, only genuine concern.

"I'm fine. Well ... better now."

To see him, in the flesh, not broken as my imagination had told me, all but sprang the cords of tension. I dropped my head back, relieved. His smile widened.

"Let's get you out of here."

Polar took me to the Ice Quarters, rooms I'd yet to see. The set-up was similar to the Poison layout, with a royal foyer upon entry. Unlike the thrones in the Poison Quarters, however, both seats were nearly the same size, only one was more intricate to offset the weight of power. They were carved from driftwood, beaten by sand and faded from years of unobstructed sunshine.

The room, draped in cool tones, managed to balance ice and sea. The colors, the decor, everything was the opposite of the Poison rooms. And, best of all, there were no plants.

"Frigid kills them," Polar said, as he watched me scan. "She can't help it, she's always radiating a chill, and the plants can't stand the cold."

Score, Frigid.

He went farther into his rooms and motioned for me to follow. His quarters were less opulent than what I'd seen to date, as if he didn't care about impressions or painting a picture of wealth and glory. He wasn't a pompous ass needing to put on a show. The hallways were covered in family photos —nearly wallpapered with memories—and my throat swelled when I spotted a teenage Gram hanging in the center of it all. I stopped in my tracks, and Polar stepped up behind me.

"She was such a lovely thing, wasn't she?"

I nodded. Gram was tiny, fierce, and good. Polar touched the frame, smiling wistfully.

"I miss her," I said.

"I do too."

A thought occurred to me. "Does Frigid mind you having pictures of Gram on your wall?"

"Not at all. She actually insisted. And if my memory serves me correctly"—he dropped his touch—"she was the one to hang this up. Picked the photo and spot."

"Not the jealous type, then?"

"She loves me," Polar said. "Her love is one of the purest things I've ever known and, honestly, I don't think I deserve her." He looked around the hall, his gaze touching every image.

I followed suit and found myself traveling back in time, surrounded by Polar's and Frigid's histories. There were photos of Ferno, Plague, some before their transformation, others after. There were the sisters—Ember and Scream. And then there were others that took me by complete surprise.

Thorn as a young girl, posing in the middle of a garden, her smile bright and uncorrupted.

A very pregnant Amelia standing next to a dark-haired boy with large eyes, who held onto one of her unsheathed claws.

Dolly pushing a girl on a swing, the child very much a copy of the Doppelgänger leader.

Dad and me.

Me.

Then there were pictures of Camille and her daughters taken at various stages. One in particular sucked me in.

The girls were all grown. Camille was sitting on a bench, Dreams to her right, Torti to her left, and sprawled across both Torti and Camille's laps was Fantasia. She was the only one looking at the camera and she was smiling with her eyes, while the others were connected, but wistful and far away. Dreams held Camille's hand, and Torti rested her head on her mother's shoulder, looking down at Fantasia with pure unadulterated love.

"I love that photo," Polar said. "I like to fill my home with good memories."

I reached out and touched the picture.

"If you'd like," Polar said, "I'd be happy to make a copy for you."

"Yeah, that'd be great."

He clapped me on the back and we went farther down the

corridor, my eyes roaming over every image, greedily absorbing them.

It was a menagerie of photographs. So many faces. More images of Thorn, of Camille and her girls, of Dad and me. Every Seven hung on the wall, all during various stages of their lives. All carefully selected.

For such icy quarters, this was the friendliest place in the castle.

And that theme continued as we entered a room in the far back.

Because it seemed the Ice rulers didn't give a rat's ass about image. They'd abandoned the trappings of power and chosen to be themselves—unapologetically so.

The cream-colored sofas were so worn they appeared second-hand, and all the furnishings had at least one chip or scar. If I had to guess, I'd say the look was intentional. Nothing went together, it was a hodgepodge collection. But somehow it all fit.

Hand-stitched afghans.

Lamps from the seventies.

Rugs so worn they were literally threadbare.

It was, without a doubt, the best damned thing I'd seen. It was a space for you to drop your guard.

A space that promoted normal breathing.

Polar sat down and smiled at the shit-eating grin I wore. "Seems you approve of our lodgings?"

"Would it be stupid to say this is the best surprise I've had since coming here?"

He draped his arms over the back of the couch, spanning the width. "Not at all." He motioned to a spot across from him. "Now take a seat and tell me what I've missed."

Polar was patient as I covered everything, not just Jester, but all the events that'd occurred since he was sent away.

A few times I tripped over my words, the memories stinging. He listened, with only the occasional nod to keep the momentum going.

Polar, in return, gave me very little. He said virtually nothing. Not a word about his time spent on the Southside, even when I asked about it. He skirted the subject of Ferno, and he avoided Thorn's name.

He tried to make small talk, which he sucked at, and his focus kept wandering to the wall where a cheap, plastic clock was mounted. It was the type of item you'd find at a rummage sale, its geriatric face so clouded it was hard to see the hands.

He seemed to be stalling and constantly fidgeted, as if he were waiting for something.

When the clock hit the eleventh hour, he gave me a crooked smile and told me to sit still. Then he left, retreating deeper into his quarters.

Far away, a door opened, the hinges loud enough even a human could hear.

And when he came back, he had a new swagger to his step.

Because behind him was a surprise I wasn't expecting.

Fantasia.

She looked exactly the same. Nothing about her had changed, well, except for the sadness shrouding her. Her black hair still shimmered, her olive skin glowed, her lavender eyes turned me dumb. In other words: beautifully perfect.

I froze, in shock, gratitude. *Disbelief.*

Then she smiled, and I smiled back feeling stupid happy.

Because I was stupidly, over-the-moon, ecstatically happy.

"You have ten minutes. If anyone comes in and sees you two alone, tell them I'm chaperoning and call for me." Polar looked at Fantasia. "We have no working cameras in our quarters and all our hinges are squeaky. Pay attention. And since I'm a lousy chaperone, I'll be in my room for ... Ten. Minutes. Exactly." He gave me a pointed look and nodded toward the clock. "Use your time wisely."

We were two magnets. The moment Polar left, we dove into each other's arms.

For the longest minutes of our lives, we stood silent, letting our hands say everything our voices couldn't.

Her skin smelled the same. Holding her was like coming home—and even the gloves covering my skin didn't deter me.

Our fingers explored every inch of flesh. Fantasia memorized my shoulders and chest with her touch. I couldn't get enough of her neck and lower back. If I could've dissolved into her, I would have.

Damned if I didn't try.

She placed her face against the bare skin in the crook of my neck, and my nerves jumped from the sensation. I was thankful her healing properties allowed us to touch, that my poison wasn't a match for her unique gifts. It's like we were made for each other.

When she pulled away to get a better look at me, her eyes were infinitely more vibrant with my immortal sight.

She cupped my face. "I've been so worried about you," she whispered.

I laughed. A real, true laugh. "*You* were worried about *me*? I thought you were dead. Imagine how that felt."

She rested her forehead against mine, her breath so close it crept into my lungs. "It was a mean trick."

"It was a mean thing to see." I raked her hair with my fingers. "How long has that marker been there?"

"A while. It was made after Chugknot."

His name pierced. I know it's stupid to be jealous of a dead guy, but some things can't be helped. Memories hold power, and he'd made himself infinitely fierce in Fantasia's past. And although I didn't know the details surrounding his death, I was able to guess a few things.

For example, that he was good and had conviction. That his taste was impeccable since he tried to pair up with Fantasia.

That I hated the sound of his name coming off her lips.

"I'm going to make that tombstone a lie," I vowed.

She shrugged it off. "I imagine it's only a matter of time before it comes true."

"Why would you say that?"

"Because it's my fate. I'm not willing to be their puppet and do everything they tell me to." Her voice brimmed with pride. "Even now, when they give me orders, I'm finding ways to undercut their authority." She gave me a wicked smile.

I wanted to shake her until some sense stuck.

This. This was why Torti came to me. To stop Fantasia from walking toward her death. To use our bond—the one I still felt—to end her recklessness.

"What are you going to do?" I asked.

She shook her head. "It's tricky."

"Don't pull that crap with me." I studied her face. "What are you doing?"

She folded her arms. "I have it under control, Daniel."

"Then it shouldn't bother you to fill me in."

"If you must know, it has to do with the human they're making me recruit. And it's fine. I have it under control."

"You've already said that."

She turned angry so fast it blazed. "You know they've never asked me to recruit a human. Not once. But now all of a sudden I'm a valuable asset and need to play my part in building our beloved society." She snorted. "I've only ever assisted. My sisters are the recruiters, but now Thorn's sidelined them. It's total crap and I'm gonna make her regret it." She stepped up to me and jabbed her finger into my chest. "They can't control me. *She* can't control me."

"Fancy—"

"Don't Fancy me." She socked her fist into my chest. The hit wasn't painful, it was what it represented that stung. "And don't you even think about schooling me. I get enough of that from my sisters."

I tried to touch her arm and she pulled away.

Her face flushed, and I realized she wasn't angry so much as upset. She bit her lip, doing her damnedest to keep it from trembling.

She was like her mom, handling anger better than fear, so that's the look she wore.

I didn't want to spend the small amount of time we had together fighting. She already felt like crap and I didn't want to make it worse. I gave her a sheepish grin and leaned down a fraction to catch her gaze.

"Let's talk about something else."

"I'd like that."

"Good, me too."

Fantasia swallowed and nodded. "I shouldn't have snapped."

"I'm already over it."

She went right back into my arms.

"So what shall we talk about?" I asked.

She smiled and cupped her hand around the base of my neck. A lover's embrace. "How about how much I've missed you? How I've been trying to find ways to get to you. I've walked past your window countless times, but someone was always nearby. I could feel their eyes even when they were lost in shadow." She pursed her lips. "They've been watching you so closely. I thought this moment would never come. I'm so thankful for Polar." She grew soft. "If it wasn't for him this wouldn't have been possible."

"So you're saying I owe Polar a big thank you."

"Only a lifetime's worth of gratitude."

"I think I can manage that."

She smiled, only it was stained with sadness. "I'm sorry about everything, Daniel. I'm sorry...." she choked on a sob and I shushed her.

"No more bad things. Not right now." I looked to the clock and was horrified to see how much time had passed—the world wasn't gracious enough to stop spinning on its axis. "We only have two minutes and thirty-five seconds left."

"No more bad things then." She rested her head against my shoulder and I squeezed her tighter. "You know what I've been thinking?" she asked.

I breathed into her ear. "No idea. I don't have that talent."

"I keep thinking I'm still a stranger to you. And you're a stranger to me. And yet," she sighed, "and yet you dominate all my thoughts. And I don't know why."

If I could've pulled her tighter, I would have.

Deep inside me, something lurched. For the longest time I'd worried it was fake. My feelings, the borderline obsession, it didn't make sense. I'd convinced myself nothing this real could be true. I thought my connection to her was tied to my human fragility, predator-prey as Jester said. A trick.

Anything but real.

And yet, here I was, a Velore, and the bond still pulled.

Torti. Dreams. They both believed in our connection.

Why shouldn't we?

"I can't explain it either. And I honestly don't care what it is." I ran my thumb down her cheek. "I just don't want it to go away."

"Me either."

We were alone, in the midst of an opportunity we might not get again. Or at least not for a long while.

And I'd had enough of rules. I tilted her head up and she moved in sync.

Our lips were only a hair's width apart when a door hinge squeaked, and we froze in a compromising position.

Polar stood in the doorway, wearing a look I couldn't place. He hesitated before clearing his throat and turning his back. "I forgot something in my room," he said and disappeared, giving us a few more desperate moments alone.

Fantasia smiled, and our lips came together in a direct violation of Narivous' laws. She tasted even better than I remembered.

I was grateful for my heightened senses.

And for my badass grandfather.

⚬⚬⚬

AFTERWARD, Polar escorted me back to the Poison Quarters, and I thanked him till his ears bled. He told me to keep it under wraps, a warning I didn't need. Aside from that, he was strangely silent, and I wondered if he regretted allowing me those stolen moments with Fantasia. He shoved his hands into his pockets to hide his anxiety.

He moved a lot like me when I was nervous.

When we reached my door, he paused, and looked toward the skull-lined mantels. I didn't follow his gaze. Instead, I focused on the lower half of his face, where white stubble shadowed his jawline.

He shook his head, barely a twitch, and pulled his hands out, only to crack his knuckles.

"Daniel," he started, "there's something I've got to tell you, and you're not going to like it." He swallowed, piercing me with his gaze. "You're to meet with the Seven tomorrow." My adrenaline spiked, and Polar placed his hand on my shoulder. "It's protocol for events like this. Standard. Don't let it get to you. It's really not a big deal."

"Then why does it feel like a big deal?"

He gave me a coy smile. "Alright," he conceded. "Maybe it *is* a big deal. But you have nothing to worry about. You've done nothing wrong when it comes to Jester. Just tell the truth and it'll all work out."

"Will you be there?"

He shook his head. "No, only the Seven, but I'll take you as far as the chambers. Hopefully, once they get their fill of what happened, that'll be the end of this whole ... *regrettable event.* And afterward"—he took a deep breath—"Thorn is going to have a private audience with you."

Everything went cold, and it wasn't because I was standing next to a man of ice. Fear gripped me, reaching deep inside to strangle my nerves.

"Look at me, Daniel. It's going to be okay. She's not angry anymore. She's done being angry. I spoke with her before coming to see you. She wants to move on. And to be honest, this meeting is long overdue. It was going to happen sooner or later, Jester was just the catalyst to get the ball rolling."

And to get the lab completed.

I almost asked him about it. To see how much he knew of the safe-hold being resurrected in secret. He was sent away for a reason, to stop his interference, and now it was probably too late. Despite Torti's assurance, I doubted I could make Thorn like me. I was the blemish in her reign. Proof others had gone against her.

Who wouldn't want to cut me out?

"A lot's happened today." Polar's eyes were kind, and he let go of my shoulder. "Get some sleep, and tomorrow will be better."

He walked away before I could argue.

And somehow he managed to steal the warmth, even though he took the draft with him.

CHAPTER 7
TRIAL

The next morning Scream was at my door, holding clothing in a garment bag, prodding me to get ready. She didn't mention Jester, or sneaking out, or plastering my cell with her power.

Nothing about my time in lockdown, or the investigation. Her mind was one track—*impress Thorn.*

So help me, I needed to.

"The suit's been tailored to fit you," she said as she draped it across the bed. "It's formal, designed to be worn for official meetings. Since you're now a member of our clan, you'll wear our emblem." She surveyed me from head to toe, looking for imperfections. "See to it you shower, shave, and comb your hair. You've been a bit unkempt lately. You have an hour." She gave me a tight smile and swept from the room.

I lingered in the shower, attempting to use up every drop of water to scrub away my memories. Jester's death clung to my skin, the way decay hugs a corpse.

I'd obsessed over Jester all night. Small pockets of information were starting to bleed through, and I wasn't sure if they were real or fabricated.

There was a vague snapshot of Jester rotting on the ground while I stood over him, a grin cracking my face.

His features were in an active state of erosion, as my powers crawled beneath the surface of his body.

They were connected to me. Every particle answered to my will. A minuscule army of soldiers. Mine to control. Mine to invade.

Mine.

And I could've made them stop if I wanted to.

But I didn't. Their hunger became my hunger, and I wanted them to devour, to eradicate Jester, making him nothing more than slime and rot. To taint Thorn's soil with his decay.

I looked into his eyeless sockets and urged them on as my body lighted with warmth, a cocoon enveloping me. It took a second to place what I was feeling: happiness.

True, bonafide happiness.

And the thing that got me, really got me, was the lack of guilt. Power blasted me, and I enjoyed every second of it. It was, without a doubt, one of the greatest moments of my life.

The sensation of control—I wanted it back. I craved it.

For the first time in my life, I was on the fringe of addiction, and it scared the living shit out of me.

⚒

I GOT DRESSED ON AUTOPILOT. The clothing selected for me was unlike anything I'd ever worn. It was too rich for me, well above my station. They'd clearly confused me with someone else, someone important. The black jacket was cut close to my body, and on one shoulder, stitched in a dark thread and barely discernible, was a spider web. A brand of strength, subtle enough to seem unobtrusive, but nonetheless there to make a statement. Slacks, onyx as night, draped the way quality fabric does.

As I stood in front of the mirror, a tidal wave of power tugged at me.

I smiled, thinking for a second I might be okay. Marveling at how a change in skin could warp my morbid thoughts into something more hopeful.

When Scream came to the door, a look of satisfaction played over her beautiful features. She let out a low whistle.

"Why, look at you," she said, crossing her arms. "I knew there was a handsome man behind all that slovenliness."

I fought back a scowl and tugged on my jacket.

Scream came up behind me and wrapped her arms around my shoulders. She looked at me through the mirror.

For a moment, I forgot about her dormant power. She had the ability to strike people dumb. Her lips nearly grazed my ear. "There will be a vote today, and I know it will be in your favor."

The blood drained from my face, and Scream squeezed me tighter. "Ah, don't worry, my darling. Just retell your story as is. Don't deviate from the truth. Thorn is a good woman. A fair queen. And you, my beautiful love, already own a piece of my heart." Her jasmine cloaked me. "You're like the son I never had. The child I always wanted, and I told her as much. Please," she whispered, turning me around, "mind your tongue and make me proud. I want nothing more than for you two to like each other. To understand each other." She stepped away. "She must come to like you. She must." And in her eyes I saw the truth. Scream knew about the lab's resurrection, she knew what was at stake.

She wanted me to make it all go away.

"Any advice?" I asked.

"Tell the truth." She stood on her tiptoes and kissed my forehead. "And you'll be fine."

It sounded like a lie.

POLAR WAS WAITING for me in the greeting room of the Poison Quarters. He and Scream exchanged a perfunctory kiss before she left to meet with the other Seven.

I had just enough time to throw back a cup of tea before Polar indicated it was time to go.

We started toward the back of the castle, and I bit my tongue as we neared the entrance with the rose emblem. Bad memories lived behind those doors. I hadn't been in that room since Tony's death, and I doubted my translucency could handle a frolic through such ugly history.

Thankfully, we veered to the right, where a stone staircase took us down deeper corridors, into the underbelly of the castle.

My thankfulness began to wane the farther we went.

Each hallway, with its jagged corners and confusing twists, made my brain swim. I tried to focus on our route, the direction we were headed in, but every passageway looked the same. It confused the crap out of me and set a hive of wasps fluttering in my gut.

The same stonework. The same shadows. The same depressing scent, a mixture of rotted dreams and abandoned hope.

And then, of course, my mind was elsewhere. Too wrapped up in what was to come to focus on much else.

I kept circling back to Fantasia and her covert methods. She was actively undercutting Thorn's authority, and I wanted details.

Knowing she was somehow using her recruit to do it only made me more curious.

For the umpteenth time in the past hour, I wanted our time back, simply so I could press harder and pry the information out of her. She was too strong willed. Her morals never wavered, and she was infuriatingly stubborn.

And I couldn't help but wonder—what if that was our last time together?

If I were to die, I wanted to go with only the best memories.

And if I lived, I'd convince Thorn I was the best, most obedient Velore she could ever hope for.

We finally stopped when we reached a tall, domed door made of black steel.

Polar rubbed his hands together and gave me a slight nod. "Just don't lie, and don't skim over details. And then the vote will follow. It goes without saying that the vote is a formality. Thorn has ultimate say, so see to it she speaks in your favor." His eyes moved around the empty corridor.

I swallowed and raked in the threshold. It scared the bejeezus out of me.

Polar leaned in and spoke in a voice barely above a whisper. "Afterward, she'll have everyone else leave. It'll just be you and her. Please, be on your best behavior. No smart-ass comments, don't talk back, show her the respect she deserves."

He meant beg.

Polar didn't miss my look of disgust and snatched me by the lapels. "She is our queen, Daniel. And no matter your personal opinion, she deserves our respect. Bow and honor, do you understand?"

I bobbed my head and he released me. My gaze wandered back to the door. The smile Polar gave was as colorless as his hair.

"Don't fail me," he said and reached for the knob.

EVERYTHING HAPPENED FAST. Polar must've suspected my nerves were about to short, because he didn't give me the opportunity to stall.

Instead, he ripped open the door and gave me a gentle but firm push and slammed it closed behind me.

Thankfully, I remembered to bow, because the power in the room was suffocating.

The room was large, circular, and commanding. The walls were lined with tiered rows of seats for prospective spectators that were, thankfully, all empty. In the center of the room, much like a bullseye, was a podium. Even though it was on the ground floor, it felt like a pit, especially since the room was built up around it. In front of the podium, a healthy distance away, was a platform with seven thrones. The seats flanked out in a V formation, with the largest and grandest at the front.

Each one was occupied by a regal woman, royally dressed —although they all paled in comparison to the one at the apex.

Not even dull lighting could fade the shine of her strength, nor the spark from her crown. Each golden thorn glinted.

Thorn gave me a smile, not the least bit friendly, and nodded toward the podium.

I took my place and stared up at my predators. The reckless side of me wanted to laugh. To have thought my poison afforded me protection was comical now that I stood in the maw of the beast.

For they were the seven masters of death.

The rulers were dazzling, and even though I'd only met a few aside from Scream, I knew who they were. I tallied my knowledge of the other clans. Two were unmarried—Thorn and Dolly. Serpent was the only Seven to be doomed along with her sweetheart. Amelia enjoyed eating her human kills. Ember held little humor. Frigid battled lucidity.

And Thorn commanded them all. Her neck was stiff with righteous power, framed by waves of auburn hair. Her hazel eyes, more vibrant with my immortal vision, captured the mellow lighting of the room, setting them afire.

Ember and Amelia, Fire and Animal, sat to Thorn's right and left. Amelia's feline face and mean smile tugged on my power, but the buzzing didn't surface. It was dormant—and I hoped it'd stay that way. Behind them were Serpent and Scream. Of all the Seven, I knew least of the Water leader. She had a snake cuff slinking up her arm and, despite the serious-ness of the situation, looked as if she were stifling a laugh. Mirth shone in her eyes, and it took a bit of the pressure off.

Scream snuck me a wink. It helped alleviate even more of the tension. But perhaps the most disturbing part was that no one seemed upset over Jester's death.

Was he a throw-away Velore?

I chose not to look at Dolly or Frigid. Both had eyes of ice, and where one was sharp the other was lost.

I gripped the podium and kept my spine straight as I waited for the interrogation to begin. Ember, surprisingly, took the lead. She unfolded from her throne and passed Thorn, her dress of liquid fire whispering against the polished steps. A smile of affection passed between the two.

It was a smile that couldn't be faked.

Ember's bright-red hair was tied back in a large bun, ruby studs pinning it in place. She wasn't wearing a tiara, but she still had a grace only the elite could pull off.

"Daniel," she purred, descending the raised platform to stop and stand in front of me. "We're going to make this as painless as possible." She motioned toward the other six, Thorn's face the most unreadable. My stomach somersaulted. "The events surrounding Jester's death seem straightforward, but we would like to hear your version of events." Her grin turned apologetic. "Propriety dictates such formality." She patted my hand, the way a mother would placate a child.

I looked down and steadied my breathing, gripping the podium like a buoy at sea. I allowed myself three breaths to mellow my nerves before going all in, spilling my guts with complete truth. Every morsel of honesty I owned went into my confession.

I told them why I left my room in the first place, threw the assholes who led me out under the bus.

I told them about Jester's tour and the words he spoke.

I told them everything.

Not a single detail was skimmed over, not an informational sliver omitted.

Besides, something told me they already knew.

Make Thorn like you, pinged over and over, not only a reminder but a silent prayer, too.

For Fantasia.

What took an eternity in my mind passed by with relative swiftness.

I lifted my head after I finished and looked from Ember to Scream. Both nodded, pleased, and my muscles slackened.

Ember moved in front of the podium, in a sense shielding me as she addressed the other six. "Is Daniel's testimony enough to satisfy Your Majesties?" she asked.

They answered in sequence, starting in the back with Dolly. She nodded and said, "Yea," followed by the others, each member granting their approval. Amelia hesitated, but followed suit. Ember was the last to voice her satisfaction.

Then it was Thorn's turn.

She stayed silent for a nasty amount of time. Dicking

around, making me squirm. She stood up and waved for Ember to take her place behind her.

I was left to stand alone in the pit, and it was as if the power shifted, as if Ember took away the little bit of strength I had.

Thorn's cheek flinched.

The vote is a formality. Polar's warning reverberated through me. Thorn could veto all of them and send me to the lab for execution.

She must've known I knew, because she waited.

And only after the tension built into a fog, when my fear had built to a subtle buzzing at the back of my skull, did she deliver her verdict.

If she had a gavel, it would've splintered on impact.

"Daniel," Thorn spoke my name and set my veins on fire. The other six stared. Even Amelia and Frigid lost their boredom. Thorn took a step away from her throne, each movement controlled.

She moved with lethal finesse. Her silk cape, the color of Fantasia's eyes, shimmered with each step.

Time was her weapon, and she sought to wield it in long, punishing strokes.

When she reached the ground floor and we were eye to eye, and a dozen feet apart, she said, "I've decided to let this infraction slide."

I nearly melted. She held up her hand and narrowed her eyes.

"Let's not get ahead of ourselves." She looked at me crookedly. "I believe it's time you and I have a chat."

She tried to make it sound spontaneous, but I knew better.

Thank you, Polar.

I nodded and stepped to the side of the podium, but didn't

move in her direction. She was leading the show and I'd be damned if I messed up her performance.

I bowed respectfully, to demonstrate my compliance, and when I unfolded she was peering behind her shoulder at the other six, as if weighing her options. Dolly raised her hand, tentatively, but the ice of her blue Doppelgänger eyes belied something more sinister churning behind her cherubic appearance.

"Yes, Dolly?" Thorn said.

Dolly stood and smoothed her dress, taking up a painful amount of time. She looked at me and flashed her teeth. "Will you be naming him?" she asked.

Thorn scrutinized me, as if the thought of giving me a new name was something she hadn't considered until that very moment.

A lie.

"Why, yes," Thorn said carefully, "I think I will."

"May I make a suggestion?" Dolly asked, her voice managing to be both silky and acidic.

Thorn wouldn't pull her gaze from me. "Why, of course, Dolly. You make such wonderful suggestions."

Behind her, my aunts started to fidget, Scream shuffling in her seat, her laced hand covering her mouth. Dolly's grin only grew. "I like his gloves," she said. "Perhaps you should name him Mittens."

Thorn yipped with laughter, even the others chuckled. Only Dolly remained stoic, as if affronted her suggestion wasn't being taken seriously.

It dawned on me this could be a test. Dolly had gotten into my head while I was still human, back when Chanticlaim's brain blockers had kept every other Doppelgänger out. She worked me like a robot, forcing words from my mouth that didn't belong to me.

She showed me images—some my own, others foreign.

She held me hostage while Thorn destroyed Tony.

And then, in a move I wasn't expecting, she pretended she couldn't see into my mind at all and told Thorn as much, which enraged our queen to the point she stormed out of the room, roiling with anger—giving Plague the opportunity to turn me into ... *this*.

Now we were standing across from each other, her blue eyes big and innocent. This was her way of showing me she wasn't afraid.

Yes, she lied to Thorn, but the dirt she had on me was greater than the dirt I had on her.

Because she knew it all. She knew who I'd fight to keep alive. Hell, I nearly desecrated an entire graveyard when I thought Fantasia was dead. And then there were the others....

Aunt Marie, Uncle Dean, and Lacey.

Charlie and my cousin Eric.

Polar.

She was sending a clear message: *I own your ass.*

And that's why she glowed with bravado, eager to poke the nest of wasps, daring me to open my mouth and spill my secrets—or my toxin.

Because she knew there was no way in hell I was going to do that.

I crossed my arms and bit back a snide remark. Thorn merely waved, snuffing the laughter, as she turned on her heel.

"If you will," she instructed the other six, "leave us. Mittens and I have a lot to discuss."

They all rose, silks and lace rustling as they moved toward the exit.

My eyes scanned over Scream as she brushed past, letting her hand trickle along my arm. "Take the joke," she lipped, before slipping out.

Dolly was last to leave, lingering long enough to shoot me a glare that should've incinerated me to ash.

Seems she may have saved me back when I was human only to resent me as a Velore.

Little did she know it no longer bothered me.

I was well used to it.

THORN'S FOOTSTEPS were so light it seemed she didn't touch the ground. She went back to her throne and sat.

I shoved my hands in my pockets and took to inspecting the floor.

"Come up here," she ordered, jutting her chin toward Ember's empty throne. "Shouting at you from across the room is a waste of energy."

I practically stumbled up the steps, my immortal grace failing me. Somehow, Thorn managed to appear neutral through it all, although her eyes never lost their piercing edge.

I went to sit in Ember's throne and Thorn growled. "Don't you dare." She leaned to the side, her expression bright and powerful. "That is a seat of honor, and you"—she pointed at me with disgust—"have not earned that right. You will stand as I address you."

"My apologies, Your Highness," I mumbled.

Her lips pulled into a calculating smile and she spoke softly, barely above a whisper. "Oh, how fun this will be."

CHAPTER 8

THORN

I switched schools so often I considered myself a nomad. The earlier years were the hardest. I was young, naive, and told myself stories. Big whopper tales.

Like this would be the last school and it was safe to make lasting friends.

That people wouldn't care I was poor. Or my dad was in jail, and my mom smelled like an ashtray drenched in tequila. That, by default, I smelled like smoke too, since I lived with churning chimneys of nicotine.

Oh, how I lied.

But if that wasn't bad enough, at my ninth school, in the middle of my fifth-grade year, I met a kid hell-bent on making my already miserable existence even more miserable.

A feat he mastered with little effort.

His name was Clint, and his life was as crummy as mine. But whereas you'd expect it to build a bond, it created a divide. Primarily because my dad and his dad hated each other.

Thing is, even dirtbags have a code of ethics, and my dad couldn't even abide by those.

He narced.

The greatest, most awful offense a sleazeball can make. And my dad did it, with very little goading. A cop found his stash and a dirty needle, and Dad went belly up, offering Clint's dad in exchange for leniency.

Word got around pretty fast, and when Clint made the connection I was the son of the bastard who ruined his family, their feud became our feud.

And Clint had about twenty pounds of lard on me, which he liked to throw around when no one was looking.

He punched.

Kicked.

Slapped, smacked, and walloped.

Always when teachers weren't looking.

He was a bully, and it offered him a layer of protection. No one went against Clint.

And I'd be damned if I told. That would make me my father's son—not just in blood, but actions—and the insult would hurt worse than the injuries.

No, thank you.

So I found another way to end it. I was vigilant, a master of invisibility, and one day I caught him looking at two sketches he kept hidden in his cubby. They were prison pieces, drawn on lined paper—portraits of Clint and his dad. There was some crud scrawled on the bottom, stupid words about how much his dad loved him. Called him his boy. Said he was proud. Missed him. Bullshit I never heard, not even once, from my own dad. Blah, blah, blah ... It tinted my blood green.

Clint thought no one knew, or maybe he thought he was untouchable. Either way, he was wrong.

I jacked the drawings and used them as collateral.

I told him I ripped up one and flushed it down the toilet.

Clint's bottom lip started to tremble, but he had the sense to bite down and stop it.

It made me smile.

Clint's small, meaty hands balled into tight fists. "What are you gonna do?" he asked, and I told him that depended on him. The meaner he was, the more likely I'd flush the other, too.

He threatened to tell, and I turned on him. Called him a narc, and asked how proud his papa would be to have a spineless bastard for a son.

I shut him down with his own code.

And two months later, when Mom got evicted from our slimy apartment and I had to switch schools, I made sure to put both pictures back in his cubby.

Because the truth of the matter was I didn't destroy either, even though I wanted to. I hung onto them because I wasn't entirely sure I could rip his memories to shreds.

Maybe I was weak.

But whatever, it still worked. By pretending to destroy one, it made him desperate for the other.

I only had to make him believe.

Because that's what life is—a farce.

And I was getting good at pretending.

Now, with Thorn in front of me, her polished nails stroking the arm of her throne, I had to convince her I was worthy.

That I would do her bidding.

Make her believe.

I tucked my hand behind my back and bowed again, keeping my smile respectful and my eyes dutifully downcast.

The whole shtick made me want to hurl, but she seemed to buy it.

Still, she made me stand in front of an open seat, to show my place. The back of my legs hit the cushioned pad of Ember's throne.

Thorn cocked her head and appraised me, the glint in her eye softening slightly. "This conversation's been long overdue."

I nodded, unsure if my voice would hold up. But she waited on me, so I said, "I've been looking forward to it." And even I was surprised with how genuine it sounded.

"Oh?" Her brows arched.

"Yeah. I've been wanting to tell you how sorry I am for all the trouble I've caused."

Eat my lies....

Thorn's cheeks blushed with subtle color. The silence was too quiet, if that were such a thing, and I sought to fill it with groveling.

Because she clearly liked groveling.

"And I promise to be a good citizen, to follow your orders. I won't be a problem anymore."

"Sit down," she ordered, her voice leaving icy slivers.

She indicated the step and I fell into place, she atop a pedestal, me at her feet.

Thorn raised her chin so slightly, had it not been for my sharpened vision I would've missed it.

"You say you won't be a problem," she began, "but Jester's decaying corpse tells another story."

My mouth had run dry. Everything about Thorn screamed danger, that is, aside from her appearance. She was a trap, her looks a subtle weapon to lure in prey, and now her focus was on me.

"He, uh, he provoked me." I wrung the back of my neck,

nerves on edge. "I tried to take the Dexitrol to stop it, but he knocked it away."

"Yes, but you shouldn't have been in that graveyard to begin with. Had you followed my orders Jester would still be alive. You own more responsibility than you care to admit."

Something inside me cracked, and I hung my head. Of all the scenarios I'd played out in my head, that was the one I'd been too afraid to touch. She was right.

My hands were covered in Jester's blood.

"I saw the body, you know," she said, her tone caressing. "And I have to say, you worked quite the number on him."

Was it possible for her words to splinter my lungs? The icy message nearly froze my heart mid-thud. I focused on keeping my face flat, unmoving.

"Fortunately for you," Thorn continued, "I never really cared for Jester." She was staring so intently, waiting for me to react. Adopting a conspiratorial tone, she leaned forward. "And at least he had the good sense to kill himself in the graveyard. Made cleanup easier." She chuckled, and somehow, miraculously, I managed not to recoil. "Although, to be fair, after you'd finished with him there wasn't much left to bury." She clapped her hands, amused, before letting her laughter fade.

"The body was such a mess." Her voice had a lazy quality to it. She looked at me with a bright gleam. "He was barely recognizable. Nothing but rotted skin and bones, lying in a pool of congealed blood, dark as death itself." Her shoulders sagged, and she closed her eyes and dipped her head back, reliving the scene. Her neck, smooth and beautiful, arched as she basked in the pleasure of a memory that was a nightmare for me, a daydream for her. She sighed and opened her eyes. "Not to mention the sad state of the cemetery. I had to go in and regrow the plants you killed, which is difficult to do with a layer of that"—she circled her hand—"goop."

Guilt churned in my stomach and anger burned my veins. Jester had taken something good from me. He'd used me as a vessel for his own personal gain. He'd used me as everyone else used me. I bit my lip and stared at my lap, managing to choke out a pitiful, "I'm sorry."

I didn't so much see Thorn stand as felt the atmosphere shift. She weaved herself between the thrones, touching each one with careful strokes, before folding her manicured hands behind her. She stopped at the last one in the far back. The one with cherubs and eyes—Dolly's insignia—and kept her expression shielded.

"No need to apologize," she said generously. "Jester contributed to the issue, and seeing he's dead, we might as well let it go. But I will say this, I was impressed with your level of destruction. It shows you have potential."

What?

She turned, her face stern but excited. "I like to think I'm rarely surprised. I've almost always found life predictable. People, predictable. But you ..." She paused and her eyes flashed. "You've proven to be quite the little conundrum. I'm both angry with your existence and ... *intrigued*. You know, it took years for your aunt to wield such catastrophic results." Her face split with a smile. "And now you have me thinking, perhaps, with some work, we can alter your mistaken transformation into a beneficial one. One that will benefit me. Because, Daniel, everything and everyone in Narivous is here to serve me."

My back pulled tight. Torti said Thorn loved power above all else, that my mistake may be the catalyst to make her like me. Her prophecy was eerily accurate.

"I've learned to adapt," Thorn continued. "That's what being queen is all about. Adaption, power. Your *creation*"—she paused again, testing the word in her mouth, her features pinched—"was an abomination against my rule. I've forbidden the making of any new Poison members for very good reason. Their powers are unpredictable and dangerous to my beloved society."

I kept my face flat. She spoke of her society, when really she meant herself. She couldn't control the Poisons—the only Velores capable of surviving death by topiary. Control was lost on them. On me.

It vexed her.

She walked toward her throne and positioned herself behind it, running her hands along the top. Her face shadowed over. "You shouldn't have been made," she continued. "I can't have my subjects disobeying me, regardless of their motives, it makes for a very sloppy court. Do you know I considered killing your makers? They would've earned it too." She arched a brow and waited for my reaction. My intestines twisted into an angry knot.

Whatever my face belied, it made her happy, because one cheek lifted with a half-hearted smile.

"You know why I didn't?" she asked. "I thought to myself, if I kill them, would it take away from my control? My leverage?" She laughed with an insane lilt. "By keeping them alive, I have more power."

Breathe in and out. In and out. Don't let her see you fold.

She saw anyway.

"I have to pick my sacrifices wisely. I only want ripples, not tidal waves," she said, malice infusing each word. "I want boats to rock, but not capsize. For the boats belong to me. As does the water. The land. Everything. They are mine and are here to serve my needs."

She paused. "And I can't decide with you. If I should keep you or capsize you."

Appearances were important to Thorn. She wanted her

citizens to see her as omnipresent, all encompassing. Queen and God in one stroke. By simply allowing me to breathe, it made her look weak.

Thorn gave me a smile from her poisoned lips, her face darkening over.

I had the good sense to say nothing.

"I think you and I should get to know each other better, before I make such lofty decisions," she continued, as she took her seat, her eyes never leaving me. "And if you answer the way I hope, perhaps I can find a use for you yet. Everything I've heard is secondhand—and secondhand gossip is always skewed. So, Daniel, tell me ..." She ran her tongue along her lips. "What do you think of the human world?"

A test. It was so painfully clear she might as well have handed me a sheet of paper and a No. 2 pencil.

I knew what she wanted to hear. So I went with it.

"The human world blows."

She smiled wide. "Oh? How's that?"

I thought back to my nomad years, the nights I'd been discarded for bigger and better things, i.e., drugs, gambling, and booze.

How drugs dilute blood, erasing familial bonds, turning parents into strangers.

What I spilled next wasn't a lie, but honesty in its rawest form.

"It's filled with shitty people, with shitty agendas. Opportunists who look for kind-hearted people, taking from them until there's nothing left to take. They ruin them, one stab in the back at a time." I looked down at my gloved hands and wished I could see the flesh underneath. I used to have my hands memorized. All the bad years when ugly words were shouted by ugly people—I'd stare at them. I'd focus until my palms blurred.

I knew them well.

They were a safe sight when my world was crumbling. It didn't matter where I was.

Sitting outside in the cold, while Mom and Dad had a row.

Sleeping in our car after being evicted.

Waiting to be picked up after school, knowing all along they'd forgotten about me.

I turned my palms over and hated how they were lost beneath the mesh.

I wanted them back.

"I'd have to agree with you," Thorn said, grabbing back my attention. "Humans are too easily swayed by mortal vices. My Velores are stronger. Better." She tapped her head. "Our bodies are not as fallible to addiction or weaknesses of the spirit."

I nodded. Fantasia had pretty much said the same thing, minus the boasting.

Thorn cocked her head. "Tell me about your parents."

"Not a lot to tell, really."

Weak.

"You're not a good liar, Daniel," Thorn mused. "Which may work in my favor." She folded her hands in her lap. "Out with it. This is us getting to know each other. I won't have you holding back. Not only is it rude, but it's very unbecoming behavior to display in front of your sovereign. That and, need I remind you, lying to me is a punishable offense. So unless you're prepared to suffer the consequences of my displeasure, I suggest you loosen your tongue and speak honestly."

"Sorry, it's just ..." I ran my fingers through my hair. "They weren't very good parents. They weren't even good people. I don't think they even wanted me, but they had no problem using me when it suited them." My jaw clenched. "All I have are scars and crappy memories I'd rather forget."

Something flashed in Thorn's expression. She nodded, as if

I'd said something so profound I stunned her. She leaned forward in her chair. "Would you believe me if I said I understood?" She smiled at my surprise and shook her head. "We can move on." She looked toward the door, and I recognized something I never expected to see—a morsel of her humanity. I thought back to the memorials in the graveyard. There was something festering in her past.

I felt a tug. Understanding, maybe? Pity? Or perhaps camaraderie?

When she looked back, she'd changed. Become stiffer, more determined. Perhaps edging closer to anger. Whatever memory she pulled up, it wasn't a pleasant one. "So tell me, how do you like my society?"

The test was back.

I shrugged my shoulders. "I can't really say. I've been stuck in my rooms for so long, I barely remember what your city looks like. It's kind of made me stir crazy. And, well, no one really talks to me."

I tried to keep my tone fair, but it had an accusing quality to it.

Thorn met it defensively.

"It's for the best." She gave me a syrupy smile. "New Velores are tricky creatures. They wake up from death, alert and often afraid, armed with powers beyond their wildest dreams. These gifts are foreign, wholly unnatural, and many slip into translucency straight away. It simply cannot be helped. Mind you, not all gifts are threatening. The Doppelgängers come to mind. Waters are equally un-lethal, considering, of course, you're nowhere near a significant source of liquid. But then we have clans such as yours that amplify our need for precautions. What you hold within your body could decimate a great portion of my population. What kind of ruler would I be if I let one of my deadliest Velores—a novice with fresh power—walk around my city without any safeguards? Even for a sliver of time? Even the insane would consider that mad. *Reckless.* If Jester weren't a puddle of goop, we could ask him to recount how quickly you slipped."

She hesitated for only a moment, her eyes luminescent. My silence was all the incentive she needed. "So how do you like them?" she asked, indicating my gloves.

She was trying her best to provoke me.

And stupid me let her crawl under my skin.

"I understand why you put them on," I said. She started to smile and it pissed me off. Her unpredictability was infuriating. I wanted out. She was suffocating the room, and in a lapse of judgement, I allowed my defiant mouth to run away with me. "I think gluing them on wasn't necessary."

The shadow smile on Thorn's face fell.

"Don't you talk to me like that," she hissed. Hairline cracks formed around her eyes and the whites flashed with power.

It was a stark reminder of what lay beneath the surface. A flicker of her deadly abilities.

Self-preservation kicked in.

"I'm sorry," I said, desperate to backtrack, if not for me, then for Fantasia.

Make Thorn like you.

"I-I just meant I'd do anything you asked. I'd wear them indefinitely if you told me to. Your order would be as good as glue. I didn't mean anything by it."

"On your knees," she barked.

I followed her orders, every muscle protesting. Embarrassment brought on a heated rush, and I hung my head.

"Listen good," she said, "and look at me when I speak."

I lifted my jaw and saw Thorn losing herself in anger. She'd risen from her throne and was looming over me. Her translucent phase was quickly building. Her skin turned to moss, with dark fissures creeping and breaking across her complexion. Then there were her eyes, light framing black orbs, the hazel gone.

She leaned down and shot her hand out, the move quick as a blur. With angry fingers, she latched onto my face, her nails digging into bare skin.

And she wasn't wearing gloves.

Pain tugged on her demonic features, but she refused to let go. Almost nose to nose, she spoke soft, threatening words. "You may be deadly, Daniel, but so am I. And hear this now. *You. Can't. Kill. Me.*" Each word enunciated carefully. "Do you understand?"

She flung me away and pulled her wounded hand to her chest. Her fingers flexed in search of relief.

"Get out of my sight," she ordered.

I scrambled down the platform, and as I reached the midway point to the door, near the podium, she called out.

"You're indeed dangerous, Daniel," she started. "And mark my words, death will follow you, whether you want it to or not. Jester's slaughter is now yours. He's left his mark. He will be the first of many. And for that, I will give you a name to remind you of your curse."

The smile she gave me was full of hatred.

"Your new name shall be 'Death.'"

A ripple raced down my spine.

"Now leave me."

I couldn't get to the door fast enough.

CHAPTER 9
A FRIGID GREETING

I stumbled into the hallway, shell-shocked and disorientated. A guard, who wasn't there when I went in, stood vigil outside the door. He looked the part of menacing: tall, pale, with obsidian eyes. He had might.

"I think Thorn needs help," I stammered, and he cocked his head, taking me in, baring his teeth.

"Did you injure our queen?" he snarled, taking a threatening step toward me.

I shook my head and tried to move away, but the door hit me in the ass.

"No. She touched me." I wasn't sure how badly she was hurt, but I didn't want the blame to fall on my shoulders. Not that it would matter—her word was law. If she said I attacked her, there would be little I could do to argue against it.

But somehow, confession felt ... *right*. Like it could help balance the scales, even if only a marginal amount.

"She's been exposed to your poison?" His face took on a powerful scowl.

"She did it to prove a point." I attempted to meld to the door, as fear sucked the power from my skull.

He weighed the information and after a few tense moments said, "I'll see to her." I jumped aside as he pushed his way through the threshold, the hinges cracking from the force of his swing.

I took off at a run.

I should've paid attention to the twists and turns of the corridor when Polar guided me below the castle, but the impending meeting with Thorn threw my internal compass and ruined my good sense.

It wasn't long after making a few wrong turns—or maybe one wrong turn that went on forever—that I found myself lost in the pit of the castle. Far below ground, everything was darker. The castle grew above and below the surface.

The hallways were stone silent, and as I attempted to retrace my footsteps, a noise reached my ears. Breathing and whispers. I followed the sound, eager, since I was at the point of staying lost indefinitely unless I located someone.

It seemed whoever it was heard my footsteps, no matter how quiet I tried to make them, because they clammed up.

A static charge bounced off the stonework.

Not being alone and not being able to see who was with me pitted my gut. I wondered if I was being stalked.

You're not helpless anymore. You're deadly, Daniel.

Or is that Death? I shook my head. I'd never accept that name. Thorn branded me, gave me a title to weigh me down. Jester's crime a reminder every time anyone addressed me.

Calculating bitch.

The light was lacking, with only a few faint sconces showing the way, but my refined vision needed very little and I took each turn with bravado. Not letting the dark shadows intimidate me.

I hit a few dead ends, with nothing but doors and corridors looping into confusing circles. The arches and angles promised to keep me wandering for ages.

Then I captured a smell. One that was fragrant and full of comfort.

I let the scent guide me and followed the aromatic trail. It led me back to the same corridor where I'd detected breathing, the section that held too many shadows to count. It was a hub within the castle, a long hallway with a half-dozen corridors snaking from the main body.

Why was I foolish enough to focus only on my hearing and sight? How had I missed the scent before? Perhaps a draft now carried it toward me? Regardless, I tracked the smell, creeping along the wall, careful not to spook whoever was hiding in the recesses.

There were no visible cameras, unlike most places within the castle, and not having a glass eye on me alleviated a touch of stress.

After a few steps I spotted who was occupying the space. And it wasn't one, but two someones.

I froze. They were distracted and had no idea they had an audience. Because they weren't trailing me at all, but were engaged with each other.

In the dark, away from prying eyes, Polar's white hair was a beacon against the black. His head was bowed and his eyes closed, as he leaned his forehead against the smooth, pale skin of a beautiful female.

And it wasn't his wife, Frigid.

Camille's golden coils gently swayed in the drafty corridor. Polar's one hand was on her lower back; the other rested against her cheek. Camille's arms were wrapped loosely around his shoulders. They stood silently, as if breathing the other in.

What the hell?

It felt too intimate to be appropriate.

I cleared my throat and they both jumped, whipping around to look at me, their faces the color of embarrassment.

They recovered quickly. Camille turned her blue eyes down and smoothed the fabric of her shirt, tugging it even though it draped perfectly over her frame.

Polar flashed his teeth.

"Daniel," he clapped his hands, all smiles and pleasantries. "I was wondering when you'd get back."

I looked between the two, and Camille curled her lip into a defiant snarl.

"Did I interrupt something?" I asked.

Polar's reaction wasn't the least bit forced. He squinted his eyes as if my question was ludicrous. "Of course not. Camille had some information to share with me, and we were just digesting it."

"That's a unique way to digest it."

He shrugged and gave Camille a short glance. The smile she offered didn't light up her face. "You can go now," he said to her, and she quickly bowed before heading past me, careful to avoid my touch. When she'd disappeared, taking the scent I'd followed with her, Polar took a step forward and lost his friendly prose.

"Don't question me in front of subordinates," he shot.

"Don't lie to me and I won't."

"What makes you think I was lying?"

I snorted and crossed my arms across my chest. "Really?" *How was that anything but inappropriate?* "You two looked like you were about to kiss."

"Did you see us kiss?" His question came out more accusatory than inquiry, as if he knew the answer, and before I could reply he leaned in closer. "Of course you didn't, because we weren't kissing. And to spread a rumor like that would do neither of us any favors." His blue eyes held my own. Not petitioning really, more like demanding. "We were talking, Daniel, that's it. She's had some rough news, and we have a history."

"A history?"

"I suppose not everything Jester told you was a lie."

Whoa ... "What?"

Polar's shoulders slumped and he leaned against the wall. He shoved his hands in his pockets, in a move very much like my own. "What he said about recruiters and the bond they have with their recruited. I think there may be some truth to that." He cleared his throat and dodged my gaze. "Camille was mine and, well, we've always had a bond. From the very first day I met her." Polar shifted his feet. When he looked back up, he wore a mask of wistfulness. He glanced behind me in the direction Camille had fled, as if he could still see her. "We became friends. Close friends, and that bond never really went away. Maybe because she was the first person I knew here, aside from my brothers, but regardless, she's special to me, and I make no apologies for that."

My face cramped. If that were true, could that mean the connection between Fantasia and I was false? The thread linking us nothing but a farce?

A warped sense of Stockholm syndrome?

Polar searched my crestfallen face and attempted to backtrack. "It's different for everyone, though. Camille recruited my brothers, too, and they don't have anywhere near the same connection we do."

I wanted to ask, to see how deep his feelings went for Camille. To see if they mirrored my own for Fantasia. But fear embedded itself deep in my throat, blocking my voice. All I managed to get out was a pitiful, "Okay."

"Can you do me a favor, though?" he asked, his voice splintering in a way that told me he really didn't want to say what was coming next.

"Sure."

"Don't tell Frigid. About what you just saw, I mean." His shoulders slumped. "She's fragile."

Something told me it was a bit more than that, but I agreed, because it was none of my business. Besides, he was keeping my secrets too, and I wanted to repay the favor.

But of all the things to bother me, it wasn't the sneaking around or lying, it was the sadness he wore. It wasn't fitting— it wasn't Polar—and I didn't like it.

Not one bit.

⁂

NEWS CAME THAT EVENING: I had a gentle release on my confinement. Scream was all smiles, not the least bit aware of the painful ending to my meeting with Thorn.

"A gentle release?" I asked.

"You're allowed to roam the castle and, at night, when most of Narivous is sleeping, to explore the royal grounds." Scream clapped her hands.

My smile wasn't convincing.

"There's more, though," she said, determined to earn a more excited response. She paced my bedroom. "Right now, I have it on good authority you'll get to sit in the royal conjunction box at the Dawning Rose Celebration."

I grinned at her enthusiasm, although I was confused as hell. I'd heard of the Dawning Rose Celebration, and knew it was a ritual in honor of Thorn. Marking not her birthday, but her resurrection day. But aside from that, the details were foggy. This was the first I'd heard of a viewing box.

Scream filled in the blanks. "It's a grand display. All the

Sevens play a role—you'll get to see us in action." She shot me a wink and squeezed my fingers. "And because you're family, you'll get one of the best seats in the house. This year it'll be even more special because you'll be with us." She lifted my hand to her lips and kissed it. "And, as it so happens, Thorn is selecting two new guards. You'll get to see the Trials of Worthiness." She sighed, her contentment running from her hand through my arm. "It's my favorite time of year."

"Um, as helpful as all that is, I'm still confused. What's the Trials of Worthiness?"

"Just what it sounds like. Velores wanting the guard positions compete. They showcase their talents and only the very best get selected. It's a title of honor and prestige. And, if they're new recruits, the recruiters get a reward too. So even if they don't qualify for guard duty, it gives them incentive to bring in others who will."

All news to me. But she'd piqued my interest. "What kind of rewards?"

She shrugged. "It depends. I've seen monetary gifts. Homes. Land. Familial protection. It's all contingent on the desires of the winners."

"Familial protection?"

"The human family members of Velores are protected. They can't be collateral if the Velore screws up."

Priceless.

Scream continued. "We've also extended protection by destroying their enemies. A lot of our recruits come from less than ideal circumstances, and riffraff follows them. Most of them are afraid of immortality, not for their souls, but for leaving their loved ones behind unprotected. We take out their threats and soften their worries."

She kissed my hand for a second time. "Obedience and loyal servitude are highly rewarded here."

So it seemed.

I wasn't going to utilize my newfound freedom—it felt too much like a lengthened chain and not liberation. But Polar practically shoved me out the door as soon as the moon rose. "You have a pass for fresh air—use it," he snapped.

The royal gardens stretched to the far right of the castle, thriving despite the thick grove and looming overhead branches.

Out in the open, I could feel eyes on me but chose to ignore it, instead focusing on the feel of real air. On how nice it tasted.

There were fountains and benches. Trellises wrapped in ivy, birdbaths of concrete. Roses of the rainbow and statues, including another memorial to Thorn's mother. The carver sculpted her from soapstone, displaying her sitting on the ground, a wreath of wildflowers twined in her hair. It was a beautiful space filled with romantic archways and colorful petals, and one I would've paid more attention to had it not been for the scent of cinnamon.

Maybe the eyes watching me were the eyes I wanted to see.

Thorn's greenery was everywhere, and to the back was a reaching hedgerow. The base was littered with flowers. I followed it to where it cut off abruptly and realized it wasn't a wall, but a maze. Cinnamon mixed with earth, and I stepped inside and followed the trail.

The moonlight found fractional pockets to spill across my path, and unlike the mazes I'd seen in picture books, Thorn's had trees growing inside it. The limbs defied gravity by growing off spindly trunks, keeping Narivous under the concealment it craves.

I wasn't sure if it was off limits or not; I simply followed my nose.

And the scent of cinnamon grew. I made wrong turn after wrong turn, passing little cherubs and gargoyles sitting amongst roses and other perennials tucked into decorative niches.

The walls loomed, and gnarly branches threw shadows.

And then I heard a voice call out my name.

"Daniel?"

Fancy. She was on the other side of the hedge. I edged as close as I could without making contact with the shrubbery. I didn't want to kill Thorn's plants.

"I'm gonna come find you," I whispered.

"No, don't." I could feel her on the other side. So close yet so far away. "It's safer this way."

Our words barely breached the barrier of topiary. It seemed fitting Thorn's magic was standing between us.

"Did you know I'd be out here? Or are you just some hot chick who likes hiding out in the bushes?"

She smiled, I could feel it. "A man of ice may have tipped me off. He told me Thorn gave you some leeway."

Now I smiled. "Looks like I owe Polar another one. And, yeah, they're broadening my cage."

"So the meeting with Thorn went okay?"

"Well, kinda." I looked around the maze and sniffed the air. The only person I felt or experienced was Fantasia. Still, I dropped my voice to a near breath. "The first part was okay, but the second part got a bit complicated."

"Details?"

I was grateful for the divide between us. She wouldn't see the heat in my expression. "She asked me questions about my past. About my parents. And then she got all hostile." I omitted the part about my smart mouth, knowing Fantasia would lecture. "Thorn grabbed my skin without any gloves on to prove I couldn't kill her."

"Heavy."

"Yeah, and, uh, she gave me my new name."

"I heard. How do you feel about it?"

"How do you think I feel about it? Shitty."

"It's not *that* bad...."

"Liar."

"No, it's true. It makes you sound like a badass."

"Your flattery's weak."

"Ah, yes. But you're smiling, I can tell."

She was right. So many questions barreled through my brain. Answers I needed to know. I wanted to ask about her mom and Polar. I wanted to ask about the rose ceremony. If she knew what Thorn was planning to do with me.

"They stopped the lab," she whispered.

"What?"

"Thorn's no longer having it built. She ordered the work halted."

"Are you sure?"

Her words grew eager. "Yes. She actually had the workers pulled out right after your meeting with her. You stopped it, Daniel. You stopped it."

Daniel. My smile grew.

"But why?"

"I dunno," she breathed. "But you must've impressed her."

Crickets filled the silence.

"Fantasia?"

"Yes?"

"You look really pretty."

She gave a happy snort. "You can't see me."

I smiled. "Ah, yes, but I'm picturing you right now."

"Oh yeah?"

"Yeah, you're naked and look great. I admire your boldness."

She snickered in an attempt to suppress a laugh. It made me smile even wider.

Seconds. Then a minute. Quiet calm, until she cleared her throat and shifted the tone.

"Daniel?"

"Yes?"

"Before I go ... I have to tell you something."

"Why don't I like the sound of that?"

I felt her creep closer to the other side of the hedge. "Tomorrow some bad stuff might happen. And I need you to know it's the only thing I could come up with. Forgive me."

"What are you doing, Fantasia?"

Her breathing shallowed. "I'm sorry," she said, and then, to my horror, her footsteps retreated.

"Stop!" I called out, louder than all our stolen words put together.

I ran farther into the maze, but the turns twisted me, and by the time I reached the other side, her scent was already dissolving. I was surrounded by dark, empty shadows, and the eyes I felt were only a memory.

She was gone.

⚬

THAT NIGHT, after I found Polar to thank him, I asked if I could crash in his apartment.

He didn't even seem phased when I requested the couch over the spare room. It's like he understood me and, as was the norm, let me have my way.

The Ice Quarters, despite the pervasive chill, was warmer. More inviting.

It felt like home.

I woke up the next morning when the temperature in the room dropped. I opened my eyes to find Frigid lounging in a chair opposite me. She had her legs folded under her in a child-like pose, cradling a cup, her fingers wrapped tight against the porcelain. She was wearing a loose gown and her customary choker pinned around her neck.

Her blue eyes, normally swimming with insanity, were vividly clear. The smile she gave me was open and eager.

She wasn't lost in her madness.

It was enough to make me bolt upright. I ran my fingers through my hair and rubbed the sleep from my face.

"Hey," I croaked, and she flashed her teeth in a beautiful, angelic smile.

Damn, I'd never seen her like this, and it threw me off balance.

"Hey, yourself." Her voice was as melodic as I remembered, back in the forest, when I was lured by her siren song. Only now there was no trap lingering beneath her words.

This was, without a doubt, her. The real her.

"How'd you sleep?" she asked.

"Good. Really good, actually." The couch, the worn feel of the leather, the exhaustion over the past few days, all of it merged. I'd slept like the dead.

"I'm so happy to have you here, D. I've been wanting to talk with you for a while, but well ... you know ..." She looked to the cup she held in her hand, embarrassed by her shoddy mind.

Everything about her was soft. Her mannerisms, her long white hair, her beautiful porcelain skin.

And the fact she called me D, which meant she knew my new name and didn't want to rub it in.

I now understood why Fantasia said Frigid was good, when her mind allowed her to be.

"It's alright," I said.

"No." She shook her head and loosed a deep sigh. I swear a chilly breeze touched my skin. "It's not. Not really. But, no matter how hard I try, I can't keep it away. The hardest part is not remembering. It's like having pieces of time stolen away. Not having control ..." She placed the cup on the table, and looked toward the ceiling, almost as if she were in silent prayer. When she pulled her head back, her face was ravaged with despair. "I hate not having control."

"I so understand," I mumbled, thinking back to my powers in the cemetery. She nodded.

"Jester was a tormented soul." She pegged my thoughts. "Every time I saw him he was always in the same spot, sitting by himself atop a tombstone. Even for a city of outcasts, he was a bit more of an outsider than the rest of us. My only hope is he'll have found the peace he was so desperate for."

She painted a pathetic picture. "Me too," I said.

"Maybe one of these days, when you're feeling up to it, you'll share the details of what happened with me."

I smarted, pulling my head back to peer at her curiously. She was in the Throne Room when I gave my testimony.

"Um, I already told you everything."

She cocked her head, confusion tugging her brows in.

"Back at the council meeting, remember?" I said. "Yester-day? When you voted to let me off the hook?"

She grabbed a strand of her hair, pulling it between her fingers, her mouth shaped into a small 'O,' before she said, "Oh that." Her laughter was nervous, and she looked away, embar-rassed. "They often drug me for public appearances. It's how they manage me when they're putting on a show, especially if I'm displaying behavior that's less than becoming." She continued to stroke her hair nervously. "It's a bit shameful, really, but Narivous is all for show, and no one wants to demote me. So they have no choice but to put me in a trance. But the drugs wear off rather quickly, so it's more like an ill-fitting bandage."

"That sounds kinda awful."

"It is. It really is. I'm just glad I voted in your favor." She tried to make it sound light, but her tenor was too tight. She bit her lip. "Thing is ... I don't really know who I am anymore. Somehow, over time, I've forgotten. I miss not having an identity."

A shudder built along her shoulders and crept down her torso, and it wasn't from the cold.

She shook her head, dislodging some painful thought, and looked at me. "There's something I've been wanting to ask you," she said. "I wanted it to be the right moment, when I was in the right place." She tapped her temple.

She had my full attention. I folded my hands in my lap. They were starting to shake, and something told me she wouldn't miss it.

I marveled at how rapidly, and completely, she could transform from insanity to clarity. Her piercing blue eyes as sharp as a hawk's.

"When I turn, I don't always forget *everything*. Pieces break through, kind of like snapshots. They're short and don't tell me much. And honestly, it really depends on how deep I am in my translucency." She cleared her throat. "Thing is, I have a snapshot of a time in the forest. With a boy much like you. Same build. Same height. Same lopsided smile. I remember that boy, and for a time, I worried I may have killed him. He was so handsome, reminded me of a younger version of my Polar. I went back the next day, when my head was clear, to search for evidence. I even went so far as to ask a few Velores if they dumped any bodies on my behalf." She paused and blinked her eyes. "They've done that, in the past, you know. Removed corpses to spare my feelings. Everyone is always bending over backward for me. But this time ... well, this time they all said no. And now, looking at you ... I think I know why."

My nerves lit up, and I raked my fingers through my hair.

She knew.

She remembered me when I first came into the forest. Only a few Velores deep in our confidences, like Fantasia's sisters, her mother, and Chanticlaim, were privy to those details. And Dolly—but there was nothing we could do about that.

But here was another breathing soul aware of the dangerous secrets Fantasia and I shared. Secrets that could land Fantasia in a grave.

My vision grew blotchy, tongue heavy, and Frigid held up her palm to quiet my screaming mind.

"Calm," she said, her tone so soft and powerful I felt the thrum of her energy. I took it. "I don't want to know what happened," she said honestly. "And although this does not need to be said, I feel a responsibility to both you and Polar." She placed her hand over her heart. "Tell no one. No. One." Each word came out crisp. "You couldn't have escaped Narivous on your own accord. No one ever does. That means someone helped you." She stood up and came to sit by my side, grabbing my hand with ferocity. Her icy powers leaked through my glove, numbing my fingers and trickling up my arm. Her breath brushed my ear as she leaned in close to whisper. "And they are good girls," she said. "Good, lovely girls. I love seeing them, they make me smile—even knowing what I know. Keep your lips sealed and your secrets hidden."

Fantasia. Her message wasn't entirely cryptic. She knew who'd helped me escape, perhaps she had a snapshot of the scene, a clip of Fantasia wrenching me away. Her mask hiding her beauty, her patchwork cloak covering her frame, but still unmistakably Fantasia.

Frigid leaned back, her face so very sad.

"I think you're a good boy," she said, before her face started to crack and light began to build from somewhere deep inside.

The temperature in the room plummeted even further. My skin started to prickle, as the cold air swirled. The blues of Frigid's eyes were slowly turning to black, her pale skin to powder, her lips to chapped ice.

She was losing herself.

But I didn't pull away. Something deep in her powers tugged on me. It was comfort. Peace.

She was leaving me in plain sight, but I wouldn't leave her —even knowing she was about to cover her room in ice crystals.

I gripped her hand harder, as her translucency bled over to my fingers. A tingle started to form and we both smiled, ready for the sensation to take us from reality.

But then there was a scream.

And it wasn't from me.

CHAPTER 10
SACRIFICIAL GIFT

The scream was much more than a scream. It was a howl, full of rage and fear, and it sounded human. The walls trembled with the owner's wrath.

Frigid only smiled, her expression cloudy. She was looped up on her power and beyond reach. The room continued to plunge in degrees, and I managed to pull from her supernatural lure.

The screaming continued to build, and it was greater than Frigid's icy magic.

Something told me this was what Fantasia warned me about.

I cracked open the door and peered into the hallway. Velores were gathered in the corridor, and I took a swig of Dexitrol powder for safe measure.

Because to kill a suicidal Velore was one thing, but to take the life of a human was another.

And the person wailing in the center of the corridor was very much human.

I may be undead, but I wasn't a monster.

At least, not yet.

A SMALL CROWD HAD GATHERED, guards included, with some hanging back at exit points and others near the heart of the action.

A few sharp Velore eyes landed on me, but the commotion occurring in real time took away my spotlight. I faded to wallpaper.

Which was just fine by me.

I shut the door behind me, but kept my hand on the handle, in case I needed to dart back inside. I wasn't sure where I stood with the isolation decree, and if I was even allowed in the hallways with this much activity.

Yet I couldn't pull away.

The man was young, early twenties, and on his knees. His movements were jerky, his eyes wide, as he looked from his audience to the shelves of skulls and back again.

Each glance amplified his horror and his muscles tightened, cords of raw fear bulging along his neck. The more he looked up, the more panicked he became.

He was relatively isolated in the center of the corridor, with only a pair of Velores within touching distance. Even though no one held him down, their presence kept him contained.

Or maybe his legs had turned to gelatin.

I saw what he saw, and I had to suck in gulps of air to stop the thrumming along my skull—despite the Dexitrol in my system—to keep my fear from fetching my powers. Not here. Not this close to someone so fragile.

Because I could easily put myself in his place, surrounded by a group of oddly dressed people. A few wearing masks.

Almost all wearing cloaks. And some with glowing eyes and infant cracks branching across their attractive features.

Fear built a layer of sweat along his brow. Not a single samaritan offered help.

"Please," he begged, clasping his hands in prayer. "I'll do whatever you want, just let me go."

Someone laughed from the far back, before the crowd quieted to phantom levels. A few parted to make way, and there, as I expected, was Thorn. Everyone, in a unified move, bowed deep.

I followed suit.

Thorn was whole again, no sign or indicator of my leached poison. She stepped toward the human pleading for his life and everyone stood up, synchronized movements too abnormally perfect.

For a fleeting second, Thorn captured my attention and, to my surprise, winked.

It wasn't a move that passed unnoticed. A few Velores shot me glares, as if she'd bestowed me some sort of honor.

"My, my, my," Thorn began. "What do we have here?"

The man went mute, his instinct shutting off his voice so only his ragged breathing could be heard.

Chanticlaim came forward. He'd been in the back, waiting for this moment. I cringed at the sight of him, at the hard lines around his mouth, the regret in his shoulders. He got onto one knee next to the human and held his palms up in submission. "My Queen," he said, his voice docile but strong. "The human you requested."

A sacrifice.

"Get up," Thorn ordered, and Chanticlaim stood, stepping away to give her room with the man who was quickly fraying at the hem.

His aura was strong and rich, a deep periwinkle blue. Of

course she'd want him. He had the makings of a powerful weapon.

And Thorn loved her weapons.

"I said, GET UP!" Thorn barked, her gaze locking on the man who still hadn't left the ground. He stumbled to his feet, his brown hair fading to ash, the same as his complexion. Thorn took the man's chin in her hands. "Tell me, my boy. What's your name?"

"C-Colby, ma'am."

She let out a low hiss, and her fingers squeezed tighter. "It's 'My Queen,'" she snarled, before tilting his head to the side, inspecting his profile. She ran a finger along his jaw and licked her lips. "Now address me properly." She leaned in and, in a whisper every immortal could hear, said, "And see to it I like how it sounds."

His nod was barely a dip. Thorn's grasp remained unyielding. "My Queen." He managed not to stutter, and Thorn's brow arched ever so slightly.

"Tsk, tsk." She inched her nose to his, almost touching. To his credit, Colby didn't pull away. "That's not what I meant, you foolish boy. I ask your name, you give it to me, and see to it you follow it with my proper title. Start over."

Colby's chest heaved, his fear palpating the air. "My name is Colby, My Queen."

Thorn let out a slow smile. "Very good, Colby." Her words were stilted, careful. She released him, pushing him back into a stumble. "I think we may just get along. Now, my pet, get on your knees, where I find you most pretty."

Colby buckled from both obedience and fright.

Thorn circled him, the same as she'd done with me, taking in her citizens, even bestowing a few generous, near authentic smiles. Recipients of her good graces earned scowls from the leftovers.

"Tell me, Colby. How is it you've come to our fine city?"

Colby looked around the room, as if he held out hope someone would answer for him. When no one did, he said, "I was supposed to meet a girl here. I didn't know this place was off limits."

Thorn stopped pacing and shot him a pointed look. Colby recovered with, "My Queen."

"A girl?" Thorn mused. "Oh, Colby, you are just a hot-blooded male, aren't you? And what's this girl's name?"

"Her name is Sarah, My Queen."

Thorn pivoted and gave the crowd a confused look. "A Sarah, you say? Well, I'll admit my population has grown rather quickly, but I don't know of a Sarah in my city. Or in my army. Although the name does seem slightly familiar. Perhaps you'd care to describe her for me."

"She's beautiful, like, like ..." He indicated all the perfection surrounding him, his eyes stalling on a few gazes turned demonic, their translucency coming through. He looked at Thorn. "She has black hair."

My stomach turned to lead. Thorn glanced over her shoulder and shot me a smile. We both knew what was coming.

"And lavender eyes."

Thorn's smile stretched, and she lifted her chin.

This was going to end badly. There was something wrong with this recruit, I knew as much from Fantasia's warning. But looking at him, with his vibrant aura, it seemed Fantasia had collected a real prize.

And for whatever sick trick, she'd masqueraded under the name of my ex-girlfriend.

"Ah, yes. I know who your Sarah is. Very pretty girl. A heartbreaker"—she clicked her tongue—"and unfortunately for you, a liar."

Colby's head shot up in surprise.

"Where is our 'Sarah'?" Thorn made air quotes, and Colby searched the room.

I hated how desperate he looked. I hated how I stood back. I hated how I did nothing.

Watching should've been a crime.

Chanticlaim took the lead. "I'm sorry, My Queen." He bowed again. "I'm not sure where she is. Perhaps she's working another mission on your behest?"

Thorn stepped closer to Chanticlaim. "I can assure you this was her only task. It seems rather strange she'd want me to receive him without her being here." She clicked her tongue again, clearly her signature move, before staring down a female spectator. "Bring her to me—and do it quickly," she ordered. The Velore, who had a gold "G" emblazoned on her chest, gave a curt bow and disappeared. Thorn cocked her head at Chanticlaim and flashed her mean smile. "It wouldn't be right to receive my gift without her."

He nodded as Thorn turned her hungry eyes back on Colby. Chanticlaim's face pulled down the moment Thorn's back was turned.

He knew something was wrong with this recruit, too.

The waiting seemed endless, going on for days, years, before Fantasia showed. I worried Thorn would grow impatient. That it would piss her off. But instead she took the opportunity to mingle with her citizens, leaving Colby to tremble in the hallway's heart.

She laughed. She kidded. She accepted the praise of her subordinates with a magnanimous air. In turn, every Velore basked in her approval.

Her ability to twist a situation, to make herself the nucleus of their worlds, was stupefying.

She stopped near my hideout, so close she nearly grazed my arm. My bow was deep enough to garner a gracious smile.

"I'm so glad you're here to see this." She leaned in and poured whispers into my ear. "In a sense, you're to be thanked for this generous offering." I nodded, and she added, "One of many to come, I'm sure, my darling."

Thorn looked back at Colby, who wouldn't—or perhaps, couldn't—stop gawking at the skull-lined ceiling, before moving on, her cloak spilling behind her. She continued to make her rounds, charming every Velore in her wake.

They adored her. It was so sickeningly obvious.

When the doors creaked and Fantasia emerged, she wore her mask. I had no doubt it was shielding her gnawing emotions.

"Ah." Thorn clapped her hands and approached Fantasia, who took to her knees and held her palms up, a pose I was beginning to recognize as a favored one.

"Get up, get up," Thorn said, waving Fancy to her feet. "Oh, and remove that dreadful thing. I think Colby would like to see your pretty face."

Fantasia peeled the mask off, her eyes unnaturally hard. She didn't look around, but kept her focus trained on Thorn.

Colby nearly cried out with relief. "Sarah?"

Fantasia didn't flinch. She wouldn't acknowledge him.

All the while, I tried to figure out what was wrong with her candidate. On the surface he looked perfect, marking all the boxes Narivous favors.

Strong aura. *Check.*

Vibrant color. *Check.*

Decent cower. *Check.*

Ability to beg shamelessly. *Check.*

"Well?" Thorn prompted Fantasia. "Aren't you going to greet him?"

Fantasia looked at Colby as if he were see-through. "It's nice to see you again, Colby." Fantasia's neck was straight and stiff, her voice icier than Frigid's breath.

Thorn looped her arm through Fantasia's and somehow managed to yank a small smile from Fancy's lips.

"You've done well," Thorn whispered loud enough for all to hear. "I think he's beautiful."

She was referring to his aura and not his physical configuration. Because it was all about auras.

Fantasia managed to tweak her smile into one that straddled the line between pleased and humbled. "I searched long and hard for the right person."

It was a nasty undercut, a truthful proclamation, one so well hidden even Thorn couldn't detect it.

I winced, grateful nobody was looking at me.

Something was most certainly wrong with this human—it may not have been readily apparent, but he was a fester. Dormant and rancid.

And from the way Fantasia nibbled on her lip, she knew it was only a matter of time before Thorn discovered his shortcoming.

Damn her.

Thorn knew to not send him to his death—and resurrection—before a proper inspection. "I hope he's worthy of what we hope to give him. Chanticlaim"—Thorn tossed her head toward the door with the eye emblem—"fetch Dolly. I need to know more about our Colby."

Fantasia's skin faded. I noticed it when others were too busy feasting on Colby's fear. While they gorged on his adrenaline, I absorbed her fright.

I wanted to take it all away.

Dolly appeared, wearing a look of absolute disinterest, her face flat enough she could've been a sleepwalker.

She drifted toward our queen and took the place of Fantasia, hooking her arm through Thorn's, a move so affectionate it transformed the two, for a heartbeat, into a pair of beautiful friends.

Thorn patted Dolly's arm and gestured to the kneeling human. "Isn't he lovely," she said, her voice filled with longing. "A gift for me from this beautiful creature." Her hand swept over Fantasia, who bowed her head and faked a look of pride.

"A beautiful aura indeed," Dolly replied, snapping a smile at Fantasia. "Lots of potential."

Colby stayed still as stone, his head cemented to his neck. Only his eyes pivoted, swiveling from hazel, to blue, to lavender. A trio of women, all of them wanting something.

Fancy shot me an apologetic look.

"But as you know"—Thorn unhooked her arm and gave Dolly space—"I need to make sure my humans are worthy of the greatest gift they could ever hope for. Please, read him and tell me if he'll enhance our society. If he's as valuable as he looks."

Dolly smiled brightly at Colby, whose knees had to ache from the kneel he was forced to remain in.

"Absolutely." Dolly placed her hands on the sides of Colby's face. He had a hungry look to him, as if he were gazing upon his savior. He'd already dismissed Fantasia, seeing her for a fraud.

Now he pleaded with Dolly, using only his eyes.

Dolly had that way about her. The blue irises, the porcelain skin. Even her clothing, pastels of lace, spoke of innocence and goodness. But it was pretend—a predator lurked behind her angelic presence, otherwise she wouldn't be in such a powerful position.

She took a few moments, and the crowd started to shift. Dolly's lashes fluttered. She didn't like what she saw.

Some Velores leaned in, while others fidgeted.

Dolly took a step away and scanned the room. Regret ran her skin a shade lighter. Two Velores wearing eye emblems caught her attention. They bowed their heads, and she gave them a polite nod in recognition.

Then she took another step, as if to distance herself from Colby. From the truth.

"I'm sorry, Thorn. But I don't think he'll work out."

I knew it was coming, but it still slammed into me. A box-train of velocity.

Thorn rippled, literally. She emanated rage, sending it off in waves. We could all feel it. The crowd around me lost their eagerness—it was quickly replaced by fear. They turned to granite.

And Colby.

Colby started to weep.

"N-no," he stammered. "I'm a good person. I'm a good person. I've made m-mistakes, but that's normal. T-that's human."

No one acknowledged him. It was as if he were already dead.

Thorn approached Dolly, her crown catching her ire, the spikes sparking and the room crackling with frenetic energy.

"Tell me why he fails," she bit out.

Dolly shook her head. "He isn't a loyal human, Thorn. We overlook many shortcomings—murder, addiction, violence, thievery—but it's often because they've been corrupted by the weight of drugs, or life has given them cruel circumstances that have exacerbated their depravity. In a sense, they become their own strangers. But this one"—she waved her hand in Colby's direction—"this one does not know the meaning of loyalty. He is sober. Clean of drugs, and still wicked. There is no redemption for him, for he is a man with no conviction."

"No!" Colby screamed and stood up, but he barely managed a step before vines whispered along the stones, moving at a runner's speed, grabbing his ankles and clambering up his body. He froze, shock locking his joints. Thorn was slipping into her evil ego, and it threatened to swallow the room.

No one dared move when Thorn was at full translucency, least of all Fantasia. She seemed to have stopped breathing. Her eyes were as big as sand dollars.

Thorn's creamy perfection was gangrenous, cracks overtook her face. She hovered at a deadly level of power.

"Tell me it isn't so," Thorn hissed, willing Dolly to recant.

Please, please, take it back.

Dolly ducked her head, and her face crumpled with regret.

"I wish I could. He's ideal otherwise. But"—she pinched her mouth—"he will be unreliable. He will move whichever way the wind blows, light and weak as a soap bubble. Unsubstantial. A nothing."

"So my gift isn't really a gift at all, but a total waste." Thorn's hands clenched. She snarled at Fantasia and stepped so close she breached her breathing room. "A TOTAL WASTE!"

Thorn's powers touched us all. My vision blotted. It was as if her energy had a magnetism, testing our willpower, tempting us. My hand hovered over my pocket, where the weight of the vial lingered.

If she went after Fancy …

I'd have to stop it.

The thought was a painful blade.

Thorn stood over Fantasia, who'd dropped to her knees. "Explain it to me, Fantasia." Thorn, speaking her name, ramped up my own translucency.

The thrumming was begging, the Dexitrol nearly eradicated from my system.

"His color is beautiful." Fantasia's tenor was meek. "I thought he could change, that he could be groomed into a good fit. Aren't humans easily swayed when given a gift worth fighting for?"

"You know better." Thorn stared her down. "You know what we look for. You know what I want. And"—she jabbed a finger at Colby—"you most assuredly know what I don't want."

"I'm new at this. I'm new. I thought his color would be an asset."

My tongue wanted to meld to the bottom of my mouth.

Someone placed a hand on my shoulder, and I turned to see Plague standing behind me. He moved with a stalker's grace. With the shake of his head, he delivered a clear warning: *interrupt and it'll get worse.*

Fortunately, Thorn wasn't working her vines around Fantasia's body, but Colby's.

A good sign.

She was building him a suit of greenery, and Colby could barely twitch against the branches. Thorn kept him on his knees, pinned in place.

Yet, she never glanced at him, instead she stared Fantasia into oblivion, seeing if she'd protest or argue in his favor.

For once, Fantasia chose common sense. She kept quiet.

Colby was in an active state of deterioration. The vines crawled and roped, transforming his yelps of fear to whimpers of pain.

His breath started to come out in short rasps. Thorn stepped away to survey her handiwork.

But her eyes found me first, and a smile bloomed.

Thorn switched directions, approaching me. All eyes followed, including Fantasia's. Thorn held out her hand, and I had little power other than to reach for it.

"Come, my darling," she cooed.

She led me toward Colby, and every inch of my flesh heated. Dolly gave me a curious look, before turning her attention back on Thorn.

Fantasia appeared as petrified as I felt.

"Colby," Thorn said. "See this darling boy here?"

Colby didn't speak. How could he? He could barely move, but his eyes, which were now tearing up, managed to hone in on my face.

Thorn stroked my arm, careful to avoid my flesh. "This was a gift from Fantasia, or"—she clicked her tongue—"as you lovingly like to call her, your Sarah. And he's lovely. Perfect. And mine. All mine."

I didn't shiver. I didn't react. Although having her lay claim to me, in such an open fashion, brought bile to the back of my throat. Instead I found a smile, a good-for-nothing smile, as if her branding me was the greatest gift one could ever hope for.

I hated myself.

She let go of me and stepped closer. "We named him Death," she announced happily, addressing both Colby and the crowd. "And it's a name so fitting. For he has the power to kill with a single touch. Amazing, isn't it?" The vines started to wrap around Colby's face, giving him a mask of Thorn's making. She left his mouth, his nose, his eyes free. "Death serves me as I see fit."

She leaned down and touched the top of Colby's head, and then, to my surprise, started to remove some of her vises—the ones around his right hand. It was the only part of his flesh still visible.

He looked like a living topiary, carved not with hedge clippers, but Thorn's power.

And I could see it then, what she was going to have me do. He wasn't viable for resurrection. He was unworthy of their gift. They can overlook murder, and torture, as long as a human plucked from the cesspool was capable of swearing fealty to Thorn. This one may not have committed any heinous crime, but in the eyes of Narivous he was unworthy. He was the most despicable type of human. One who stood for nothing, only his own gain.

A nobody.

And since he wouldn't be resurrected, his method of death wouldn't matter. She could kill him any way she wanted.

And she kept looking at me.

I chanced at a glance at Fantasia. She'd wilted.

"It's a shame," Thorn said, addressing me, "we glued your gloves on. But there are other parts free of clothing." She was looking at my face, smiling, ever eager.

I didn't want another life on my conscience.

Not so soon.

My powers continued to build without my consent.

Thorn saw my shaking hands, recognized my weakness, while the other Velores fidgeted, angling themselves toward the exits, calculating the distance it would take to evacuate if I accidentally unleashed.

It only made Thorn brighten, black pupils and all.

She held up a palm and gestured to Colby, the vines manipulating his free arm, grabbing and twisting to hold it out, waiting for my touch.

"Death, please come forward, let's show—"

"He deserves this," Dolly whispered, and Thorn halted and turned. Dolly was wringing her laced hands in front of her, twisting them as if she pulled some dark information from the deep recesses of Colby's mind. "He abandoned his own little girl."

Thorn grew hotter.

"He blamed the mother, said she kept him away, but the

truth is, he left her," Dolly said. "He didn't want her because she was female. Because he believes males are better."

It was the killing shot.

The group around us hissed.

And our queen magnified in acidic energy.

Thorn snapped completely, shockwaves rippled through the crowd, and I was long forgotten.

Fantasia was forgotten.

Every Velore was forgotten.

Thorn abandoned the world, and now it was just her and Colby. He was in her path, and she was a city-sized tornado.

Colby tried to shake his head, but failed against his restraints.

It was too late anyway.

Thorn dug her vines into his body, starting with his mouth. He tried to scream, a distorted "No," but they were already too deep.

Green life feeding death.

And then she dropped him.

Unlike Tony, she didn't force the vines to bloom.

She stood over his lifeless body, his nerves firing with a last stab at life, convulsing in stuttering jabs. And in a move far from queenly, she kicked his head.

Her purple cloak grazed his blood, her hem leaving a trail of sticky gore as she walked toward the door with the rose emblem. Two guards opened it. Thorn paused in the threshold and bored into Fantasia.

"You will now recruit two humans to make up for this failed one." Righteousness twisted Thorn's lips. "One will be a child, younger than ten. To teach you a lesson. For we can train a child, infuse loyalty, and perhaps in the future we will avoid such mishaps."

Thorn disappeared without another word.

Fantasia's color faded to nothing. But she managed to stand and hold her head high.

She was breaking, internalizing it all.

She'd gambled and lost.

And as she exited the hallway, she never once glanced at Colby. She didn't look at her fellow Velores. She didn't look at me.

Despite the bravado, no one could miss the defeat in her exit.

Her heart was almost as dead as Colby's.

CHAPTER II

DAWNING ROSE

Fantasia fell off the face of the earth. For a week, she was practically unseen, unheard of, materialized in thought only. I wanted to talk to her. I needed to talk to her. Shake her until sense stuck—and not just on her poor choice of recruit.

Part of me was ticked she used Sarah's name as her own.

Part of me knew she had some warped logic for doing it.

Either way, I wanted answers.

Optimism took me to the garden each night, where I memorized the lines of the maze, mastering every angle and turn, hoping to catch a whiff of her scent.

Not even a trace lingered.

Disappointment followed me back to the castle, where I was torn between quarters. Scream liked having me in her apartment, Polar preferred his.

I felt a desire to please both and waffled between the pairs, although I gravitated toward Ice.

Frozen, cold, and lived in.

Stranger still, terrified wails began to trickle in. There were no patterns to their occurrence. They would just show up, at random intervals, rattling the daylight hours or shocking the night awake. Most were male, one was female.

All were human.

And even though I didn't want to see, I still looked. From whichever rooms I was staying in, I'd crack open the door and peer out into the skull corridor.

It was the same scene every time, with shadows to exaggerate their suffering, a disturbing puppet show of sorts. Hands would always be folded in prayer. Knees well used. Sometimes fetal positions employed, showcasing backs, hiding centers.

Pain in the rawest form of measure.

And I couldn't stop looking.

I must've lacked willpower. Maybe I was a glutton for punishment, or—most frightening of all—perhaps I enjoyed feeding off their suffering.

Because their pain took away from my pain—and I hated myself for needing it.

I was becoming someone I no longer recognized—the old Daniel a ghost, the new one a monster.

All the strangers were led away alive, and later, when I was surrounded only by my own breathing, I'd convince myself they'd be okay. Perhaps Narivous would be an improvement over their former lives. Maybe they wanted to be part of a society where they wouldn't be lost amongst the fold. A recognized member. Popular simply because the numbers were less severe, a small-town-vibe sort of thing.

But then logic would ruin my pep talk.

They had shitty auras, so had no worth in Narivous society.

On the sixth day, another human was brought in. Not quite a man and no longer a boy, he was trapped in that awkward phase of puberty. He had shaggy hair dyed green and acne so heavy his face was covered in cratered pockets of pus. His over-sized, threadbare clothing dripped from his frame.

Ugly years for most anyone—more so for him. He was grappling the line between human and troll.

I felt dirty looking at him.

He wept large, sloppy tears as a Velore wearing a guard uniform wrestled him by the collar. His aura was nonexistent, the color of a jellyfish—damn near transparent.

After he was properly inspected by Dolly, the guard hauled him underground, where the human prisoners were kept.

The tower was only for Velores.

And as much as I wanted to ask what was going on, I decided to live in my imagination, where I forced shit to work out, because that's how my brain operated.

I'd learned, from years of violence, that the truth is the carnage beneath a bloody bandage. Yes, some had to look, but those who didn't suffered no real scars. You can't un-see stuff, and my imagination was kinder for the sake of my sanity. Some people call it denial, I call it survival.

Three days later, the Dawning Rose Celebration started, and I found out the humans' purpose.

Narivous ripped off the bandage.

They made me look.

<hr>

I TRIED to absorb the city. Daylight and freedom were an exotic pairing. I had yet to see Narivous without a nightly veil, at least not with my immortal eyes, and for this once, I'd been gifted both. For only an hour, but whatever, beggars can't be choosers.

Only rule, I was to keep a healthy dose of Dexitrol powder with me at all times.

Which was kind of my standard, but I didn't point out the obvious. A pass was a pass, and I wasn't going to piss on the opportunity. My sarcasm took a back seat.

"Trumpets will announce the starting of the celebration. When you hear them, head toward the arena at the northeast corner of the city." Polar laid out the specifics as he leaned against the doorframe to my room and fought a grin. He was the most polished I'd ever seen him, fitted together in a suit of ivory with a snowflake emblem stitched in silver on his vest pocket. For once, he acted like he cared about appearances. Even his white hair had been tamed, brushed back, opening his face and making the paleness of his eyes jump. I kind of preferred the more slovenly version. It was more relatable. "You can't miss it. But if you get confused, just follow the crowd."

I nodded.

"And be careful to mind your touch." This time he didn't try to stifle his smile. It flashed. "Have fun exploring your new home."

So that's how I found myself, the day of the Dawning Rose Celebration, standing in the city center, squinting at the light. For once we weren't under a dense cloud cover and the trees couldn't block the powerful spring sunshine. It infiltrated the evergreens, finding the smallest pockets to spark the city. My eagle eyes drank up every piece of it.

Everything looked different. Immortality refined my sight, sharpening lines, brightening colors, making me think I'd spent my entire life with subpar senses.

Every house, no matter the size, was perfection. Details. Narivous was all about the details.

Around me, Velores bustled. Excitement crackled the air, and I tried my best to become nothing more than an optical illusion.

I was still gaped at, however, but not in an unkind way. It was hard to place into words the looks they shot in my direction. It was a curious mixture of fear and something I wasn't anticipating—*admiration*. My aura, my clan, my lineage, all of it represented strength. And in a city where power was coveted, I was on top of the heap.

Even though no one could touch me, girls gave me flirty smiles and winks. Guys were tinted in jealousy. Heads bowed slightly when I passed them on the walkway, a move of respect.

I was, for the first time in my life, popular. Revered. So much so, they seemed too afraid to approach, but their expressions were open and hungry—urging me to come to them, to start up a conversation I didn't want to have, but they were ravenous for.

They were going to starve. I had no desire for a superficial, monotonous back and forth.

So while they gawked, I stopped to stare at the fountain of Thorn, the heartbeat of the city.

It was beautiful, no doubt.

And crafted in near likeness.

She had hands open wide, roses blooming from her palms, feeding life with her powerful magic. Behind her, water cascaded from a broken stump, pooling around the concrete basin of vines and flowers.

Cobblestone houses, with copper roofs covered in fuzzy patina, provided a fairytale backdrop. The paver path spread like spindles of a spider web, reaching every door, tying them together.

Large trees spotted the space, hedges acted as fences, and groves walled off houses. Despite what they represented, I found myself appreciating their beauty.

It was something you didn't find in modern cities, where

trees were a burden, hacked down to make room for parking lots and malls. Mother Nature an inconvenience to the ambitions of man.

Here she was embraced, since the ruler was born of her blood.

Flowers sprouted everywhere. It would've put a botanical garden to shame.

And despite it all—the tyrannical ruler, the deviant Velores, the slippery scruples—I found my new home inviting.

Most every place I'd lived in was unloved, and looked the part. Leaky roofs, peeling paint, the stench of mold and desolation. Only Gram's house bucked the pattern.

But this, this was different.

Narivous was a peculiar sort. It was polished pride. So strange, and bizarrely welcoming.

It was the shortest hour of my life. I couldn't move quickly enough, taking in as much of the city as possible, but there was too much ground and not enough time. When the trumpets rang, I ambled toward the arena.

Polar was right, I couldn't miss it. It was ginormous, domed, and built from white stone. On the outside, in perfect placement, were tall trees on spindly trunks. They acted as overgrown bushes, leaning over the masonry shell, covering the upper part of the stadium and blocking it from aerial eyes. Another impressive display of magic.

I passed one of the many garden parks on my way to the event. Since there were still other Velores behind me, I decided it was safe to take my time. I detoured into the labyrinth of flowers and nature. This particular park was only a touch smaller than the royal setup, but nearly as grand. There were water fountains with nymphs, gazebos draped in honeysuckle, small bridges spanning ponds filled with lily pads and framed by cattails. Dragonflies zipped across the smooth surface of the water, while weeping willows dipped into their own images. There were trees of every sort, all in bloom. Cherry blossoms the shade of cotton candy, magnolia petals the color of vanilla. Pink and white, and lots of green.

And in the middle there was a statue. Only it wasn't of Thorn, but of Scream, carved from black granite. I had a feeling each of the Seven had their own monument.

But this one ...

It sucked me in.

There was something peculiarly wonderful about it. Scream's hands were clasped tightly to her chest. She wore a diadem of jewels connected to a veil covering her hair. Somehow it defied gravity, turning stone to air. The dress puddled near her feet, black movement frozen in time.

Her neck arched toward the sky. Her expression both longing and tormented.

I could've stared at it all day, it had that magnetic effect, but time had gone stupid.

The trumpets blared again.

I moved along, but looked over my shoulder, trying to gulp the image in deep, thirsty swallows. It wasn't just the statue that got me, it was that they seemed to have carved her on her wedding day.

And she didn't look happy.

⚡

EVERYONE WAS HOLDING their breath in the brimming arena—or at least it felt that way. Packed tight with powerful auras, weak auras, magic of every sort, the air was saturated with lethal potential.

And expectation.

The event was due to start any minute, and the atmosphere rippled.

Banners hung, evenly spaced, each bearing a clan's insignia, but there was no order to who sat where, everyone intermingled.

The stadium floor was made of compacted dirt and along the walls were doors of various sizes, all made from solid iron.

The rulers, of course, had the best seats in the house, an open balcony box equipped with thrones, jutting out far enough to give them an unobstructed view. All were in their places, aside from Dolly, who was notably absent.

Off to the sides of the royal station were smaller units, occupied by husbands of the Seven, family, and other high-ranking officials.

I happened to be among them, in the smallest box at the farthest left-hand flank. I was alone and someone clearly was worried about my stability, since there was an extra vial of Dexitrol powder waiting on my seat.

I sat and looked over at the box housing Polar and my uncles. It was the first time I'd seen Ferno since his banishment. He was dressed in formal attire, but he still had on his trademark stocking cap to hide his scars. Since his balcony jutted out farther than my own, I was left staring at his back, but he must've sensed my gaze, since he turned in his seat and shot me a wink. He waved a short hello before the crowd stilled, then turned back toward the center of the arena, where Dolly had surfaced in the hub.

Thorn, for the occasion, had manipulated the overhead branches so there was a break in the foliage and sun could spotlight the stage. It gave off the impression she controlled more than plants, that even the universe bent to her will.

Dolly was frustratingly beautiful in her lace dress. She wore her incorrigible half smile. The ribbon around her waist matched her blue cape and for some reason I fixated on it. I suppose it reminded me of the finishing touches to a well-planned costume. The whole I-promise-you-can-trust-me look she was so very fond of, it made her seem innocent and fragile, especially when she widened her cherub eyes for the audience.

She held up her hand, sheathed in a glove of white, and the crowd roared.

A gate of wrought iron lifted from the ground floor. Two members of the guard emerged, holding one of the humans captured earlier in the week.

The man dragged his feet, his large belly swinging like a lard-filled pendulum. His girth, although impressive, didn't slow the guards.

The stadium took to its feet, jeering and catcalling. The bleachers rattled. The guards forced the man to kneel in front of Dolly. He was a blubbery mess, snot trailing from his nose, past his lips, and into his mouth.

The man was pleading with Dolly, who stood innocently enough in front of him. His pleas were lost to the crowd's roar.

The guards stepped away and the human tried to stand. He even managed to shift a knee before he stopped.

Or, more accurately, froze.

His mouth didn't move, his hands stopped shaking, his blubber stilled. The crowd "oohed" and "aahed."

Dolly's blue eyes hollowed into dark, bottomless pits, the whites framing her dilated pupils. The porcelain visage she carried so well eroded with tiny hairpin cracks.

She was a living demonic doll and the human didn't see it. Dolly had shut out his senses.

With the flick of her hand, the human stood.

And it hit me what the Dawning Rose Celebration was—a talent show for the undead. A reminder of the betters who sat on thrones, of our place beneath them.

Dolly forced the man's body to move, dictating every step. He skipped around the arena, clumsy despite the hold of his cerebral master. When he finished, the ovation was deafening. And so were the mean-spirited taunts.

I scanned the bleachers, thinking Jester got it wrong. It wasn't just the guards who were heathens, but the whole lot of Narivous. Everyone applauded. *Everyone.*

Even Fantasia, who I located across the way, politely brought her palms together. She was sitting with her sisters and mom, her mask concealing her emotions. Fred was perched on Dreams' shoulder, a yellow dot of happiness in a blanket of bleak.

From the angle of Fantasia's neck, and the way she sat stiff shouldered, she was doing her damnedest to avoid glancing in my direction.

The crowd grew eerily quiet and my attention turned back to Dolly, who started to fold her fat human into impossible positions. The silence was so the audience could hear his bones crack and his joints pop.

When she'd thoroughly broken him, to the point he was near limp, Dolly took a bow and the cheers returned. I thought it was over until she forced him back to his knees and handed him a knife. The sun glinted off the steel blade.

I grabbed the vial of Dexitrol, my heart sinking, as I realized I was about to witness an execution.

So help me, I couldn't look away.

Dolly flashed her teeth and the crowd stomped their feet. The beating gained volume, moving into a rhythm, a crescendo.

The man, still lost in Dolly's fog, tilted his head back. His eyes had no luster, as if he were already dead.

He held the knife and angled the blade along his exposed neck.

Dolly slashed her hand through the air, a theatrical move.

And the human mimicked her.

He plunged and pulled, hitting an artery, spraying his blood over the dirt floor.

His death was slow. Dolly released his mind as soon as the blade sliced its path. The crowd quieted and I realized it wasn't a solemn hush, but an eager one.

How else were they to hear him gargle? To hear his choking? They wanted to feed on his failing heartbeat.

With the earth stained red and his twitching ended, the crowd went feral. The sound rattled my skull.

Dolly took off her gloves and dipped them in his blood. Velores in the stands waved their hands and jumped up and down. She flung them, equal parts red and white, at her adoring fans, who scrambled in the stadium, fighting over the sick trophy.

I stared at my shoes as they hauled the body away, then prepared myself for an encore, inhaling half the bottle of Dexitrol powder. Six more rulers to go.

⁂

THIS IS how it went down.

Serpent, unable to perform her water abilities on dry land, took to using snakes to illustrate her power. Pythons, anacondas, and a cobra danced to her instructions. She even had an infant rattlesnake slither down her throat, only to hock it back up.

I gagged.

For her finale she sicced her most venomous snakes on a human sacrifice. It took forever for him to die.

Ember lured her kill with her siren song. Then she set him on fire.

Scream, too, lured her kill with her siren song. Then rotted his flesh clean off.

Amelia played with her kill—the only woman of the group—giving her superficial wounds, stretching her agony into ages, before filleting her in true testament to her depravity.

Frigid's display had an accidental edge to it. The younger boy with the green hair, the one I'd seen carted around by the collar in the castle, had been transformed. His face was free of grease, his hair dyed to a more presentable shade of wet sand, and he was dressed in a costume, clothing from an era long before my time—suspenders, button-up shirt, pleated pants. His scuffed loafers had recently been polished, but still held the etchings of time.

The moment Frigid laid eyes on him she went rigid, transforming from normalcy to full-on rage. The guards barely had time to release the boy before she turned him into an ice sculpture. The crowd, aware of Frigid's fragile state, kept their tone subdued.

But the pleasure was still there.

And I was nothing more than a cowardly spectator.

When it was Thorn's time, the audience sat quietly like obedient children. She, unlike the others, didn't leave her throne. She simply raised an arm and, as she did, bushels of roses at every banister's base started to grow along the stadium's railing. A beautiful display in stark contrast to the morbidity of the other rulers.

A distinction that spoke volumes.

My strength needs no reminder, for it's impossible to forget.

It was a power play, so subtle I think many Velores overlooked it. But I knew it was a ruse.

The bitch was crafty.

THE TRIALS of Worthiness were another beast all together.

The clamoring for the two guard vacancies brought on a bout of frenzied excitement. There was a clear hierarchy in Narivous, and the role of guard was just below the desirable position of a Seven's husband.

Everyone wanted their place among the gods.

Velore after Velore showcased their talents. Each was allotted a total of five minutes to demonstrate their strengths.

Fires blazed, Ices froze, Animals slashed. Recruiters trailed fresh meat, hopeful to win a reward for bringing in the greatest prize.

Doppelgängers came forward, and since no one had Dolly's ability to control humans, they impressed the audience by flaring their auras. The Waters followed suit, since dry land wasn't conducive to their skill set.

Everything was graded on a scale. Next came the Velores that didn't fit neatly into any particular clan. They were probably assigned into whichever classification was closest.

I was shocked when two Telekinetics entered the competition. I didn't know that ability existed and tried to think of a method of death to bring about such powers.

I drew a blank.

There were Velores who allowed their bodies to be beaten to showcase their indestructibility. A few who could control electricity.

On and on and on it went.

When the last candidate finished, an intermission

followed, but it was brief, allowing just enough time for Polar to join me in my box.

"How are you?" he asked.

"Mentally scarred."

"Don't mourn the victims. It'd be a waste of energy."

I gave him a sideways glance.

He shrugged. "They were bad people. There was no fixing them." He cleared his throat and added, "We saved more lives than we took today."

Vigilante justice? I was about to ask, when Thorn entered the epicenter below.

The existing guards lined up against the far wall, ready to accept two new members into their fold.

I recognized some of them.

My prison keepers, for instance.

Volt and Spark, a sister and brother duo who could control electricity.

Cheetoh, the Animal son of Amelia, and a woman who looked like his female counterpart. Long, lean, clownish-colored hair, with the same feline stealth and mean gleam.

The candidates lined up in the center of the arena, a horizontal split of the stage. Their bodies tensed and their faces glowed with eagerness.

Thorn walked the length of them. Each one bowed as she passed.

The crowd hailed her and she allowed them a few moments of uninterrupted ovation. It was dumb how they ate out of her palm.

But the moment she lifted her hand, the crowd quieted. Obedient, brainless saps—and I was one of them.

In a voice loud but not strained, she started her address. "My darlings!"

Everything was "my darlings." I started to groan, a knee-jerk reaction, and Polar kicked me, *hard*.

"I must say, this year's Trials of Worthiness is one for the books." Thorn's voice had a happy lilt. Applause followed. "You've all made me immensely proud and I'm honored to consider myself your sovereign." More clapping. "Selection has not been easy, as all my candidates have proven themselves worthy of serving me and Narivous. But, sadly, I have limited vacancies." Hollow bobbleheads nodded.

Thorn smiled and began to glide toward a dark-skinned, dark-haired male, a newer recruit capable of sending flames thirty feet high, thick as a brick wall. His face was open and trusting as Thorn reached for his hand and held it up. He beamed, and a recruiter from far in the back stepped forward.

"This treasure," Thorn stated, "has earned his place amongst my elite. Please welcome guard member Singe."

The crowd's applause broke the sound barrier.

"As for my second guard member, I have a special treat for you." Her smile was slick and calculating as she released Singe and walked the width of her lineup. "I have, from time to time, when circumstances have aligned, selected a champion. It goes without saying this honor is rare and is only bestowed on Velores whose gifts have exceeded my expectations. This year" —she smiled at her candidates as they trembled with hope—"I have one in mind. But ..." She held up her finger before the crowd's amped-up roar could overtake her. "Circumstances have prevented him from entering our guard trials. But I will volunteer for him, for he is the most worthy." She smiled, her teeth catching the light. Cheetoh stepped forward, as if on cue.

I somehow missed the bag he was holding.

Thorn's eyes locked on me for a split second, and the world stopped spinning.

No.

Polar clapped me on the back and whispered, "Steady."

"For champion, I'd like to honor a Velore with talents of the most detrimental sort."

Inhale. *A trap. A set-up.* The buzzing began, but I managed to stop it from spreading.

Cheetoh reached inside the bag and produced a skull.

Exhale. *Nothing good could come from this.*

"It'll be okay," Polar consoled.

But it wasn't going to be okay. Okay was a word I'd never use again. Okay was a lie.

Okay didn't exist.

Thorn held the skull up to a collective intake of breath, as bodies leaned forward to take in the sight. The skull was eroded and smashed—the side dented, the maw whittled away.

From breathing in countless toxin particles.

"May I introduce our second guard member and this year's champion"—Thorn looked at me, her smile triumphant—"Death!"

The crowd took to their feet. No one seemed to care she was holding the skull of their comrade.

They only cared about the power I was capable of.

Rejoicing at my strength.

Polar stood with me and bowed his head. He whispered with his face turned from the crowd, "Bow to her and keep it respectful." When he stood back up he flashed me a smile and said, "Congratulations," loud enough to be overheard, or at least have his lips read.

Each step was an effort. When I made the ground floor, Thorn held out her hand for me. I grabbed it and she pulled me close.

And in a move I would've never expected, she jerked me forward and kissed me on the lips.

A short stab of a kiss, one so perfunctory there was no mistaking the lack of love between us. It was stiff, cold and ... *impossible.*

The crowd amplified to a frenzy, the accolade so loud the sky rolled with shock waves. It was nothing compared to the flux of emotions rippling through me, or the confusion.

How was she not in pain?

Thorn merely smiled, unfazed, and in a show of unity, raised our clasped hands high.

Her other hand presented Jester's skull, a token of my worth. I was forced to take it, and as she beamed at me, her lips cracked just the slightest.

She was wearing thick wax—a shield for her own lips—a trick that fooled everyone, even those with the sharpest sight.

And it was that simple. In a single move, Thorn managed to alter my transformation from a mar against her reign to a blessing.

It was about image, after all.

CHAPTER 12

BURIED HURTS

Thorn leaned in, her words soft so only I could hear and breathed, "Congratulations, my little pet. I've decided to forgive your existence. And I've decided to forgive your makers. That is your reward."

She pulled away a fraction, narrowing her eyes. Her cheek twitched for a second, and she added in near silence, "See to it you don't fail them." She stroked my arm and my nerves bubbled.

Her threat wasn't missed.

And to the surrounding crowd, it looked like a move of affection.

They were still cheering when she let go of my hand so she could wave and blow kisses.

She was the deliverer of death and they were the vultures, ready to consume the bodies she left behind.

Amelia entered the arena, along with her husband, Cougar, whose coloring gave me vertigo. It had a way of setting me off balance. His hair and skin were the exact same shade as Fantasia's, validating his paternity. And if that didn't do the trick, the mirror slashes on each cheek, both given by Amelia, sure as shit did.

One was for Fantasia's conception, the other for Barney, a horse he'd gifted her. Part of me wondered if it was the present itself that upset Amelia or the fact he'd showcased his affection in such an open fashion.

The pair descended on Singe, herding him toward the other guards lined along the far wall.

Dismissing the rejects without a glance.

I, however, had a different task ahead of me. When Thorn finished her sickeningly sweet performance, she indicated I was to follow and sauntered away.

Nothing good could come from meeting with Thorn alone. I shot a look at the bleachers, where Fantasia and her sisters sat.

Fantasia was still there, and even though her mask hid her emotions, her stooped neck pretty much told me she, too, knew this wasn't good.

Thorn calculated her moves and I was a useful pawn, my placement magnifying her power.

I trailed Thorn like a well-trained dog. My brain at battle with my body. I still had Jester's skull in my hand and it was making my joints ache, not from the weight—it could've been a damn feather—but from the heaviness of holding ... *him*.

No one followed us, although a few guards appeared uncomfortable to see us moving underground, alone. My newness, my toxin, their adored queen—that was a combination that didn't sit well. We followed the trail of gore, as Thorn stepped through the same exit that the bodies passed through.

"Shut the door," she barked, and I obeyed, sealing the latch behind us. The light left so quickly it hurt almost as much as the blinding sun. Fortunately, my vision rebounded.

Now it was just me and my almighty queen.

Oh, and a stack of corpses—the days' sacrifices, tossed haphazardly on the dirt floor.

The space was hard to define. I couldn't really call it a room and it wasn't quite a corridor. It was some mess in the middle. Long and relatively narrow, the ceilings hung claustrophobically low. Heavy pillars and concrete walls held up the bleachers above our heads. There were cabinets, secondhand uglies along the far side, and a few doors that undoubtedly led to other rooms beneath the arena. The floor was made of compacted dirt.

No cages. Which meant the humans, while alive, must've been kept in another section.

Thorn stood by the pile of discarded bodies, her back to me, arms folded loosely across her chest.

"Humans are such weak creatures," she said. "Gross, cruel. Self-serving."

She looked over her shoulder. Even in the darkness, the prongs of her crown managed to cast bright jabs. "My Velores are not." She turned back to the pile, staring. "You know how I know this?"

She didn't wait for an answer. "My Doppelgängers. They are my quality control. They can see the hearts of humans, which ones are worthy, and only then do we let them join our society. These people here"—she gestured to the pile—"these were scum."

A funnel of questions swirled. Polar's words about not mourning their loss centered. Thorn's stance wasn't hostile, and I chanced a question.

"If you don't mind me asking ..." Deep breath. "What was wrong with them?" She clicked her tongue and I remembered to add, "My Queen."

She nodded, pleased.

"This pile is filled with men who hurt innocents in the

most vile of ways. I won't repeat their offenses, for they are heinous." She stepped toward me.

I regarded the heap in a new light. So they were psychopaths destroyed by other psychopaths. A shudder crawled along my shoulders. Thorn surprised me by stroking my arm.

"When you say innocents, you mean children, right?" My eyes lingered on the one woman of the group.

She sighed. "Yes, children, or the very old. Hurting them in one way or another. All unwarranted."

Is it ever warranted?

I didn't ask, because I didn't want to know. She had one of those personalities, a justifiable mindset, someone who could convince herself anything was okay as long as it fed a greater purpose.

Unfortunate means for an exceptional cause.

She'd do anything to maintain her grip on power, even leveraging the lives of children.

I must've had a telling expression.

"I know what you're thinking," she said, and I made my face flat. "How can I possibly recruit human children if I find crimes against them so horrid?"

Not exactly ...

She gave me a small smile. "It's because I trust they will be happy here."

She grabbed Jester's skull, removing the unsettling weight, and set him on the ground. She took my hands, a move that was kind and gracious.

"I'm a good ruler, a fair ruler. The cheers out there? When I stepped into the arena? Did they feel authentic to you?"

All too much. I nodded.

She flashed her teeth in a smile I didn't think she could make. It transformed her. "It's because they love me. I saved them, and they're happy here. I've given them peace, a sense of family. A life they didn't know they could have. I've pulled them from their demons, from people who have hurt them, and I gave them power to overcome their tragic beginnings."

There was a knock on the door and she dropped my hands, but hesitated, as if she wanted to maintain her hold on them.

One of Amelia's dark haired-boys, which one I still wasn't sure, came in. He gave a bow and a ready smile. Very much un-Animal like. His scalp fell just shy of touching the low ceiling.

"I'm sorry to interrupt, but I wanted to know if I could lend a hand." He nudged his head toward the pile of bodies.

"You're such a good boy, JC. Have you met Death yet?" Thorn asked.

"Not formally." He gave me a kind nod. "Hello."

"Hello."

Thorn clapped her hands. "Very well, then." She stepped away, her movements light and unhurried. "Would you two dispose of the bodies? Remember to bring me the heads." She pointed to Jester's skull and looked at me. "That's my gift to you," she said, her words almost nurturing, her face filled with expectation.

JC, from behind Thorn's back, mouthed, "Thank her."

I bowed and said, "It's very kind of you, My Queen." She smiled, and brushed my arm one last time.

"I'm very much looking forward to our new start," she said with not even a touch of threat. It was unsettling how quickly she transformed.

And then an impossibility happened—I smiled. And it wasn't faked. Part of me wanted to believe her.

Part of me knew I never could.

But I took the offering, since I was running out of hope. Desperation does strange things to the psyche.

"Don't worry," JC said as soon as she left. "I can do the cutting."

I THOUGHT we'd need a ton of help moving the bodies, but JC was a pro.

I stood back in the corner, my hand wrapped around my vial, as he claimed the heads. He laid down a tarp to collect most of the blood, but still, the ground had a carpet of gore by the time he finished.

It was surprising how fast he hacked them off. One minute the bodies were whole, and the next they weren't.

It was like a bad B horror movie and I was an extra on set.

He pulled a strong coated netting—more like a breathable wire—from a cupboard and placed four of the headless corpses into the sack.

The other two he left on the dirt floor. Dolly's kill, by far the bulkiest, was one of them.

The bag, set up like an oversized hammock, had flexible cords attached to handles spoking along the perimeter. "We'll carry these four, and then I'll come back for the other two," JC said.

We each grabbed a set of handholds and lifted. It was surprisingly light.

Or my strength had improved.

Most likely the latter.

"The heads add a lot of weight. And most of these guys were lightweights to begin with." JC shrugged, and placed a rolled-up towel over his shoulder so he could rest the cord against it. "Immortality beefs up our muscles, too. So yeah ..."

The sun was falling when we trekked through the forest. A

few Velores offered to help carry, but JC dismissed them with an easy smile and some bogus excuse saying I needed exercise.

It was pretty clear he held a ton of power.

They all ogled him as if he were some sort of divine being. But, surprisingly, JC wasn't arrogant about it. Another un-Animal-like characteristic. I wondered where he fell in Amelia's litter order.

It took us forever and a few breaks, on account of the weight and distance, to reach the graveyard. But I was surprised we managed to do it at all.

Immortality had increased my stamina.

There were six empty holes already dug and we quickly filled up four.

JC handed me a shovel. "I'll go back and get the other two. You can start shoveling."

Being left alone, in a graveyard with four fresh bodies, should've wigged me out, but I'd seen too much, too soon. Desensitization was already settling in. And the freedom, despite the macabre circumstances, softened the tension. Manual labor had a soothing effect.

I focused on my task. Shoveling, building a rhythm, doing everything within my power to stop myself from surveying the Velore side of the cemetery where Jester's marker sat. Guilt made it stick out. Thorn had already grown back the grass and it blended well, but I recognized the motley fool's hat carved from stone, with three bells at the end of each triangular fold. I knew who was underneath.

I'd filled up two holes by the time JC made it back with the leftovers.

He picked up a shovel and got to work. Solid minutes passed with only the sound of disturbed dirt raining between us, before he spoke.

"She was going to have you get rid of the bodies," JC said,

and I paused to look at him. "Just in case you were wondering. She usually has a new guard do it, and since you followed and not Singe, it was pretty obvious you were her pick."

"Oh." The thought hadn't really crossed my mind. "Well, thanks for helping."

JC shrugged. He had a bit of a Greek god look about him. The chiseled jaw, dark eyes, onyx skin. Cougar's heritage so clearly imprinted. Same as Fantasia. No wonder Amelia hated the sight of Fancy. She was a walking reminder of the night she came second to Camille.

He stopped and spiked the ground with the head of the shovel, leaning against the handle like an oversized cane. "I also wanted an opportunity to talk to you."

I paused again. "Why's that?"

He searched the forest line, his eyes narrowing, and I followed his trail of sight. I recognized the move, it was one Fantasia made when she first saved my ass. Surveillance.

"Because Fancy recruited you."

My attention was completely his.

"Look, I just wanted you to know we're not all the same."

"I never—"

"I didn't say you did. I just know how I'd feel if I were in your shoes." He tried on indifference, but it fell short. "I'm sure you got an earful on Mom, and I'm not going to lie and say she's been fair to Fancy. But, well, she doesn't do well with betrayal."

"Duly noted."

He smiled. "But she's really not a bad person."

If you say so. I grunted and gathered another pile of soil, giving him a less than convincing "Sure." It was the best I could do given the circumstances, and simply to change the subject I asked, "So how many siblings do you have?"

"Four full, one half," he said. "I'm the oldest, then there's

Cheetoh and Cheetah—they're twins." I recalled the matching red-haired female in the arena. I wondered if they shared similar asshole-ish dispositions. "And then there's Jaguar. He looks a lot like me, just a shade smaller. And worlds more immature." JC waited a moment and added, "Not to alarm you, but it seems we have a little birdie listening in."

He was looking toward the forest line, where a bright sphere fluffed its feathers on a branch.

Fred.

Dreams emerged after him and moseyed over.

She was dressed, again, in an unusual getup, with a bedazzled vest, a skirt made of feathers, and purple hair underneath the waterfall of blonde, which, for the record, had somehow made it to her ankles.

"Wild Saturday night, huh?" she asked, eyeing the graves.

"We're in the company of some real party animals," JC said. "They went out and lost their heads."

"I see that."

"Who says we don't know how to party?" JC winked, and she tucked a strand of hair behind her ear.

"Speaking of parties, you two are missing a spectacular one back at the city."

"Is that so? Seems you're missing it too."

Dreams fidgeted, eyeing the forest. She shifted her weight, and Fred flittered to JC's shoulder. He stopped shoveling and considered her. "Is everything okay?"

She shook her head and looked at me, her blue eyes swelling into quarters, her bottom lip nipped with nerves.

JC took less than a second to piece it together and started to put on a performance, dropping his voice. "We have about ten more minutes' worth of work. Why don't you go for a walk, Dreams, maybe leave Fred behind so if we need to find you he can lead the way?"

She nearly slumped over and looked at him with gratitude. "Thank you," she lipped.

He swallowed, his Adam's apple bobbing with effort.

"I know," he replied.

She left Fred twittering and prancing along JC's shoulders. He chirped at being left behind, but stayed, even though I never saw Dreams deliver an order. It's like he knew his role and clearly disliked it.

Or she had a magic over him.

After Dreams disappeared into the yawning blackness of the forest, Fred traded JC's shoulder for a nearby tombstone, bouncing along the edge like a light orb. JC gave me a look and indicated we should work closer together.

"It seems suspicious if you two leave together," he mumbled. "The graveyard is too open, less places to hide, and because of the celebration, we're most likely being watched."

I cleared my throat to indicate I'd heard him.

"In ten minutes, Fred will fly into the trees. If we work fast, we can get this done in time. Just follow him and he'll take you to her."

"I feel like I've missed something."

"No, you're just new. I've known Dreams forever and can read her like a book. She needs to talk to you, and if I had any guesses, it has to do with Fantasia."

I nodded and started stabbing mounds of dirt, pummeling like a madman.

"Why are you helping her?"

"I told you, just because Mom hates Fancy doesn't mean we all do." He hesitated for only a moment. "Dreams is pretty great too. Amazing, actually."

There was a thick undercurrent, an intimacy.

"Are you two dating?"

He almost laughed. "No, not at all. Although I've always wanted to."

My pace didn't stop. "Why don't you then? Your mom?"

"No, I'm not her type."

Surprise ruined my aim and my last shovelful missed the mark. JC was not only sculpted like a gladiator, but adored. The few girls we passed in the city nearly fell at his feet.

"Impossible standards?" I asked.

He laughed. "No, but thanks for the boost in confidence."

"But you're like a freakin' Adonis."

"Again, thanks for the boost in confidence."

"If you're not her type, then who is?"

He snickered. "Aphrodite."

"Oh ..." It never crossed my mind Dreams might be gay. Probably because she lured in Tony by dating him, I simply assumed she preferred guys.

"Yeah, I've tried converting her, but she says it doesn't work that way." His grin didn't falter. "I'm gonna keep working at it."

"You'll have to let me know how that goes."

"Only if I succeed."

"So that means never, huh?"

"Probably."

I shook my head, a smile taking over my face. We managed to fill the last pit just as Fred took off for the forest line.

Almost like clockwork.

There was nothing forced when JC wished me luck on my way out. Needless to say, I liked him.

⚮

FRED WAS about a dozen trees in. He took off deeper into the forest as soon as I breached the border.

Night had fallen over an hour earlier, and the forest was about as black as a darkroom for developing film.

Every so often Fred would stop and chirp.

Or so it seemed.

I'd heard of smart birds. Trainable birds. But this was twenty shades past ridiculous.

Eventually, Fred flew into a thick pocket of trees and landed on a redwood, a tree not common in the Cascade Mountains.

Dreams was sitting on an oversized root, her hands twisting in her lap. She saw me and brightened, hope making her eyes glisten.

"Hey, Rapunzel," I said.

She stood and smiled so big it fed my own.

"Thanks for coming."

"Of course." We stood uncomfortably, neither one of us knowing how to move forward.

When I couldn't stand the silence, I took a step closer and asked, "Is everything okay?"

That's when she came apart at the seams. The smile. The sparkling eyes. It wasn't real. It was theater, all of it, and now she was out of character.

She buried her head in her hands and hiccuped a sob.

This was bad. So very, very bad.

"She's so screwed up right now," Dreams breathed, lifting her face from her palms. "So screwed up. I can't get her out of it. She keeps making stupid decisions, all because she thinks it's right. She knows better, but she doesn't care. And now she's slipped into this bad depression and we can't get her out of it. We've all tried, Mom, Torti, me. We can't break through. It's like she's trapped."

Fantasia *was* trapped. She was stuck between morals and obedience. I saw the stakes Thorn placed on her. How she exited the corridor after her newest assignment, her spirit shattered.

I shook my head, and looked anywhere and everywhere but at the broken woman in front of me. Dreams' pain was robbing her color, it stung and burned. I felt her heartache, it synced with my own.

Dreams grabbed my hand, forcing me to look at her. "Help us bring her back."

"I don't know what to do."

She squeezed so forcefully a knuckle popped. "I don't either, but right now we're running out of options. You're kind of our last hope."

Icy fear breezed along my skin. "How screwed up?"

"Really screwed up."

"Specifics?"

Dreams looked away and attempted to gather some inner strength. "You know that time I talked to you in the gym? When I told you about the lab being built?"

"Yeah."

"Remember how you smiled?"

I nodded. It was an unforgettable sensation, thinking I was going to die and wanting it to happen.

Dreams leaned in. "She told me she wasn't going to do it, not with the child, and I told her if she didn't they'd kill her. She can't go against Thorn like that. And you know what she did?" She stepped away, her eyes straining around the corners. "She gave me the same smile you gave me."

No, no, no, no, no. The mantra flipped on repeat, swirling in my head. Panic thrummed, my heart caught. "She can't," I whispered.

"I think she's going to."

"I won't let her."

"That's what we're banking on.

"Where is she?"

"In her cave."

"Take me there."

Dreams allotted a small smile and did a quick survey of the forest. "I knew you were good for something."

She took off at a run, and I was right on her heels.

We made the cave in record time. The rope dangled from a precipice, a noose without a loop. I'd already leapt off one mountain, I'd do it again. All for her.

"Make it better," Dreams said.

"You can count on it."

Dreams gave me another smile, before letting the forest absorb her as if she were nothing more than mist and shadow.

I grabbed the rope, took a deep swallow, and threw myself over the ledge.

CHAPTER 13

A CAVE OF SORROWS

Fear threatened to turn my bones to jello. The rope was too vulnerable for my liking—a simple method, yes, but not an innocuous one. I mean, it would've taken only one vindictive asshole to cut the fibers above my head or, more likely, one bad grip to send me spiraling to the cliff base. I didn't trust my hands.

I think my nerves bore the brunt of the workout even though my arms carried all the weight.

When I reached the hollowed-out pocket, dangling like a worm on a line, I tried to steady my fear. And then, like the eye of a hurricane, it was gone.

Because she was there. Fantasia was there. Waiting.

My dead heart thumped.

***

She pulled me into the cave and, when my feet landed on solid ground, led me to the back where light couldn't touch us. We faded into obscurity, two silhouettes surrendering to the darkness. She wrapped her arms around me, her grip fierce, her touch desperate. So help me, I forgot everything. I forgot my anger. I lost my whirlpool of questions. I dipped my head into her hair and tried to breathe her in.

And it was like I transformed into who I used to be. I was just a boy in the arms of a beautiful girl. A girl so far out of my league it seemed as if the universe had finally bestowed an act of kindness to make up for all the shit heaped on me throughout the years.

Not necessarily a reward, since Fantasia wasn't a prize to be won, but more like a godsend, a stroke of luck.

Like the last time, we let our hands do the talking.

Only hers were infinitely more ravenous. She grabbed my face, a move so quick I barely had time to lift my chin before her lips covered mine, her kiss deep and searching.

It lasted for a full millennium.

Her taste was perfect. The way she moved her mouth was perfect. The length of her body against mine was perfect.

Air was a luxury we opted to forgo.

Every one of our instincts kicked in. My hands went everywhere, exploring, searching, committing her flesh to memory. I wanted to rip off my gloves and hated the glue keeping them on.

But her touch, that was something I could feel. Her fingers moved inside my shirt, running up my chest. When she finally broke the kiss, we were both short of breath. Her eyes glowed.

Neither of us apologetic over broken rules.

I was ready for another go at it.

"Well, that's quite the greeting," I said, combing my fingers through her hair.

She smiled and asked, "How'd you know I was here?"

I leaned in, my lips only a hair's width away. "Can't you just see it?"

"No." She pressed her lips to mine. "You'll have to tell me."

"Dreams," I replied. Kissing her again. I swear, I'd never tire of touching her. "She said you could use a pep talk." I cradled her face in my palms, and we melted. She kissed me a final time, the move more of a punctuation mark, and stepped away.

"My sister's a busybody." She rolled her eyes and grabbed my hand. "Come. Have a seat." She led me to the pair of chairs housed in her rock pit sanctuary.

We folded into them and leaned forward, so our breath became a breeze of solidarity.

"So what did Dreams tell you?"

"She said you're a wreck, and she's worried you're gonna do something stupid."

Her smile made my hairs bristle.

I squeezed her hand and with the other lifted her chin with steadfast fingers. "Look at me," I demanded. And as I expected, her lavender metamorphosed to stone, hard and cutting. "You've got to stop this."

Her face fell and she bit her lip. "I can't, though...."

"Of course you can."

"You're asking the impossible, Daniel. You're asking me to sacrifice my morals."

"C'mon, be reasonable."

"No. I can't make more of us." Her prideful voice dropped, stumbling into regret. "It's wrong. We're wrong."

Her sadness drifted around the cave, swarming in great billowy tendrils. She was stuck on stubborn, so much so I decided to alter the trajectory of our conversation.

And since the timing would never be perfect, I went all in, head first.

"Why'd you pretend your name was Sarah when you recruited Colby?" I looked away, fighting the fear curling around me. *Sarah*. I wanted her safe—away from Narivous, away from me. Simply thinking her name was too much, panic hammered in my chest.

Fantasia let go of my hand and bent over, her head nearly touching her lap. "Because I'm stupid. And because I'm jealous. And because I'd seen her the day I found Colby. You were in her thoughts, and I hated it. I wanted her memories. To be her. To know what it's like to lay claim to you in such an open way. She's going to always have that, and I never will. And when Colby asked my name, it just kind of ..." She looked up and pinched her mouth, digging for an answer. "Shot out. I couldn't stop thinking about her, and then it was too late to take it back. Because you can't take back a name. You just can't." Her whole body clenched and her eyes watered with black tears. She blinked them back, and I reclaimed her hand.

"Okay, then."

"I'm sorry."

"It's okay."

"No, it's not."

"Let me be the judge of that."

She smiled and I kissed her, ending the argument.

Through a film of grief, she said, "Thank you."

I shook my head. "Don't thank me yet, we still have some shit to hash out. Like you bringing in crappy recruits."

"I can't do it, Daniel. I can't condemn people."

I took a deep breath. Defiance ran deep, the crux of her morals, and telling her not to do something was an invitation for rebellion. She wouldn't listen, so there was only one option —select a different path—and Thorn had unwittingly handed me a map. I was banking on Fantasia's answers, hoping to cash in on my instincts, willing her to respond the way I needed her to.

Even if I didn't agree with my own argument. Even if I hated every excuse I was about to give her. None of it mattered. I needed to keep her cooperative and ... *alive*. I'd say anything.

It was time to start checking off boxes.

"What are you hoping to achieve?" I asked.

She relaxed, bolstered by the openness I shoved into my voice. I felt bloated by fraud. "Freedom," she whispered.

Check.

"You want to leave Narivous?"

"No, not necessarily. I just don't want to be forced to do things I find unethical."

Check.

"And you think recruiting humans is unethical?"

"Of course it is. Death would be better than this life." She bared her teeth and ripped her hand away. *Check.* "How could you even ask that?"

Check. I knew how to station my answers, and questions.

"What if that's not true? What if this life *is* a better alternative?"

She flinched. "You can't be serious. Tell me you're not serious." She leaned back, folding her arms across her chest, closing off her body along with her mind.

"Look, Fantasia."

"This is stupi—"

"Thorn said some things," I started, and she took a breath so heavy all the oxygen funneled from the cave into her lungs. Her jaw clenched and I held up my hands. "Relax."

She didn't.

I leaned farther forward and made my voice a damn lullaby. "If you could see my thoughts you wouldn't be mad, so

I'm guessing your sight is blocked right now." I still hadn't figured out how Fantasia's mind-reading capabilities worked, if it was dependent on the Velore, the clan, or translucency levels.

But one thing was clear, she had no access to my mind, at least not at the moment. Favor was on my side.

"Okay, then." *Steady*. "Do you think the cheers in the crowd, when Thorn entered the stadium, were fake?"

"Some of them...."

"But the majority?"

She rolled her eyes.

"That's what I thought." I stared above her head, at the jagged stone ceiling. Dank and dark as the argument I was about to build. "Those people out there love her, which tells me she pulled them from something far worse. They like it here. She even said so, and as much as I hate to admit it, I think she's right."

"It's not natural."

We aren't either.... I stopped myself from saying it. I needed to support my case, not hurt it. I took a breath and gave a more benign response. "Neither is technology. Cars. Pesticides. All of it. If you want natural, you're in the wrong era."

"That's a bit of a stretch...."

"Maybe so, but listen"—I reached for her hand, pulling it from its shelter against her chest—"I know how bad it can be. I've seen it. How ugly people get. What drugs do. They melt brains, rip apart families, make you think your entire lineage is hexed. Those people in the stadiums know exactly what I'm talking about because they've lived through it. Whether they were the addict or just collateral of the addiction, it doesn't matter. They've known the very worst of society. And Thorn" —I squeezed Fantasia's hand—"Thorn made it better. She took them from it. She knows they're indebted to her, and you know it, too." I stopped and winced at my own painful memories.

The wreckage of my former life. The rage. The beatings. The pangs of hunger.

The hatred that clung to me like a hostile aura.

On a good day I was unwanted, and on a bad one, an obstacle. It stripped away my humanity, reducing me to a hinderance, an object others had to work around.

"But they can never leave," Fantasia whispered.

"And I bet a lot of them are okay with that."

"What about the ones that do want to leave?"

I hesitated before vomiting my answer. "I don't think they should."

She ripped her hand away for a second time and turned her face, slighting me in form and message. "How can you say that?" Her voice broke. "Everyone deserves freedom, the right to choose their own path. The right to decide for themselves who they want to be, what they'll become. It's like you've switched sides."

One. Two. Three. Breathe.

"I'll always be on your side. Nothing will ever change that." I looked around the cave, at the dew hanging off the stone, at the starkness of our cold shell. This was her peace. In a city of beauty, it was the rawness of her cave, the sterility, that told no lies. Ugly and honest.

"Then why are you saying this? Why the change?" she asked.

"Because I want you safe. Because things aren't always black and white. There are gray areas, and that's okay. It's normal. And ..." I leaned back and braced myself for the sting.

"And?"

"And I talked to Frigid."

"So?"

"So, she's just as you said. Sweet. Good. But I never would've known that if she had her way with me the first time I came into the forest." I leaned forward. "I'd be dead, another person to weigh on her conscience. She isn't safe, and she needs to stay here. For herself, for others. Unless, of course"—I paused and raised a brow—"you'd like to see her killed off permanently."

Fantasia let out a low-grade hiss, her tongue forking into a reptilian dialect. "Of course I don't want that."

"Then don't you see?" I held my hands open wide. "She needs to stay here. She can't have freedom. It's too dangerous."

She leaned forward and pierced me with her stare. "And don't you see, that's exactly why there shouldn't be more of us made. We're too deadly, too powerful, and Thorn likes human recruits with questionable ethics. She doesn't care if they murder or steal, as long as they'll be loyal. They'll be monsters with gifts they don't deserve, gifts they shouldn't have. You don't give power to people like that."

She let her final thought hang.

"And yet, you're forgetting one thing," I countered.

Her righteous glow started to crumble at my slow smile. I had a big argument still awaiting its release.

"You're now on recruiting duty. You get to pick. Choose someone who isn't a criminal. Choose someone who has a shitty background but still has their morals. Someone like ..." I put my hand on her leg and squeezed. She didn't try to brush it away. "Pick someone like Tony." I hesitated, then added, "Or like me."

She opened her mouth, then quickly sealed it. She either lost her words or didn't have the courage to speak them.

Either way, I took her moment of weakness and expanded on it. Eroding her dangerous thoughts into bits of dust.

I stood up and kneeled next to her chair, my fingers stroking her thigh.

"Instead of looking at your new assignment as a curse, look at it as a blessing. It's all about context." I gave her a smile she didn't return. "You have an amazing ability. You can see thoughts. Use it to our advantage. Find humans who have it hard, harder than their life will be here, and give them this gift."

"But ... Thorn, and her power. We'll be giving her more."

"I didn't say to recruit bad people."

"But they have to be loyal."

"Loyalties change. The good will do what's right."

"But Colby ..."

"Colby was weak. That's why you picked him, right? Or was it because he hated women?"

"He didn't hate women."

I stood up, surprised. "*What?*"

She gave me a sly smile. "I think Dolly made that up so you wouldn't have to take his life. As a kindness to you. Colby didn't hate his daughter, he loved her. It was the mom he hated." Fantasia tucked a strand of hair behind her ear. "It was a bold move on Dolly's part. There were other Doppelgängers who could've easily read the lie from Colby's thoughts, but I imagine it doesn't really matter, no one's gonna argue against Dolly. And her powers are so much stronger. She can always say she saw what others missed."

"You can't be serious." Anger turned my vision black. "She lied? For me? But what about you?"

"Excuse me?"

"Could you've been killed over her saving me? By saying he hates women?" One flaw was bad enough, her recruit was already garbage, but to give him another for my sake was more rank than shit.

Fantasia gave a grim laugh. "No. It was only because she was ticked. Thorn actually takes the greatest pleasure in male recruits who think they're better than females. Those are the ones she likes to break. It feeds her ego. I've seen her give them the lowliest jobs, just because she can. She used one as a footrest for over a year, broke him into nothing, and then executed him because she worried he would never get over the slight. They're a challenge—and she always wins."

I shook my head, amazed how a crisis can transform details. Dolly had looked to the other Doppelgängers, I remembered the eye emblems, I remembered how she'd stepped away from Colby right after she'd done so. I recalled Dolly's undecipherable look when Thorn beckoned me to her side. Was she preparing for the worst, knowing Colby wasn't viable?

"So Dolly was protecting me?"

Fantasia nodded. "Yeah."

"That's the second time...." I muttered.

"What does that mean?"

Did she really not know? I was again questioning Fantasia's Velore mind-reading abilities. She was almost certifiably blind.

"The day Tony was killed, she got in my head and stopped me. She knows ... *everything*."

"Oh ..." Fantasia frowned, but didn't seem surprised. "Makes sense, you were acting strange and, well, Dolly's powers are tough to beat."

"You're not worried about her knowing?" I tapped my temple.

"Can't do anything about it now," she said honestly.

"I don't really like that answer."

"Yeah, well, it's either that or give you a lie." She grinned coyly. "Plus, if she's protecting you, that means she likes you. I doubt she'll say anything." Fantasia finished with a shrug.

I shook my head. We were falling off track anyhow.

"Come here." I held out my hand. She hesitated, eyeing it as if it were a trap, but then accepted my waiting palm. I made sure my squeeze was both comforting and steady. She let some of her edge dull, and I needed to keep at it. To transform her sharp blade to a butter knife.

I pulled Fantasia to her feet and wrapped my arms around her, letting my grip deepen in the divots of her lower back. "Let's start off small," I murmured. "Something manageable and easy. Let's play in the gray area...." I nestled into her neck, kissing her. She let her head fall back, opening herself to me.

My lips ran a line from her collarbone to her earlobe. My hands slid under her shirt, feeling every rib, melding to her rivets. I breathed into her ear. "Recruit the adult first. Pick a spectacular one. Someone good. Someone bright. Someone loyal. Someone with conviction."

Her voice grew soft and wispy. "And then what?"

"Maybe that'll be enough, maybe she'll let the child go."

She shook her head. "It won't be enough."

I looped my fingers through her hair, holding her steady, and kissed her lips. "We have to try. That's all we can do. One step at a time. Bring her someone who will make her forget about Colby, make her forget why she's mad." I spoke into her mouth. She matched my words with her own, both of us talking, kissing, feeding.

"And if we fail?"

"We come up with something different," I murmured. "But you can't be reckless. You can't leave us."

She wanted to shake her head, I could tell, but I rested my forehead against her own, stilling it. "Please," I whispered, and the string between us, the invisible link, strong as spider silk, thick as rope, stretched taut. "Don't leave me."

"I don't want to leave you."

"Then don't."

"Tell me again."

"Tell you what?"

"That it's okay. Convince me." Fantasia's voice barely breached a whisper.

"It's okay," I promised, letting my hands creep, nearly losing myself against her. She moaned and slid her hand up my neck, pulling my mouth closer. "I can honestly say, in this moment"—my smile landed against hers—"that being resurrected was the best thing to ever happen to me."

"Smooth," she replied, and our hands resumed their frenzied pace. She never said it, but I knew she'd agreed to my terms. I felt it in her energy.

She would recruit the human. And I would do everything within my power to eradicate her guilt.

We kissed. And then kissed some more. Our bodies swayed together. I wanted to rip her clothes off and kept working at it. She thwarted my every move, modesty a worthy adversary, but I still gained ground and the flesh of her torso become more visible with each touch. When air became a desperation, she pulled her lips away and searched my face, tugging her clothes back into position. I winced, all my hard work gone, *poof.* "We can't keep doing this," she said.

"But I wanna keep doing this."

"If we're caught...."

That stalled us, turning our happy jaunt into a grim one. We both inched away, a minuscule amount equivalent to a yawning divide. I tried to give her a grin, to bring back the moment, but she winced.

She was holding something back.

"What?" I asked, and sure enough, she nervously bit her lip. "Out with it, Fantasia."

"There's something that's been bothering me and, well, I've been waiting for the right time to tell you."

"What is it?"

Rather than answer, Fantasia walked toward the back where a worn saddle bag was discarded like dirty laundry. It was ancient, the leather pale as clay, the straps limp. She picked it up and rifled through it.

Paper rustled from inside, and her body steadied when she landed on what she was looking for. She gave me an uncertain look as she plucked a flyer from inside.

"You need to see this," she said, thrusting out the paper. "Here."

I took it and smoothed it out. The image was saturated in color, the sign of a professional print job, and I struggled to wrap my head around the person staring back at me.

Because it was me. Well, the old me.

Human me.

I'd forgotten who I was. My original blond hair and blue eyes took me back. No streaks of ash, no deepening of the irises. I was ordinary, in every sense of the word. At the top, thick letters read: Missing. Daniel Thatcher. 17 years old, six foot, 165 pounds. That was followed by contact information. I recognized Aunt Marie's and Uncle Dean's numbers, along with a desperate request for my safe return.

And a reward that was well beyond my worth. She was offering $10,000 for verifiable information leading to my whereabouts. *Information.* A trail to follow. Something to give her hope.

For me.

"She won't stop," Fantasia said, tapping the paper. "Every few weeks she increases the reward, makes more, and passes them out. She refuses to think you're a runaway. She took out an ad in the paper, filed a police report, and has you splattered all over social media."

"This is impossible. She doesn't have this kind of money."

"She's using her inheritance."

My cheeks heated as I fought both a smile and a grimace. Translucency started to spring on me. Fantasia laid her head on my chest. "Pull it back," she said.

"I didn't think she'd look for me. Not this hard." My throat hurt from the emotional lump lodged there.

"She won't *stop* looking for you. Neither will your Uncle Dean. They're wallpapering every town that produces a lead. She refuses to sell your grandmother's house because she thinks you'll come back." Fantasia ran her hand along my arm and from her steady stroke, I realized I was trembling.

She gently took back the flyer and tucked it into her pocket. She stepped away so she could look me straight on, grabbing my hands. "I can't stay away from you, Daniel. But I will, if you ask me to, because you have more to lose than me. You have humans close by who are expendable. What we're doing right now, it's against the law. And you need to know what could happen if we're caught."

"But my family, for this?" *Way too extreme.*

Fantasia shrugged. "It's hard to say. If Thorn's having a bad week, anything could happen. Or worse, Amelia could find out. She'd have no problem slaying them, with or without Thorn's approval. She's impulsive like that. You need to know the risk you're running."

"You're running one too."

She shook her head. "They need me. I'm their one healer, remember? And they need my sisters, because they bring in revenue and recruits. They could make an example out of you, though. Out of your family."

I shook my head and searched the ceiling, desperate to stop my slow heartbeat from punching through my ribcage. This was why Fantasia didn't want any more Velores made. This. Right. Here. Our powerless situation.

And I'd just convinced her to make another.

All to keep her alive, so she'd be near me, knowing all along I couldn't have her.

The defiance she was so very fond of infected me.

When I looked back at her, my eyes flashed. She dropped my hands only to cup my face.

"Tell me to let you go and I will," she said. She was absent of tears, but they were coming. Her mouth pinched in an effort to steady her face. "We're practically strangers, anyway. Maybe this stupid thing we have, maybe it isn't real and if we stop feeding it it'll just go away."

It's like she found my old thoughts, the ones I'd already cataloged as bullshit. I refused to believe this was fake. I needed it to be real.

For once, I had to believe something good could happen to me.

It was real. I willed it.

"I don't want to stop feeding it," I replied.

"Really?" Her face flushed, optimism making her infinitely more beautiful.

I kissed her, so deep she'd be left with no doubt. "Yes, really. I believe in it, Fantasia."

"So what are we gonna do?"

I looked down and she mistook my gesture for one of defeat. She stepped away and grabbed a strand of hair, anxiously stroking it. "You're not going to risk it, are you? I wouldn't blame you."

"Fantas—"

"It's okay, really."

"You've missed your mark."

"How do you mean?"

I reclaimed her hands and smiled. "We just need to think in the gray area." I kissed her hand. "We need to make my family leave. Send them far away, like Polar did with Gram. Because I can't give you up. Not with ..." I shuddered. "Not with everything else."

I attempted to quash the thoughts flickering behind my eyes. Because "everything else" was grim.

It was all encompassing. It was my future, what life would be like without Fantasia. I couldn't survive my cage if I didn't have her to hope for. I'd pull into myself, fading till I was nothing more than a hazy memory.

Today I convinced Fantasia that recruiting humans was okay. I hated my logic. I hated how it made sense. I hated myself.

Fantasia looked at me, and misread my thoughts—*again*.

"So I'm guessing you know," she said.

I shook my head, lost. "Know what?"

"About guard duty initiations."

"I'm not following...."

"Oh, I-I thought ..." She faded with a stammer. "I just assumed." She choked, placing her hand over her lips, as if she could will the words back into her mouth. "I'm sorry."

"Sorry for what?"

"About the sacrifice."

"The ones we just buried?" JC'd said a new guard member always disposed of the freshly dead. But when she shook her head, my stomach pitted.

"No." She leaned against my chest and wrapped her arms tight around me. "Oh, Daniel," she moaned. "They're going to make you kill a human."

"No ..."

She nodded. "It's mandatory for all guard members." Her woeful eyes looked into mine.

I was going to hurl.

Thorn was hellbent on turning me into the monster she wanted me to be, both body and soul.

And I'd just convinced Fantasia to make her more.

Fantasia was right, we shouldn't exist.

We were the wicked.

CHAPTER 14

VEINS OF FIRE

Fred collected me shortly after Fantasia delivered her bombshell. He fluttered into the cave and swooped around the cavernous hole. Fantasia peeled herself away.

We'd kissed so much my lips chapped. She touched them and with a soft glow put them back to the way they were. It kind of sucked. It was like she erased our moments, and I was gonna have to feed off those memories to get me through the next few days.

The sacrificial human thing plagued me.

So much so, when I climbed the rope, I barely acknowledged the potential fall.

Dreams was standing uncomfortably at the top. And Fred fluttered to her shoulder. "They're starting to wonder where you are," she whispered while scanning the area. "JC told them you went for a walk down toward the quarry."

I nodded.

"You have to say quarry, 'cause there are no cameras there. Got it?"

"Got it."

We started on the narrow, trampled path, dodging ferns and briars. "Did you have any luck?" she whispered, as she ducked under a tree branch. She never really looked at me, instead she focused on the surrounding brush.

"She's gonna recruit," I mumbled back.

"She's not just saying that?"

Well, technically no. But I wasn't gonna serve that answer.

"Nope. It's for real."

We reached a main thoroughfare. Dreams did a little back kick, folding her hands together and letting out a childlike squeal, a very un-paranoid move, too loud for my liking. "Thank goodness!" she sang. "Torti and Mom are gonna be so relieved." She reached out and squeezed my arm. "Nice job." She flashed her teeth and even Fred picked up on her happiness. He chirped.

I pointed to the bird. "How?"

"We have a connection," she replied, shooting me a wink and skipping ahead.

By the time we made it back to the city, the Dawning Rose Celebration was winding down. We hesitated at the entrance. Guards weren't in their places, most likely exempt for the night. Too many active Velores for anyone to sneak up on the city, anyhow.

People were still out, singing, dancing. Off in the distance, on the palace front lawn, were two spots of white. They barely landed in my line of sight, since they were tucked off to the side, partially concealed by a massive evergreen. Polar and Frigid were dancing, if you could call it that. He held her tight in his grip, leaning over her, and they were swaying to music I couldn't hear. She was lucid, that much was clear, and from the desperation of his hold, he was trying to keep her that way.

As if his clutch could save her mind from falling apart. I looked away.

It was too painful.

There were small bonfires—very small bonfires—controlled by Fire members in designated concrete hollows. The smoke was minimal and the tree cover directly above the plumes was at a higher elevation.

"So it doesn't look like a forest fire," Dreams said when she saw my interest. "Fire watch hasn't really started yet, but still, we like to play it safe. We only burn clean hardwoods, so the smoke is less, and only on special days. Because aside from a real forest fire, having humans think there's a fire is probably our greatest threat."

Sending firefighters in droves to Narivous would be a disaster, with or without real flames. The consequences would be far reaching.

"What happens when fires do break out?"

"We have ways of stopping them."

"How's that?"

Her smile was all teeth. She squeezed my arm, never afraid of touching me, trusting my clothes to keep her safe. "Why, silly—*you*." She laughed. "Or, rather, your aunt. But now that you're here, I'm sure they'll use you too. Fire can't get past the particles. Scream goes along the border, lets out a wail, and coats the trees."

"But wouldn't it turn the trees into kindling by killing them?"

"Yeah, but there's more to it. Kinda a multifaceted process. Thorn follows behind and forces green trees to grow. Saplings, or something like that, only they're the size of real trees. She sucks all the moisture from deep wells to keep them raw and wet. And then the Fire clan comes along and warps the blaze, making it go back the way it came.

They've stopped countless. But it requires a ton of work and energy."

"Can't Fires just stop the flames?"

She shook her head. "The only one who can really stop them is Ferno. But when they reach forest-fire proportions, it's too much for one man."

"Ember can't stop them?"

Dreams shook her head. "She can build fire, she can make it explode, warp it, walk through it, but she can't quench it."

"And Ferno can? I don't get it."

"I thought Fantasia told you about the auras?"

"She did."

"And about methods of death."

"She did."

"So?"

I went palms up. "Okay, so obviously I missed something."

Fred fluttered to a branch overhead. "Have you not really looked at Ember? At Ferno?"

Of course I had. And then I realized her implication. Ferno wore a stocking cap to hide the nasty scars around his head. I'd never seen the rest of his flesh, he was careful to keep covered. More most likely lurked. Immortality had not healed his wounds, but Ember, Ember was beautiful, unmarred, skin smooth as porcelain. "Oh ..." I said.

They were killed differently.

As were the other Fires. Singe, for example, had perfect skin. I'd only seen scars on Ferno.

"Why don't they make more like Ferno?" I almost asked *how* he died, but figured I had enough scar tissue coating my brain for one day. My head needed a break.

"They've tried," Dreams said. "But they also have the tricky aura component to contend with. And"—she moved her head from side to side—"it's a bit difficult making them like Ferno, without destroying the body, that is. Ferno was more luck than anything else."

"I can't believe I didn't see it."

"I can." Dreams squinted at me. "Fantasia keeps saying you're smart, but I'm not really buying it."

"Gee, thanks."

"You're welcome," she said sincerely.

I rolled my eyes and laughed, and she surprised me by wrapping her arms around my chest. She rested her cheek on my shoulder. "Thank you," she said. "For keeping her safe." She stepped away, a bit embarrassed by her display of affection. "I'm glad you're here," she said honestly. "Even if you *are* stupid."

I laughed. She gave me a sparkling smile and bowed before leaving, shooting me a wink on her way back to the festivities. Free of worry, Dreams was light as her feathered friend.

Her kindness was not missed, nor was her bravery.

And not only that, but the details she rained down. Fire was feared. Narivous had a weakness.

It was information worth keeping.

⁂

"There you are!" Scream's voice, always one to carry, echoed along the skull corridor. She was wearing a tiara with a spiderweb design, black jewels encrusted in every hub. It was the most regal adornment I'd seen her wear, and it glowed almost as much as her expression.

She grabbed my hands and planted a kiss on each of my cheeks. "My darling boy," she said. "I've been waiting to congratulate you all evening. The honor. Not only a guard member, but our champion." She shook her head with proud wonder. She leaned in and spoke into my ear. "We haven't had a champion in a long time, I honestly thought we never would after the last one."

"What happened with the last one?"

She wrinkled her nose. "I shouldn't have said anything. It's just I'm surprised she reinstated the honor. And it's yours. *Yours.*" She grabbed my hand and shook it for emphasis. "My clan." She closed her eyes, trying to lock in the moment. "My clan recognized. And did you see how happy Thorn was? Oh, it was delightful."

I couldn't move beyond the champion honor—or, more accurately, my predecessor. It was a wad of discarded gum on a hot day, overlooked until stepped in.

Now it stuck.

"So Thorn gave me an honor you thought she'd never give out again?"

"Yes. It's wonderful, isn't it?"

"Maybe." My mouth had gone dry. "I think it depends on what happened to the other guy."

A grimace stole her glimmer, but then she brightened. "No. No unpleasantries right now. We have too much to celebrate to let ghosts ruin our moment. We shall leave them where they belong, a chapter in a history book. So, tell me, are you still riding the high of being our most adored Velore?"

"Sure."

When I didn't feed into her excitement, she patted me on the shoulder and said, "I know you must be exhausted. I heard you had the privilege of burying our dead today."

Privilege?

"But if you're up for it," she started, pulling me toward our quarters, "I have one more surprise for you."

She stopped outside my room and grinned. With fanfare, she opened my door to a grotesque scene, one she was clearly proud of.

Jester's skull sat on a shelf built specifically for him—someone must've retrieved him while I was out and crafted a place to keep my grisly trophy. But perhaps even more horrific was what was waiting on my bed.

It had my aunt bouncing with excitement.

And left me wanting to suck up a week's worth of Dexitrol.

"Your new life officially starts," Scream breathed into my ear.

I cringed and stared at the uniform. It wasn't the forest green vest with the G emblem that ignited my nerves, but the other two pieces: a black cloak and a mask to cover my upper face. Garb to fit my new name, my new title.

New identity.

Scream squeezed my hand, intertwining her fingers, and smiled with every ounce of herself. Pride laced her voice. "You are a treasure to our society. May the world fear you."

It was almost as if she willed it to be true, and it dawned on me, as kind as my aunt was, her views were radically different than my own. Hers were in line with the majority of Narivous' logic. Beautiful and deadly, she held power in the highest regard.

I wondered who broke her.

And who would eventually break me.

"Look for the birch trees," JC said. We were toward the eastern side of Narivous, hugging the outer perimeter. Day five of guard training and I was finally being introduced to the lay of the land. "Birch trees with yellow roses mark our borders," he continued, pointing to a pair growing close to each other. "They're also tucking points."

"Tucking points?"

He nodded and motioned for me to follow. The rain dumped, slapping the hood of my cloak, soaking the fabric, weighing it down.

"This," he said, as he reached for a piece of paper-like bark. Only it wasn't bark, but a hidden door. He punched in a code, put his eye against a black reader, and the camouflage lifted. The rain continued to pelt.

None of the Animals wore outdoor gear. "It's restrictive," JC replied when I asked about it. We'd just stepped out into an active monsoon, and his clothing adhered like a second skin. "I'd rather take the rain over my muscles being bound."

"A cloak isn't really binding, though."

He shook his head, the black strands already glued to his forehead. "It's an obstacle when we're running, kicking, flipping, like what we do at our sparring stations."

Made sense. I got to see the training sessions in person. It seemed every Animal was a member of the guard. A long time ago, Fantasia had said it was their superlative senses that made them ideal hunters. They had the ability to detect human interference from miles away. Animals could hear breathing, smell fear; they were the ultimate predator. Humans couldn't hide.

Since I was unable to touch anyone, I had to stand back while practice took place. We congregated in the domed arena that housed the Dawning Rose Celebration. There, I witnessed the same lethal dramatics as during trials; only difference, the wheat had already been separated from the chaff. The group I now belonged to was of the cruelest abilities.

Cheetoh and his twin, Cheetah, went against each other in great bouts of power. Claws and blood showered the dirt floor, and they smiled with each wound they earned.

Pride in pain.

Their kitty instincts were a strange sort.

And they definitely couldn't perform their pouncing maneuvers with a cloak.

JC took out a rectangular tin, the size of a fat book, from deep inside the birch and crouched low, indicating I should follow. He grabbed a corner of my cloak and held it over the metal box, giving it shelter. "Not really the best weather to be pulling this out," he mumbled. "But you never know with Oregon."

"I hear ya."

He opened the lid and showed me a series of pills in plastic bottles, powders in vials with cork toppers. There were even hypodermic needles with some sort of sickly yellow liquid; it looked like phlegm.

"These are our emergency provisions. Once in a while things get out of hand and we need some extra help." He pointed to each item and named its purpose. Knock out. Suicide. Sedation. Amnesia. Happiness. Hallucinogen. And because I was in training, he asked, "Can you think of why we'd need these?"

"To bring back humans alive?"

He nodded, pleased. "Yeah, pretty much. We can kill with no issues, but if we find a human who might be a good recruit, we're supposed to bring them to Thorn. Also, if they have kids with them, or other people who really aren't important but don't necessarily deserve to die, then we like to give them the amnesia pills. It turns their memories into bad dreams. They'll remember fragments, but they'll think it's a nightmare or something."

"That's surprisingly merciful."

JC scowled.

"What?" I asked.

"It's not really merciful," he said, then leaned closer. "And if I tell you something, you've got to promise not to say anything. Got it?" His face went hard, the water darted off in sharp jabs, his expression angular.

"Got it."

"Okay." He took a breath. "We spare people, not to be kind, but to keep control. It's calculating. Thorn tells people it's for mercy, but really it's to keep a hold over her new recruits, until she has them, for lack of a better word, *brainwashed*." JC shook his head and looked around, checking the perimeter.

Of course. Because anyone found in the forest would be an unwilling volunteer.

There was no predicting what they'd get.

"It's all about breaking people, taking them down to the studs, and then rebuilding them to Thorn's standards. Conditioning, or whatever," JC said. "I've seen even the strongest fall."

He was staring, not really at me, but others in the past. My time was coming.

"Why don't the other Seven try to stop it?"

"They'll never go against Thorn."

"Why? It can't be because they're afraid of dying."

"I thought it was obvious."

I shook my head.

"They love her. They really love her. You can't rewrite history." JC swayed a sliver closer. "Every human, every Velore, is going against a past no one can undo, a prologue that binds the Seven. Not even your grandfather or uncles can stop Thorn."

"But Frigid and my aunts—"

"Will always side with Thorn."

"So they'll let her break me?"

"They don't consider breaking a bad thing. It's a good thing—*necessary*—as long as they rebuild you better and stronger. In their heads, they're doing you a favor."

"That's why I have to kill a human, isn't it?"

He nodded, as a roll of thunder rumbled. "Especially for guard duty. They need the deadliest and most compliant. And they don't want you hesitating to kill if need be. Best way to do that is to have you kill on their terms. The first is always the hardest. It comes easier after that."

Lightning flashed and my face fell.

I kept replaying my argument with Fantasia. Convincing her to bring in another recruit.

"Do you know when it's gonna happen?"

"No, but it'll be soon. Romeo's in charge with bringing someone in, and he's been working pretty hard at it."

"Does he know who the person's gonna be?"

"I think so."

I swallowed and took my mask off, dropping it, trying to catch my breath.

"You need some Dexitrol?"

I shook my head. "No, I need a way to fix this."

"You can't. You're sand."

"Sand?"

"Yeah, sand. That's what everyone is. Too small to be put back into rock and shells."

"That's heavy."

He shrugged.

"Do you suppose the person I'm supposed to kill will be bad?" Finding a new angle was my only hope at easing my conscience. It's amazing how insidious guilt can be. It slips through the smallest cracks in your exterior. Cracks you don't even realize you have until a memory sneaks in and stings.

I needed my sacrifice to be the worst of the worse. Despicable. Like the scum at the Dawning Rose Celebration. It would make it easier, less painful. Perhaps even a good thing.

Maybe.

JC looked away, and the sky rumbled for a second time. He measured his words carefully. After a few unsteady moments, just as another flash lit up the forest and his mournful face, he stepped close enough I could feel his warmth. He used the rain to keep our words locked between us.

"Thorn gave Romeo specific instructions, but none of us know what they are. He's keeping it under lock and key. But I can tell you this—Thorn's afraid of you," he whispered. "I knew it the moment she made you champion. You know how I know?" He didn't wait for an answer. "Because the last guy in your shoes went against her and had his head taken off for it. She wants to show the world she's not afraid. That even her champions can't take her out. That even the strongest are not as strong as her. She's gonna work extra hard on breaking you. Because she has to break you. She needs to prove a point. That even the most deadly bow to her."

I already knew the answer before I asked, "Who was the guy before me?"

"Chugknot. His name was Chugknot." JC's smile was grim. "Word to the wise. The fall from grace happens fast, so weigh your decisions carefully."

Damn. I knew it. I knew it back when Scream mentioned my predecessor. I just didn't want to face it—or the implications it carried. I still didn't want to face it.

"Just remember," JC added, "Thorn's all about image."

"So I've heard." I started to turn away, bogged down and tired, and for the first time, JC actually chanced a touch. He grabbed my arm and forced me to face him.

He searched the trees and said, "Being guard doesn't mean we always have to be the bad guy." He took a step closer. "The amnesia pills are great. The closer you use them to the actual event, the fewer pieces the human remembers, but the longer you wait, the more they can recall—up to 12 hours of false memories." He clenched his jaw. "They don't keep track of who logs in and what's used. Only guards, Brilliants, the Seven, and a few runners are allowed in the birch trees, so I suppose they trust who has access."

As the rain started to slow, his candor picked up. He dropped his head and pinched the bridge of his nose. "I can't read minds, but I can still sense a person's worth and I do what feels right in the moment. I've done what I've felt was ethical, even if it's not according to code, or even law. It's a risk, like everything else but, well, I was always told being brave brings benefits."

He stepped away and his body, normally coiled with Animal power, unraveled. He leaned against a tree, tossing his head back, letting the water wash him of his sins.

He didn't have to finish what he was going to say.

I could read between the lines.

They didn't keep track and the birch trees were filled with mercy medicine.

I wondered how many human minds he'd erased, simply to give them a second chance at mortal normalcy. If somehow he could tip the scales between good and bad, and keep his soul on the winning end.

Seems rebellion ran on the Animal side of Fantasia's blood. Their veins were filled with fire.

⬥

FANTASIA AND I, back in the cave days earlier, came to an unspoken conclusion. We'd be true to ourselves.

Narivous may control our deeds, but not our hearts.

We would be with each other, even if only in bursts of stolen moments. And we would do it carefully, since getting caught was not an option. The little things, we needed the little things.

And we made a rule—no heavy topics. Recruits, sacrifices, death, despair, all forbidden. I wouldn't mention Chugknot, even though I wanted to. Nor would I ask if she could see Romeo's thoughts.

If we only had pockets of time, we weren't going to fill them with sadness.

We were going to nourish hope and starve anguish.

And we had a feathered friend to help us.

Fred was our accomplice—and through him, Dreams. Somehow Fantasia wrangled her into our plans. I assumed it was Dreams' gratitude for keeping Fantasia obedient. This was her way of contributing to her little sister's safekeeping. A happy Fantasia was a compliant Fantasia.

Narivous, although worlds different, was still a working city. There were bakeries, eateries, a school, community centers, and plenty of places to creep off and cop a feel.

So this is how it went: the day following the Dawning Rose Celebration, after my orientation, I was out in the garden roaming the hedge maze, hoping to find Fantasia waiting in one of the alcoves, when Fred fluttered in front of me. He twittered, danced, and shot past a corner. I went after him. He led me from the royal gardens to a narrow alleyway between two houses hugging the far bank of the city.

And there was Fantasia, standing in the shadows, tucked behind a large incinerator—what Narivous used in place of dumpsters. The city had strong protocols on discarding waste and most everything that could be reused, was.

Fantasia and I only had a few minutes, but it was enough. We kissed, touched, breathed each other in, enjoying the taste of liberation.

And then she gave me a new time, a new place, to look for

Fred. "As long as we don't establish a pattern and keep it sporadic, we'll fly under the radar."

I kissed her, agreeing to anything.

"If Fred swoops and flies off, then that means abort, and just keep walking as if nothing unusual has happened."

"On it."

The next day, we met under the bleachers of the arena. She talked about everything and nothing. I did the same, both of us pausing to taste the other. She made me alive, and my face ached from smiling.

"How is this possible?" she asked.

"I've stopped trying to figure that out."

"You," was all she said before kissing me until I forgot my name.

The following night we found a patch of starlight down by the unregulated quarry and danced. We were huddled near a rock base, two stony-planed walls giving us cover. Our kissing took precedence over our footwork, and I used the opportunity to touch her.

She let me. Damn, did she let me.

I cursed the gloves.

We continued to rotate time and spots. On greedy days we'd meet more than once.

A secluded plot of garden in the morning.

An underground tunnel, decommissioned and void of cameras, in the afternoon.

The night of the rainstorm, when I learned JC was as rebellious as his half-sister, I found Fred perched on Dolly's statue. Dolly's was perhaps the most depressing to date. As I expected, every Seven had her own monument, and some had multiple. Even other notable Velores, Brilliants included, had one.

Narivous loved sculptures.

Dolly's was carved from soapstone and heartache. Her hair

was straighter, her face younger. In her arms she held a small girl wrapped in a blanket. The child's face rested limply along Dolly's unmoving shoulder, so you could barely make out her features. And whereas Dolly gripped the girl for dear life, the child draped like a limp doll.

Rain from the storm blended with the carved tears on Dolly's frozen face.

For the life of me, I marveled at the artist's ability to bring each statue to life. Narivous had an artistic genius in its midst.

Near her feet was a small cross, but it was almost lost amongst a sea of white. Because Dolly's statue existed in a meadow of tulips the color of fresh snow, all in bloom, under groves of willow trees.

It was one of the more open places in Narivous.

Fred took off, and I traced the space around me before casually following in his direction, careful to make it appear organic.

He led me to a spot secluded inside weeping branches, a curtain I was careful not to touch with my bare flesh.

Fantasia was waiting.

And something was very wrong.

CHAPTER 15

NEVER TO BE FOUND

Fantasia was holding her mask in a tight grip. I peeled off my own, loving how the air brushed my skin.

"You look like you're going to break our 'no heavy' rule."

She dropped her shoulders. "Trust me, I'm not happy about it. Come." She held out her hand and guided me farther into the willow grove, to a tree with a stone base. There was a door leading underground. She lifted the lid and motioned for me to follow.

It was a narrow pit, a storage closet for shovels, hoes, and rakes organized on pegboards. She kept the door open, and Fred perched on a branch directly above us. I spotted her bag, laying in a discarded heap, at the foot of the stairs.

We were now in a hole, lost deep in a tulip meadow, with only a small exit. Fantasia was slipping off her rocker. I set my mask on the ground and crossed my arms.

"Don't give me that look," she said. "This was the best I could do. Dreams is keeping watch. If Fred takes off, that's our cue someone's coming."

"And then what?"

"I stay down here and you leave, shutting the door behind you. Dreams will get me when it's safe."

"I don't like this at all."

"Oh yeah?" Fantasia pulled out a piece of paper tucked in the folds of her cloak. It was another flyer. Marie and Dean had upped the ante to 20k. "If you ask me," she whispered, tapping the paper, "this takes precedence. We've got to get them to leave. And besides"—she gestured to Fred—"the grove is on the outer bank. No one really comes here. Dolly's statue depresses them. And Dreams has great visibility. She's sitting in one of the tallest willows. She'll have plenty of time to warn us."

I couldn't stop staring at Aunt Marie's flyer. At my face. At the cash reward plastered along the top of it. Holy shit, she was getting desperate.

"We don't have a lot of time," Fantasia continued, reaching for her bag. She pulled out a satellite phone—a damn near brick—and placed it in my hand.

"Delilah got this for us," Fantasia explained. I recalled the day I met Delilah, down by the river, back when Tony was alive and my blood still ran red. And even though she reminded me of a porcelain doll with her short stature, blue eyes and golden ringlets, her power was impossible to miss. Velores straightened when she spoke.

I gave Fantasia a curious look. "Don't let her size fool you, she's a Brilliant. This is on loan, and we only have a small window." Fantasia arched her neck to check Fred, who sat calmly on a branch. "Chanticlaim's cell blocker won't interfere with the signal," she explained, tapping the phone in my hand. "The number will come up with an out-of-state area code, somewhere in Texas, I think."

I groaned and craned my neck to look at Fred, and Fantasia

looped her fingers through my hair, guiding me back to meet her eyes.

"I'm so sorry, Daniel. But you gotta do this. We have to get her to call off the search party."

"What should I tell her?"

"Tell her you ran to Texas, 'cause that's where the area code is. They'll check for sure. Your aunt is the queen of internet searches. Tell her you met a nice girl and you're rooming with two guys who work at a local pizza parlor." She leaned her forehead against mine, closing her eyes. "Tell her you're happy, and you just needed a break."

"Do you think that'll be enough?"

"There's only one way to find out. Call her."

I punched in Marie's number before I lost my willpower. It rang a few times before going to voicemail.

I lipped "voicemail" to Fantasia, and she gave me a thumbs up. "Even better," she mouthed. "She can't talk back."

I regurgitated Fancy's story, telling Marie I was okay. I was happy. Feeding her so much BS she'd no doubt bloat by ingesting it all. Before I hung up, I told her I loved her and that this phone was on loan, indicating she couldn't reach me if she tried calling back later.

Hanging up felt like severing a tie.

Fantasia cupped my face in her hands. "I'm sorry you had to do that."

"Me too."

"You know what?"

"What?"

She pointed to the flyer, at Dean's number. "Why don't you call Dean too? Hit it from both angles."

I groaned. And she put her hand on my lips to silence me. "We have to get it over with. He won't be as hard to convince as Marie. Just do it."

Unlike Marie, Dean picked up. The moment he heard my voice, his words jumped. "Daniel! It's you! Where are you? We've been worried sick."

"I'm sorry, it's just—"

"Tell me where you are right now."

"I—"

"Do you have any idea the amount of stress you've put us through?"

"I'm sorry, it's just—"

"You're coming home. I won't accept any other answer." I held my hand over the mouthpiece and lipped to Fantasia, "He's going berserk."

She rolled her hands. "Stick with it," she whispered.

"Look, Dean, I'm in Texas right now, so I can't just come back. But I wanted to let you know I'm okay. I just needed a break."

"Why the hell are you in Texas?"

"I needed a change of scenery."

"Daniel, bud, look, we all grieve differently and I know you're hurting right now, but Lillian wouldn't want you to throw your future away. She'd want you to come home, finish school. I'll pay for your plane ticket. I can do it right now."

Background tapping, like Morse code, came through. Dean must've been at his computer. "And I promise I won't ride your ass when you make it home. You have a pass, okay?"

"Dean—"

"What part of Texas are you in? I'll get a one-way from the nearest airport."

"Dean, listen—"

"Do you need a taxi? I can arrange that too."

More tapping. "Dean, I'm sorry, but I'm not—"

"Hear me out," he begged, and damn, it was like a spear to my heart. The typing stopped, he was giving me his undivided attention. "Marie and I have your room all set up. I know you're worried about being a burden, but you're not. I have a brand-new fishing rod waiting for you, and Lacey wants a fishing buddy just as bad as I do. I've already promised her we'll hit the lakes when you get home."

I didn't want to break, not now, but he kept puncturing me.

"Lacey asks about you every day. And Marie and I've talked about it, if you need to move into Lil's house until you've finished school, so be it. We'll pack up and move in too. You can have your old room. We just want you home."

My throat caught. His sincerity was stronger than my lies.

"You have to sell Gram's house," I reminded him.

"We're fighting it, bud. We're fighting it for you. We've got lawyers working on it, and right now we have it bound up in probate. We want you home and if that house is what you need, then that's what we'll get you. I'll throw all my money at it to break the will. Just come home."

Oh, man. This was bad. Fantasia wrapped her arms around me as I fought the urge to bawl. He was chiseling at me, throwing out a life that no longer existed. I started to tremble, my powers rattling as much as my voice.

"I'm sor—"

"Stop saying you're sorry. You reacted to a loss, a tragic loss, and we understand. We love you, Daniel. And think of it, when it's time for college, you'll have a place to live—free of rent. Marie and I will cover the taxes. You can just keep it up. How does that sound?"

Fantasia breathed into my ear, "End it now, Daniel."

"I'm so sorry." My words shattered, I could feel my voice crack, I was disintegrating to shards. "I'm so sorry, Dean. I love you and Marie. I love Lacey. I'm sorry, but I can't."

"Danie—"

"I'm not coming back."

He was mid-argument when I hung up.

The phone rang seconds later, and Fantasia shut it off. I plopped onto the steps and tried to suck in air, taking the time to force my powers back. I was getting better at repression, but it was still a challenge. Like new paint in a humid zip code—I was gonna be tacky for a long time.

"What if he leaves a voicemail?"

"We'll check and delete. Delilah will kill the number the moment I return it." Fantasia spoke slowly. She sat on the ground and wedged herself between my legs, placing her head against my thigh. The weight gave comfort. I leaned forward and buried myself in her hair.

"I don't want to hear the message."

She twisted her body, craned her neck, and looked up. "Okay," she said softly.

"They're fighting the will," I replied.

"I know ... I know ..."

"And I won't give you up."

Everything, even her smile, was sad. "I don't want you to." She took my gloved hand and planted a kiss inside it. "You're kind of my hope right now."

"So that leaves one thing to do."

She nodded, biting her lip. "I wish there was another way."

"Me too." It seemed I was destined to hate myself.

⁓❧⁓

WE WAITED for the timing to be perfect. So as the days passed, I took to learning the customary spokes of Narivous. They were strong, long, and constantly in rotation.

I was grateful to be off duty when a set of unfortunates, the first since becoming guard, trespassed onto our land.

A pair of hunters lost their bearings and it wasn't even a

guard member who found them, but one of the many Velores who roamed the forest desperate to prove their worth.

Since their auras were nonexistent, and the Velore was in a pissed-off mood, he crushed both their heads with his bare hands.

"It happens," Spark said. We were in the Enlightenment Center, a building for furthering our education. It was large, steepled, and reminded me of a church/school hybrid. All Velores were expected to attend classes, and guards had a mandatory five days every month, on rotation. I was in C group.

A dark-haired girl with black eyes, a copy of Delilah aside from her coloring, stood in front with a laser pointer and a map of the Cascades. The projector beam washed over her every time she crossed in front of it.

She completely forewent the podium, since she couldn't even breach the top.

Spark, with his square shoulders and even squarer jaw, kept mumbling in my ear, piecing in the parts he thought I needed to know, his bald head bowed so his moving lips were blocked.

"Lots of them do that, ya know. I've even heard they bait."

On my other side was Fantasia's half-brother, the younger copy of JC, the one who was notorious for acting his shoe size instead of his age. Jaguar always wore a smile and liked to laugh. Although the youngest, he already had permanent crinkles around his eyes.

And now that I'd gotten to know him, I was fairly confident he was the guard I'd seen that night in the gym.

The one who'd let Dreams in.

Jaguar leaned in and whispered, "Dude, Spark, he's not gonna know what that means." Jaguar squinted at me, as if he were appraising me for the first time. "And I think he may need it explained more than once."

"Asshole," I hissed.

Both grinned, and Spark continued. "Okay, so here's the thing, we're awesome."

"But I'm the most awesome," Jaguar whispered back.

"The hell you are," Spark said.

"I'm sorry if the truth hurts."

"You're delusional and distracting, so shut your piehole, and lemme finish before Esther climbs down our throats and makes us stay late." Spark looked toward the front. Esther's dark coils bounced as she glanced over her shoulder. Turned out Delilah was the oldest of a set of Brilliant triplets. Esther was the youngest, and the middle sister I'd yet to meet.

"She likes to hide," Jaguar explained before class. "People stare and it makes Ruth uncomfortable." When I asked why, Jaguar shot me a blank look, blinked, and said, "Because she's half and half."

A riddle so far over my head it soared.

Now Esther was doing her best to ignore our whispering, and from her pinched lips and consistent momentum, she was well practiced.

Jaguar was a walking distraction—you just had to accept it and move on, otherwise you'd go in circles.

"Okay," Spark said, "so guards are pretty great, right? We get to do pretty much anything we want. We don't have to ask for things, shit is handed to us. And we get respect for just breathing."

"It's a good life," Jaguar followed.

"Yeah, and not to mention the chicks."

"Dude, Spark, he can't touch anyone."

"Oh, shit. Sorry."

"Just ignore him, Deadly," Jaguar said. "Spark can only use one of his heads—and it's not the one on his shoulders."

Nicknames were a popular trend in Narivous. Jaguar gifted me "Deadly" the day he refused to shake my hand. Said he didn't want to rot and I should keep my "nasty-festerish" flesh to myself. Apparently he didn't trust my gloves and claimed he was too pretty to ruin his looks on the likes of me.

Somehow, he managed to make it sound like a compliment.

"So, yeah ..." Spark waved his hand, shrouded in a rubber glove, ignoring Jaguar and moving on. "Some Velores try to get this job by doing surveillance and killing in grand fashion, thinking they can get guard duty by some overdone display in the field."

"It never works."

"Yeah, guards are only made during trials. And only demoted if they commit treason."

"And when he says demoted, he means head on a pike," Jaguar clarified.

"Yeah," Spark nodded, a bit more solemn. "That's pretty much what I mean."

"But still, you get some desperate Velores."

"Really desperate."

"They even lure humans in so they have someone to kill," Jaguar added, shaking his head. "Pathetic."

"Yeah. They're like cats who give their owners dead mice, thinking it'll earn them favors." Spark's smile electrified and he looked straight at Jaguar. "Cats are stupid."

"Why you gotta be so mean?" Jaguar shot out a little too loud, and Esther halted her lesson.

"Do I need to separate you three?" she asked.

And in sync, both of them pointed at me and said in unison, "It's his fault."

Dillholes.

Total dillholes.

But they were my speed.

I TRIED to focus on the positive. On Fantasia and the conversation we had earlier. How she was going to present her gift to Thorn by the end of the week, the human recruit she described as "perfect."

And as pathetic as that good news was, it was infinitely better than where I stood, a paper crumpled in my hand.

The stars shone brighter without a moon, and I let my head fall back, taking in every dotted crystal.

The wind had free rein. No trees to block its path, no magic in its way. And when I righted my neck, I was left with an ache.

The sight was soul crushing. I was looking at what was left of Gram.

Her yellow house, with its lavender bushes and brick steps, a tangible reminder of times long past. Inside there'd be bright cupboards, wallpapered walls, doilies, and frills.

Pieces of her.

I'd painted the trim. Helped Gram with the shrubs. Mowed the lawn.

It was her. Love and freedom. So simple, and yet so far away.

I'd watched the weather system, waiting for a dry spell, and then, when I got three consecutive days of no rain, set my plan in motion.

Chanticlaim was kind enough to turn off the cameras in the underground parking garage—maintenance, he said. JC graciously took up my guard shift—off the books, of course, and since guards worked in pairs, Jaguar politely chose not to notice. And Delilah, well, she thoughtfully provided the phones—satellites for inside Narivous and a burner for my back pocket.

And everyone was nice enough to not ask questions.

Deniability, I'm sure. Guard members have certain privileges and rights. If I wanted a day off, and had it covered, there was no reason anyone should mind. Least of all question my motives.

And I discovered, rather quickly, you can disappear while on patrol. You only had to avoid certain spots where cameras lurked, most often in statues randomly placed throughout the forest, since their eyes weren't of stone, but of tattletale lenses.

Jaguar often slept in a tree with his raccoon Bonnie. He'd perch himself on a branch in one of the oak trees leading into the forest, his little masked pet on his lap. "Humans are no different than stampeding elephants, Deadly," he said on the first day he was supposed to be training me. "They can't sneak up on me even in my sleep." He faked a yawn. "And I don't know about you, but I need a nap." When I asked him what I was supposed to do, he suggested "jacking off" and then climbed the oak, dismissing me.

Spark spent his time trying to get laid, which, I found out in an uncomfortable fashion, he was rather successful at.

My eyes hurt from catching him mid-act.

Cheetoh and Cheetah were dust. They liked to run and used the perimeter as a race track.

JC hid.

And the other guards kind of did their own thing. Unless you were a sentry placed outside the gates, you could fade into the scenery.

No one really said boo, because guards were still the most powerful. The brightest auras, the strongest collection, and even goofing off they effectively kept the land free of human interference.

But it did explain how two hunters got in without the guards' detection. Sure, they would've found them before too long, but the whole I'm-keeping-eagle-eyes-on-the-forest bit was a bunch of BS.

Bless their hearts, they sure pretended, though. And everyone happily swallowed their lies.

Fantasia, Torti, and Dreams took Delilah's satellite loans— they knew my plan and where I was going. They were my surveillance.

Fantasia offered to do the dirty work, but this was my job.

After I'd hung up with Dean in the willow grove, in a span of thirty minutes he and Marie had left seven voicemails.

All deleted without being listened to.

My windbreaker, so human it made me want to hurl, flapped softly against the breeze. I wasn't human anymore, and dressing like one seemed stupid. The absurdity of the lie made my stomach curdle.

I smoothed out the crumpled ball in my hand and stared at my old face.

The old me.

I didn't bother going inside the house.

I couldn't chance losing my nerve.

This house was a binding glue. A beating heart of hope. Marie wouldn't leave Oregon as long as there was a chance she could claim it. I pulled out the lighter I brought for the occasion and flicked the wheel to life. The wind paused for a moment, and the fire danced upright, as if the universe had given me its blessing. I hovered Marie's flyer over the open flame. It ignited, and I watched my face erode to nothing.

"I'm sorry," I said, tossing the burning slip at the base of the house where a trail of gasoline lingered.

The blaze erupted. It was almost as if the house wanted to die.

The flames licked the trim, corrupting the white, charring it to black, turning our memories to ash and smoke. I waited for full engulfment, a total loss, before using my unearthly speed to flee. I followed the Velore code, parking miles away, and made it to the car in record time. Fire engines soon whirled, sirens eating away the country peace.

I looked in the rearview mirror as I knocked the shifter into drive.

The night sky was glowing, the fire dissolving Gram's old life.

Another part of me died with that fire. My dead heart hollowed a bit more.

But I willed it to be enough.

CHAPTER 16

LOVE AND PUNISHMENT

I paced the hedge maze near an alcove with a bench, its legs drowning in bushels of tulips. I selected one of the wider pockets, off center, with three exits to choose from. Random placement. Fantasia, at that very moment, was presenting her gift to Thorn. A woman whose name I never even bothered to learn. Fred would show her the way to me as soon as she'd finished, and then he'd be our sentry while she filled me in.

The whole time, under my breath, I wished, willed, damn near forced Thorn to take away the child recruit. It would break Fancy, and I couldn't handle the thought.

My mind went to every possible scenario, and I grazed my empty pocket. It was void of Dexitrol powder.

Laquet, Cougar's older brother, was in charge of guard training, particularly the sparring stations. He would oversee pounces and flames, icy assaults, and brawny attacks. The day I showed up for my first session, he gave me a tight smile. He looked like all the others—JC, Jaguar, Cougar. Same colossal height, dark hair, dark eyes. Only he appeared younger than Cougar, far from older. He wasn't heavily scarred, and he didn't have life's disappointments lining his features.

He asked me to watch from the wall. "You're kind of our backup," he said. "We'll only use you in the field when we've exhausted all other tools, since you're as likely to kill the person you're trying to save as the person you're trying to destroy. Assuming, of course, we're not working off touch." I nodded, and he added, "I've already discussed training measures with Scream and Plague. I'm going to give you private lessons in your rooms, where we can test and have a safe place for you to vent." The screaming room was a precious commodity.

True to his word, Laquet came and pushed me. He brought tools to force my translucency out and taught me methods to reel it back in. The first few times, I exploded.

I was left shaking and weak. Sweat and toxin clinging like a stench.

But I got better, to a point he suggested I ditch the Dexitrol powder. "Working without a safety net improves our balance on the tight rope."

Seemed analogies were popular with all Animals. When I cringed, he added with a kind nod, "I don't think you really need it, anyhow."

The next day, my vial went missing. Someone removed it while I was out. I had only myself, which was a frightening prospect.

Now I sat alone in an alcove with a brimming head and no vial, feeling vulnerable without that stupid bottle.

I turned when padding came into earshot. Fantasia barreled around the corner. She wasn't wearing her mask—there were too many tears.

She collapsed into my arms, and Fred fluttered overhead, landing in an inconspicuous section of maze, barely in my sight.

She gasped in short bursts, leaning into me, willing us to become one. I pulled off my own mask, letting it fall next to hers at our feet, and wrapped my arms around her.

I buried my face in her scalp and did my best to quiet the sobs.

Her pain bled through me.

"Shhh ... Shhh ... It's okay, Fantasia. It's okay."

She shook her head. "It's not, it's not, it's not."

I guided her to the bench and tried to get her to breathe. Cracks of translucency fissured around her eyes, the first time I'd ever even seen her powers, and my insides plummeted.

"You've got to calm down."

She hiccuped air. The cracks went away so fast, I was impressed with her level of hold. But the cord keeping her tethered was clearly taut. I wondered what it would take to break it.

"It wasn't e-enough," she choked out. "The h-human recruit. Thorn loves her, was so happy she even k-kissed me." Fantasia wiped her eyes, a trail of black liquid staining her hand. Her words came out in short jabs. Gasps of a story. "She told me h-how proud she w-was." Fantasia swallowed. "And th-then she said she c-couldn't wait to see the child I b-brought back."

"Oh, baby, I'm—"

"That's not e-even the worst part." She threw her head back, every line of her neck a ladder of vulnerability. She continued to wipe her face, her cheeks perpetually wet. When she looked back, something deep inside her was missing.

The lavender was hollow.

"I'm now an o-official recruiter," she said. "I-I have to

constantly c-condemn people." She pulled her knees to her chest and wrapped her arms around herself, dipping her face into her own cradle.

I felt like a total ass.

"It's not that bad," I said.

She wouldn't look at me. "You're right. It's worse."

"No. No, it's not." I took a breath. "Just ... just keep recruiting people like we talked about. Nothing's changed. Not really. Save them from worse—"

"Don't you get it?" She bored into me. "I searched forever to find one who would work. One who wouldn't kill my soul. And it took me forever. *Forever*. To find just *one*. I can't do this. I just can't."

"But you've got to."

The smile she gave me was the same smile Dreams was afraid of.

It was the smile I never wanted to see.

I grabbed her hand. "Don't you do that," I said. "You can't give up."

"It's gotta stop...."

"Baby." I coaxed her onto my lap. She didn't resist, folding over me, building an arc around my neck with her arms. She let her forehead fall against my own. We sat there, quietly, as I racked my brain for a solution—when a chuckle caught us off guard.

And life quickly eroded from bad to shit.

"Well, what do we have here?" Amelia stalked toward us, her eyes shining, angry.

Seething.

Fantasia jumped from my lap and landed on her knees. I simultaneously froze and went dumb, my mouth hanging open like a Venus flytrap. Amelia's spindly fingers were wrapped around something bright and small.

Fred. Tight in her palm, he was desperately trying to wiggle his way free, chirping in either pain or anger. Maybe both.

Amelia, triumphant, raised her chin and neared us, her body lithe, strong, and coiled with righteous indignation.

"Come out, Dreams," she called. "I know you're here. Otherwise I'll crush your little feathered friend."

Dreams came from around a corner and I realized, all at once, the maze was a stupid place for a rendezvous. There were too many loops to close. Dreams couldn't keep an eye on every entrance, the hedges were too tall for a proper lookout and, not to mention, we were out in broad daylight. *Stupid.*

"Ah, there you are," Amelia said. She smiled, her feline teeth sharp and biting like the rest of her face.

Dreams had lopped her hair since the last time I'd seen her. It was now at her shoulders, shaved on one side, dyed a rose pink. She was trembling, her face flushed with fear.

In the span of forever, I managed to regain a bit of reflex. I found my knees and bowed my head. I tried to recall the exact moment she'd stumbled upon us and was relieved there'd been no kissing.

We could argue this.

Fantasia was shaking beside me.

I didn't dare reach out and comfort her.

"Get over here, Dreams." Amelia's green irises flickered.

"Please don't hurt him," Dreams pleaded, her full attention on Amelia's closed hand. Both Fantasia and I stayed stock-still, afraid to even breathe.

Amelia's hand shot out as soon as Dreams was in reaching distance. She grabbed a fistful of hair, the locks a perfect harnessing tool. Amelia shook the base of her skull, and Dreams bit her lip to stifle her cry.

Fantasia put her hands to her mouth in horror.

The buzzing started to rattle, and my heart leapt.

"What is this?" Amelia asked, holding Dreams by one hand, Fred by the other. She was shaking Fred, locked in her fist. The bird struggled.

"I was just going for a walk."

Amelia narrowed her eyes and her gaze raked over Fantasia and me. Fancy's hands were still in front of her mouth, but she'd steepled them, as if she were praying.

Perhaps she was.

"Liar," Amelia replied. And then, to our horror, she clenched her hand and, so help us, we heard every one of Fred's bones break, his final chirp, a cry for help. The crunch was worse than the scream that followed.

Dreams came unglued and started to wail, only Amelia shut her down before she could build to full volume, slapping her hard across the face.

She whimpered, biting her lip, forcing her shattered heart back down her throat.

Fantasia leapt, going from a kneel to a full-on pounce, her eyes murderous. I lunged and managed to grab her shins, forcing her to the ground. I covered her body with my own, fighting to keep her still.

Amelia dropped the dead bird at Dreams' feet, and Dreams went to reach for him, as if she could piece him back together.

Amelia used the opportunity to jerk her leg up, shooting her knee into Dreams' face. For a second time we heard crunching, only now it was the cartilage in Dreams' nose. Purple blood rained and Dreams stood up, cupping her hands to stop the spray, and in a move so sadistic it hinged on heinous, Amelia swooped down, collected the bird, and slammed his broken form into the side of her face.

The gash left behind was a mix of both Fred's and Dreams' blood.

Feathers of yellow floated in the air, like a post-pillow fight, and Dreams fell to the ground, crying in a heap, curling into herself.

Amelia smiled.

"Well then, as for you two ..."

I was still on top of Fantasia, her body heaving in angry fits. Her energy fed my energy and my tongue grew heavy, but I abated the power, forced it back. Fantasia may have been able to withstand my toxic wail, but Dreams was another story.

Loosing it would mean losing her.

Two guards—Spark and Splint—barreled into the maze, stuttering to a stop behind Amelia. The noise must have drawn them to us.

Their complexions blanched to cream, petrified and gaping as they pieced together the scene. "I have this," Amelia said, holding her hand to still them. Spark ran his rubber gloves over his bare scalp and edged toward Dreams.

You could feel his conflict, the need to comfort, to help.

Amelia growled him back. "Don't you dare," she said. "She's earned her place and needs to wallow in her pain." Spark bowed his head, taking only a half-step away. He shot me a look, and the distance cackled with wattage.

Amelia only grew bigger, taller, more imposing. "But I'm glad my guards are here, for we have punishments to dole out."

She looked directly at me, and I realized she needed them to keep me from exploding. Upping the ante by placing innocents within breathing distance.

"Death, darling. Let her up."

I crawled off Fantasia and took to my feet.

Fantasia stood, and I saw her fill with anger. Her skin rippled. She wasn't looking at Amelia, but at Dreams, who was cradling what was left of Fred to her chest.

Cooing to the bird as if he could still hear her.

Dreams' face covered with the gore of Amelia's violence made the blue of her eyes brighter, more defined, and they were boring into Fantasia's. Without a sound, Dreams sat up and behind Amelia's back mouthed, "Be good."

Fantasia took her eyes away, putting them back on Amelia. She lifted her jaw in a manner that most assuredly wasn't "good."

"Did you want to attack me?" Amelia asked, snaking closer, leaving Dreams to shudder in painful convulsions.

Dreams and I locked eyes, and she formed the word "help." It left me feeling hopeless.

"Answer me, Fantasia."

Fantasia gave her most defiant smile. She was going to bite, and I had to stop it. Find the muzzle and cinch it in place. "Of course—"

I darted in front of Fantasia, knocking her shoulder in the process. She took a shuffle back, not even a full step, and her words fell away. I used my body as a block, and blurted, "She'd never think of hurting you."

Thankfully, Fantasia didn't contradict me. I could feel her against the length of me, her breath touching my neck. My nerves billowed.

Aside from throwing my hand over her mouth, leaping in front was the most indiscreet move I could've made, drowning out her answer with my own.

But desperate times call for desperate measures.

Amelia reared, her translucency pulling out her claws, her skin cracking in every direction.

Her eyes blazed—*at me*.

"HOW DARE YOU!" she shouted. "STEP AWAY FROM HER!"

I twisted in place, away from Amelia and toward Fantasia, and mouthed, "Don't you do it."

"GET AWAY, DEATH!"

I dipped my head in Amelia's direction, a submissive move delivered far too late, and stepped to the side. Fantasia turned to stare at me, and dread wrapped my lungs in a tourniquet. Her lavender was lost to onyx, the whites glowing, and fissures, similar to Amelia's, blossomed around Fantasia's eyes. She was looking at me and seeing nothing.

Amelia edged closer, outraged. "AND DO NOT COACH HER ON WHAT TO SAY TO ME, YOU STUPID, FOOLISH BOY!"

I flinched, right as a soothing voice, tentative and unsure, disrupted the pattern of vexation.

"Mom?"

Amelia whipped around. JC stood next to Spark and Splint, a hand on Dreams' head.

"DON'T TOUCH HER."

JC fed the fire. He didn't let up, a bold act of defiance. He stroked his thumb along Dreams' shaved hair and spoke calmly, as if addressing a frightened animal. "Mom, Dreams needs help. And he's still new and unstable."

He was looking at me. Somewhere, in the mix of moments, my powers began to pull—*again*.

My skin was alive, sizzling with voltage. Recognizing it, I tried to force it back under.

Amelia regarded me. "Well, then," she said, "I suppose it's a good idea you leave, JC."

"Mom."

"Now."

"Mom, just—"

"GET OUT!"

JC shook his head, his jaw clenching. "I'm a guard, I'll stay and help."

Amelia whirled and pounced, sheathing her claws and throwing a hit at JC's temple. He took it, his massive head absorbing the blow, barely bucking. His face flushed, not from pain, but from reprimand. Amelia grabbed his shirt and flexed her claws against his chest. "I gave you an order. You *will* obey." Too much defiance in such a narrow window. "You're making it worse for them," Amelia said when JC hesitated. Her soft smile was more frightening than her snarl. "I'll take a chunk of Dreams' head."

JC's shoulders dropped, and Amelia released him. He paused for only a second before turning and disappearing behind the hedge corner.

"You!" Amelia pointed to Splint. She indicated the space behind me. "Block his path."

Splint obeyed, growing paler with each step, his own magic tugging.

It was a tough gig holding me, the bomb, in place.

She smiled at Spark and ordered him to take the last spoke. Now every escape was clotted. Dreams, Spark, and Splint breathing locks.

It made sense, why she sent JC away. She didn't want to risk him. He'd be at the mercy of my toxin if I exploded.

That's why JC tried to stay. Amelia wouldn't poke the nest if one of her kittens were nearby.

He knew it. She knew it.

We all knew it.

Amelia descended on us and ordered Spark and Splint to kneel, as if they were waiting for an executioner's sword.

And the hilt was in my hand.

"You have no right to go against a direct order, Death," she said. "I asked her a question, and I expect an answer from her."

"I'm sorry," I said. "I'm so sorry, but I promise we weren't doing—"

"SHUT UP!"

I didn't listen. I could still formulate words, and I needed those words to keep the tide back. Talking was one of the few indicators I still had control, over my powers at least, and I needed control.

Because the pressure was gaining ground.

"But it's my fault—"

"I said SHUT UP!"

Fantasia silenced me by touching my arm. She'd managed to pull back her own energy. Her eyes no longer glowed. Self-control in its fiercest form.

It must've been the "I'll take a chunk of Dreams' skull" that calmed her inner storm.

She'd sacrifice herself, but never her sisters.

Amelia narrowed at the move, too intimate for her liking. "Stop touching him," she growled, and before Fantasia could pull away, Amelia's palm, fast as a whiplash, slammed across her cheek. The slap ricocheted off the hedges. We all felt it, and my restraint cracked.

Fantasia's face flooded, a color burst mushrooming along her cheekbone.

The crevice breaching my control became a divide, and I went bold. I wedged myself between the pair, for a second time using my body as a toxic barrier. Seeing Fantasia hit so violently rattled not only my head, but my entire core. I was going to lose my translucent battle unless everyone stopped.

Amelia took a step back, her eyes dark as space.

"You treasonous little bastard," she hissed. "You'll wish you hadn't done that."

I shook my head, not knowing which direction to turn, both in body and argument. Anger flashed in my eyes, and Amelia matched it with her own.

"Dexitrol," I managed to spit out. I needed Dexitrol.

Everything was charring—my vision, my lungs, my self-control.

My tongue was growing stiff, the air fuzzy. Amelia recognized the transition and snarled. She wasn't afraid. She wanted me to do it.

Amelia could probably outrun the spill with her Animal speed, but the others ...

Fantasia grabbed my collar and yanked me back, before falling to her knees in front of Amelia. She arched her neck and begged with woven fingers. "He doesn't have any Dexitrol. Please, just give me my punishment and let him go."

Amelia smiled and stretched her claws, the tips sharpened to impaling points.

I was rolling with energy.

Their outlines blurred. Fantasia shook her head. "Keep it back, Death," she said. "Keep it back."

"If he unleashes, it'll be your fault," Amelia said.

Someone grabbed my leg, and I could make out Splint's form—his face clouded, features a blend. Only desperation would make him touch me. He was on his knees. "C'mon, man," he pleaded.

Amelia laughed. *She. Laughed.* She was enjoying herself, getting high off their fear.

She wanted me to shatter. To prove a point.

And like hell was I going to let her. I dug deep into my wells of self-control.

Laquet had told me to make it a color, to push it so deep it became nothing but a shadow of itself.

Focus.

I willed it to fade.

And so help me, I turned it from a blinding primary to a dim pastel—but it was still there, immersing my thoughts in a heavy cloud.

Amelia spotted the change and it displeased her. She cocked her head and started to pace as her guards kept station. She stopped to take in the sight and smiled at Fantasia, who'd gone pitiful.

Amelia was the director, and we were the unwilling cast.

"You, Fantasia, are off limits. You've always been off limits. And you will always be off limits. That will never change. You understand?" Amelia looked at me. "She is a mistake, Death."

My bones leadened.

She wasn't a mistake.

Never a mistake.

This was why Fantasia hated Narivous. It wasn't the recruits.

It wasn't the sacrifices.

It wasn't the power Thorn continued to accumulate. Nor the power she allotted this feline bitch to have.

It was the deprivation of affection.

Fantasia wanted freedom. Liberation from a crime she never committed. She wanted to love—and Narivous would never allow that.

Maybe that's why our connection was so strong. Neither one of us was supposed to exist.

Amelia stepped close enough to Fantasia she could swipe her paw and leave a trail of scars behind.

"You are filth," she spat in Fantasia's face. "Filth. Garbage. Just like your whore mother." She smirked. "I'd like to say I'm surprised, but I expected this of you. To spread your legs, to be the little slut you were born to be. I knew it was only a matter of time before we caught you. And now here we are."

She held her arms wide, indicating our small circle.

"And look at the chaos you've caused. Yes? Bringing Death into your mess."

Fantasia nodded.

I started to shake my head, and Amelia shot out her leg, knocking my feet from under me. I landed hard, my limbs absolutely worthless. I'd gone sluggishly slow.

"STOP DISAGREEING WITH ME!" she barked.

The move filled my head with pressure.

Amelia continued, staring down Fantasia. "Your punishment will come in two forms. First, you'll be whipped." She pointed to me. "Death will deliver the blows. I will watch and keep count."

No.

"Fifty lashes. If I catch you messing with him again, you'll get a hundred, and the numbers will double henceforth, until you beg us to clear your head from your shoulders. Do you understand me, little whore?"

Fantasia nodded, black tears running down her face.

No.

"I will also take a pound of your flesh in a spot so open you'll never forget this day. Consider it a mercy since I'd much rather dispose of you."

No.

"Now kiss my feet and thank me for my kindness."

No.

I wanted to call out, to stop this. To plead our innocence—even though we weren't innocent. But I was brimming. Swollen, and my tongue wouldn't move. The rattling in my skull was tighter, quicker, frenzied fast.

I kept the color to nothing but darkness—but it wasn't enough.

Everything was different.

People were shouting. Our group had grown.

I couldn't see Fantasia anymore, but I recognized her shadow as she crouched to kiss that bitch's feet.

It was just shapes. Lots of shapes.
Amelia's shape jolted.
Fantasia screamed.
And I lost sight of everything, as I faded to nothing.

CHAPTER 17

LIES

A shard of ice pierced my heart, crystallizing my blood, forcing the darkness away.

The chill was pretty much what lifted my lids, and the only thing keeping that iron veil from falling back into place.

And I wanted to let it fall back, to stifle the pain, to erase my memories, which had already grown murky. My ribs hurt under every breath, my throat burned, my joints ached with a dull throb—and that was me lying on top of a padded mattress.

The duvet was frozen and crisp—and so was I.

Polar stood next to the king-sized bed, its posts so dented and marred the crevices held layers of frost. I was inside the Ice Quarters spare room, the one that was unofficially mine. The walls were dressed in snowflake paper, silver against cream, and the eclectic furniture looked as if it was selected with little fuss but lots of love. On the chipped, green dresser—the type you'd find at a rummage sale—were photographs of my former life.

Gram, Eric, Marie, Dean, Lacey, Charlie, Mom and Dad. All of them stared back at me from their gilded frames, the only expensive items in the entire apartment.

Every time I switched rooms, swapping between the Poison Quarters and Ice, Polar managed to put in a new piece intended to alleviate some of my homesickness. It usually just made me sad.

Polar fell into a chair beside me, his shoulders slumping with relief. "Finally," he said. "I was getting desperate." He turned his head and spoke to someone I couldn't see. "Let's give him a moment, let him regain his bearings."

Polar peered at me, his blue eyes emerging from the black, his glow in recession.

He'd been in translucency. The chill was from him, and I placed my hand on top of my chest where a glacier thumped. I wasn't wearing a shirt and my gloves were gone.

Feeling my skin, hands exposed, was about as surprising as the energy flitting through the room.

"I knew that would bring him to. We should've done that hours ago," Chanticlaim said, checking a latch at the door before padding across the ivory carpet to stand on the other side of my bed.

Hours ago?

"Your talents are as good as an ice bath, Polar."

Their focus intensified, and from the looks on their faces, whatever was happening was far from good.

I jostled slightly and felt the room swim. I closed my eyes and attempted to ask, "What happened," but got only as far as "Wha" before rust and pain erupted in my larynx. I winced, and Chanticlaim shushed me.

"Take a moment. You've had quite the ordeal. Here." Chanticlaim thrust a glass of water at me, sleeved in an insulated hold to stop the water from freezing over.

Each swallow was a salve and a fan against the fog.

My hazy recollections sharpened around the edges, and the garden pulled into focus.

"Fantasia," I croaked, and Polar's concerned expression leapt from sorrow to anger in a quick beat.

He shook his head and looked to Chanticlaim.

Neither one spoke, locked in a stalemate.

I sat up and my vision reared, as did the roar in my ears. Waves of blood whooshed, and if I hadn't been sitting, I would've tipped, my equilibrium gone to shit. I gripped my head and waited for the room to steady.

My vision wasn't the best—it was stuttering. Blur, sharp, dotted, clear, it couldn't make up its mind.

"She's recovering," Polar finally said.

Chanticlaim held out Dexitrol in his gloved hand. I refused to take it, and he shifted his weight.

"Do I need to leave?" Chanticlaim asked, eyeing me with uncertainty. "I can't survive the poison, and I don't want to be here if he lets loose."

Polar stood and grabbed the vial from Chanticlaim; he thrust it under my nose. His demeanor was stiff as the blanket covering me.

"Take it," he ordered. "A healthy dose."

So. Very. Bad.

I obeyed and emptied half the vial, while they both stared at me as if I were some sort of exotic animal.

Polar's attention flicked between me and Chanticlaim before he broke the silence, his words crisp. "Everyone's alive ..." he started, careful with his phrasing. "You've been out for almost twenty-four hours. We've been waiting for you to wake. You didn't let out your wail, and no one was injured in the maze ... well, aside from Dreams."

He took a moment and ran his tongue over his lips. His eyes flashed with conflict.

"I'm angry you brought her into this." Polar's fingers rolled into tight fists. "I know she's an adult, but still.... To meet with Fantasia like that in such an open fashion, using her as a look-out." He shook his head, disgusted.

I noticed he didn't condemn the fact I was meeting Fantasia, just the method we chose.

We'd gotten sloppy.

Chanticlaim didn't act surprised. Instead, he shuffled his feet and shoved his gloved hands in his pockets.

Polar cleared his throat and nudged his head toward the door. "Chanticlaim, on second thought, why don't you step outside for a second? Thank you for providing the Dexitrol. I think it was well needed. Their poison is impossible to get out of the drapes." Polar tried to smile, but it slipped into a glower.

Chanticlaim ducked his head and mumbled, "Of course," before exiting the room, sealing the door behind him.

Polar's scrutiny magnified.

"What were you thinking?" he hissed.

"I'm sorry."

His face darkened. "Sorry isn't going to cover it, not this time."

His rage freaked me out. "Look, she's had a lot going on. Me too. We were just talking it over."

"A lot going on, huh?" Polar stood up and leaned in. "I've had a lot going on, too. Want to know what I've had going on?" He didn't wait for an answer. "I've been cleaning up your mess for over a week. That's what I've been doing. It's busy work trying to cover your ass."

His anger slipped into disappointment. He ran his fingers through his hair and said, "I'm not your enemy, and if you have a problem, you should come to me."

"What are—"

"I know about Lil's house." He plopped onto the bed beside me. He placed his feet on the frame and folded like a paper spring, situating his forearms on his knees, letting his anger drop.

"How did you know?"

"Because I'm not stupid," he said, looking at me sideways. "And because Charlie privately reached out to me." Uncle Charlie, Gram's brother, was a liaison for Narivous, a Protector who helps keep our society secret. Apparently, he was also a gossip. Polar lifted his chin. "When he told me about the fire, I talked to Chanticlaim about the cameras in the parking garage, and when he told me they were shut down for *maintenance*, I knew it was you. I confirmed with Camille." He stared at the wall, not really looking at me. Probably too ashamed. "I kept waiting for you to tell me, thinking you just needed some time, and now I see you've been hiding a lot more than I thought."

"I'm sorry," I rasped, the texture of my throat road rash. "I thought it was better if I kept it to myself. I didn't want to involve you."

"But you were willing to involve Dreams? Torti, maybe? Fantasia for sure."

I winced, his disappointment more painful than the slivers of ice he'd directed at my chest.

"I wasn't thinking."

"I know you weren't. And it was reckless. *Stupid*"—his whole body clenched—"on all counts. Narivous doesn't adhere to human law, so it's really not the arson that matters, but the reason behind it." He cracked his knuckles. "Care to tell me why?"

"Isn't it obvious?"

This time, when Polar looked at me, suspicion turned him dark. He was no longer light—even his blue eyes were deepening like the depths of the ocean. "I have my theories. The innocent theories, the ones I try to lean toward, all have you coming to talk to me. The ones Amelia is building are another story."

"What do you mean, Amelia's building?"

"Tell me why."

I dropped my shoulders. "Fantasia's why," I said, feeling alone. Petrified, too, if I wanted to describe the heart of it.

Polar's muscles relaxed.

"That's what I thought ... honestly, that's what I hoped."

"Why would you hope for that?"

"Because Amelia's been spreading far worse, and with your silence, I thought maybe something more heinous was going on."

"How could you think that of me?"

"It's not necessarily you I'm worried about, but Fantasia. That girl ..." He didn't finish, and I was thankful for it. She was a rebellious spirit, but the oppression, the lack of love, would make anyone want to chew off their arm, as long as the manacles were taken off with it.

"What's Amelia been saying?" Nothing connected, as if we were building a picture with two different puzzles. The pieces wouldn't fit, and even if they did, it would never look right.

"She said you two looked too comfortable for that to be a one-time meeting. She thinks you've been plotting against the crown."

"No ..."

He swallowed and brushed white strands of hair from his forehead. "Yeah."

"Does anyone believe it?"

The strain around Polar's eyes deepened. "What do you think?" he asked, and when the pressure in my head swelled like a helium balloon, he tapped my hand, the one holding the

Dexitrol. "Take more if you need it. There are some things we need to go over, and we need to do it quickly."

I nodded and took another hefty dose. The swelling subsided.

"When I learned about the house, I spoke with Ferno. He's set three homes on fire in two days. All vacant. Trying to throw off suspicion. Now it looks like there's an arsonist going around. I hope it's enough."

Guilt seized my chest. All this time, before the maze, Polar had been covering my ass, waiting for me to come to him. I should've. I should've told him the truth.

He was my ally.

"My fear," Polar continued, "is they'll find out about the house and say you were trying to force your family to leave for other reasons. It would've probably been fine, had you not been caught. But, well, the maze incident changes everything."

I looked at the almost empty bottle and experienced a void as hollow as the glass.

"But it's just a house," I muttered.

"No, it's not. And you damn well know it. You burned down that house to drive your family away. There are many tangents someone can draw from that. One scares me above all others." He waited a moment and then filled in the blanks. "They can say you were trying to keep your family safe and far away in case your attempt to overthrow Thorn failed. You were removing collateral. If that's the route they go, then we have a very challenging battle ahead of us. Worse yet, it's not like you can tell them the real reason without compromising Camille's daughter."

How I managed to screw up, even while being careful, was a damn near art form. It's like I was the Da Vinci of crappy mistakes, every decision a brilliantly idiotic brush stroke.

And it didn't pass unnoticed that Polar referred to Fantasia as Camille's daughter. By going after my own heart, I could very well have punctured his.

"Amelia hates that girl," Polar continued. "She's wanted to be rid of her for ages. Her healing properties have kept her safe, otherwise she would've been killed a long time ago. But now, Amelia's using this opportunity to further her motives. She wants Fantasia dead and, unfortunately, you may have given her the ammunition she needs."

I groaned, recalling Fantasia's shadowy figure leaning forward, the shriek of pain.

"Is she okay?"

He shot me a searing look, and my stomach curdled.

"She's alive, if that's what you're asking."

Well, kind of.

"But she's okay?"

Polar stayed silent for far too long. "Nothing's okay right now."

"Polar, you're scaring me."

"Good. You need to be scared. Scared means you'll start making better choices."

"But I thought ..."

"You thought what?"

"That you approved of us."

His attention turned toward the door as if it'd grown ears. "I didn't say otherwise, I just hoped you wouldn't be so stupid as to meet out in the open. You know she's off limits."

"Of course I do—"

"I thought I set up a precedent, that you would come through me. That we understood each other and I didn't have to spell it out for you."

"I'm sorry."

"It doesn't matter. Not anymore. You're not allowed to see her ever again. The risk is too great."

"Don't say that."

"You think this is easy?" He held out his hands, palms up. "I know what you're going through. I know the feelings you're experiencing. I've been there. I'm still there." The Camille reference was a strong undercurrent. He ran his fingers through his hair, frustrated. "But there's no other option. You are never to see her again. And that's assuming neither one of you gets buried for what you did."

I winced, and he took a bit of the bite from his frost.

"You think they'll kill her?" I asked.

"Her healing abilities keep her safe. And right now, what you managed to pull in the maze is keeping you safe. But if they do a ton of digging and find out you've been up to something worse, even more treasonous, I'm not sure your asset or Fantasia's will be enough to save the two of you. So if there's anything you need to confess, now is the time. I can't help you if you're keeping secrets."

"I'm not plotting against the crown. I just wanted to—" I stopped as his words sunk in. "Wait, what? What do you mean, what I pulled in the maze? I didn't do anything other than black out."

The hazy memories, the few I could still retrieve, hurt like a mofo.

Fantasia's shadow, leaning down and kissing Amelia's feet. Her scream. The most painful sound in the world.

My question ripped the darkness off Polar.

"You did much more than black out." He fought a smile. "You did something we didn't think possible. It has Thorn extremely happy. *Eager.* And that's the only reason she's willing to accept another path." He leaned closer, his tone colluded. "Why she *wants* you to give her another path."

"I don't understa—"

"You took away your aura. You stole away your poison. You

were touchable by everyone, and it's given her hope." He had a proud look about him. "You don't know what that means, I'm guessing."

"No clue."

"It means you might be the link she's looking for. The link that ends the Poison curse." He stood up and started to pace, his footsteps silent along the pale Berber carpet. He continued to lighten with every passing second. "The Brilliants have always wondered if the key to the solution, either ending the deadly touch or removing the powers altogether, rested in the ability to kill it before it leaves the body. If ultimate suppression existed. But they needed a Velore that could possibly abate it. There was a rumor, once upon a time, that Scream managed the task on a single occasion. She's never been able to replicate it, and there are those who question if it even happened. Either way, it's always been the wild card. But making other Poisons was always forbidden—even if it meant possibly finding someone who could be our key to curing it."

Polar gave me a real smile. "But now you're here, and you've done something no one thought possible. I need you to make me a promise." Polar again looked toward the door before approaching my bedside, leaning in, and speaking in hushed tones. "Thorn is going to ask you if you can replicate what happened in the maze. Say yes, even if you think you can't. Even if you're unsure. Just say yes."

"And then what?"

"I don't know," he answered honestly. "But Thorn is going to ask, and you're going to tell her you can do it. Time. We need time, for things to calm down. For things to get better. And then, well, we go from there." He shrugged and started toward the door.

But I wasn't done with him, not when there were gaps I still needed filled.

"What happened to Fantasia?"

Polar let off a wave of ice. The bed, drapes, rug, all of it crystallized under his strength. He turned, and his eyes went black.

"That can wait until later. Right now I need your head in the game. I was supposed to send for the guards the moment you woke up."

I gripped the blanket and went to throw it off me, only to realize I wasn't wearing any clothes aside from a pair of boxer shorts—and the room was still frosted. Someone had stripped me while I was out. Small, red ink marks were drawn all over my body, random placement of minuscule x's.

Bizarre.

"No." I made my voice strong. "You can't do this, Polar. Imagine how you'd feel if it were the other way around. If it were ... Frigid."

I almost said Camille, but changed my mind. He hadn't openly revealed his relationship and this wasn't the time to call him on it.

His expression softened, and I added, "Just tell me, please."

My desperation must've tugged on him, because his stubbornness faded. "Do you think you can handle it?"

"Not knowing is worse. You don't even wanna know what my mind's working up."

Which was true. Every horrible scenario, all of them stemming from the scream that serenaded me into my coma, told me Fantasia would never recover from Amelia.

He looked on the brink, and I gave him an extra shove.

"I'll tell Thorn whatever you want, but please, just give it up. Tell me, what happened to Fantasia?" My heart was thumping in the darkest recesses of my chest. "I need to know. I can't *not* know."

"She's been lashed, and since you were *indisposed*, Dreams delivered the blows."

I groaned and almost dropped my head, but the angle of his jaw stopped me.

There was more.

Polar waited, surveying me for cracks, and then closed his eyes, cinching them shut as if blinding himself from the truth. His pale complexion turned ashen.

"What else?"

"I'm sorry, Daniel."

He called me Daniel. I started to stand. If my feet froze to the floor, so be it. He wasn't leaving me dumb.

He relented and said, "Amelia cut off the ring finger on her left hand. As a message to anyone who comes in contact with her."

The room spun, and Polar came back over. He gripped my shoulder, his icy fingers slicing beyond my skin.

The walls went from white to black. Rage wasn't the color of blood, but of unending night.

I was gonna kill Amelia.

So help me, I would see her dead. And I'd take ultimate pleasure in it.

"Calm down," Polar urged. The heat whittled away the Dexitrol. Soon it'd be nothing more than cinders—ruined fragments.

"I need you to be calm," he reiterated. "This is not the time. You need to be on your best behavior. For yourself. For me. For Fantasia."

That toned it down. "Where is she?"

"They have her locked up. As a precaution while they're undergoing their investigation. Look, Daniel, Thorn wants to believe this was a one-time situation. Messing with Fantasia isn't as bad of an offense as trying to dethrone Thorn."

"But I can't tell her that, can I? I mean, what would happen to Fantasia if she knew we were trying to be together?"

"I honestly don't know." Polar let go of my shoulder and folded his arms across his chest. "And I don't want to find out. Thorn is giddy over the aura suppression, and I need you to play on that. She wants it bad—a fix to the poison."

A dark thought slammed into me. Fantasia was helpful because she could heal—in particular the toxin. If Thorn found a way around the poison, either through salve or elimination, would Fancy's talent no longer be useful?

"But I can't, Polar."

He jerked and shot me a cruel look. "Of course you can! Why would you even say that?"

"Because if I'm the key to finding a cure to the toxin, then what happens to Fantasia? If they don't need her anymore, they'll get rid of her."

Polar leaned down and spoke through gritted teeth. "As long as she's obedient, she won't have to bank on her talents. That's it, Daniel. That's it."

"But Amelia—"

He hissed. "Amelia doesn't decide who's eliminated, that decision falls solely on Thorn, and Thorn won't destroy her without cause."

I turned my face and Polar grabbed my jaw, forcing me to look at him.

"I'm serious, Daniel. Think of the shock waves Fantasia's death would cause if Thorn killed her simply to appease Amelia." He scoffed, releasing me. "Her sisters are some of the best recruiters we have. Camille is exceptional as well. The chaos Fantasia's death would bring, *if it wasn't justified*"—he was careful to enunciate this last part—"would disrupt the balance Thorn's worked so very hard to keep. Fantasia only has to be obedient. It's all up to her."

His lack of compassion hit a nerve. I bristled. Polar squared his shoulders and took a step back.

"This is your one chance. Thorn is paranoid by nature, it won't take much for Amelia to convince her you're plotting. If she hasn't already done so."

"But you said she wanted to believe."

"Oh, she does." He paused and dodged my gaze. He'd been holding back this entire time. I could see it.

"What is it? What are you keeping from me?"

"There's an underground lab built specifically to handle toxin particles." He stopped, choking on emotion.

Guilt, not fear, left me heavy. Another secret I'd kept from him. But I couldn't mention the lab, because Fantasia most likely learned of it through illicit means.

"They went to work a few hours ago, piecing it back together," Polar said.

Too many falsehoods to grab from, none of which he deserved, so I found the mute button and shut my trap.

The lab was back in, which could mean many things.

Death.

Test-rat.

Torture.

All of the above.

"That lab scares me, Daniel." Polar went over to the dresser and picked up a picture of Dad and me. He spoke to the photograph, doing his best to keep the quiver from his voice. "I don't want to lose you." He ran two fingers across the image, before putting it back in its place. "Narivous took Richard from me, it took Lil, and I can't have it take you." Polar waited a moment, still staring at the photo, and in a voice so low I wasn't sure I was supposed to hear said, "I'm not letting them take you."

He scratched his cheek, a nervous tick, and spoke directly at me. "That lab is either going to be used to test on you or put you in a coffin. I honestly don't know which direction they're heading in, but you have the ability to stop it."

He squinted around the room, and nodded to himself. "You're going to stop it," he repeated, as if he could will it by saying it aloud. He went toward the door, pausing with his hand on the knob. "I've got to go get the guards. It's going to be okay." He gave me a pretend smile, one that didn't reach his eyes, before disappearing from the room.

But I knew then.

Why he was so desperate to talk with me. Why he waited —no doubt—by my bedside.

He knew they were leaning toward treason, that the only thing stopping the guillotine from crashing down was my unexpected trick.

And in order to buy more time, I had to become a magician. Learn how to recreate the "impossible task." Pull a rabbit out of a hat and make the audience believe I'd done it from thin air.

I was doomed.

CHAPTER 18

SCYTHE

It would always feel wrong. Be wrong. The sound of metal bars snapping shut, the lock slinking into place.

It stole something of my humanity, made me feel more animal than man. I was an inconvenient pet, pushed aside, latched in a kennel so the owners could pretend I didn't exist.

It demoralized me in ways being undead never could.

I'd yet to meet with Thorn. As soon as the Seven heard I was awake, I was ordered to the tower. Fantasia was in a similar placement, in another wing. They didn't want us conspiring.

Confined and beaten down, probably, just like me.

They gave me the same cell with the bed and window—the one I stayed in after rotting Jester. I considered carving my name into the stonework, to mark my territory. At least my room had one of the best barred views of the city, so I could overlook Hades from a fantastic vantage point.

Polar, Splint, and Spark were the ones to escort me to my cage.

The latter two moved to the beat of a funeral march. Spark kept shooting glances in my direction, even Splint lost his strut, but no one chanced a word.

They didn't chance a touch either.

Orders, I'm guessing.

"This is just a precaution," Polar said, as Splint sealed the door and walked off, Spark close on his heels. They were kind enough to give us a moment alone. After receiving word I was going into lockup, I'd been watched without fail.

I even had to get dressed under supervision.

Polar put his hands on the bars and spoke swiftly. "She'll be coming soon. See to it you take your medication." His gaze shot toward the camera. He dipped his head, formal like, and spoke so the lens couldn't capture his moving lips. "Remember what I told you. That's your card to play."

He left without looking back, and I was stuck in purgatory with nothing but regrets, an overactive imagination, and twiddling thumbs.

Occasionally I'd gape at my hands.

The guards hadn't returned my gloves—for whatever baleful reason—and now I couldn't help but stare. My hands had become foreign appendages.

Either from lack of sunlight or from the poison, they'd taken on a gangrenous tint.

My nails, once pink, had gone gray. The lines in my palms were deeper, more conspicuous. If anything gave away my immortality it was the hideous attachments at the ends of my arms.

I'd become Frankenstein. It's like they'd severed hands from a corpse and stitched them onto my obliging wrists.

I never thought it would happen, but I missed the gloves.

SOMEHOW, I fell asleep on the poorly padded bed. My mind refused to let up. It force-fed me sick images. Marie and Dean, stubborn and filled with love, waiting for me back home, only to be snatched away by a pride of claw-fisted Animals and dragged to the land of the dead.

The executioners wore black hoods over their faces, but I recognized their frames. Knew Cheetah and Cheetoh held Marie and Dean, still wearing their pajamas, lining them next to a large swimming pool.

Jaguar held Lacey. He was cradling her, as if giving her comfort, while she slept against his shoulder. Her chest lifted with short, unhurried breaths, her face slack and soft. The hood hid his expression, and I wondered if Jaguar was smiling or sobbing. His fingers flexed, claws poking out, kneading the skin on her arm. He reverberated with a low purr.

Amelia didn't bother to wear a mask. She smiled, her teeth flashing. She waved Cheetoh forward and they forced Dean to kneel in his plaid fleece bottoms, next to the pool.

I tried to call out, but a warm body pressed against my back and a hand missing a ring finger clamped over my mouth.

"This has to happen," Fantasia whispered. Her arms were impossibly strong, like unyielding steel, and I couldn't fight her off.

Her touch made my skin crawl, our unexplainable bond severed. She was now all Animal—the breed I hated most— the side she kept hidden from me. She'd lost her allure, her cinnamon replaced with an overpowering, repugnant feline musk. I resented her, hated the way her flesh felt, how her breath trickled into my ear.

I grabbed her hand and drove my fingers in, but she wouldn't let go. If anything, she got stronger.

So I gnashed my teeth and bit her hand. She only laughed and nibbled on my ear.

Out of nowhere, Polar materialized and grabbed my arm. His eyes were liquid pools of tar, dark as the devil.

"Atonement," he said.

He nodded toward the pool, and I watched as they forced Dean's head into the water and snuffed out his heartbeat. Marie came next.

Lacey was last.

Amelia looked at me as she coiled her hand in Lacey's long, brown hair, the same move she'd used to incapacitate Dreams, twining it at the base of her neck, a perfect handhold for control. Lacey's mouth fell open as if she wanted to cry out, only she emitted no sound. Amelia's smile grew. She shot me a wink and then plunged.

I woke drenched in sweat and took an entire bottle of Dexitrol to stop the thrumming. And because I really had nothing to stay awake for, and I was a glutton for punishment, I fell asleep for a second time.

It was mercifully free of dreams.

A DOOR CREAKED OPEN, and there was a shuffle along the stones, the way rich fabric whispers against a hard surface.

I sat up, the fog of sleep dissolving in an instant.

Thorn had come alone, unaided by guards, dressed down and wearing an expression I couldn't read. She stood outside the bars, touching nothing, her hands hanging limply at her sides.

She didn't belong in this part of the castle, I could feel it.

I stood up and fell to my knees, bowing my head in total submission.

She didn't flinch. No smile, no amusement. When groveling didn't elicit a response, I knew I was in far too deep.

As I'd been trained, I waited to be addressed. She took a million eternities, to the point my knees began to crumble. The ache crawled up my joints, giving me sudden onset arthritis.

"You are an asset and a burden," she began, her words barely above a whisper, so soft not even the walls could claim them. "A threat and a promise, and for the life of me, I can't decide what to do with you." She took a step forward and stared me down.

I kept to my knees. It was the safest place, cowering. A cold breeze swept through the corridor, not too uncommon in the dankness of the cells. I shivered.

"I'm here for your side of the story, Death. Tell me, what happened in the maze?"

Everything I had, all the sincerity I could muster, went into my tenor—to add credence to my confession. Polar said she needed to believe. She *wanted* to believe. And I was offering something far better than Amelia's lies. A promise of greater power, for ultimate domination.

Her heart's greatest desire.

Thorn once said she didn't want to capsize her ships, just disrupt their calm seas with strong ripples. Death was a game with the steepest ramifications, and once I was gone, she couldn't get me back. If I really was the link she was missing, to remove me would only hurt her cause.

We both wanted to believe I was the answer.

"I asked Fantasia to come meet me," I said, the acoustics of the tower ricocheting my voice into an echo. Making it appear as if I were speaking twice over. To take the blame more than once.

That's what I needed to do, to own all the faults. Diverging from Fantasia, altering the trajectory of their suspicion.

She'd been punished enough.

"She's my friend," I started, taking deep breaths with each

punctuation. "And I knew she was giving you a new recruit. I only wanted to know how it went since it's as important to me as it is to her, that you're happy. We want you to be happy."

She nodded, the first indicator I was doing something right.

"She was sad, though, because she was worried she wouldn't be a good recruiter. She's afraid of failing you. And I tried to comfort her. Amelia walked in on a situation that looked bad, but really, it was innocent. We weren't doing anything." *For once.* "I was just trying to be a friend."

Another nod. I thanked the stars we hadn't been kissing.

"Then everything went bad, and I didn't have my Dexitrol on me. I was scared and freaked out." I ran my tongue along my lips. This is where I needed to place it. Make her think I did it intentionally. That I could do it again—over and over if need be.

This was where.

"I could feel the thrumming, ya know? And, I, uh, made my powers a color, just like Laquet taught me, and I felt it change. Become more condensed or something. And then, well, I forced it far under, and next thing I know I'm waking up in the Ice Quarters."

Thorn smoothed her hands down the front of her dress. Her composure didn't falter, but I detected the slight tremor in her fingers. Excitement bleeding through her stoicism.

"Amelia thinks you and Fantasia have been plotting against me. That you've been doing it for some time." She lifted her chin a fraction.

"No. Never. We'd never plot against you." I steepled my hands, and ducked my head. A poster boy of subservience. When I met her eyes, I did my best to well them, force black tears to pool. Somehow, perhaps from the stress, the bleakness of the situation, I managed.

This time she smiled.

"I don't know why Amelia would think that," I continued. "We just want to make you happy. That's why Fantasia was upset, that's why I was comforting her, all because we were fearful of letting you down."

Thorn's gaze roamed over my quarters, taking in the bed, the barred window, the stark walls, the pitiful blankets I'd been using to try and stave off the perpetual chill of the cell. They were moth eaten, and smelled like mold and tragedy.

Something was whirling inside her head, and she wasn't sharing.

"Stand up," she ordered.

My knees ached as I stumbled to my feet.

She motioned for me to approach the bars, surveying my bare hands.

"You think you can suppress your abilities again?"

"Absolutely." Hell, even I was convinced of it. That's what desperation does. Makes even the impossible seem plausible. I could be a magician.

She nodded, pleased.

"And you say this moment of comfort was due to her fear of failing me?"

"Yes."

"And that's the one thing you don't want to do?"

"Neither one of us wants to fail you."

She mulled on it, turning away, her informal dress skimming along the cold concrete. "Tell me, Death," she said, her back turned. "How has your friendship with Fantasia blossomed, when you've had so little free time? When no one has seen you two together? How have you managed to maintain that connection?"

She pivoted and grinned in a mean way.

Before I could answer, before I could grease my mental

cogs, she spat out a reply. "I think you've been sneaking around. And I can't help but wonder why. Part of me believes it's because you fancy her. You are a foolish hot-blooded male, susceptible to a pretty face. And she has one of the prettiest faces, doesn't she?" She angled her head, taking me in. "I'd hate for something—or someone—to come along and ruin it for her."

I lost the breath in my lungs, I almost lost the ability to stand. She clicked her tongue and pressed forward. "And then the other side wonders if she's up to the same tricks I've long suspected of her. Which, if that's the case, means she won't have to worry about her pretty face, since we'll slice her head clean off her neck. Let the crows eat her eyes and my beetles her flesh. So?" She arched a brow. "Which one is it?"

It was an answerless question. Anything I gave her would be wrong. It was almost as if she wanted Fantasia dead.

Same as Amelia.

I shook my head and stuffed my hands in my pockets. Everything in me gave way, and I fed her a morsel of honesty. "I have a crush on her. Jester told me it's common to fall for your recruiter. He told me that right before, well, right before his death. But, I promise you, we're only friends. That's it. I know she's off limits, and Fantasia'd never go against an official order. Besides, I don't think I'm her type. If she even had a type. Well, you know." Stupid. I was so stupid. Thorn smirked.

"How did you know to meet in the maze?"

She was looking for the accomplice—Dreams—and I wasn't giving her up. I began to pummel Amelia's story with jabs of my own.

I had to make her believe.

"I ran into Fantasia on guard duty. And, uh, she told me she was bringing in her recruit. I convinced her to meet me in the garden. It was all me. I should've known better. But she was my first friend here, and I wanted to help her, ya know."

Thorn nodded.

"You'll stay put, Death." She gave a terse smile at my drafty kennel. "Here, until the investigation is complete."

She started to walk away, and two guards, waiting on her cue, opened the door. I was already snapped in two, giving her a kowtowing bow, when she stopped to give me a final glance.

"You say you can replicate what happened in the maze, yes?"

I nodded, my neck springing like a jack-in-the-box.

"For your sake, let's hope that's true."

And then she was gone. All I could do was wait.

A DAY PASSED. Then another. No one came to visit, aside from Polar, who delivered meals and spoke in snippets turned from the camera.

So far the house had yet to be discovered.

But Amelia was sniffing hard, and as each hour ticked by, she grew more determined. Polar worried the string of arsons wouldn't be enough to keep attention away.

Particularly because Ferno set the fires in a different manner—and the fire chief noted it. Another fail on my end. Had I been honest, they could've replicated my methods, made it seem one and the same.

Something else I failed to account for was our own scent trail. The Animals were hound dogs after an escaped convict. They were checking perimeters, using my clothing as a guide. Locating every spot I'd visited in the past two weeks.

And every spot Fantasia visited.

It made me wonder how often the Animal clan did this,

using their senses to track. Polar managed to tell me, with his hand carefully placed in front of his mouth, that they don't normally search for specific scents. There are simply too many and they get flooded with information, overwhelming their receptors.

This was just a special circumstance. Lucky me.

They picked up our scent in her cave—strike one.

They detected it by the rock quarry—strike two.

And by day three, they found my scent in the one place I wasn't authorized to be in: the parking garage.

Polar wasn't allowed to visit me after that, or so I assumed, since he didn't deliver my food. Instead, guards with masks over their faces and builds I didn't recognize dropped off my meals.

It was only a matter of time before they discovered the house.

I waited for the blade to fall.

⁂

Two guards, complete strangers, smiled at me from outside the bars. One was tall and lanky, with shaggy brown hair haphazardly brushed back. He had tattoos sketched all over his skin, peeking from the edges of his uniform—a walking billboard. He held the key to my cage in one lean fist.

The other had a babyface, which was in stark contrast to his cut frame. When he smiled, it looked wrong. He held a black bag, weighted down by an unseen object, and he swung it like a pendulum, as if he wanted me to take note of it.

Neither one appeared friendly, their grins more like snarls.

I knew this was coming. Hours earlier, I'd had my Dexitrol removed, accompanied by an order to shower and shave.

"C'mon, princess," Tattoo spat. "It's time for you to earn your keep."

The other reached into his bag and produced my gloves. He also tossed me my cloak. My mask was absent, and I thought better than to ask after it.

I slipped the mesh over my fingers, thankful no glue was being used, and secured my cloak. Everything smelled strange—rancid and nasty—my pores retracted against the fabric, and it took a second to place the scent. When I noted it, I jolted with repulsion.

Amelia. My gear smelled like Amelia.

These were the items she used to track my movements. Putting them on was like letting her close to me. It made me want to shower with boiling water, burning my skin off along with her memory.

Of all signs, sending strangers to escort me was perhaps the most ominous—and it didn't matter where we were going. They might as well have had scythes and palls.

There was a funeral to attend.

I just wasn't sure whose.

We descended the narrow stone staircase, and every step hurt in both spirit and body.

At the bottom of the stairs, two more guards—or at least I assumed they were guards—were waiting. More strangers. One had a flattened nose and brawny arms, the other was a female with bright green eyes and bleached blonde hair.

Both held the same black bags as Babyface. Tattoo was handed a spare.

The new pair weren't wearing gold G's, but they held themselves as if they occupied the job. Suited in the same material used for my gloves, they wore head-to-toe clothing of black mesh and looked ready for war.

Armor for whatever was going to happen.

No one said a word. No introductions, nothing. I had to mentally assign them nicknames to keep the order straight. The two official guards led the way, and the others followed at the rear.

We made our way through the castle, passing the main corridor. For once, I looked up, drinking in the skulls, wondering where mine would sit. Resolve and sorrow sat heavier than the fabric of my cloak.

I'd run out of tricks.

I couldn't stand the sound of our footsteps. The castle was hollow.

"Where is everyone?" I asked.

"Out," Tattoo said.

"Where?"

"Does it matter?"

The pair snickered behind me. They lost their smiles when I glared back at them.

"Where are we going?"

"Patience." Tattoo shot me a grin. "You'll know soon enough."

Outside the castle, the city was a ghost town. Only a few Velores crept along the walkways, and even fewer dared to look our way. Spark was there, however, next to one of the many indistinguishable cottages. He flexed his hands and nodded in recognition, but his jovial side was asleep.

Something was happening.

There were no guards stationed at the gate, and the quad surprised me by passing through the exit, leading me into the forest and not into an underground compartment. Perhaps death wasn't in the cards for me today.

The black bags swung.

Babyface spoke as we headed toward the oak trees and the meadow.

"You get to kill your humans today."

I stopped, and one of the half-guards bumped into me. He reared in a panic, running his gloved hands over his exposed flesh, fearful I'd actually made contact.

"You sure you're up to this, Iron?" Tattoo asked. "Things are about to get a lot worse."

Iron glared and nodded. "Oh, yeah. I've got this."

"What do you mean humans?" I shot out.

No one answered.

I got louder. "You said humans. *Plural*. What do you mean?"

Tattoo, the clear leader, stepped close to me. "Well, poppet, it means there's more than one."

"But I was told I'd only have to kill one."

"Who told you that?"

I shook my head and muttered, "Never mind." It wouldn't make a difference. If I had to kill more than one to prove my worth, I was resigned to do it.

Even if I stumbled through it, by the end of the day, they'd have what they wanted: my soul, morals, whatever.

I'd given up.

Proving my worth—and showing how committed I was to being a good, obedient Velore—was my only task.

Maybe, if I did a good enough job, they'd let Fantasia off the hook.

"Let's get on with it," I said, and Tattoo shot me a wink.

"This is gonna be fun," he said. He jutted his chin at the others and barked, "Suit up."

They dug into their bags and produced gas masks, quickly putting them in place.

Breathe, Daniel. Make it fast. My body responded. The tingling built on command—it was almost as if I held a semblance of control, but I wasn't foolish enough to accept the mirage. Although I wanted to.

Anything to keep my family safe.

To keep Fantasia safe.

We hit the trail leading to the oak trees, a healthy distance from the meadow's entrance, and stationed ourselves in a deep elbow, where trees eclipsed our presence. All we had to do was step out and bam, we'd be in ambush mode.

The forest represented so many things to me. I still loved the scent of wet earth and crisp pine needles, of fermented berries and rotting plants. It was still natural, even with Thorn's hold on it.

A land of freedom and entrapment.

We entered the silent part of our territory. Where birds and woodland creatures disappeared. They sensed danger and did their best to skirt the area. It made me marvel at Jaguar's raccoon, Bonnie, and Fred, back when he was alive. How they could attach themselves to us, the apex predator.

But what I missed when I was human, I picked up as a Velore. Life still lingered. I could hear remnants of the river, of bugs whisking through the air, of pinecones dropping.

I pulled my hood up and leaned against a tree. Trying to stop the thrumming from rising too quickly. Each second added to the pressure.

I put my fingers in my ears, not wanting to hear the humans approach. I was going to treat this like a fast, clean break.

Through my blotted sight, the quad started to shift. Although their expressions were blocked by the gas masks, I could tell they were smiling. Their bodies had that easy movement. The girl even rubbed her gloved hands together in anticipation.

Why the asshats liked pain so much was beyond me.

Probably a trait common in the cesspool Narivous liked to pluck from.

Heathens.

Babyface shot me a thumbs up. I could hear the voices, and Tattoo nodded it was time.

They stepped out, and I dropped my hands.

Do this. Make it quick.

I followed their lead and made my entrance. My head bloated with the whirling poison and determination to follow through.

On the trail, with mouths open in shock and hope, were Aunt Marie and Uncle Dean.

Life fell away.

CHAPTER 19
SETUP

After Marie moved to Oregon, I only saw her on special occasions. I missed her, the warmness of her smile, the way she owned life, her confidence.

I also missed the way she'd tell my dad off when he'd done something particularly stupid.

Aunt Marie was fearless that way.

She wasn't malleable like Dad, who'd do anything for a fix. Aunt Marie was made of stronger stuff.

If Dad were clay, she'd be cement.

One time, while Dad was on a long junkie jaunt—having disappeared for over three months—Marie accompanied Gram to Maine for a birthday visit. I was turning ten.

Gram bought me my first grown-up bike, and Marie got me all the stuff to go with it: padlock, chain, helmet.

Overkill, but I know why they did it. To make up for the void in my life. As if shine and ribbons could fill in the hole my dad's absence left behind.

They even got me a cake, which never happened when it was just Mom and me. It was chocolate with fudge filling and had frilly little ribbons of frosting along the edge. There was a plastic bike, no bigger than my thumb, cruising along a cookie crumble path, outlined with plastic trees and candy rocks.

It made me feel special.

But on the day of, when evening arrived and Dad still hadn't called to wish me a happy birthday, Marie flew into a fit. She stomped through the house, said words she rarely used, made everyone uncomfortable with the weight of her anger.

Gram tried to ignore it. She sat on the couch, paying close attention to her knitting needles, breaking off at random intervals to give my hand a comforting squeeze. I'd always squeeze back.

"I think I know where he's staying," Mom said after Marie dropped her fifteenth F-bomb in half an hour. Marie pounced. It's a rare thing indeed when a junkie can be tracked down with a working phone number.

I could overhear snippets of the conversation when she got Dad on the phone.

She knew how to bait.

"Yes, we're in town." "Mom wants to see you." "It's your son's birthday." "Well if you don't have a ride we can call a cab." "We're not an ATM." "Maybe. Depends on how you act—just get your ass over here for your son." "Last time."

It was never the last time.

Never.

Marie managed the impossible—she got Dad at the table to sing me "Happy Birthday." He was jittery, amped up. Meth made him hyper and talkative.

He barely paid me notice, he was too focused on bumming money from Gram, but my bike was another story. He couldn't stop staring at it.

That night, after we'd all gone to sleep, the bike—unsurprisingly—went missing. The chain lock severed, a pair of bolt cutters snatched from a neighbor's shed discarded near the disjointed links.

I sobbed when I found it missing. Not so much for the loss of the bike—although that sucked—but for the destruction of Dad's memory. It didn't take a genius to know who'd jacked it.

Marie found me staring at the spot where my bike last sat, chain in hand. When she reached for me, I took off for a field behind our house.

She called my name, desperate. I ran faster. Not wanting her to see me cry, to know how badly I was hurting.

Her voice held sadness and unease in one note.

The same as it did now.

She broke between syllables while crying out my name. She couldn't decide whether to look at me or the guards wearing gas masks.

A flash of movement darted from the bushes and trees. Three Animals, tall and lanky, claws on showcase, stepped into the open. Cougar, Fantasia's father, among them. The other two were unfamiliar and not related to Amelia's brood.

Cougar wasn't smiling, but glaring. His cut jaw and mirror scars flexed from a mouth clenched tight.

I'd been so focused on shutting out my senses, I'd ignored all the other scents intermingling with the pines. The musk of dangerous bodies poised to strike, waiting and eager.

Marie froze, a limp piece of paper dangling from her fist. Her face was as pale as her knuckles, and her mouth hung slightly ajar.

Dean grabbed her and forced her to take a step back. She stumbled into place, as Dean's other hand crept for his hip, where the outline of his polo shirt rested awkwardly against an object hidden beneath it.

Always the cautious one, Dean would never venture into the woods without his gun.

My four escorts held their positions, two in back, two in front. But the Animals, they crept closer to Marie and Dean. One of them, with sand hair, eyed Dean's hovering hand and rasped out a warning.

"I wouldn't reach for that if I were you."

Dean froze, his hand just centimeters from his pistol.

The Animals smiled, all but Cougar, and split to cover the sides, creating an aisle for me.

No one moved for an infinite amount of time. Seconds, most likely, but they went on forever. Marie's and Dean's chests didn't lift. They'd stopped breathing.

And the thrumming I was so eager to claim, I pushed back.

Because I wasn't playing their game. I was done being their pawn. If they didn't have a reason to kill me before, they would have one in a minute. Because there would be death, but it wouldn't be Marie's and Dean's.

Every cell in my body went into hyperdrive. Dean locked eyes on me and held his hand out.

The other stayed floating over the gun in his holster.

"Daniel." He managed to keep his voice from shaking. Impressive considering the warped circumstances. "Why don't we take off, son."

I heard him swallow, even from a distance.

I started to take a step toward them and Cougar cut me off, his back in front of me. Even without seeing his face, I felt him smile. He curled his fingers, flexing his claws, but I wouldn't let him block me. I sidestepped and paralleled him.

"Aunt Marie, Uncle Dean, why don't you guys head back to the car." I kept my neck upright, refusing to flex even a fraction. They weren't getting my subservience, not after this. Not ever again.

"Oh, I don't know," Cougar replied. "I think they should

stay. They came here for you, after all, and it wouldn't be fair for them to leave so ... *prematurely*."

The Animals flanking the path smiled. I was going to erode their lips away.

The skin rippled under my gloves. My mouth went dry as I made the anger, the rage, the indignation, transcend from floating poison particles—the airborne type—to pores and sweat.

My touch was going to land the Animals in a world of hurt.

Marie opened her mouth, then closed it, before Dean spoke. He took a step toward us.

"We don't want any trouble." He looked at Cougar, his vision darting from Cougar's face to his hands. Disbelief coated Dean's words. "And we won't ask any questions. We just came for our nephew." He nudged his head toward me, not letting his gaze slip, so he wouldn't see the masks, so he wouldn't focus on their imposing builds.

Or on the power they emitted.

To keep the illusion this was all some delusion brought on by stress.

I could see his mind formulating plausible explanations, because this type of thing wasn't real.

"He's only seventeen, a minor, and needs to be with his family," Dean said.

Marie found her height and a stroke of courage. She motioned for me. "C'mon, Daniel. We're going home."

Cougar chuckled and stroked his claws, drawing Dean's attention, refusing him blinders.

Desperate, Dean shook his head and spoke rationally. "As impressive as your props are, they're of little importance in the grand scheme of things, and I'm more than happy to overlook them. Whatever it is you guys have going on, I really don't care. The solution's an easy fix. Just let Daniel go and we'll leave. No need to overcomplicate the situation. We won't bother you again." He and Marie began to motion with their hands, beckoning me to their sides.

"He's not going anywhere," Cougar snarled. His power curled around him, a predatory mist. He flexed his knuckles and his neck muscles bulged.

Calling his claws a prop was the ultimate insult.

Both Marie and Dean blinked, they saw the flash of energy bursting from Cougar, and Marie started to weep as Cougar took a step toward them.

I matched it.

"Please," she muttered, and I held up my hand, giving her my best smile. The decrepit company really stole from the effect.

"Aunt Marie, Uncle Dean, please go back to the car."

Dean shook his head. "Not without—"

"GO!"

He took a step back, the shuffle making the Animal pair snicker. One of them blasted into a blurred outline to block their exit.

To contain us all.

I moved between Cougar and my family, using my body as a shield. I wouldn't look at Marie or Dean—couldn't, really. Instead, I turned and glowered at Cougar, trying to keep his focus on my face as I did my best to free my greatest weapon, the one I could control, the one he couldn't defeat.

Complacency was nothing more than a memory. I was ready for a fight.

"If you think, even for a second, I'm going to do this, then you're more batshit crazy than your batshit crazy wife," I said, and Cougar's face went from bronze to burnt.

He grabbed me by the shirt, not caring how close he was to making contact with my skin.

He was also absolutely unaware my flesh was sizzling—I'd managed to manifest the toxin into a layer of film. It crawled over me, the buzzing making my fingers tingle.

"Apologize," he growled.

"I guess that answers it then." I gave him my most infuriating smile. His color grew, and he shook me—but my plan was working. He was distracted, too caught up in his own righteous hierarchy to capture the movement beneath my cloak. The small jabs of a glove being subtly worked off. I snorted. "If you think I'm gonna say sorry for speaking the truth, you're an absolute whack-job."

He roiled beneath the surface, his face warping into a demon's mask.

I met his foul face with another smile.

He lifted me by the collar, till I was far off the ground. The fabric started to crack, the pressure too much, before it tore clean away.

My reflexes didn't falter. I landed on my feet, the tatters exposing my chest. Thankfully, my cape concealed my hand— he couldn't see the glove was nearly off.

It bolstered my confidence, because the fool had given me another access point. More skin to touch.

For someone with razor sharp vision, he missed it all. He grabbed my lapels and knitted them together, yanking me back toward him.

"You won't talk to me that way," he growled.

"The hell I won't." His strength expanded, bristling down his arm, staining my own energy with his slimy film.

"You filthy little—"

"Big talk coming from the coward who can't even stand up for his own daughter."

"How dare you!"

"I don't take orders from losers." I smirked. "I won't do this."

Cougar roared, primal. All beast, no human. The tenor of his rage rattled the forest around him, yet I remained steadfast and frozen.

Where he shook, I stilled.

Two forces at odds. His power was full of brawn and strength, mine was subtly discreet and far more effective.

He threw me to the ground, my back absorbing the blow. Muscles barked and bones creaked, threatening to snap if he added even the slightest pressure. It seemed Cougar was more powerful than gravity and a jagged cliff, the strength of his Animal blood strong enough to shatter immortal skeletons.

His temper tantrum—that final burst of violence—was what I needed. On the ground, feigning vulnerability, I managed to slip the glove off and tucked it beneath me.

Things were going to get interesting.

Somewhere in the chaos, Marie started to scream, the attack from Cougar activating her vocal cords. It assaulted my ears, scraping the insides and threatening to bleed out my canals.

Cougar bent over me, his face within reaching distance. "You will do this or suffer the consequences."

I shot him a smile, one full of teeth, and spat, "Well then, I'll suffer the consequences."

I threw my bare hand forward and clutched his face, forcing every piece of death into my exposed palm. I gripped so deeply his features dimpled from both pressure and burn. My smart mouth had made him stupid and slow, and the pause was enough to sink my blow.

He screamed and ripped himself away. It gave me power. And a smile fell on my face like a long-lost memory. The other Animals sprung, but jumped back when I whipped my bare arm around. I found my feet as they retreated like skittish kittens, facing the maw of an angry, rabid dog.

Now it was their fear I was smelling. It was more alluring than the scent of cinnamon. I wanted to bottle it and wear it like cologne.

The guards pounced, confident in their bodysuits, but they failed to account for the vulnerable patches the gas masks left uncovered. Small targets, but I was up for a challenge.

I dodged their attempt to corral me, twisting my free arm away, the one they wanted to pin. They knew containment was their only chance at defeating me.

Blondie was the first to chance a grab, snagging my feet and throwing me off balance. She sent me to the ground, but not before I clutched the front of her fabric armor and pulled her atop me. Reflex sprang my fingers, and I found her pocket of skin.

She started to spasm on contact and her wail took over Cougar's, who was breathing in short stabs, his lungs on the fritz. He searched in one of the black discarded bags, his face scrunched. One Animal stayed beside him, whispering words I couldn't hear because of Blondie's shrieking.

For some reason, her screams were even more acoustically pleasing—it made my toes curl—and I recognized the power building within, fogging my ethics. I willed it to strengthen. I needed more of it, to keep my morals at bay, to keep the wrath centered, to make it so powerful all of Narivous would feel it.

I expected Marie and Dean to run, but instead they rooted —or, more accurately, Marie rooted, her mouth contorted into a silent scream.

Dean wouldn't leave without her—she became his shackle.

Iron took the place of Blondie, trying to wrangle my free arm. He wasn't much for grace, however, and I managed to buck and knock his gas mask. It slipped, giving me more exposure. And as he tried to reposition it back in place, his foot caught Blondie's withering frame and he tripped, landing straight in my trajectory.

I dug my finger into his eye and it burst like a crushed grape.

He gripped his face and fell away, coiling into a tight ball, the ground turning both black and red, bane and blood.

He thrashed like a snake severed in half.

The air held a metallic tang. Pine and iron, two scents synonymous with Narivous.

His howl added to the cacophony serenading the forest. It was an opera-worthy performance, the screams the sweetest sounds I'd ever heard.

Blondie and Iron down, the other two guards circled. But they were moving differently, with a lot more care, practiced hunters careful with their placement. It hit me then, why the two I'd just decimated were here—they were wannabes. They wanted to be guards and had opted for this task to try and earn their badges.

The other two were the real deal—most likely stationed on the Southside. Pros, unattached, and ready to come at me with everything they had.

Without any worthless sentiments to get in the way.

I kept reaching, searching, willing my touch to make contact with as much flesh as possible. I grabbed Tattoo's foot and jerked, forcing him off balance and sending him to the ground, where I had easier access to his face. I dug for skin.

It took only a swatch to get to his nerves and set them afire. His powers flared, and my body took flight, almost as if I were an orb.

It took a second to place what was happening. Why I was hovering. Why gravity no longer mattered.

Tattoo was a telekinetic. And although he was withering,

he was a fighter, a warrior to the core, suspending me with his mind, as he fought the poison ravaging beneath the surface of his flesh.

He held me parallel to the trail, with nothing to grab, nothing to touch. *Nothing.* He took away the one weapon I could control.

We were tethered, he and I, by an invisible cerebral link. He grunted from the exertion of keeping me off the ground and ripped off his gas mask to help focus. His face was beginning to deteriorate from where my fingerprints left their bite. Fissures bloomed along his features and they weren't just his powers shining, but mine too.

I was attached to them, my particles. They'd materialized from anger and ire, cords of atrocities that looked as ugly as they felt.

And they were moving in waves on my command. They were still mine.

He had a hold on me, and I had a hold on him.

One of the unknown Animals, his face out of focus, had a bag in his hand. Cougar, his face still twisted in pain, held one too. They were cupping the fabric brim, as if preparing to cocoon it over something.

Or someone.

Tattoo's power was stronger than I could've expected. He kept me suspended, eliminating the only tool I could use, my touch.

If I were to wail, I'd kill everyone—including Dean and Marie.

Still, I grabbed for the second glove, desperate to wrench my hand free, only Tattoo's mind froze me in place, robbing me of all movement.

I wanted to scream, the toxins dancing on my tongue. My body went reactive. Instinct and predatory prowess pulled from the deep wells of my body, far below my self-control, to an internal part that knew no awareness, knew no thought. Wild, free, and wholly primitive.

My lungs grew texture.

My eyes blazed.

Tattoo continued to hold me, allowing for a pissed off Cougar to approach.

Movement cornered around the bend, as two more Velores descended.

Behind, in a different zip code, Marie and Dean fought back.

A shot rang out.

It boomed, louder than anything I'd ever heard. It made my ears bleed, my head clear, and it nullified Tattoo's spell, knocking me free and zapping the buzzing as I collided with the earth.

Faces came into focus.

Cougar buckled, his hands over his ears, his broad shoulders twisting, responding almost as severely as he had to my rancid touch.

No blood. He wasn't hit, it was just the sound. His heightened senses reacted as if someone lit a bomb near his ears.

All the Animals were buckling over, screeching inside their heads.

It made me smile.

But then I laid eyes on Marie. The other guard, Babyface, was holding her in his grasp, his gas mask removed. A dark plum was blooming under Marie's eye. The asshole had hit her, and now he'd pinned her against the earth.

His hand grazed her breast, and a growl erupted from inside my core. He shot me a smile, his fingers flexing, feeling.

Daring me.

Dean was actively being pummeled. One of the newest

Velores who'd made the trail was taking his anger out on his skull.

I couldn't see who it was, couldn't make out anything but red.

Tattoo buckled, clutching his stomach, staunching a trail of purple with his gloved hands, so dark it ran near black.

Dean had aimed his gun at my mental prison warden. Not at the Animals trapping him. Not at the threat closest to him. But at Tattoo. Dean accepted. He accepted this unusual truth and, with it, took out the one person with the power to hold me.

And they were going to kill him for it.

Time was gone. We were all dead.

Babyface shot his attention between me and Marie, his hands roaming her body, skimming her breasts, inching toward her thighs, violating because he could.

Seeing him touch her snapped something deep inside me. The depravity of his leer, the boldness of his act. The promise of what was to come.

I thought of Gram, and Polar's mercy killing. If we were all going to die, at least I could try and make it quick.

A poison death would be painful, but it was far better than the alternative.

I rallied, shattering every shield I'd managed to maintain, and summoned the intensity scrambling to free itself. I beckoned it, and my sight blotted.

If we were going to die, so would everyone else—the gas masks had been knocked away, their lungs were free.

History was about to be made.

My tongue melded, my skin spiked, and I let my brain explode.

I was going to crash the sky on them, bring it down and take us all out.

I snapped my jaw open, unhinging to a full tilt, as my army swarmed. They clambered up my throat, dancing, bouncing, jumping with the desire to unleash.

And as they reached the apex, as the howl started to build, light became dark.

Someone tossed a fistful of Purple Magic at me, before throwing a bag over my head, locking it in, and forcing nothingness to greet me.

CHAPTER 20
A PLAN TO KILL

They left me to mold on the earthy trail, sack over my face, my poison forced down my throat.

The bags weren't just packing vessels, but tools laced in Dexitrol to suffocate my powers. I wasn't sure who slipped the coated fabric over my face, since a plume of Purple Magic assaulted me beforehand, knocking me into a sleep. Chalky film coated my nostrils and mouth. It burned my eyes.

Someone was now at my side, resting a large hand on my shoulder. Even the slightest touch agonized my muscles.

Everything was upside down.

My world. My life. My future.

My perspective twisted to a bleak screen.

I was afraid to rip the bag off, to see what was waiting for me. I kept still, to stop the burn from spreading through my limbs, using what little air leaked through the cotton fabric to brace myself for carnage and heartache.

The hand shook me gently and the bag shifted from around my head, as whoever was at my side began to pull it away.

Light shocked me into a wince.

Jaguar was leaning over, his face cut into a look of sorrow and regret.

Disgust, too, if I wanted to be completely honest.

"You need to get up," he said. "They're waiting on you at the castle."

I tried to move, but my bones ached and pain shot through me.

Jaguar grabbed my arm, using my own cloak as a barrier, and urged me into a sitting position. Everything tipped. I glanced toward the spot where I'd last seen Marie and Dean, and found it blissfully empty.

Relief lightened the pain, until I spotted gore blanketing the forest.

Blood. The color of rubies and not of amethyst, the marker of human wounds versus Velore, stuck to the earth like sap. Well on its way to drying in the midday warmth, it got me to my feet.

I staggered, my skull filling with pressure, a throb tugging on my temples.

Jaguar steadied me, letting go only when I lost my sway.

I stared at the spot where most of the blood had congealed. It had a force to it, a magnetism—I couldn't look away.

"You've got to hurry," Jaguar said. "They're expecting you."

I wanted to ask if they were okay. I really wanted to. But the answer ... I shuddered. I didn't know if I could stomach it.

I did, however, formulate one question. "Did you know?"

Had he known all along they were going to bait me with my own heart? Was this part of their play? Part of their ruse? Befriend me, confuse me, and then crush me when I let my guard down?

He shook his head, something like shame making his mammoth size smaller. "I had no clue ... about all this." He gestured toward the trail, where Dean and Marie had hemorrhaged. I tried to calculate the blood, appraise it, wondering how much they'd lost, if they could survive the deficit. "So is it true?" Jaguar asked. "Were you going to commit treason?"

He took a step away, as if voicing his suspicions could contaminate him. As if I were already guilty.

"No." I shook my head and fought back the bleating pulse. "No, I swear it. It wasn't anything like that."

He pursed his lips. "You set your grandma's house on fire."

"Yeah, but it's—"

"Mom said you were plotting to kill Thorn."

"No, I don't know—"

"And the day you set it on fire, you asked JC to cover your shift."

"I just thought it was better—"

"And I went along with it."

"I'm sor—"

"You've implicated me in your treason." He took another step away, his fingers curling into fists.

"It wasn't treason."

Jaguar stood there, his shoulders square, his muscles rigid. "Then what was it?"

"This isn't the time." I needed to muster the courage to ask about Marie and Dean, and I couldn't do it under the barrage of questioning.

A moment. I needed a moment.

"The hell it's not." He swallowed, his massive boulder of an Adam's apple bobbing. "They have your family. If you want them alive, you're gonna have to explain yourself, because Mom's convinced Thorn it was treason. She thinks you were plotting against the crown."

Hope. Something like hope flowed through my skin. He said family. Meaning both. Meaning maybe ...

I opened my mouth and then clamped it shut. A thought

struck me. "Does your mom know you and JC covered my shift?"

It was a bizarre tangent, but maybe, maybe Thorn still didn't know about the house. Maybe Amelia hadn't told her. To do so, she'd be putting her kittens at risk.

Maybe she'd convinced Thorn via another trajectory.

Maybe I could still save them.

Jaguar nodded. He turned and lifted his shirt. Lash marks stretched across his back. They were puffy and swollen, with specks of white at the edges, leftovers from a balm, perhaps.

"Mom rubbed salt into them," he said, releasing his grip. "She was so angry. Said you were likely to get us killed if Thorn found out." He kept his tone subdued, so not even the trees could hear.

"It wasn't a plot on—"

"JC got the same treatment." He leaned closer. "Thorn doesn't know we helped you. Mom punished us on her own."

I slumped and rubbed my face. "I'm sorry. I'm so sorry." And I really was. I thought since they didn't ask questions they could escape repercussions. Deniability. Instead, I'd landed them in boiling water.

"Stop being sorry and tell me why you did it. I need to know why."

"If Thorn doesn't know you helped, does she know about the house?"

He snorted. "Of course."

"But—"

"She just doesn't know how you pulled it off," he clarified. The information was priceless. I needed to know who our players were. The fewer, the better. "Mom said it was your scent at the house. Too new to be from back when you were human."

I crouched low, trying to stop the tilting of the forest. And when I stood back up, I asked, "Anyone else brought in?"

Torti, Dreams, Ferno, any of the Brilliants? The list was long.

He narrowed his gaze. "They've been checking cameras. They think it's suspicious the parking garage was out for maintenance. Known to happen though. But still, yeah. I think Chanticlaim may be in trouble. They also think it's weird arsons started picking up around the same time. But copycats usually get the idea from somewhere. And, of course ... Fancy." He moved an inch closer, his massive feet light as lion's paws. "I thought you were liking it here."

Amelia had really done it, even while rubbing salt into his wounds. If she could get to Jaguar, who I'd started to consider a friend—and who wasn't paranoid beyond reason—that meant Thorn was as good as convinced.

Screwed. We were all screwed.

"It's not what you're thinking. It's ... I did it ..." I stumbled, unsure. Fantasia's life was at stake. I glanced back at the red-stained forest floor. Each word I spoke was either going to be a nail in a coffin or a move to yank one out.

Jaguar followed my gaze.

"You could still save them."

Them. That word again. Two, not one. Both were alive.

An indication there was still time to fix this. I looked toward the bag, thankful they hadn't let me unleash. Thankful for a second chance.

"But you're gonna have to explain why you did what you did—assuming, of course, it wasn't treason. And if you can't explain it to me, then they're as good as gone. If you weren't plotting, why'd you burn it down?" Jaguar's brow furrowed, his stare strong.

"It's complicated ..."

"I think I've earned a right to know." He indicated his back, his dark eyes glinting.

A feminine voice breached our space before I could answer. "Why do you think?" Torti stepped out from behind the trees and approached us. Her stalk the same as a predator's.

She appeared more feline than Amelia.

Fantasia's sister placed her hand on my back and spoke without the slightest quiver. "His aunt wouldn't stop looking for him. Didn't believe he was a runaway. *Refused* to believe it." She pulled out a piece of paper hidden within her cloak and handed it to Jaguar. "She was papering nearby towns with flyers—his face was everywhere. Offering hefty rewards for his return." Her jaw flexed, as she twitched a smile. Even deep in boggy shit, she managed to maintain confidence. "It would only take a minimal amount of prying before they started scouting the woods. Money brings out all sorts of characters, and they'd just have to catch wind that Daniel liked the forest, and bam"—she snapped her fingers—"we'd have a search party on our hands."

Jaguar was squinting at the flyer as Torti fed me my lines.

My gratitude was beyond measure.

"Death even tried calling them, ya know?"

I winced, and Jaguar captured the move. He cocked his head, and Torti gave a convincing smile.

"It's okay," she breathed, placing her hand on my back. "You can be honest now."

Follow her lead.

I nodded.

"We tried to do it as a courtesy," Torti said. "That's why he was hanging out with Fantasia. She was his recruiter, she felt a responsibility for this mess, and they took it upon themselves to clean it up on their own. They didn't involve the Seven because they thought it was a simple fix."

"But the house?" Jaguar asked.

Torti laughed. It trickled down my spine like a cold chill. She shuffled her feet and looked down, the picture of ease. "When Death tried to convince them he was out of state, they offered the house as bait. They thought they could get him home as long as he had his grandmother's house to return to. Death, as a loyalist, sought to sever that bond. Take away their bartering tool." She squeezed my shoulder in a reassuring manner. "It'll be fine once you explain."

Jaguar handed the flyer to Torti, who put it back in the folds of her cloak.

"Why didn't you just tell us? All of this"—he spread his arms—"could've been stopped."

"No one asked," I shot out. Torti nodded. We were a united front. She'd given me a trail of breadcrumbs, and it was enough of a lead to guide us from this disaster. "I thought no one noticed. And if they did, I thought they'd ask me. Instead, they lock me up and plan sneak attacks."

I buckled, acting like I was about to heave. Not entirely an act. My stomach was churning with something awful, like regret.

Or stupidity.

The practicality of her argument, the way she wove fact with fiction, was so seamless I practically lost the ability to breathe. Locked up in my cell, with nothing but my mind for company, I should've formulated a similar answer. I should've thought of it. Screamed it at the guards, made them listen.

Jaguar lost his hostility. He squinted in the direction of the city. "Well, you better tell them that."

Torti gave me a short jab in the back and urged me to straighten up.

It was time to go.

We followed the blood trail. The scent of iron laced the forest, the smell more pungent than the evergreens.

Jaguar halted before the gates came into focus. He stumbled over his own feet, a very un-Animal-like move.

"I'm gonna go ... somewhere else."

Torti nodded, and he waited, as if she'd go with him. She didn't flinch and motioned with her head for him to go.

It made me wonder what was waiting.

I was too scared to ask.

Jaguar held out my gloves. I'd forgotten them and hadn't even noticed them in his grip. He waited for me to put them on and, as soon as I sheathed my fingers, held out his hand.

We shook, a first, and he muttered something not entirely clear.

It felt like an unsteady goodbye—final, as if he wasn't sure I'd be coming back.

He turned and left us, shooting me one more glance before launching into a full sprint, disappearing in a second.

Torti, pale as a corpse, scanned over the timber and, seemingly satisfied, tugged me into the brush. The ferns, made massive by Thorn's magic, absorbed us as if we were a figment.

She leaned in close, stopping just a sliver away from my face.

"They have Fantasia," she hissed. "I need you to pull your head out of your ass and save her."

I nodded.

"I've given you the story you need to tell. Regurgitate it, but make it your own."

She paused and looked at me. Really looked at me. What washed over her expression was an emotion hard to place.

A few tense, never-ending seconds passed before she tucked a lock of curly hair behind her ear.

Whatever she was about to share sucked the might right out of her.

"I'm sorry," she lipped. "I should've seen this. I should've caught this."

Dean. Marie.

"It's not your—"

She held up a hand and shook her head. "Let me finish. Let me say what I came here to say." She surveyed the forest. We hunkered farther down and put our heads together—two conspirators working toward a common cause.

"I never thanked you, for talking Fancy into recruiting that human." Ages ago. She was bringing up events from ages ago. And I realized then, what all this was. She was saying goodbye, too.

I could, perhaps, save my family. I could save Fantasia. But I wasn't going to save myself. Torti knew. She was familiar with the spokes and gears of Narivous, she knew how things worked out.

Or in my case, how things didn't work out.

"You'll always have my gratitude. *Always.* I'm sorry I didn't stop this. I'm ... sorry." She placed a hand over her heart and looked at me as if she could extend a piece of it. "They are going to interrogate you hard, Daniel. *Hard.* And I don't know how you'll come back from this, not after the guard attack."

I nodded. I'd figured as much.

"But I need you to ..." She waited, worrying on her lip, teeth of white against blush rose. Her shoulders lifted as she took in a breath of air. "I need you to make me a promise. No matter how hard it gets, the cruel things they say, do not, under any circumstances, tell her you burned down the house because you and Fantasia have romantic feelings for each other. Don't do it."

"Of course—"

She grabbed my hand, a move that shut me up.

"It's going to be brutal in there, but just know your fate is sealed. Don't take Fantasia to the grave with you. Please. Thorn wants to spare her, I'm certain of it. Otherwise, she'd be dead already."

I winced at her cutting words.

"Legacy, Daniel. That's the true test of immortality. Be remembered for your sacrifice, your power. Don't let them taint your memory."

Her speech was too smooth, too flawless, it felt second hand, as if she'd used it before. I wondered if she'd said as much to Chugknot right before he'd died. Had she quoted his legacy as a tool to keep him compliant?

To stop him from narcing?

I was being manipulated, I knew it. And Torti looked away as if she knew I knew. She dropped my hand, rubbing her forearms to warm herself.

Her concern was wasted.

No one was going to die today, if I could help it. Well, aside from myself. But that didn't really count.

"You're worrying over nothing," I said.

"You say that now."

"I know I'm not coming out of this alive, which is okay."

She didn't deny it.

"And I won't take Fantasia down with me."

"It's gonna be hard."

"I know."

"It's just ... she's my sister."

"Don't worry about it." I gave her a weak smile. "I'll take the fall. I'd pick her over me any day."

Her green irises shot me a look of pure gratitude.

There was also a tinge of guilt, but that was buried far

below the surface, in a vulnerable spot she wasn't accustomed to sharing.

Even my looming execution wasn't enough to break the barrier. Not that I would've asked her to.

We would pretend.

I stood up and started for the city, forcing bravado I didn't feel, and stopped when Torti grabbed my hand. She wove her fingers through mine, a gesture so affectionate I nearly broke.

She looked up, and it dawned on me how other Velores could fall head over heels for her. Her magnetism was as strong as Fantasia's, only she shared it with very few people.

It was a light, and when she chose to show it, you couldn't help but bask in its warmth.

I squeezed back. "It'll be okay."

"Daniel?"

"Yeah?"

"I'm sorry ... for everything. For ... for what's going to happen."

"It's okay," I said.

She smiled, accepting my lie.

She handed me a vial of Dexitrol powder. "Take this," she whispered. "All of it. So you don't slip up."

I did as she asked, trusting her to the core.

We walked the rest of the way in silence—hand in hand. Right before we made the main entrance, she stopped and unlaced her fingers.

"Brace yourself," she said.

I nodded, but she seemed disappointed.

"No." She shook her head. "You don't get it."

We were only an arch away from the gates.

She grabbed my hand for a second time. "It's Dean."

"What do you mean, it's Dean?" My pores tingled, despite

the Dexitrol. Dean was alive, surely. That's what they meant when they said "them."

Both Jaguar and Torti had referred to my family in plural form.

The light faded from Torti, and I heard her heart thump as color bloomed along her collarbone, reaching her neck, invading her cheeks.

"You said 'th-them,'" I stammered.

"Please, I need you to keep your wits about you."

"Who is 'them'?"

She shook her head.

"WHO?"

She pulled back and dropped my hand.

Something in me snapped. I barreled forward, bridging the distance. My feet stumbled beneath me as I came upon the wrought iron fencing, and I faltered from the garish sight dangling from a tree limb above the gates.

The rope creaked with the weight of Uncle Dean, hanging from a noose. His body turned inside out, intestines spilled.

I stopped moving, lost in a haze, burning up the Dexitrol, until the soft buzzing dulled the ache in my chest.

Despite the macabre image, the way it collapsed my heart and turned my blood to lead, it was what someone dared to carve into the flesh on his forehead, desecrating his body to send a message, that readied my body for war.

A name.

Mine.

Death.

Thorn had selected my title well.

I was going to prove her right.

CHAPTER 21

DAY OF DEATH

As Dean swayed like an ornament, my mind wrapped around the word "them."

Torti caught up and stood silently by my side. A hazy mist curled around my body, my aura as toxic as the underlying poison feeding my system.

Smoke. Smoke wove around me, weaving in and around, an enveloping fog of hatred.

There were no sentries at the gate, so it was only Dean keeping watch.

Torti and Jaguar had lied. They'd given me false hope, making me believe both Marie and Dean were still breathing. That my sacrifice could perhaps be enough to spare them.

Liars.

My eyes turned black as my soul.

Torti took a step away, recognizing my translucency, the forest backdrop a brilliant emerald curtain to showcase her fear.

A thrum of power ran beneath the surface, but I contained it—held onto it—maintaining my ability to talk.

"You're a liar," I said.

She shook her head.

"You said 'them.' You made me think he was still alive."

"I meant them." Another step away.

I smirked. Of course she did. Torti's one-track mind was cemented with Fantasia.

Not that I blamed her. But still ... *liar.* A flush of searing depravity rumbled along my veins. It sang to me, as glorious as a siren song.

Part of me wanted to unhook my maw and let her taste death.

I chose my words wisely, forcing Dean's image to stick in my mind, while dulling the color—until it was time to call upon it. I needed it to ignite my powers, to sizzle them, to make them beg.

I noted the carved flesh on his forehead. The telltale signs of puckering, inflammation, healing. He'd been branded while still alive.

"I'm going to kill them," I snapped.

Torti reached out and grabbed my arm. "No. No, you're not."

I smiled, and she cowered.

The buzzing gained rhythm, a tempo, as if my own demise buoyed my strength. I was experiencing the fearlessness of my powers. Different than the maze, more like the cemetery.

It was a good fit for the occasion.

Torti stepped closer, recognizing the fade of Dexitrol from my system. "You have to calm down, Daniel. Please. You can't go in like this."

"I can and I will. They won't live." I appraised her and nudged toward Dean, his image fully ingrained. "We can't let monsters like this live."

She grabbed the front of my cloak, and her power infiltrated me. It was as if she stabbed me with her energy.

She hesitated, her lips parting and closing, before she said, "I meant *them*." Torti took a deep breath, her green eyes starting to ignite, before she squared her shoulders and said, "They have Lacey."

Ice flooded me. She might as well have doused me with a bucket of water.

I yanked the energy back. Compartmentalizing it.

Until I was ready.

<hr>

THE CASTLE HAD BECOME A TOMB, with only our footsteps for company. Velores manifested in corners, lurking within the safety of the shadows, but they stopped breathing, afraid my treason was contagious.

Torti led me underground to the trial room. The same place I met with the Seven on account of Jester.

We reached the door where JC stood guard. On the floor, crumpled in a heap, was Dreams, her blue eyes icebergs of sorrow. JC attempted to comfort her without ditching his post, his catcher's mitt of a hand resting awkwardly atop her head, mouthing words with zero volume.

Too many sharp ears in the next room.

He glanced regretfully at Torti and me.

Dreams looked up and hiccuped. She started to sob, and Torti kneeled low, cradling her in her arms. Cooing softly and stroking her hair.

It made me want to cry.

Not just for Dean hanging from a tree branch, or Lacey, Marie, and Fantasia, but for everyone.

For Polar and Ferno, who helped cover my tracks, building a string of arsons to detract attention.

For Dreams, who lost Fred.

For Camille, Torti, Chanticlaim, Jaguar, and JC. All of them. They'd all paid a price, for a debt that wasn't theirs.

JC took a step toward me. He leaned in and said, "It's a small room inside," meaning the audience. "Take from it what you will, but it's a good sign."

I nodded, grateful.

JC righted himself and said loudly enough so any eavesdroppers behind the steel door could hear, "They've been waiting for you," and swung it open.

⚜

As JC promised, the room was rather hollow. A few spectators lounged in the seats circling the podium, and the Seven present—all except Frigid and Serpent—stood in a semi-circle around Thorn, who remained seated on her dais.

All the husbands were excluded from this event, to minimize interference, surely. Or maybe they were being penalized for their involvement—like setting fires to deflect attention. *Maybe.*

I shook the thought from my head as the rulers turned on my approach.

My eyes reached for Scream, whose face became a mask. Cold crept into her coal eyes, and she placed a hand on Thorn's shoulder. A statement of whose side she was on.

She, too, believed I was plotting against her queen.

JC said they'd always side with Thorn, that anyone going against the reign was fighting a past that couldn't be rewritten. Puncture proof.

Her resting palm spoke volumes.

I searched the room for a friendly face, wondering if I should've confided in Scream more. Told her the truth. About me, about my feelings for Fantasia. About everything.

Perhaps she could've been an ally, and while Amelia whispered words of treason, she could've whispered words of loyalty.

Too late. I was too late.

Marie, Fantasia, and Lacey were nowhere to be found.

Amelia took a few steps forward, her sharp feline face breaking into a smile. I clenched my hand and bowed low so Thorn wouldn't mistake the anger flashing in my eyes as a threat against her.

Amelia turned to Thorn, who was wearing her formal attire, crown included.

"I see the traitor has come to pay us a visit," Amelia said.

Somehow, I managed to keep my expression flat, giving her nothing, even in the face of such a petulant gloat.

Scream twitched, however, softening a fraction.

"I believe that's a bit premature, Amelia," Scream replied, her tone smooth as silk. "We haven't heard his argument."

"Yes, but he attacked my husband. He attacked our guards. That is treason with or without explanation." She pretended to be affronted—talking down to Scream as if she were an irrational child.

Scream's eyes flashed, and Amelia jutted her chin.

"He was thrown into a frightening position," Scream hissed. It seemed she hadn't lost complete faith in me. "Instinct isn't forethought. And the weight of translucency, especially for the unseasoned, is a tricky state to navigate."

"It's no excuse."

"No, it's truth. We make allowances for new Velores."

"To the extent we allow them to attack our own kind?"

"To any extent necessary!" Scream barked. "We must give them a chance to learn. And you knew—*KNEW*—the heavy toll it'd take when he encountered his own blood on that path, and still, you recommended it. You wanted him to fail. You designed it."

"We always challenge our newest members. To check their loyalties. Why should he be any different?" Amelia smirked. "Oh, that's right. Because of his 'gifts.'" She air quoted the last part. "He's special and deserves to be coddled." She leaned forward. "Considering his lethal abilities, I think we need to test him to his limit. To see if we should destroy him before he discovers the strength of his roar." Amelia threw a finger at me, her nails carved to spears, almost as sharp as the claws sheathed beneath her skin. "We can't take chances with his powers!"

"He shares the same gifts as me." Scream grew haughty. Hope continued to filter in. "And I, too, struggled to manage it in the beginning. I'm just thankful no one gave up on me. That no one threw my heart at me and told me to watch it die." Her gloved hand, still resting on Thorn's shoulder, flexed. It was barely discernible, but Thorn's lip twitched.

"Whose side are—" Amelia snarked, before Thorn shut her down.

"Enough," Thorn said, holding up her hand, silencing the pair.

Amelia huffed and lifted her angular face.

Thorn nodded toward Scream, giving her an unspoken token, one that caused Amelia to balk. Scream removed her hand to cover her mouth, hiding a smirk.

It was, without a doubt, an indicator of the direction we were heading.

So help me, things were looking better by the minute.

As long as I didn't allow myself to dwell on Dean.

"Amelia," Thorn spoke, her tapered fingers running along the arm of her throne. "Go fetch Fantasia."

Amelia ducked her head and disappeared out a back door on the far wall. Thorn's casual dismissal had sucked the wind from her sails. She shot me no more looks. It was almost enough to make me smile.

Almost.

With Amelia removed, the room lightened. Even the spectators lost their tension. I spotted Chanticlaim sitting in the far back. He fidgeted uncomfortably and, when he caught my gaze, gave me a sad smile.

Thorn motioned for the remaining rulers to take their seats, and they all obeyed. Thorn wasn't scowling, nor was she smiling. It was as if she were merely inconvenienced.

"Come closer," Thorn said, waving me forward. I positioned myself below the first step and took a knee. It earned me a glint of approval. She almost smiled.

Scream gave a subtle nod.

"My Queen."

"The investigation has been completed, my darling," Thorn said. "The findings I dare not believe."

I ducked my head even lower, before petitioning her gaze with my own. Respect, I'd give her endless respect.

And I wouldn't think of Dean.

Or Marie.

Or Lacey.

Or Fantasia.

Because those thoughts would be catastrophic. They would pull me into my powers and end all hope.

"Stand, Death," Thorn commanded. "And tell me your secrets."

I stood and righted my spine. Thorn sat stock-still, her

hands resting on the arms of her throne. Dolly and Ember both had a glazed look about them, as if detached.

But that could change quickly.

So I dove in. Regurgitating Torti's story, adding my own embellishments, punctuating it with "pleases" and "sorries."

Giving myself all the blame.

I stopped when the door swung open. I was pretty much done anyway, needing only a few more apologies to saturate the grovel. Fantasia entered, Amelia quick on her heels. Thorn motioned for me to take a few steps back.

Fantasia's hands were shackled in front of her, her rich hair heavy with grime. Dirt and body odor overpowered her cinnamon scent. Blood from where they took off her finger still stained her clothing.

They hadn't allowed her to change or clean up—not even a simple hand wash. There were dark pockets under her eyes, and her complexion was ashy. She looked starved, her movements hungry. Fantasia obviously had been kept in complete isolation.

If Torti saw her now, even she'd struggle to hold on to her composure.

Fantasia kept her head hung and fell to her knees in front of Thorn, who grew bigger by the second.

The walls were screaming, closing in.

A smug Amelia folded her arms. My nerves raged.

The manacles clanged with each breath Fantasia took. They'd broken her, ripped apart who she was, and now I was staring at a breathing shell.

Amelia stood beside her prize, broadcasting every tooth, the way a hunter poses with its kill.

Thorn watched the three of us, taking her time before speaking. "Death has recounted his version of events," she started.

"Without me?" Amelia asked, insulted.

"Tone," Thorn admonished, and Amelia gave a slight tilt of her head. "I have your account, I've heard it countless times." Thorn touched her fingers to her lips, looking between Fantasia and myself. I tried to edge closer to Fantasia when Thorn's head was turned. I managed only an inch before she captured the movement.

Thorn never missed anything.

Scream tilted her head to the side and mouthed the word, "Careful."

I froze, not daring to flinch.

Thorn cocked her head ever so slightly, aware her Poison leader was giving advice.

"Scream, darling"—Thorn's voice dropped to an intimate purr—"I excluded the others to prevent interference, please don't make me dismiss you."

Scream's black diamond hairpins flickered as she ducked her head. "My apologies."

Thorn merely smiled. "Just see to it, it doesn't happen again. You wanted to be here, and I've permitted it ... *barely*. Don't make me regret my decision."

The reprimand deflated Scream and brought a smile to Amelia, which Thorn shot down with a stabbing glance.

"I'm about to dismiss everyone," Thorn continued, her nails digging into the insignia carved along the arm rest. "Unless tongues are held." She gave me a curt smile and eyed Fantasia. "It's rather sad seeing this sorry state of affairs," she remarked, taking in her dingy clothes, her skin caked with blood and soil. "How many times, Fantasia, do we need to be here? How many times do we need to go through this? I've heard Death's recounting, and now I want to hear your version. If they match, I'm likely to be lenient."

Lenient. A beautiful word.

With Fantasia's mind-reading capabilities, no matter how spotty, we could make this work. She would know. She could read it. Unless, of course, she was having one of her blind moments.

But there were a number of Velores who'd heard my tale. She could skip down the line and choose whoever's head was easiest to gain access to.

Do. It. *Read them.*

I didn't realize I'd stopped breathing until I grew light-headed. The color of my translucency ready to flare.

Fantasia lifted her head. Her skin may have been sallow, but her eyes were bright. She gave me a look, one filled with defiance. Glinting, powerful, and strong.

I almost groaned, knowing what she was going to do right before she did it.

Either she was suicidal or she couldn't see—stress blocking her sight—or maybe she was too afraid to search the room for a more pliable head.

Whatever the reason, she threw herself over me.

"We weren't plotting against the crown," she said. Thorn nodded, expecting as much. "But I don't want to lie to you."

Thorn arched a brow, her color flushing. "Well, I would hope not, since I'd be inclined to take your head off your shoulders."

Fantasia swallowed and lipped the words, "I'm sorry," in my direction.

I shook my head, and Thorn hissed. "Don't you dare interrupt, Death." She speared a heavily dressed finger at me, her amethyst ring glinting. "You'll only make this worse. Spit it out, Fantasia."

With her head held high and her body folded on her knees, Fantasia said the one thing I was afraid of.

The one thing that would take the blame from me.

The one thing Torti asked me *not* to say.

The one thing I'd always wanted to hear.

"Death has stolen my heart. I wanted to be with him."

Thorn cackled like a witch, and Amelia's eyes blazed.

"I knew it," Amelia spoke under her breath, her canines glinting.

Thorn captured it. "What do you mean, you knew it?"

"I told you"—Amelia held her strong, thin hands in front of her—"how guilty they looked."

"No." Thorn angled forward. "You've been spending all your hours convincing me they were plotting, but this ... this tells me they were working toward something else and not my crown. And if you knew, but decided to serve your own agenda ..." Thorn leaned back and wagged her finger. "Tsk. Tsk. Bad form, Amelia. Bad form. It's enough to make me want to take your finger—the same as you took Fantasia's."

Amelia bored into me, as if Thorn's trajectory were somehow my fault, and while she was busy incinerating me with her stare, I kept my eyes on Thorn, who held a glimmer of a smile.

It was a telling upturn of the lips.

I don't think Thorn ever thought it was treason.

She just let everyone think that to justify whatever was going to happen next.

Steel couldn't be twisted, and Thorn was forged from fire. Amelia wasn't capable of manipulating her. No one was.

"Who says they weren't doing both?" Amelia spat, her eyes back on her queen. "Fantasia's a whore, and whores are practiced at using their bodies to manipulate. I wouldn't put it past her to promise him sex *and* a kingdom. She needs power to steal your reign, and Death is simply a tool."

Thorn's crown seemed to radiate. She tapped her fingers in rhythm—the only sound to be heard in a room that had grown deathly quiet. "This is all so interesting," Thorn remarked, her attention starting to wander, as if what she was going to deliver didn't matter. "Death and I spoke while he was in lockdown. You remember, right?" She turned her cunning gaze back on me.

I winced. I'd already confessed to my crush back in the cell. I said I was the one who pushed it.

Now Fantasia voiced the opposite.

I wasn't dumb enough to know the rope wasn't tightening. That she'd given us just enough to hang ourselves.

Thorn kept on. Only helping us adjust the noose.

I swallowed and nodded, willing my face not to open. "You told me you had a crush on her ... that she was the innocent. That the meeting was innocent. But now, I hear this." She snapped her fingers. "Which one of you dares lie to your sovereign?"

"He was protecting me!" Fantasia interjected. "He is an innocent. Nothing happened, so it isn't a lie. It was never a lie. I've been pursuing him. Me. It's just been me, and since neither of us have acted on it, there was nothing to confess." She gave me a sideways look before turning back to Thorn. "And I would never try to take your crown. I've only ever wanted to serve you, to make you happy."

"Well, at least one part of your story aligns. Death said as much." Thorn ran her hand along her dress, smoothing it out. "But do you really expect me to believe he didn't reciprocate in his affections?"

Fantasia shook her head. "He didn't want to go against your laws or risk my life. I was the one who pushed him."

"Fantasia, stop—" I started. Scream hissed.

Thorn pivoted in her chair, glaring at my lace-clad aunt. Scream bit her lip and tried to shrink into her throne.

Thorn stood up, and the others followed suit. She strolled

down the steps, her long lavender cloak rippling behind her, and motioned for Fantasia to stand.

Fantasia obeyed quickly, but her head never really rested comfortably on her neck. It's like she forgot how to stand tall.

Thorn looked between me and Fantasia. I wanted this act to be over with. Curtain call. End scene.

"Bring in the others," Thorn said to Amelia. "I think it's time."

I focused on the floor, centering my composure and forcing my powers back.

Amelia nearly skipped out the door. When she returned, she had Marie, her shirt stiff with blood, her sleeve ripped, a trident gash down the length of one arm.

Her face was surprisingly blank.

Thorn narrowed her gaze.

"Has she been given something?" Thorn inquired.

"It looks like it." Amelia curled her lip and said to Dolly, "You can read minds even while sedated. Who gave it to her?"

Dolly made a show of leaning forward and squinting in Marie's direction, as if my aunt were far away and not standing in front of her.

"Her mind is mist, I see nothing."

The lie poured out easily. If Chanticlaim's brain blockers couldn't shut off Dolly's switch, I doubted anything could. Not to say someone hadn't slipped Marie a cocktail—there were other Doppelgängers present, and to keep them blind, someone had to have used a selection of pharmaceuticals in Chanticlaim's stash.

Only the culprit and Dolly would know the truth.

Again, she was protecting. *Again*. If I lived past this, I was going to pay it forward.

Amelia coiled tighter. "Someone is going to suffer for this," she spat. "We'll wait it out, until it wears off."

Thorn waved her hand. "I'm not waiting it out. It's rather irrelevant, anyway."

I nearly crumbled with relief.

Someone, an angel of mercy, had numbed Marie's mind. Whatever was about to happen, she wouldn't see it, she wouldn't hear it.

She wouldn't know it.

"But surely—" Amelia started.

Thorn scowled and halted Amelia before she could push forward. "Let it go. I'm growing bored."

Fissures shattered Amelia's skin, her claws on full display. "But—"

"I said I'm done waiting. Bring in the other."

The little bit of light Amelia had was gone in an instant. I made a mental note.

Ways to hurt Amelia: take control from the control freak.

Amelia disappeared for a second time, and Thorn stepped close to Fantasia, wrinkling her nose at the odor.

"Such a sad state to be in," Thorn reiterated, just as Amelia returned, this time cradling Lacey in her arms. She, too, was heavily sedated; her eyes were shut, as if lost in sleep.

My heart hammered.

The air grew thin.

The buzzing swarmed my head, particles building, a pure, primal, instinctual reaction. The room filled with a fog, heat and rage hazing the domed underground snare.

"Easy, Death," Thorn cooed. "You're going to want to keep your mind at bay."

Amelia placed Lacey on the ground at Marie's feet. Marie remained emotionless, stiff bodied and glazed.

She was a sleepwalker in her own dream, a better alternative to the nightmare taking place in standard time.

Thorn circled the room. Heads dipped with respect as she passed.

She hesitated near the center podium and admired the sight of her rulers in silent stay, eyes on her, awaiting her command. The only one disconnected from Thorn's performance was Dolly. The once-bored Doppelgänger was now at full attention, zeroed in on Lacey.

Her blue eyes, usually shrouded with disinterest, were wide with alarm. She wrung her hands in front of her. Thorn, ever vigilant, gave Dolly a cursory smile.

"You're excused," she said, snatching Dolly's attention. Dolly's shoulders wilted at the dismissal, and she moved swiftly to the door behind me. Fleeing the trial, fleeing our future.

My stomach lurched.

Amelia's face twitched, and even though her lips remained flat, her eyes were smiling.

Thorn approached my side and surveyed me. "It's testing time," she said, her face cold and cutting, spiking my adrenaline.

The colors began to wash together, riveting prisms, a kaleidoscope no one else could see.

My power thrummed.

Thorn snapped her fingers, and Chanticlaim stepped forward from the small audience. His eyes downcast, he held a thick chain attached to an antique pocket watch with the initials R.S. carved across the face. It was in sad shape, too. Tarnished. A bit banged up. Someone had worn off the polish, as if they'd stroked the bronze metal one too many times, imprinting their mark.

Chanticlaim bowed and said, "My Queen."

"As we discussed," Thorn commanded.

Chanticlaim, with a regretful twist, tugged on his sleeves.

He went up to Marie and started to remove her shirt, unhooking each button with careful precision. He peeled it away, leaving her standing in only a bra, shivering against the cold and the company.

A horrible violation. I wanted to hug whomever dulled her senses. Embarrassment burned my ears.

Chanticlaim tied up her hair with a clip, exposing the arc of her neck. He hung the watch, which fell almost to her navel and stepped away.

I started to connect the pieces, and fear stole the blood from my limbs.

Thorn looked at me. "Take off your gloves."

I hesitated, and Thorn's face molded to menace. "Do it, or you'll make this worse."

With a tremble, I started to remove the mesh. Chanticlaim mouthed from behind Thorn's back, "Focus," before standing off to the side.

Thorn ran her hands along my shoulders. She stepped behind me and, in a voice that pulled on every fiber of my being, said, "Take the watch from her neck. Deliver it to me and I will give you leniency."

Leniency. That word again.

She could happily put it on repeat. It made my marrow light.

Leniency.

For Marie. For Lacey. For Fantasia.

There was still time to undo this.

With the aid of amnesia pills given to Marie and Lacey they could rewrite history. They could make Dean a wayward husband, running from responsibility toward a better life. They can make anyone disappear. They could feed her mirages.

There was still a way.

"You said you could replicate it," Thorn whispered into my

ear. "I've spared you. I've spared Fantasia, for this moment. Prove to me you can do it." Thorn squeezed my shoulder and pushed me forward. "Deliver the watch to me."

My vision grew blotchy.

Thorn smiled at the spectators, bodies winnowing to shadows.

Witnesses.

The walls palpitated. My power thrummed.

Amelia relaxed, practically purring, convinced I was bound to screw up.

And with every ounce of strength I possessed, I searched for the same pull back in the maze. The same sensation.

The toxin crawled beneath the surface, and Laquet's teaching echoed. I dulled the color, despite the bursting frenzy.

I approached Marie. My hands shaking. I wouldn't look toward Lacey, slumped at her feet. I couldn't. To see her, to really take her in, would shatter my resistance, which was crumbling by the second.

I became a shade of human.

I grabbed the chain, my fingers grazing flesh, real human flesh, noting the warmth of it.

Dull the color. Erase it. The mantra played over and over in my head.

The room held its breath, as I plucked the ornament from its place.

Marie's skin stayed pink.

And the room erupted into excited murmurs as I, for the second time, defeated the demon. I became a master of the monster.

It was all I had left.

I approached Thorn, the chain held out triumphantly.

Something like relief swept through my body. Thorn beamed as I delivered it into her waiting palm.

"This is how I hoped it would end," she said, her words awe-filled. She turned toward the entrance doors and gave an unspoken command. A Velore stepped forward and swung the steel open, where two masked guards were waiting. They passed through the threshold and took their place on each side of Thorn, flanking her. She nodded in my direction and took a step away, broadening our berth, her knuckles bone white around her trophy.

The guards kept their colorless eyes on me.

My gut tightened as I took in their masks, slabs of white, a hybrid between hockey and phantom. They wore head-to-toe clothing, gloves included, and held black bags—same as in the forest.

Dexitrol, along with musky fear, drifted to my nostrils.

"It has to be this way," Thorn said and nodded toward Amelia.

Amelia stepped behind Lacey.

The guards inched forward, and as I darted my gaze between the masked invaders and Amelia, a crack shattered the room.

With too-quick hands, practiced and steady, Amelia had gripped Lacey's small head and twisted.

Her neck snapped like a wishbone.

The explosion that followed rumbled the room.

It came from the depths of my soul.

EPILOGUE

They made me watch. The bags became improvised gags, thrown over my mouth to stop any potential wails. The guards pinned me in place. I was too dulled by the Dexitrol-laced fabric to put up much fight.

Every sordid detail stained. I could've closed my eyes, but I couldn't *not* know.

The door behind Marie opened as Lacey crumpled to the floor.

Another guard, in a raven mask and a sweeping cloak of feathers, black as night, stepped forward with an ancient axe. The handle was worn and the sharpened head marred by rust.

An executioner.

Marie, lost in her fog, saw nothing.

She didn't realize her daughter lay dead at her feet.

Nor that the Reaper was closing in behind her.

The gloss of the feathers rippled as he lifted the axe—a bird's grace—and swung, severing her head in a single blow.

The impact was so forceful, her head rolled to a stop just

feet from me. Her eyes were brighter in death than they were in sedation.

Amelia laughed like a deranged hyena, placing her hand over her stomach.

My body sang with fury.

Chanticlaim approached Lacey. He held his hand over her neck, where the break most likely took place, and nodded to Thorn.

He produced a syringe from his jacket. It was filled with something ugly, and my muscles succumbed to rigor mortis. He slipped the needle into her vein and her body began to convulse, twitching with violent spasms. Chanticlaim swooped her into his arms and darted from the room, clenching her to his chest, as the serum began to work its way through her system, bringing her back to life.

Fantasia's face went slack.

Thorn collected Marie's severed head, grasping her locks, and approached the dais.

She held Marie high, angling her so I had the very best view, and gave a speech that went on for decades. It left me shattered.

The gist of it was simple: this was my fault, regardless of intentions.

Had I not burned down the house—motives be damned—Marie and Dean would be alive. Originally, I was set to kill two random females, but since my actions, treason or not, were a direct violation of Narivous' policies they'd altered their decision and chosen my own blood for their ritualistic slaughter. And since Thorn was in a giving mood, and ruling the intent wasn't malicious, she would consider Marie's and Dean's deaths my human sacrifices.

Lucky me.

Thorn accepted Lacey as Fantasia's child recruit, "to free

her conscience." They would make Lacey an Animal, turn her into claws, angles, and sinewy muscles—and Amelia would raise her as her own.

She never said it, but I knew what this was: bait for my obedience. To stop any potential acts against the crown. Thorn had me. Utterly had me.

My heart folded.

I WAS A ZOMBIE.

Literally and figuratively.

I downed enough sedatives that night to put a bull to sleep and allowed darkness to swallow me whole.

But sleep was stolen from me when someone jarred me awake with an urgent shake.

Scream stood over my bed, her gown scandalously revealing—the V dipping to her navel. Formal wear. She must've come from a meeting.

I groggily checked the clock; it was early enough the stars were still out.

"I need to talk with you."

I sat up, wiping the sleep from my eyes, and Scream tutted and snapped her fingers. "Come," she said and disappeared, leaving behind a trail of jasmine to follow. It led me to the screaming room.

Scream sealed the door behind us. The fact she wanted to have a conversation in our toxic closet, where soundproof provisions encapsulated us, sobered me. I stiffened, alert.

"What Amelia did to you was abhorrent." Her flawless face twisted with rage. Black crow's feet, indicators of her power, flexed along her complexion. She grabbed the sides of my jaw, running her thumb against the start of stubble. "But that foolish woman may have hurt her own cause." She released me and stepped back. A smile broke the heavy tone.

My brow furrowed. "What are—"

She held up a hand and spoke slowly. "Do you know why Amelia went after you so hard?"

"Because she hates Fantasia? And thought I was having a relationship with her?"

"Close, but not quite."

I cocked my head, and her teeth glinted.

"She sees the aura pull," she clarified.

"Aura pull?" *Way* over my head.

Scream folded her arms. "It's a rare connection—but an undeniable one. It's a sensation very few Velores experience, but for those who do, they find themselves bound. Tied. We think it has to do with original aura colors. You were—before turned—the exact same shade as Polar. Perhaps a little brighter, but the hue down to a tee. And it's a rarity to find someone who matches perfectly. None of us are certain, but we all suspect Camille was the same shade before she came to Narivous. Our old king brought her here—already changed— so we have no way of knowing, but we've suspected. And, well ..." Conflict flashed over her features. "Polar and Camille have this weird thing. He tries to hide it, and he's tried to quit her countless times, but we all know." When I forgot to feign surprise, she smirked. "Looks like someone's already filled you in."

"I kind of suspected."

"It's okay," she said softly, grabbing my hand and raising it to her lips. A kiss of forgiveness. "Fridge knows, too. It's not a well-kept secret. And I know Polar loves my sister—I've never seen a man so conflicted. And as much as I hate him for it, I can't blame him. Not with ..." She tapped her head, indicating how often Frigid disappeared.

"So this aura pull?" I needed to hear more. I needed something good. Anything. Anything to distract ...

"I think you and Fantasia have matching bases. That's why you two feel such a compulsion toward each other. You're linked by bonding colors. Amelia suspects it too."

This strange thing between us, what her sisters told me was real—was. It made sense.

They would know. Their mother was linked to Polar.

And I was linked to Fantasia. All of a sudden, I wasn't just some stupid, lustful guy. But a bound one.

I wanted to ask a million questions. Why the bond happened with Fantasia. Why I didn't feel the tug with her sisters. Do aura colors remain consistent through generations? From sibling to sibling? What about color consistency when mixed with other Velores? Fantasia was a hybrid after all.

Before I could settle on a single inquiry, Scream continued.

"Amelia will always hate you. She will search for a way to destroy you, because you're a threat to Fantasia's isolation."

I shrugged. "I can't be with her anyway, so I doubt she has much to worry about."

"Don't be so sure." She met my shocked eyes with an arched brow.

"What do you—"

"There's an underground lab."

Again, I forgot to feign surprise, and disgust twisted Scream's mouth.

"Sounds like your little birdie's been busy."

"I, uh. Well ..." I twisted my neck, and my temperature fevered.

"Relax." She waved her hand. "I don't care. But learn to manage your expressions better. Don't let surprise steal your secrets." She angled her head, appraising me. "That lab has been a splinter in my palm. I was so angry when Thorn started having it rebuilt. She tried to hide it, but gossip is a hard force to defeat."

Scream tried to pace, but the closet didn't allow for much stride. "When I questioned her, she told me it was a precaution." Scream snorted, irritated. "And then she used those guards to lure you out of your room and off a cliff, so you'd injure your body and spill poison into the atmosphere. She wanted to justify that stupid room—prove your impulsiveness and cement her case to destroy you. She was excited when you killed Jester. Thought she could end you for it, and we would just accept your death because you'd earned it."

I turned ghost.

"WHAT?"

I don't know why it came as a surprise, Thorn being the mastermind and all, but it did. She'd given me a guilt trip, laying all the blame on my head, when all along it had been her.

My body smoldered.

Scream let out a nervous laugh and touched her throat. "I assumed you knew," she said.

My unhinged jaw said otherwise.

We'd never really discussed Jester. He was the elephant we worked very hard to step around.

"Didn't you wonder why I got so upset when you recounted your story about Jester's passing?" Scream asked.

"Well ... no." Truth was, I was too wrapped up in my own shit to give it much thought.

"It's because the set-up was too convenient. I know how Thorn operates, her mark was all over it."

The edges around my sight blurred, and Scream held up a hand to calm me. "Don't let it fray you. Think of where she was coming from. We scare her. It's the power thrumming through our veins. You know firsthand how powerful we are. It's a legitimate fear." She pulled me into her embrace to soften the blow.

I forced the color down.

"I confronted her and she admitted to the deception," she continued.

"But I proved her right. I was unpredictable."

"No, darling. You proved you have a heart. That's all. And I pointed that out. I also pointed out how insanely gifted you are. I suggested she make you a guard." She grew taller with pride. "I may have even guilted her a little, but that's between you and me." Scream shot me a wink. "And now I'll share another secret with you. I hate Amelia and would like nothing more than to see her rot." She paused and gave me a smile. "Expressions, darling," she admonished. "You must master that face of yours."

"You hate Amelia?" I choked out. The Seven presented themselves as a united front. Even when they disagreed, they were still joined.

"I imagine you share the same sentiment."

I nodded. Hate was a trivialization.

"Once the lab is complete," she said, "we'll hurt her in ways she'll never recover from. We can end the poison curse and torture her in one fell swoop."

"So, you think it's a curse too?"

"It's hard not being able to touch anyone. To always be fearful someone will graze my skin and I'll cause them unnecessary pain. For ages—ever since the day of my transformation —I've wanted to be rid of this malediction. This damned cloud that follows me. And you, you may be my way out. That room was built eons ago, to test on both Plague and me. They even tested on animals specifically made into Poisons. But the testing ... well, the testing is tricky. We couldn't get adequate information out of Plague, because the poison isn't what killed him. And as for me ..." Her voice drifted, and her eyes grew soft. "Thorn forbid any additional testing. But you ..." She rested her forehead against my own. "You may be what we're looking for. And Thorn is prepared to give you anything you want."

I sucked in a lungful of air, not daring to dream.

Scream smiled, and I was blinded.

"You help our cause, and Thorn will give you Fantasia."

The room spun.

Scream cupped my face, our happiness flocking the space. "We will torture Amelia where it hurts. Her pride, her husband's infidelity, will fester. It will be a slow, painful assault, and perhaps, if we get her frazzled enough, we can find a way to eliminate her."

I matched her wicked smile with my own.

"She'll regret her mistakes," Scream said. "Amelia will regret us all."

THE LEGEND

He couldn't figure out if the shake was from rage or annoyance.

Either way, it was a bad sign.

His momma's hands were folded in her lap, fingers intertwined, so strongly clasped even her fleshy knuckles shone bone white—all to stop the tremble. Her obsidian eyes were glossed over; they had a cutting edge to them.

The boy stood uncomfortably in front of her, as if he were on trial, shifting his weight, hoping beyond measure she'd see him. That she'd *really* see him.

For once, he needed her to care.

He shoved his hands into his pockets. Her face, although round and soft, grew sharp with resentment. His stomach lurched, and he wrapped his hand around the pocket watch he kept hidden within the folds of fabric, feeling the ticking heartbeat, trying to pull courage from it.

"You selfish boy," she said. "How can you do this to me?"

He swallowed and tried to fight back tears.

He knew it. Deep down, he knew she wouldn't save him, but she was his last hope. His last chance. Everything else had already been stolen from him.

He had nothing left.

"ANSWER ME!" his momma demanded.

"What do you mean, Momma? Do what?"

She sprang from the couch, moving quicker than he thought possible, and slapped him across the cheek. The move burned in flesh and spirit.

Salt when he sought salve.

"You and your lying mouth!" she spat. He was only an inch or so shorter, but his momma would always tower, and she used her imposing presence to shrink his nerve. "Your father was a worthless man, content to let us sleep with empty bellies in a house full of holes and drafts. Then he died, with no provisions in place to look after us, and we went from poor to nothing!" She thrust him away and lifted her double chin. "Your stepdaddy was kind enough to give us a home, *a home*, with food and clothes on our backs—a warm, soft place to lay. And you want to throw out lies? *Lies?*" She jabbed a finger in his chest. "And in the home he so kindly provided for us?"

"It's not a lie, Momma."

She smiled, so cold it turned his blood to ice—and he knew then, he saw her truth.

She knew where her husband went every night. She knew what he did under the cover of darkness.

She knew.

And she didn't care.

His stepdaddy gave his momma financial support and, in payment, she gave him her son's innocence.

"It's a story you'll never repeat again," she hissed. "And if you do, I'll see to it you regret it."

Shattered, he lost his ability to speak and bolted as

scalding tears trailed down his cheeks. He could hear his momma's heavy breathing, as she sucked in air, taking up all the oxygen in an attempt to calm her rage. He ran to his room and slammed the door behind him. He leaned against it, as if he could keep out the haunting memories that stalked him like a shadow.

He slid to the ground, pulled his knees to his chest, and wept on the floor. He wouldn't cry in his bed, it had already claimed too much from him.

He pulled out the pocket watch and rubbed his thumb across the initials engraved on the cover. His daddy had given it to him. He called it an "heirloom." It was the nicest thing his daddy had owned. The boy stared at it, trying to remember the time when his stomach was empty, but his heart was full.

He wanted his father back.

He was starving again, only this was infinitely worse. He was hollow from lack of love. From cruelty.

⁂

His momma let it go on for years—encouraged it—turning a blind eye, thankful she didn't have to look after the needs of her own husband, content to allow nightfall to shield their secrets.

When the boy entered his thirteenth year, the family picked up and moved to a cabin along the edge of a forest. Whispers had cloaked them for far too long, and they sought privacy where eyes couldn't reach them and ears couldn't eavesdrop.

So the stepfather could fulfill his wicked desires without the threat of interference.

In a surprising twist, the boy found a small measure of happiness in the move, because he had a forest to absolve his hurt. He found comfort in the isolation of timber, in the company of plants, in the suffering of animals.

He filled his time taking back his control. He honed his hunting skills and took down animals of all sizes. He killed squirrels and birds, trapping them in clever nets, taking their lives for no purpose at all.

Aside from the pleasure.

He pinned bird wings to bark, drove nails through the abdomens of squirrels, skinned baby possums alive, hung rabbits from their ears—all for the sake of power.

He would sit and watch until their rapid breathing slowed and their hearts stopped altogether.

He left his mark everywhere and kept track of the landscape by stationing his sacrifices. Horrid ornaments mapping his territory.

As isolated as the forest seemed, it wasn't without occupants. The greenery swallowed independent cabins, homes far from civilization. Humans, just like him, who hated people and preferred the unfeeling company of unanimated timber. He wondered what they were hiding.

And it was a midday summer afternoon, when the sun shone brightest, that the forest's darkest secrets unfolded for him. He came upon a girl sitting on a fallen log next to a riverbed and hid himself behind a tree. To watch her. To drink in her innocence. She was pretty—so pretty he felt a twitch at the auburn hair, hazel eyes, and skin browned by the sun. Evil thoughts ran through his head. Things he could do to her. Things he wanted to do to her. She could make him come alive.

It would be easy.

He smiled, careful not to breathe, not to make a sound.

The girl hummed to herself as she lolled her head from side to side, swaying to her own song. She held her hands parallel to the earth and quieted her tune. Concentration flashed across her features. She wiggled her fingers and took deep, long breaths. A flicker of movement captured his attention as a seedling emerged from the soil, sprouting toward her waiting palms.

He blinked.

And blinked again.

Another stalk grew, and she made it climb to her will.

He gasped, too afraid of his unraveling mind, and her head shot up. The stalks stilled as her eyes took on a demonic flair— solid black surrounded by shining light.

He ran for his life.

All this time he'd thought he was the scariest thing in the forest.

He wasn't even close.

He spent weeks searching for her. Instinct told him to be afraid, but curiosity got the better of him. He became obsessed with the earth girl, and began to hover and hunt, desperate to find her, to see if his eyes would betray him a second time. But she'd vanished.

Then one early autumn evening, as the sun started to fall below the horizon and he was making the regretful trudge home, he felt the pull of a presence. He stopped mid-stride and turned, letting his eyes graze over the path behind him. The moon was in half-form, and the amount of light beyond the foliage was minimal. His fingertips started to heat with fear.

"Don't run," a man's voice said. "I can see you want to and, I assure you, that won't be to your benefit."

The boy tried to blink away the night.

"For someone who prides himself a predator, you seem awfully scared." The voice came closer, and it soon became an outline—the escaped shadow of a demon—before the pearlescent glow of the half-moon gave away the voice's identity. The man had a hunter's grace, with features that straddled the line between handsome and intimidating.

"So, are you the boy who was spying on my daughter?"

The man smiled with hints of wolf.

"Too many girls have caught your eye, huh? Don't remember which one I'm talking about? She was down by the riverbed."

Not even the lack of light could hide the fade from the boy's face. This was the father of the girl who tripped his fascination.

"Why would a lad like yourself spy on such a young girl?"

Fear drove the boy silent.

"I asked you a question," the man said with another step. He was now within striking distance. The air grew thin as the boy's heart raced.

"I've seen your work," the man said. "You're the one leaving dead animals pinned to trees, am I correct?" He arched an eyebrow and waited. "Suddenly shy, eh?" The man laughed, and the boy's hairs hackled. "I'll tell you what, Junior. Do you mind me calling you Junior?" He shook his head and clicked his tongue. "I don't particularly care if you mind, I'll call you what I want. I think you and I need to establish a few ground rules. I don't like cowards. You're old enough to man up, so when I ask you a question, I expect you to answer, got that?"

The boy nodded, and the man smirked. "I don't take kindly to disobedience," he said. "It's rude. Didn't your momma teach you any manners?"

At the mention of his mother, the boy flexed his hands and clenched his jaw. The stranger's smile amplified—and it wasn't a kind one.

"Ah," the man said, as if he understood who the boy was. As if he saw through his exterior and spotted the broken heart that continued to pump blood, but lacked feeling. "I think you're just who I'm looking for." The man bridged the last few steps and placed his hand on Junior's shoulder. "Don't be frightened." His lips peeled from his teeth, somewhere between a smile and a snarl. "My name's Urrel, and I believe we were meant to find each other."

JUNIOR TOOK to his new name the same way he took to his mentor. Urrel gave him purpose. He taught him greater tricks. From tracking to hunting.

"Trapping is an art," Urrel said. "There are exponential ways to doom an animal—you're limited only to your imagination. But"—he held up a finger—"if you ever decide to eat your prey rather than waste it for whatever senseless reason you have, then it's best you kill it quick. You'll want a clean meal. Fear, a rather wonderful emotion to witness, is dreadful to eat. The animals pump adrenaline and it turns the meat gamey. I don't recommend it. Although ..." Urrel stroked his chin in contemplation. "You're a strange buck. I bet you'd like tainted meat, which opens up a lot of possibilities."

Urrel had a way of doing that. Slipping in insults the way bark slides beneath the skin.

But Junior didn't care. Since the death of his father, here was a man who wasn't using him. Who didn't hurt him.

Urrel would ask questions, displaying genuine interest, and before long Junior was revealing his past. Urrel remained quiet as Junior poured out the heaviness of his heart, sharing his darkest secrets.

He waited for Urrel's reaction to the secret that left his heart cold, stroking the pocket watch—the same as he had done years before when he'd confessed to his mother—and willed Urrel to see him.

Urrel took the information stoically, before placing his hand on the boy's shoulder and giving him a kind shake. Junior nearly buckled—for once someone listened.

Someone cared.

"Women are such weak creatures," he said, with a disgustful shake. "Not to say your stepfather is a good man, far from it, but she is the one who has a responsibility to protect you. She has failed you. She is filth." He leaned down a fraction, so Junior was forced to look him in the eyes. "Those sins do not belong to you," he said. "They belong to him. To her."

Urrel grew bigger, more important, in Junior's eyes.

Junior smiled, and Urrel matched it with his own.

⚜

WEEKS AFTER HIS CONFESSION, Junior was on his way to meet Urrel when a whistle blew past him. A hatchet swiped across his field of vision. It landed with a *thud* into the trunk of an evergreen. It happened so fast, so close, Junior barely reacted. A few more steps in the wrong direction and the head of its sharpened blade would've landed square in Junior's skull.

Urrel's laugh courted the hatchet's trail.

"What's wrong with you?" Junior said. "You could've killed me."

The laughter fell away as Urrel's face molded into indignation.

"You ungrateful little shit," Urrel hissed. "I was testing you. Seeing if you were fit for glory, and that's the tone you take with me." In a fit, Urrel stalked up to Junior and grabbed him by his collar. "I was going to offer you the opportunity of a lifetime. Something no mere mortal deserves. And now you wag your vile tongue and make me question my own judgement." Urrel released him with a violent push. The boy fell to the ground. He met Urrel's accusing stare from the damp earth. "Tell me I haven't wasted my time on you."

"No, Urrel. I-I'm sorry. It scared me is all."

Urrel crouched low and took the boy's jaw between his fingers, forcing their eyes to lock.

"That answer bothers me even more," Urrel began. "I need brave men to join me on my journey."

"What journey?"

Urrel pulled him to his feet and grabbed the hatchet from the tree trunk. He ran his hand along the blade.

"Why is it you never ask me about my daughter?"

The question came out of nowhere. Since meeting Urrel, Junior avoided any mention of the girl who could control the earth. It was a bizarre phenomenon: every time he attempted to ask, fear would seize his throat and rob him of his nerve.

Would Urrel ask him what he knew?

How much he knew?

Was he even supposed to know?

The question loomed between them, and Junior had to answer. Because he couldn't *not* answer.

"I was waiting for you to mention her first." Junior's words came out slow and measured.

"Oh really? That seems a bit strange. Since I confronted you for following her. Why were you waiting on me?"

"Well, I ... I thought ..." Junior sagged. "Well, I wasn't sure ..." He lost his voice.

Urrel surprised him with a smile.

"You wanted to ask about the plants? Isn't that right? You're worried I'll be mad you know our secret."

Junior relaxed. "How does she do it?"

"I gave her that gift." Urrel lifted his chin and gave a prideful grin. "I found the secret to everlasting life, the cure to mortality. It took years of finessing, but I finally unleashed its powerful capabilities, and I used it on my beloved daughter. I did it to save her." He leaned in and whispered. "Her crazy mother buried her alive. Can you imagine? That's why I hate women. Cunning, unstable creatures. She tried to kill my only child. I dug Thorn out from her shallow grave with my bare hands, cleared the soil from her mouth, and poured the serum down her throat. I used every last drop." Urrel's voice grew wistful. "It was the best moment of my life."

"You brought her back from the dead?" Junior whispered in awe.

"I did. Now Thorn can move plants. A bit of a worthless talent, if you ask me. Especially considering the possibilities. There is a greater power to be had. I don't need pretty flowers, or vines with berries. I need strength. I need soldiers." He looked at Junior from the corner of his eye. "And as it so happens, I've managed to reclaim some of my cure. Now I just need to find the right man willing to take a chance on greatness." He settled his gaze on Junior. "Do you suppose, despite your rather unsavory reaction moments ago, you can be that man?"

Junior stood straighter. "Absolutely! Give me a chance. I'll show you I'm the right one."

"How do you plan to show me?"

"Whatever you want. I'll do whatever you want."

Urrel's smile was slow and steady. "Now, boy, that's exactly wanted I wanted to hear. I have a chore for you."

⁂

THE FIRST SNOWFALL of the season brought a smile to Urrel's face. The crisp air, the blanket of white, all of it meant it was time.

He went to the window of their ramshackle cabin, his eyes

drifting to the stack of railroad ties ready for a flame, and pulled out his watch—a stolen treasure—and knew Junior was doing the same.

Junior's watch was a cheap thing—Urrel's a better quality—but the kid held onto it like it was a priceless relic.

Sentiment's a stupid waste of energy.

Urrel glanced over his shoulder at Thorn, who'd risen early to mend shirts. She looked up as Urrel pretended to scowl at the sight of winter.

"We've got snow," he said, folding his face into a grim expression. "This is just the beginning of winter, Thorn. We're going to have to buckle down. Do you suppose you're strong enough to grow some decent vegetables for us? Unlike last year ..." He shook his head and clicked his tongue. "You were quite the failure. For a moment I believed you almost had it. Such a foolish thought." Thorn didn't flinch and continued to pierce the fabric, her fingers well practiced from years of servitude. Each stitch was tight and precise, just as he'd taught her.

"I will, Father. I made carrots grow this past spring, remember? And, I've ..."

Her voice tapered off, and Urrel's brow arched.

"And you've what?" he asked. "Do you have something more you'd like to contribute? As far as those carrots, it was spring, when the weather was in your favor. I dare say the earth did all the work. Now it'll be cold, uncompromising, and much harder to fight for."

"I'm getting stronger."

Urrel folded his arms behind his back and gave her his full attention. "Oh, really?" he asked. "What makes you so sure?"

Thorn's fingers stilled, the needle poised to strike.

"I've been working very hard. I've managed to grow a few more since then."

"So you say."

Thorn felt the tension between them crackle, and her eyes reached for their glow. She looked down so Urrel wouldn't see. He hated when her eyes sparked. He considered it an act of defiance.

"But you haven't brought any here," he continued. "I simply assumed you were unsuccessful—as you usually are. Have you been growing vegetables and not bringing them home?"

Thorn sat quietly, her eyes hidden. "Yes," she spoke carefully. "Yes, I've grown some potatoes and onions."

"Why did you not bring them home?"

Urrel knew the answer, but he wanted to see if she was daring enough to tell it honestly.

"Because they weren't perfect," she said. "I wanted to bring home food that was perfect."

Liar.

Urrel's lips almost twitched into a smile. Soon, very soon, she'd learn the consequences of speaking such mistruths.

Weeks before he met the boy, she started growing bold. Slipping away during the day, almost always in the morning and evening. Going to the same place. Every single time.

She said she was practicing her gifts.

She thought he didn't know. But Urrel knew everything.

"Food is food, Thorn. You should've let me be the judge of whether or not it was worthy of consumption. Your judgement is lacking. You're not as smart as me."

Thorn bobbed her head. "I'm sorry, Father."

"So you think you're stronger? Competent?" Urrel went back to the window.

"Yes." Thorn stilled. "I am stronger."

"I look forward to seeing your improved strength against this cold."

"You'll be happy."

"Hmmm ..." Urrel pretended to contemplate. "This weather is going to lock us in, that's for sure. I doubt you'll be able to venture out and play much longer. You might want to prepare for staying in. Cabin fever comes on quickly."

Half an hour later, as Urrel predicted, Thorn snuck away. Before she left, he surprised her with a new set of earmuffs and swallowed back the bile as she lit up with gratitude. She wore her emotions so openly—it only fed his revulsion.

"Thank you, Daddy." She held them up to her ears. "But what do I do with my old ones?"

"It's always good to have a spare."

Thorn smiled and wrapped her thin coat along her shoulders.

Stupid child didn't even stop to think how odd it was he bought her a second pair of earmuffs, when she didn't even have a proper jacket. Hell, she'd outgrown her shoes, to the point her toes were peeking out the front.

Still, she did not question.

When she left, proudly wearing her new earmuffs, the other set was tucked under her threadbare sweater.

Urrel smiled to himself, commending his own brilliance.

He knew where she was going. Who she was going to meet. He knew she would give up her only pair of earmuffs to help the other, so it was crucial she had another set.

"Every little bit helps. May it be enough to block the screams," he said softly, as the last of Thorn's retreating frame vanished into the sleeping forest. It would take her hours upon hours—she was painfully slow with her worthless skills and that, too, made it awfully convenient.

He sighed, almost wishing they wouldn't make it so easy. He glanced at his pocket watch and noted the time.

He waited five more minutes, till the short hand landed on the ten, and went out and set his burn pile on fire. The railroad ties were coated in tar—it sent billowing tendrils of black smoke into the sky.

The signal.

He timed it, made the journey countless times. How long it would take to reach the cabin, how long it would take to reach the meadow.

The ravine.

All of it. Urrel had paid close attention, marking every minute.

Waiting was the worst part. Truth be told, he didn't have much faith the boy would execute his plans without error. As the minutes ticked by, Urrel paced in the heart of their hovel, until it was time. He stepped out and followed Thorn's footsteps, trailing her snow-marked path. Winter was coming in gentle, the amount of snowfall on the ground minimal.

Another perfect aspect to his plans. Because he needed snow, enough to show tracks, but not heavy enough to erase them. Still, the tree cover allowed for a few bare spots where snow couldn't breach the overhead foliage. He made sure to place his steps in wet soil.

He wanted to whistle. He always wanted to whistle. Especially when he thought of his beloved Rose. The wife he took with an axe—severing her pretty head from the rest of her pretty body.

He was often conflicted in his memories of her. Loving her and hating her in equal measure.

The scales always tipped to hatred when he looked at Thorn, turning his annoyance into spikes of venom.

He bit down on his bottom lip and flipped the collar of his

thick coat up around his ears. Winter may be kind, but it wouldn't be for long.

Halfway along Thorn's course, Urrel stepped off her path and made his way to a seasonal creek bed. Not much wider than a couple of feet, it was ideal for snow tracking.

The water had enough force to remain unfrozen, and the snow couldn't yet stick. That meant he could walk along the bank, keeping his footsteps hidden. He followed it, and it wasn't long before he located Junior waiting at the ravine, sitting on the frozen ground, his knees pulled up to lock in the warmth. There was a trail of blood following the disturbed snow, and a discarded knife, coated in red, lying next to him. He was trembling, shaking in a jacket too thin to keep out the stabs of ice.

All according to plan. Urrel stood over Junior and smiled.

"Did you say what I told you to say?" he asked.

Junior nodded.

"How many were there?"

"Two."

Urrel nudged his head in the direction of the bloodied trail. "And is she dead?"

"Yes."

"Did you leave the other alive?"

"I think s-so."

"And where is the bat?"

"I l-left it outside th-the cabin."

"Did they scream?"

"I caught th-them off guard." Junior's lips had purpled in the cold, and he moved in such disjointed fashion it was comical. "The oldest I hit on the doorstep as sh-she was g-gathering wood, and the other ..." His teeth began to chatter, clacking together. "I-I t-told her t-to keep q-q-quiet or I'd h-hurt her."

"Good."

Urrel noticed Junior's pants were unbuckled, and he wondered if the deviant boy had done more than they'd discussed.

"Now you'll m-make m-me immortal, l-like you p-promised?" Junior stuttered.

"Of course. You've proven yourself worthy." Urrel handed Junior a vial. "Take this," he ordered. "It's the first step." Junior took it in his numb hands, blood stained, and fumbled with the stopper. Urrel, annoyed, removed it for him and dumped the fluid down his throat.

Moments later, the boy's heart broke into a crescendo, as the poison Urrel gave him arrested his organs, forcing them to shut down—along with his ability to speak.

With worried eyes, he looked to Urrel and managed to grunt as he fell to the side, the snow enveloping him.

Urrel leaned down into his ear and whispered, "You're such a tragic waste, and I've done the world a favor by killing you. I would never think of making you immortal. But since I'm a good man, I'll see to it you get a proper burial, even though you deserve to have your bones picked clean by vermin." Urrel reached into Junior's pocket and plucked from it the watch he held so dear. "I'm going to keep this, as a trophy."

Junior's eyes bulged, his tongue swelling three times in bulk.

Urrel grabbed him, dancing close to death, and positioned his body in the creek bed, letting the icy water intensify his pain.

"To wash away your sins," Urrel said, leaving the boy to die alone.

Urrel made it back to the cabin minutes before Thorn. She was frantic and begged him to follow.

Something tragic had happened. It took all his energy not to grin.

They went to a meadow, and there, as Urrel expected, was a blonde girl without a heartbeat, still and frozen as the winter falling on them. Blood pooled near her throat and thighs. Junior had indeed taken liberties, stealing her innocence before her life.

She was being cradled by a girl nearing womanhood, with locks of flame. A dark knot swelled on the side of her head, tears frozen to her face. She was pleading to the limp child in her arms.

Willing her to wake up.

Thorn went to stand next to another girl—older than the dead and younger than the fire—whose wail struck the atmosphere. Her lungs were as dark as her hair. Thorn patted the girl's back, and he overheard Thorn whisper, "Daddy will fix it."

That's right. Daddy was going to make it all better.

He stepped forward and crouched.

"What is this?" he asked.

The redhead, with eyes of a doe, took charge. A teenage boy broke into their house, she explained. He had a bat and wild eyes. He hit her in the head, knocking her unconscious. She woke to find her little sister gone, and a trail of footsteps. She followed them and found her sister lying in her own blood.

She stopped to point at the disturbed snow leading away.

"He did this to her," the eldest whispered. "He did this, and I couldn't stop him. Tabitha says he's dead down by a creek bed."

The raven-haired child, the one Thorn was busy trying to comfort, had discovered Junior's corpse. She'd finally stopped wailing, having gone mute with grief, and allowed her elder sister to do the talking.

"Why would a monster do such a thing?" Urrel asked.

"Can you help her?"

"I need answers first," he said, looking up into Thorn's guilt-stricken face.

"But you can save her?" the redhead asked.

"Yes." Urrel waved to Thorn. "I saved Thorn when her mother killed her, and I can do the same for you. But answers ... I need answers." He looked down into the face of the little body he took into his arms. "And time is running out. I can't possibly bring her back from the dead when your parents may have an objection. It'd be disrespectful and perhaps a sin against their beliefs."

"It doesn't matter."

"Of course it does. It may be unholy in the eyes of their God. Before I proceed I must seek their approval. I can't move forward without speaking to them." Urrel paused. "Where are your parents?"

"Mother died in childbirth, and Daddy ... hasn't come home. It's been two months now. I think ... I think maybe he abandoned us. So you see"—she wiped at her nose—"we have no one but each other."

Urrel ducked his head into the small child's neck, to make it look as if he were checking for a lingering life-force, when really he was hiding his smile. Their father was buried in a shallow grave of Urrel's making. He was, after all, an obstacle.

"If only I'd been there," the dark-eyed child, Tabitha, finally said. Thorn went to wrap her arms around her shoulders, but she brushed them off. Thorn's face fell into an even sorrier state of dejection, and it made Urrel's blood sing.

Thorn wore pain well.

"Why weren't you there?" Urrel asked, looking between the two. He raised a brow. "Thorn? Do you have something to tell me?"

"She was with me," Thorn admitted. "I was growing her vegetables for winter."

Urrel nodded, solemn. "Then this death is on your hands," he replied. "For something tells me had she been there, the numbers could've stopped this tragedy."

Both girls began to weep, and he thought he heard the red-haired child whisper, "That's what the intruder said."

Urrel hid his pleasure. Junior had indeed followed orders.

Meanwhile, Thorn's heart bled into the open. This is what she got for keeping secrets. Urrel had taught her a valuable lesson.

And she would live with the guilt for the rest of her life—rightly so.

"Since you're responsible for this tragedy, Thorn"—Urrel managed to crack his voice—"I will do my best to make this right." He gave them a smile and dug out a vial from his pocket. "I will bring her back, but first I need the ultimate sacrifice."

"Anything," the red haired-girl said.

The other nodded and parroted, "Yes, anything."

"Very well." Stars danced in Urrel's vision. He stood up and looked to the frozen girl child. "She will be my Ice. And you will both die to save her."

Acknowledgments

I can't believe I'm here again, at the back of a book. And I can't believe I just used the word "again" to describe this process. Is it normal to suffer shock over a year later? Because I feel like it is. I'm living it.

And it's amazing.

The support. The cheerleading. The kindness. All of it has blown me away. That's why this section is perhaps my most favorite. It's the place I get to acknowledge all the wonderful people in my life, my crusaders, my badass tribe. The awesomeness I get to interact with on a daily basis. So brace yourself, it's about to get all mushy (as it rightly should ... you can never say thank you enough). Okay, here we go ...

Thank you to my husband, Chris. You are, without a doubt, one of the greatest things to ever happen to me. You are such a supporter of my books, of my stories, of my quirky traits, and I'm super lucky to have you in my life. I love you.

To my kids, Frank and Sam, I love you guys with all my heart. You two are the reason I mustered up the courage to go after this wacky dream of mine, and I hope someday you'll look back on my work and be proud.

Thank you to Karen Petersen, my editor. You rocked this novel. I know I was super picky—and a bit difficult at times—but your patience, kindness, and mad editing skills continue to awe me. Thanks for going on this journey and cleaning up this beast of a book.

Amanda, again, you are the BEST cover model a girl could hope for. Thanks for going with me three times to get this shot. Oh, and on the next shoot, please, please, please bring your EpiPen. Bees are attracted to you, and as much as you like to joke that your lifeless body will make the shoot more "real," I don't find it funny. Not at all. Bring. The. Pen. (Oh, and I hope your mom reads this and yells at you. You're welcome.)

So this part is gonna get tricky. Apparently I'm drawn to Rachels. It has a nice ring to it, right? The name Rachel? It's like, hey, I like that name, and the person attached to it must be a total badass who needs to be my friend. And then I get all pushy, make them friend me, and we live happily ever after. I guess what I'm getting at (aside from my love of Rachels), is that I have two to thank. For simplicity purposes, I shall say one is friend Rachel, and one is beta Rachel (although beta Rachel is also a friend). And yes, I could break it up by using initials, but then I wouldn't need this extra paragraph, and I like this paragraph so, yeah, I'm gonna do things the hard way. Damn I feel like this is getting complicated (and totally on purpose).

Okay, friend Rachel. Thanks for listening to all my talk about this venture (and never acting like I talk all the time about this venture). You've been amazing through it all. I love your honesty, your kindness, the way you look at the world. You are, without a doubt, someone I admire. If I could be more like you, I'd be winning at life. Thanks for being in my world and encouraging me every step of the way.

Beta Rachel, you rocked this beta thing. Seriously, I'd read your notes, sit back, and say to myself, "Damn, she's smart!" Thanks for reading Shades, for your feedback, for every thoughtful response you gave me. You have one of the most brilliant minds, and the fact you volunteered to help me is humbling. Thanks for being such a fantastic beta and friend.

Katherine, thank you for being the first to read Shades (aside from the Legend ... I held out so you'd have a little surprise when the book was released). Thanks for your feedback, for talking with me, for just being the type of person I want in my world. I hope someday we'll live closer together. I miss you!

Brittany! Oh, my lovely Brittany. You were an unexpected, most wonderful, fabulous surprise on my publishing journey. When I released Colors, I wasn't expecting to find you, and now that I have, I'm keeping you forever. Thank you for pushing Colors, for sharing it, for taking a chance on me. I love that we're learning things together, and I have you in my corner. Thank you for being one of the greatest friends I could hope for.

Britney Cawrse (I guess I have a fondness for Britneys, too!), the cloaks you made for the cover shoot ... A.M.A.Z.I.N.G. I love them and when I was snapping photos, I kept thinking of your incredible talent. If anyone needs some custom work done, find this girl. She does kickass work. KICKASS!

My mom and dad, CJ, Brandi, Todd, Kevin, Kristie and all my peeps, thanks for being in my world. You know you guys own a chunk of my heart, forever and always.

Oh, and of course, thank you to my readers. To all who picked up Colors and gave a newbie a shot. Yeah, you guys rock.

About the Author

J.M. Muller lives in Oregon with her husband, twin boys, and her darling fur babies. She has a plethora of skills (okay, that's a lie), but does enjoy writing and creating—to the very best of her abilities.

www.jmmuller.com